"I want us to be ~~married before~~ you have the baby."

"Mick, that's not possible." Hana tried to sit up, but a nurse pressed her back.

"Hana, listen to me. If we're married, the baby has my last name. The birth certificate will say *Callen*. This baby will be ours—yours and mine. I'll be the one, the only, father."

Hana's tear-swollen eyes sought the doctor. "Is it crazy or is it possible? I'd like that…a lot." With her free hand she touched her stomach.

Dr. Walsh shrugged. "It's crazy, all right. You'd need a license and that takes time.…"

"We have our license. They processed it today. It's…uh, at the house."

"Then we can do it," the doctor said. "Somebody find the hospital chaplain and get him up here on the double. Mick, you run home and get the license."

Mick nodded, then slid his hand up to cradle the back of Hana's head. "I know this isn't the way we planned it.…" He grinned. "But at least we'll have a Christmas wedding."

2

Dear Reader,

When I first thought of writing a story that centered on twins who fly mercy flights in a wilderness area, I imagined it as two stories in one book. But I hadn't even finished the synopsis of Marlee's story before I realized her brother Mick needed a life, a love, a book of his own. My editor agreed.

Mick had been wounded in Afghanistan, healed, and had rebuilt his grandfather's charter flight service to what it had once been. Mick Callen enticed his sister to come home, only to have her leave again when she found her true love. The twins' grandfather died over the summer. I just couldn't leave Mick alone and lonely.

Certain books come together more easily than others, and Mick and Hana's story was one of them. I love both of these characters. Plus I like writing about families who face the challenges real people face in real life.

I hope you enjoy reading the second of the Angel Fleet books. The men and women (and the various organizations) who make mercy flights accessible to people in remote sites share a unique strength and compassion. I admire them one and all. However, Mick's story, like his sister's, is pure fiction and not patterned on any of the many real mercy flying services.

Roz Denny Fox

P.S. I love hearing from readers. You can reach me at P.O. Box 17480-101, Tucson, AZ 85731 or via e-mail at rdfox@worldnet.att.net.

ON ANGEL WINGS
Roz Denny Fox

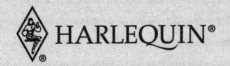

TORONTO • NEW YORK • LONDON
AMSTERDAM • PARIS • SYDNEY • HAMBURG
STOCKHOLM • ATHENS • TOKYO • MILAN • MADRID
PRAGUE • WARSAW • BUDAPEST • AUCKLAND

ISBN-13: 978-0-373-71388-2
ISBN-10:   0-373-71388-6

ON ANGEL WINGS

Copyright © 2006 by Rosaline Fox.

This edition published by arrangement with Harlequin Books S.A.

® and TM are trademarks of the publisher. Trademarks indicated with ® are registered in the United States Patent and Trademark Office, the Canadian Trade Marks Office and in other countries.

www.eHarlequin.com

Printed in U.S.A.

ABOUT THE AUTHOR

Roz made her first sale to the Harlequin Romance line in 1989 and sold six Harlequin Romance titles, writing as Roz Denny. After transferring to the Harlequin Superromance series, she began writing as Roz Denny Fox. In addition to the many stories she's written for Harlequin Superromance, she's also written two Harlequin American Romance books and two Harlequin Signature books. Her novel for Harlequin's new series, Everlasting, will be coming out in August 2007.

Roz has been a RITA® Award finalist and has placed in a number of other contests; her books have also appeared on the Waldenbooks bestseller list. She's happy to have received her twenty-five-book pin with Harlequin, and would one day love to get the pin for fifty books.

Roz currently resides in Tucson, Arizona, with her husband, Denny. They have two daughters.

Books by Roz Denny Fox

HARLEQUIN SUPERROMANCE
1069–THE SEVEN YEAR SECRET
1108–SOMEONE TO
    WATCH OVER ME
1128–THE SECRET DAUGHTER
1148–MARRIED IN HASTE
1184–A COWBOY AT HEART
1220–DADDY'S LITTLE
    MATCHMAKER
1254–SHE WALKS THE LINE
1290–A MOM FOR MATTHEW
1320–MORE TO TEXAS
    THAN COWBOYS
1368–ANGELS OF THE BIG SKY

**HARLEQUIN
AMERICAN ROMANCE**
1036–TOO MANY
    BROTHERS
1087–THE SECRET
    WEDDING DRESS

**HARLEQUIN
SIGNATURE**
COFFEE IN
  THE MORNING
HOT CHOCOLATE
  ON A COLD DAY

CHAPTER ONE

MICK CALLEN MOVED a step higher on the twelve-foot ladder that was propped against the battered Huey. It was the only helicopter in a fleet of three aircraft belonging to Cloud Chasers, Mick's company, which delivered freight throughout remote northwest Montana.

He stretched to dab lubricant on the far side of the rotor pitch. The pain in his hip at the movement was a sharp reminder that he'd reached too far for the titanium socket a surgeon had installed a year ago. He adjusted his weight and breathed more easily. Damn, how long would it be before he'd remember he didn't have the same range of motion anymore? But setting limits wasn't easy for a man who, at thirty-five, ought to be in the prime of his life.

Frustrated, he raised a greasy hand to swipe a stubborn lock of hair out of his eyes, then caught himself and first rubbed the grease down his coveralls so he wouldn't have a black streak through his blond hair. Mick shifted again and rested the can on the top rung. From this vantage point he could see a row of white-capped peaks in the distance. A slice of the Rocky Mountains.

Intent on servicing the Huey, Mick hadn't noticed the added nip in the morning air until this minute. The sky was a deep, cloudless blue. Pappy Jack would've said it was a perfect day for cloud chasing. Hence the name of their company.

A pang seared Mick's chest. This pain wasn't related to the injuries he'd sustained in the military when he'd been shot down during his last mission in Afghanistan. Nor was it the result of the many subsequent surgeries. Mick recognized this ache. He'd diagnosed it weeks ago as he tinkered with his plane engines. This pain struck each time he left the house to work solo.

Since mid-May he'd shopped solo, cooked solo, ate solo, flew solo and walked Wingman, his mutt, solo.

Here it was, already late October. It had been six damned months and he still expected to see his grandfather moving around the property. Pappy Jack Callen, Mick's mentor and grandfather, had always been the real heart and soul of Cloud Chasers.

At Jack's funeral late last spring, scores of residents from the nearby community of Whitepine had come to pay their respects. More than a few of Pappy's old friends had claimed Mick and Jack were lucky that Pappy had said good-night as usual one night and then simply didn't wake up the next morning. They said that when they died, they hoped it happened that way.

Except they weren't the ones who'd found Pappy lifeless in his bed. Mick had. And not a day passed that he didn't think of a hundred things he should've said the night before to the man who'd long been the rock for Mick and his twin sister, Marlee. Pappy had been everything to them after they'd lost their parents in a senseless car accident some twenty years ago.

Marlee assured Mick over and over in the days following the funeral that Pappy knew they loved him. But his sister, newly married and pregnant, didn't have endless empty hours to fill with nothing but rambling thoughts. *Should've*, *could've*, *would've*. These seemed to define Mick's existence lately. Not the touchy-feely type, he'd never been a big one for vocalizing how he felt. A fault he'd have to live with, or change. Damn, but change didn't come easy, either.

At eighty-six, their grandfather had lived a full life. Jack Callen proudly boasted a distinguished military career. He'd married the love of his life. Had built his home and business from the ground up. He'd raised a son and shepherded twin grandkids toward becoming fine navy flyers and otherwise all-around productive citizens.

By comparison, Mick felt his own life was going nowhere fast.

His new brother-in-law, Glacier Park forest ranger Wylie Ames, said what Mick needed was to find a good woman. His sister took every opportunity to nag him to phone Tammy Skidmore, a nurse in Kalispell who'd shown enough interest to hand him her phone number the day he'd checked out of the hospital.

He scowled as he slopped grease on the underside of the rotor. Huh, maybe he *should* pick up the phone and call Tammy. But something held him back. Mick jokingly told Marlee it'd be hard to date a woman who had jammed needle after needle into his bare butt. Although that didn't ring true. Mick had lost all modesty after his accident. With Tammy, at least, if they ever reached the point of doing the deed, he wouldn't have to explain the ugly puckered skin that ran from hip to ankle where he'd been riddled by shrapnel. Mick probably didn't have a single physical asset Tammy Skidmore hadn't clinically observed, so that was pretty much a nonissue.

And if he crossed Tammy off his list of available females he was left with slim pickin's. Available, suitable women didn't grow on trees and there was little more than trees in this backcountry. Though a couple of old schoolmates in White-pine had let him know at Pappy's funeral that they were back in circulation. One was too straitlaced to suit Mick. The other lacked any scruples.

A little voice in the back of his mind niggled. *What about Hana Egan?*

What about her? Last fall, Pappy had told his twin sister that Mick was "sweet" on the smoke jumper. Mick had tripped over his teeth to deny it.

"Mick!" Hearing his name drifting up from the foot of his ladder jerked Mick out of his daydream. He hastily jammed a lid on the grease bucket and began to make his way down the rickety ladder.

Stella Gibson was waiting for him at the bottom. Judging by her worried expression, she'd anxiously followed his slow progress. The matronly widow, who lived in a cabin down the hill, had helped Mick in a variety of capacities since his medical discharge from the navy. She'd cleaned the house and left enough meals in the refrigerator to keep him and Pappy from starving.

Those months when Mick had been laid up, when Marlee moved home and flew his route, Stella took care of Mick, Pappy and sometimes Marlee's daughter, Jo Beth. But she had never made a secret of the fact that she was looking for a permanent job. It was only after Marlee married Wylie, and Pappy passed away, that Mick got smart and hired Stella to work half-time cleaning house, and the other half keeping order in Cloud Chasers' office. That was a task his sister repeatedly said he was bad at.

Hands on hips, Stella was obviously ready to give him a motherly lecture. "When I left yesterday, Mick Callen, you told me Josh Manley would be in today to service the helicopter. Why are you up on that ladder?"

Mick set down the bucket, pulled a rag out of his back pocket and wiped the excess goop off his fingers. "Yeah, well, Josh's mom phoned. His girlfriend conned Josh into driving her and a coworker into Kalispell today. Apparently they're all invited to an early Halloween party at the home of his girl-friend's boss, who happens to have an opening for a corporate pilot. I know Josh really wants that job. He's a good pilot, and I can't use him full-time."

"If he gets the job, who'll help you, Mick? Between the upswing in freight orders and the mercy missions with Angel Fleet, it seems to me you need a full-time flying partner."

"With winter coming on, it's a matter of weeks before I'd have to cut Josh's hours. That's the nature of the freight business in upper Montana."

"Running in high gear these last six or seven months, I never thought to ask. Will my hours be cut over the winter?"

Wingman bounded up, his tongue hanging out. The part Lab, part shepherd, part some unknown breed, nosed Mick's leg until he crouched to rub the dog's furry head. "Actually, Stella, I've been juggling my finances, hoping I can afford to spend the winter bumming around some island with white sandy beaches, ice-cold margaritas and bikini-clad babes. I'd like you to look after the place. You know, see the pipes don't break and my planes don't blow away. Up to now, no one's had time to scan in all the old accounts or shred the mountains of paperwork Pappy stored in those damned cardboard boxes, either. I'll pay you to handle everything."

"I can do that. Are you planning to take the dog?"

Mick let the animal lick his chin. "I wish. But this guy's a cold-weather mutt. I intend to corner Marlee and Wylie and ask them if I can pay his son to take care of Wingman until I get back in the spring. Last time I visited them for a weekend, I let Dean take care of my dog. Since Jo Beth has Piston, it evened the odds in their 'yours, mine and ours household.'"

Stella's dark brown eyes sparkled when she laughed. "You'd do that to your poor sister? Add another creature when she's dealing with Thanksgiving, Christmas and having a baby? Last time we talked, she said Dean had rescued a half-grown grizzly who'd been shot by a neighboring rancher. That boy already has twin wolf cubs and numerous small animals in various stages of healing."

"Was Marlee complaining?"

"No. She sounded happy, in fact."

"Yeah, she does." Mick straightened and patted the dog. He gazed blankly at the horizon. "I was just thinking, Stella, it's perfect flying weather. I should shake out the chopper and see if the maintenance I did takes care of the rotor wobble Josh was complaining about. Last week when I flew to Missoula for my last visit with the physical therapist, I picked up some things for the baby. I also bought a few Halloween goodies for Dean and Jo Beth. Maybe I'll take myself up to the ranger station. See if Wylie can use an extra hand with the addition he's madly building on their house."

Stella snapped her fingers. "That's why I came to find you, Mick. I took a phone order from Trudy Morgenthal at the rangers' base camp, and the smoke jumpers would also like some supplies delivered no later than tomorrow afternoon."

Mick's grease-stained fingers fondled the dog's silky ear. "I delivered Captain Martin's winter supplies weeks ago. He said he wouldn't need anything until spring."

"I gather this is private supplies for the smoke jumpers. None of them are in your billing system, which brings up the next question. Will you fly out such a small order for cash? Jess Hargitay promised to pay on delivery."

"I guess. Jess has been with Martin for a few years. Not all the jumpers return each season." He frowned. "I've never known any of them to request private supplies. In fact, I understood they were all leaving next week, except Captain Martin and his assistant."

"Mr. Hargitay mentioned that a group is planning a farewell

climb in Glacier Park. One of the taller peaks, but I don't recall which. They've ordered ready-to-eat meals, long johns and miscellaneous stuff."

"Huh. Long johns for sure. I see there's quite a bit of snow up along the ridge."

"If the report I heard this morning is correct, we're liable to lose this fine weather soon. They predict we'll see snow in the valley by early next week."

Mick laughed. "Stella, you can't trust the news channel weather staff to get it right. If you want the skinny on the weather, you need to phone the service pilots use."

She tipped back her head and scanned the sky that was visible through a row of majestic pine trees that blocked north winds from battering the house. "You're right." She looked at him again. "So, then, you want me to phone Trudy and this Jess guy and say you'll take both jobs?"

"Sure. Sounds good. I never turn down an opportunity to earn money. What's today? Thursday? Ask Trudy if tomorrow's soon enough to deliver her order. I'll fly to Kalispell this afternoon and fetch the supplies in the Arrow. At first light tomorrow, I'll transfer the load to the Huey. That'll allow me time to phone Wylie and Marlee, and arrange to spend a couple of nights with them."

"I'll confirm the times with Trudy ASAP. Unless you want my help in carting that big old ladder back to the work shed."

"Thanks for the offer, Stella, but my PT said I'm good as new. Maybe better than, what with all the hardware installed in my hip," Mick said with a wink. He forgot the condition of his hand and raked still-greasy fingers through hair that needed more than a trim, as curls fell over his eyes and skimmed the lower edge of his collar.

"You look kind of shaggy. But unless there's someone out

in the great beyond you want to impress, I'd say you can get by for another week without a barber."

Again, a clear vision of perky Hana Egan popped into Mick's mind. Probably because Stella had mentioned Jess Hargitay. Jess gave the impression that he was hot stuff in the eyes of female smoke jumpers. Mick had seen Jess act possessive of several women who'd rotated in and out of the camp. A few years ago he'd heard there were allegations of Jess inappropriately harassing a partner, a female. She quit forestry and Mick heard she'd dropped charges rather than fight a losing battle in court. Mick had seen Jess move on Hana. But maybe she returned his interest. Probably did. Mick's trips to the camp were sporadic, so it wasn't as if he knew anything for sure.

"Stella, if Trudy needs her order today, buzz me on the house intercom. I'm going to store the ladder and grease, then go clean up."

They parted, and Mick returned the ladder to the shed. On his trip to the house, he took out his cell phone and punched in his sister's number. Her phone rang three times before she answered, and then she sounded out of breath.

"Hey, sis, did I catch you on the run?"

"Mick?" His twin's voice reflected both surprise and delight. "I had my head in the oven when the phone rang. I stopped to take out two pies before I picked up."

"You're baking pies? What's the occasion?"

"I'll have you know I cook a lot more since I acquired a family of two hungry males. Thankfully, Rose sent me her favorite recipes," Marlee said, referring to her former mother-in-law, Rose Stein. Marlee's marriage to Wylie Ames was his twin's second marriage. Her first husband had died after a prolonged bout with cancer. She'd had some problems with her ex-mom-in-law. But Marlee had met and overcome all challenges like a champ.

"These pies," Marlee continued, "are for an end-of-season potluck the park rangers are having on Saturday. I'm so nervous, Mick. Wylie said I shouldn't be, but this'll be the first time most of his ranger buddies will have met me and Jo Beth. Bud and Ellen Russell—Bud is Wylie's closest friend— came by to deliver a wedding gift from the whole crew. Outside of them, I won't know a single soul at the gathering," she admitted. "I hope my offerings at the potluck are edible, or the women will feel sorry for Wylie. They're probably all wondering how he met me, anyway."

Mick didn't comment. He was trying to piece together the significance of what his sister had said.

"Mick, are you still there? Is something wrong? Oh, no, don't tell me the report from your physical therapist was bad? I meant to phone, but we had a lot going on, what with trying to get the addition finished so Rose has a place to sleep when she comes here for Christmas. You know she's going to help when the baby's born? And do you remember Emmett Nelson, Rose's neighbor from San Diego? They'll be traveling together. I think they're an item. Are you listening to me, Mick?"

"Yes. I'm fine according to the PT. It's just…I scheduled a couple of deliveries up your way tomorrow. I figured on spending the weekend with you guys. That was before you mentioned having plans for Saturday. Maybe I'll swoop in for a minute tomorrow afternoon and drop off the Halloween treats I bought for Dean and Jo Beth."

"You will *not* just pop in and out. I have an order sitting at the Kalispell airpark that you can bring. And you'll stay for the potluck. So, if I don't pass muster with Wylie's coworkers, I can hang out with my brother instead of looking like a wall-flower."

"Why wouldn't you pass muster? Anyway, the only important thing is how much Wylie and Dean love you. Hey, come on! You flew choppers in a war for pity's sake. Which of the other ranger wives can claim that kind of guts?" He shook his head. "Are you okay, sis? I've never known you to be insecure."

"You never saw me when I was pregnant last time. Feeling frumpy comes with the territory."

"Hmm, that explains it. I haven't been around a pregnant woman—except one in that fender bender a couple of weeks ago. She went into labor at the side of the highway near White-fish. Angel Fleet had me fly her and her husband to Kalispell. He was a basket case. I hope Wylie won't be like that."

"He won't. Wylie delivered Dean. Although, he wants me to stay in town the last weeks. I'd much prefer the local midwife come here. If the weather doesn't permit that, I'd still be fine with just Wylie and Rose on hand. Out of curiosity, what did the woman have, a boy or a girl?"

"A boy. Cute little dude. The dad acted goofy, tapping on the nursery glass and making goo-goo noises. He gave me a blue bubblegum cigar. I tried to picture myself in his shoes, but I'm positive I would've acted way cooler."

"If you don't get on the stick and meet a woman, Mick Callen, you won't ever have kids—and we'll never know if you'd act cool or not."

"Yeah, yeah! Time to hang up. I've gotta go shower and then fly to Kalispell and collect the orders for delivery tomorrow."

"If you don't have to fly on Monday, stay over with us for an extra day. We'd all like that."

"We'll see. I'll toss in a duffle and see what Wylie thinks about me crashing his company barbecue. Isn't your weather too nippy for a barbecue?"

"The gathering's always at the park picnic grounds—to cele-brate closing the park for the winter. Closing is Sunday. If that storm hanging out in Canada blows down, Trudy Morgenthal says we can eat in the wildlife lecture room at the base ranger camp."

"Stella heard about that storm. I'll have to check reports. Maybe I will stay over. How bad are they predicting it'll be? Nothing like the doozy last June that surprised the heck out of everybody? Never seen such high winds."

"Nothing so major, thank goodness. Wylie said he'd never seen a storm cause as much damage as that one. I think this forecast is for a few inches of snow, that's all. The kids have their fingers crossed. Probably because Wylie built them sleds out of scrap lumber."

"All right! If I wasn't planning to stay over before, that would've tipped the scales. It's been years since I did any sledding. Expect me around lunchtime tomorrow. I'll see if your kitchen skills have improved." Mick clicked off before the sputtering began.

As MICK FIRED UP the Huey, the breaking dawn gave no indication that the weather wouldn't be a repeat of the previous day. Streaks of purple, pink and gold edged out the deep gray of a rapidly fading night. And there was little, if any, wind.

The thrill of the promised flight lifted his spirits, even if he'd rather be flying a navy jet than this lumbering chopper. Wingman sat in his makeshift harness, one ear perked up. Mick grinned at the dog and could swear the mutt grinned back. "We're a pair, aren't we?" Mick called. The dog raised his head and barked.

As he lifted off, Mick stopped admiring the breaking day and listened carefully for any sign of wobble in the rotors. He much preferred flying fixed-wing planes like the Arrow or the Seneca. He'd bought the chopper at an auction to entice his sister back home to Montana from San Diego. She'd flown helicopters in the navy. But if he'd known she was going to meet Wylie Ames, fall in love, and marry the guy within a year of moving back, Mick might have passed on buying the Huey. Except that it'd come in handy on several occasions during his volunteer missions for Angel Fleet. He was getting so he could land the chopper just about anywhere except in heavily treed terrain. For as fast as Montana was being built up, there was still a lot of wilderness left, thank goodness. And like Marlee claimed, the Huey was a reliable workhorse.

He'd been in the air a little under an hour when he spotted the main ranger layout below. Mick had realized yesterday that the supplies he'd picked up for Trudy Morgenthal were mostly for the weekend ranger barbecue, or potluck, whatever they were calling it. He had cartons of paper cups, paper plates, napkins. Trudy had ordered staples to get them through a winter during which no one traveled easily in this part of Glacier Park except by snowshoes or snowmobile.

He landed near the park's two smaller helicopters. Wingman got antsy waiting for the rotors to stop. Mick saw why. They were being greeted by the house dogs, a German shepherd and a good-size collie. Mick released his dog but attached a leash to his collar.

Trudy hurried down the path that led to the buildings. From her hand motions, Mick deduced that she intended to pen her dogs. He waited to open the door until she'd disappeared again.

"I know, buddy, you're disappointed to lose playmates. But maybe those dogs aren't as friendly as you. Come on. I'll walk you into the woods to do your business. Then you'll have to stay in the chopper while I unload Morgenthal's order."

Trudy reappeared about the time Mick returned to the clearing. "Where should I stack all the boxes?" he asked.

"My husband and sons and our other rangers are making

sure all of the campers have left. They'll be closing this end of the park and putting up chains across the entry roads until next season. Would it be a terrible imposition if I asked you to carry the paper goods to the canopy we've set up for the potluck? Put everything else on the porch. I don't want you reinjuring your leg. Wylie told us about your surgery. In a way, that was his good fortune. Otherwise he wouldn't have met your sister."

"Wylie's right. Marlee never would've taken over my cargo route if I hadn't been laid up. It's no problem moving your stuff, Trudy. I have a hand truck I can load boxes on."

Trudy talked incessantly as Mick loaded up cartons and trucked them around. He would've told her he'd see her the next day, as he'd been invited to the potluck, but couldn't get a word in edgewise.

"Phew, Wingman," Mick said after he'd buckled himself back in his seat. "That woman could talk the ears off a mule. I suppose she gets lonely stuck out here with her husband out tending the park."

He slipped on his earphones and promptly turned his thoughts to his next delivery. Mick wondered if he'd see Hana Egan this trip. A new kind of excitement rose in him, different from the thrill he got from flying. A month ago when he'd delivered the bulk of the winter supplies to Captain Martin, who lived year-round at the smoke jumpers' camp, Mick had managed a few words with Hana. She wasn't real talkative, and sometimes he had to cajole information out of her. She'd said she'd be going home to California soon.

As he rose above the stand of timber marking the northern-most park entrance, Mick considered how little he knew about Hana. He knew he was drawn by her red-gold curls that snapped to life when she stood bareheaded in the sun. He liked the freckles dusted across her nose. Mick probably

thought too much about kissing her shapely mouth, since odds
of that happening weren't high. He'd never seen her wear
lipstick. Of all her attributes, Mick found Hana's eyes to be
her most arresting feature. Given her coloring, a person might
expect her to have blue or green eyes, but hers were…gold.
Whiskey gold. He'd spoken with her enough to decide that her
eyes reflected her every emotion.

Time passed quickly. The smoke jumpers' camp sat halfway between the ranger station and his sister's house. The
place looked pretty deserted. He recognized Leonard Martin's
battered Ford diesel truck, and the assistant's slightly newer
SUV. The Jeep belonged to Jess Hargitay. As a rule, smoke
jumpers flew in from various camps during times of fire. But
Jess drove in. This station was the seasonal home to maybe
six men and women. And the season was at an end, Mick
lamented as he landed.

Heck, maybe he'd find out where Hana lived in California.
He'd been thinking of island vacations, but California had
plenty of white sandy beaches.

He repeated the process he'd gone through at the ranger
station. He let the rotors stop fully before he leashed Wingman
and the two of them climbed out.

"Hi, Mick."

Hana Egan's sweet voice had him spinning too fast on his
fancy titanium hip. Mick felt a deep pain buckle his newly healed
muscles. A blistering swear word escaped before he could check
himself. He dropped Wingman's leash when he was forced to
grab the upright strut on the landing skid to keep from toppling.

The petite woman was quick on her feet. She scooped up
the fleeing dog's leather leash. "I didn't mean to surprise you,
Mick. Are you okay?" Those whiskey gold eyes Mick had so
recently been thinking about turned dusky with concern.

"I'm fine," he growled. The last thing he wanted was for

Hana to judge him a lesser man than Jess Hargitay, who was swaggering toward them. Smoke jumpers tended to be agile, tough and have a penchant for danger.

"You don't act fine," she said. "Why can't men ever admit to any shortcomings?"

He tried to discreetly knead the kink out of the long muscle that ran down his thigh. He hadn't limped in a month, but he limped now as he crossed the space between them and relieved her of Wingman's leash. "I wouldn't touch that comment with rubber gloves, Hana. Suffice it to say, must be a guy thing. But I can't answer for all men." He looped the dog's leash through a cross tube at the rear of the landing skid. "I probably need to ask Jess where he wants me to stack his supplies." Still smarting from her words—and the cramp in his leg—Mick lowered his chin in dismissal and started to walk around her.

"Hold on." She touched his hand, then abruptly pulled back. "I saw you dropping down to land, and I hurried over here to catch you before anyone else butts in. I wanted to tell you goodbye, Mick."

"You're taking off for home today, then?" He halted in his tracks and idly rubbed at his hand, still feeling the rasp of her surprisingly callused palm. Although, considering the job she did, Mick didn't know why he'd be shocked to find her hand wasn't nearly as soft as it looked.

"As soon as six of us finish climbing Mt. St. Nicholas, we'll split up and go our separate ways."

"You heard there's a front moving in?"

"I'm sure Jess scoped out the weather. We're making the climb for fun. It's been a rough summer with fire after fire. This is our last hurrah as a unit before we scatter for the winter."

"Huh. So you aren't all from the same place?"

"No." The denial was accompanied by a crisp shake of her red curls.

"I imagine you're anxious to get home to your family, what with the holidays around the bend."

Mick noticed that a brittleness overtook her usually friendly demeanor. Had he crossed some kind of line? Granted, in the past they'd never got around to discussing anything personal.

"I struck out on my own at sixteen, Mick," she said briskly. "I took three part-time jobs so I could graduate from high school. Before that I was shuffled through a lot of different homes. There's none I'd remotely call family."

"So you were, what? In foster care?"

"Care? If you say so." She spat the word with distaste. "I hope that's not pity in your eyes, Mick Callen. I've done fine. This winter I'm enrolling in a couple of courses at UCLA. One day I'll have my degree in forestry." She followed that with a half-hearted laugh. "I'm surprised Jess hasn't regaled you with the fact that I'm UCLA's oldest underclassman. But I think I should qualify as a junior this semester."

Mick felt her underlying anxiety over baring so much of her soul. He usually played things cool, too, when it came to spilling his guts. Now he felt moved to share. "This past spring my grandfather died. Pappy. You probably heard about it."

"I did. Mick, I'm so sorry. You know he bragged about you something fierce. You must miss him terribly."

"Yeah. I rattle around the house." Mick dug deep to keep his voice from breaking. It was one thing to share a private grief, and another to show weakness.

"I heard your sister married Wylie Ames. Gosh, does that mean you're totally alone this holiday season?"

"Marlee and Wylie want me to spend a week with them at Thanksgiving. I probably will if I haven't winged my way to a sandy beach in some warmer clime. Their baby's due right around Christmas, and they'll have a house full with Jo Beth's grandmother coming to help with the baby. Especially if weather forces the midwife to bunk over."

Mick thought Hana's eyes looked wistful as she said eagerly, "They're having a baby? I can't believe you'd want to miss that."

"I wouldn't have a clue what to do around a newborn. By the time I come back in the spring, the kid'll be sitting up and there'll be something substantial to hang on to. They don't live far from here, Hana. Maybe if you're not off fighting a fire, I'll swing by and take you to see the baby, since you sound keen on little kids."

She gazed beyond him into the distance, and an awkwardness fell between them. "Uh…maybe."

"My sister wouldn't mind. You'll be back here next spring, right?"

She lifted one slender shoulder and Mick's heart slammed hard up into his throat at the very possibility that she might not be coming back to Montana.

Wingman started racing around and bounding to the end of his leash, barking his head off. A long shadow fell across the couple. A muscular, dark-haired man wearing a frank scowl strode up and shouldered Mick aside.

"Hana, what's taking so long? Kari said you came to collect our supplies from Mick. Everything else is loaded in my Jeep. Come on, you're holding us up. I want to make camp at the fir tree break in time to pitch tents for the night."

Hana didn't respond to Jess Hargitay's order.

Mick felt tension drawing tight as if there were a power struggle between the two. Wanting to intercede, Mick tapped Jess on the back. "Cloud Chasers' office manager said you'd pay cash for this load, Hargitay." Mick dug a wadded-up charge slip from his shirt pocket and shoved it none too gently against Jess's chest. "Soon as you cough up the *dinero,* I'll haul these supplies to your Jeep."

There had never been any love lost between the two men who glared at each other now. The dislike had existed before Hana, but intensified whenever Jess caught them talking.

Always cocky and sure of himself, Jess brushed off Mick's hand. Locking eyes with the pilot, he reached out in a too-familiar manner and filtered his fingers through Hana's curls. "Hey, babe, I'm kinda short this month. Run back and pass the hat among the rest of our climbers. I'm supplying the wheels and gas to get to the site. The least all of you can do is spring for food, canned heat and long johns."

Hana opened her mouth as if to refuse. Instead, she moved her head and ducked under the thickly muscled arm, and murmured a final farewell to Mick.

The air crackled in her wake. Neither man spoke, but they continued to take each other's measure until tall, beanpole thin Kari Dombroski loped up to hand Mick a collection of bills and coins.

He stuffed the money in his pocket without counting it. Brushing past Jess, Mick pulled the supplies out of the Huey.

As if to keep Mick from seeing Hana again, Jess relieved him of most of the load, except for the small stuff, which he snarled at Kari to grab.

Wingman lunged at the end of his leash to bark at Jess, and Mick turned his back on the smoke jumpers and bent to calm the dog. "Nice guy, huh, pooch?" he muttered. "If you could talk, I'd ask you what in hell Hana sees in that jackass."

The dog whined and licked his face as Mick untied him and hoisted him into the chopper. Before Mick had his harness and the dog's fastened, the mottled black Jeep kicked up dust farther down the dirt road.

As he lifted off, Mick noted with interest that he and Jess

were both headed toward dark clouds building over the mountain range.

He tried not to think of petite Hana Egan climbing craggy ridges topped by snow and already shrouded in a thickening gray mist.

To distract himself, he projected his worry onto Saturday's potluck. What if the wind was the first taste of the Canadian storm? If it got so bad the party was cancelled, Marlee would be devastated. Oh, his sister made noises about not wanting to attend, but Mick had seen right through her. She wanted the day to be perfect. And Mick wanted that for her, too. She and Wylie deserved to kick back a bit after nursing Dean, Wylie's son, through Burkitt's lymphoma last winter. Between worry over Dean, and Pappy's funeral not long on the heels of Dean's remission, the whole family needed a bit of fun.

CHAPTER TWO

PINE NEEDLES BLEW out from under the Huey as Mick set the lumbering chopper down on Wylie's private runway. Mick sat and admired the handsome six-seat turbo prop Merlin housed under an open shed to the left of the runway. He had helped his brother-in-law buy the plane as a surprise for his bride. Wylie had said Marlee had cried happily when she saw it.

When Mick had told Pappy, he'd merely laughed and said he'd known all along that any woman born a Callen would consider a plane an appropriate wedding gift.

Mick thought *any* woman who lived in remote Montana would think it an excellent gift. But then, he was more practical than sentimental. When he was a kid, this part of Montana was so sparsely settled, ranchers, hunters and the few recreational-sport lodge owners were dependent on small planes to fly them out in an emergency. That was still true, but to a lesser degree. Now, land was being cleared right and left. Whole towns had sprung up in areas where there used to be nothing but forest.

Mick, who was far from a recluse, nevertheless wasn't sure how he felt about all the growth. But old trail blazers like his grandfather and Finn Glenroe were either dying off or they were selling out to developers. Two weeks ago he'd heard that Finn and Mary, who'd run the isolated Glenroe Fishing Lodge for as long as Mick could remember, had accepted a buyout because Finn's arthritis had gotten so bad.

Since arriving home to nurse his war wounds, Mick had watched resort developers salivate over Finn's land. The same outfits sniffed around Cloud Chasers. The day after Pappy's funeral, Mick received three phone offers on the property. Land grabbers were worse than vultures in Mick's opinion. Pappy would turn over in his grave if Mick were to sell. And yet…

Refusing to let himself get maudlin again, he took off his earphones in time to hear the last sound of the rotors. No wobble with any of his landings. Replacing the main hub and the lubricant must have done the trick.

"Uncle Mick, Uncle Mick!" He heard his niece, Jo Beth's, excited cry the minute he cracked the forward door. It was followed by Dean's whoop and Piston's wild barking, which prompted a response in kind from Wingman.

Mick unbuckled the wiggling dog from his harness and lifted him down before climbing from the cockpit himself.

Scooping up the dark-haired girl waiting to be hugged, he marveled again at the change a year and acquiring a brother and new dad had wrought on the formerly unhappy girl. Jo Beth, now six, had been pouty and prone to tantrums when Marlee first moved home after the death of her first husband.

His twin had served two tours in the Gulf, supporting the family while Jo Beth's dad wasted away from lymphoma. Even though Marlee had fallen hard for Wylie Ames, when his son had been diagnosed with a different form of lymph cancer, Marlee had had a rough patch where she almost walked away from love. Surprisingly, Jo Beth handled Dean's illness better than her mother. The girl never wavered in her belief that her friend would recover. And now his cancer was in remission, and doctors expected it to last.

At the moment Dean looked the picture of health. The boy laughed in delight at being mobbed by the two cavorting dogs—dogs similar in size, and looking enough alike to have common parents, which was possible since they had come from the same shelter only months apart.

"Wingman remembers me," Dean said, his freckled face split in a wide grin.

"He does at that." Mick reached down and ruffled the boy's red hair. "You're looking good, my man."

"I grew an inch, too," the boy boasted. "The doctor told Mom that was excellent news."

"It sure sounds good to me! So, where are your folks?" Whenever Mick had come to visit, one or the other parent accompanied the kids to the airstrip.

Jo Beth pointed. "Mama's in the kitchen saying words Grandmother Rose wouldn't like one bit."

Jo Beth's paternal grandmother had practically raised Jo Beth until Marlee, a navy lieutenant, was discharged. That was another traumatic time for his sister. Not long after her husband, Cole's, death, Rose had petitioned family court for custody of Jo Beth. Mick thought it a testament to his sister's forgiving nature that for her daughter's sake, his twin had patched the rift with her former mother-in-law.

"I thought your mom baked pies yesterday. Don't tell me she's swearing over fixing me lunch? Granted, I've had nothing but coffee today, so I could eat a mule raw. Maybe I'll settle for nibbling on you." Mick made growly noises as he teasingly went after his niece's bony shoulder.

She giggled and shrieked until Mick set her down. "Mama's not baking pies, Uncle Mick. She made supper for tomorrow, and had it in a pan when she 'membered a 'portant in…gredient." The girl stumbled in her attempt to explain.

"Ouch, no wonder she's saying bad words. Where's Wylie?"

"Dad's out taking inventory of the campsites in his area," Dean said. "Sometimes campers steal fire grates, or mess up the trash barrels at the end of camping season. He has to make a list of the sites that need stuff stocked before the park opens in the spring. I usually help tie tarps over the leftover firewood so it stays dry for the winter," the nine-year-old said proudly. "Dad knew you were coming, so he let me stay home to help you unload Mom's supplies. He said she's not allowed to pick up anything over five pounds."

"I never turn down help, Dean. Somewhere in this monster, I believe you'll find Halloween treats for two kids who tote boxes to the house."

"Yippee!" the kids yelled out, setting the dogs off again.

Marlee hurried down the path to see what was going on. Her usually well-kept blond hair looked a fright. And at seven months pregnant, she barely fit into the men's plaid flannel shirt that stretched over her bulging middle.

Mick was shocked to see her waddle more than walk out on the asphalt. Last time he'd stopped in to visit, his sister was just starting to show.

"Wow, sis, you look like the pregnant guppy Mrs. Walters brought to our sixth grade science class. Didn't we name her Fatso?"

"Thank you, Mick." Marlee's blue-green eyes narrowed ominously. She snapped his arm hard with a dishtowel she'd used to wipe what looked like blood off her hands. When he stopped trying to evade her, Mick saw it was tomato sauce.

"I'm sorry." He apologized even as he and the kids laughed over her antics. "Honestly, Marlee, you'd better have a look-see in the mirror before Wylie gets home, or he'll beg me to take you back. No offense, but you look like hell. Okay, okay, Jo Beth! I know I said a bad word."

Since her grandmother had drilled into her head that swearing was unacceptable, Jo Beth rarely failed to point out Mick's indiscretions. Or Pappy's when he was alive.

"Spoken like a bachelor. Maybe your girlfriends are fashion plates," Marlee said, her lip quivering, "but this past month I've passed the point of getting into anything in my closet. Tell me you have freight from Mervyn's Online or I'll die. I ordered maternity clothes, and if they didn't come you'll be going to the potluck tomorrow without me." She burst into tears, further shocking Mick.

"I have them…your order," he said, trying to rectify his error of saying how awful she looked by awkwardly patting her. "Jeez, Marlee, I was teasing."

"It's okay." She smothered her face in the sauce-streaked towel, which made matters worse. "Hormones gone berserk, I guess. I swear I didn't do this with my first pregnancy."

"Is it normal? I mean, is everything okay?" Mick asked worriedly. "When did you last see a doctor?"

"When she flew me to Seattle for my checkup," Dean said, again corralling the boisterous dogs. "My dad told me and Jo Beth that's how women who are gonna have babies get."

"No kidding?" Mick frowned into one upturned face, then the other. The kids didn't seem all that positive they shouldn't be doing something to help.

"If Wylie said it, sport, it must be true. Let's give your mom some space. Come on, kids, it's getting colder. Help me haul this freight in." He flung open the door that led to the Huey's dark belly, levered himself into the cavern and began handing out the smallest cartons.

"The Polly Pocket amusement park I wanted! Is this my Halloween treat, Uncle Mick?"

"Jo Beth," Dean exclaimed, running excitedly over to his stepsiste, "Uncle Mick gave me the scary black knight and castle I've been asking Dad for."

Marlee managed to wipe most of her tears away, but left bits of tomato sauce smeared across her cheeks. "Mick, you spoil the kids. Last time you came you brought half a toy store. I told you to stop already."

"What are bachelor uncles for? Or bachelor brothers…? On my last trip to Missoula, I found some perfume to replace the bottle I broke when we moved you here. A clerk also helped me with stuff for the baby. Let's go up to the house. After you clean up, you can open boxes to your heart's content."

"What'll be left to give us when you come for Christmas?"

Her brother jumped down gingerly, and pulled a stack of various-size boxes into his arms before he shut the cargo door. "Uh, I'm thinking of taking off for parts unknown after Thanksgiving. I thought I'd find me a warm spot to ride out winter. Maybe I'll go before Turkey Day. Stella said she'll watch the house."

"Mick!" Marlee couldn't hide her disappointment. "You need family your first holiday without Pappy. Losing him was worse for you than me. I came home almost a stranger after being gone ten years. You gave him reason to live as long as he did."

Mick stared toward the mountains. "I keep expecting him to come out for breakfast or to find him puttering in the workshop. It's hard."

"I understand. After Cole died I felt like running away. Only, I had Jo Beth. But…you have us, Mick."

"I know," he said, dropping back to match his long stride to her waddle. He stopped on the path when the top box threatened to fall. "Will you grab that. I think it's your perfume. I'd hate to break a second bottle."

She took the package. "Talk to me, Mick. It's not good to hold your feelings inside. We're twins. There was a time we shared all our hopes and dreams…and sorrows."

"Back then our dreams were one and the same. To fly for the navy. It's all either of us ever wanted. Now… Life's a bitch sometimes."

"So, your wanting to get away at Christmas has to do with…losing your career? It's been six years, Mick. You rebuilt Cloud Chasers after Pappy let it slip, and it's a great success. And who'll fly mercy missions over the winter if you up and take off? To borrow Dean's term, you're Angel Fleet's best sky knight."

"Sky knight." Mick snorted.

"Apt. I overheard the kids talking on a flight to Seattle for Dean. Jo Beth bragged that she and I were sky angels. Wylie had just told us about a girl Angel Fleet asked you to fly out for a kidney transplant. Dean said angel sounded too girly for you. He's so into the knights and castles toys. He officially dubbed you Sky Knight."

They'd reached the house and Mick was saved from commenting. He was a volunteer flyer. Why gussy up his role? The coordinators of Angel Fleet raised funds to keep flights free or nearly so for needy sick and injured people living in remote locations. The staff were the real knights.

The kids had dumped their boxes on the kitchen table, and were in the living room ripping open their new toys. Both dogs had flopped in front of a fireplace that had been laid with kindling and firewood, but not lit.

Mick hadn't bought only the black knight and Polly Pocket sets for the children; he'd piled on a board game he knew they'd like, and books and music CDs. Wylie didn't have TV reception, although Mick knew he was considering installing a satellite dish.

He handed his sister her maternity clothes, and shooed her off to the bedroom. "Wait, take this, too. I noticed Wylie's belt was wearing thin. I picked him up a new one. Bison leather. It'll last a long time."

"Mick, you aren't blowing all of Pappy Jack's insurance money on us, are you? Because he'd want most of it plowed back into Cloud Chasers."

"The business made a fair profit this year. Thanks to the way you straightened out my lackadaisical billing with that computer program. Stella's done a bang-up job collecting old accounts, too. Dunning friends wasn't something Pap or I were good at. Anyway, quit giving me flak. Who else do I have to spend my money on?"

She took the belt he held out and stared into his eyes for a time, plainly itching to say something.

He assumed she was debating whether or not to deliver her usual lecture suggesting he find a wife and start his own family. Shaking his head, Mick chucked her under the chin. "Go make yourself presentable before Wylie comes in for lunch. I'll put on a pot of coffee and set the table. Your supplies will be okay stacked in the corner. We can sort out Halloween candy and baby gifts later." Mick ducked out of the room, confident Marlee wouldn't resort to yelling what was on her mind. And he was right.

MARLEE'S HUSBAND, Wylie Ames, tall, dark and usually not very talkative, arrived home after the others finished lunch. The dogs bounded to the back door to greet him, and the kids abandoned their toys to collect hugs as they regaled their dad with news of Uncle Mick's generosity.

Marlee had saved Wylie some soup and a sandwich. While Mick relaxed over a second cup of coffee, she warmed the soup in the microwave. Wylie finally pulled free of the kids and filled the arch with his broad shoulders. He was wider of chest than his brother-in-law, but not as tall. Mick had never lost the lanky body typical of a born pilot.

The men had always gotten along. They'd forged an easy camaraderie long before Marlee moved back to Montana.

Wylie clapped Mick's back in greeting before shrugging off his Park Ranger jacket. He'd left his boots in the mudroom and now padded over slick vinyl in his sock feet to kiss his wife.

"Hey, Mick, I was happy to see the Huey parked on my airstrip. There's a smell of snow in the air. We may need to use the chopper instead of the Merlin to fly up to the potluck tomorrow."

"You look windblown, Wylie. Will this storm be serious, you think, or will we only see intermittent snow flurries like one weather report predicted?" Marlee unconsciously rubbed her swollen belly.

Wylie filled a mug with black coffee, murmuring thanks to his wife when she pointed him to a chair at the table where she'd set his steaming soup.

"Don't know how bad it'll get. All I know is that this north wind has a bite we haven't seen yet this year. I wasn't sorry to find my campsites empty, just in case it snows a foot." He picked up a spoon and dipped it in the thick pea soup. Marlee and Mick chatted while Wylie finished eating.

Done, Wylie carried his plate and bowl to the sink, and noticed Marlee concocting something at the counter. "More lasagna?"

"If either of you laugh, you'll be wearing the batch I ruined," she said, shaking a wicked-looking meat fork at him. "I'd filled a big pan to the brim with beautiful layers I'd assembled before you left this morning. Then I noticed the unopened container of cottage cheese on the counter. I tried lifting noodles and putting it in, but that was a disaster. This time I'm checking off each ingredient as I add it. I can't have your friends thinking I'm a terrible cook."

Mick gulped a mouthful of coffee to hide a smile. It was only lately his sister had learned to cook. She still wasn't the best in the west.

To Wylie's credit, he assumed the proper air of concern and

kissed her again. "Mick and I will go out to the addition. That way we won't distract you."

Reaching around Marlee's belly, Wylie topped up his coffee.

Mick rose and set his cup in the sink. "Sis, that new outfit you're wearing is a big improvement over what you had on when I landed."

"Wylie didn't even notice I'm wearing real maternity clothes," she said, wrinkling her nose at her unobservant husband.

Guilt brought a flush to her husband's tanned cheeks. "You always look great to me."

"You are so full of it!" said Mick, laughing. "When I got here she had on a stretched-out pair of too-big sweats, and one of your faded flannel shirts that had a button missing right over her watermelon stomach."

The waterworks Mick had been treated to earlier erupted again.

Wylie gathered Marlee into his arms and with a hand behind her back motioned Mick out. As he clomped toward the mudroom, Mick stored this exchange for future reference. *Don't joke with pregnant women.*

He shouldn't have teased her. He knew Marlee wanted to make a good impression on Wylie's coworkers. Mick vowed he wouldn't be the cause of any more tears on this visit.

He dragged his jacket from one of several hooks lining the mudroom wall. Last time he'd toured the addition, Wylie hadn't yet installed heat. That was in September. Not half as cold as it was now. The wind whistled around the house.

Mick was pleasantly surprised when he stepped into the two new bedrooms separated by a full bath. Baseboard water heaters sizzled softly. He shed his jacket and dropped it over the doorknob.

"Whaddya think?" Wylie walked in behind Mick and gestured around at his handiwork. "The electricity in this entire section runs off a freestanding generator. I may convert the main house to another one next spring. Regular power is so iffy out here, especially if we get a bad winter, and starting the booster generator sometimes takes an hour."

He sipped from his mug. "I remember how I struggled to keep Dean warm during power outages when he was a baby. I don't want Marlee to have to go through that…." His words trailed off.

Mick knew that Wylie's first wife, Dean's mother, had walked out, leaving him with an infant. Even though he'd heard the woman was a flake, Mick had been floored when Marlee told him that Dean wasn't Wylie's biological child. Mick had never met anyone prouder of his son than Wylie Ames. At first Mick had doubted the story. Although, he'd had to admit the two looked nothing alike. Wylie had visible Native American roots; Dean was a classic blue-eyed, freckled carrot-top.

Mick pondered what he would've done in Wylie's place. Ultimately, he gave up. He couldn't imagine. Dean's mother had led Wylie to believe he'd gotten her pregnant, and Wylie must have had cause to consider it possible. Mick was glad that the navy had taught him never to have sex without protection. Not that that lesson had come into play lately. He'd had a longer dry spell than he cared to admit.

"Wylie, are you worried about Marlee's decision to have the baby at home? I mean, forecasters and the almanac are predicting a helluva winter."

Wylie stared into the depths of his mug. "I try not to dwell on it. Having babies anywhere is risky. But I love her so much, it's scary. If anything were to happen to Marlee or the baby because of me…" He shook his head at the thought and turned to look at Mick. "I can't force her to stay in Kalispell for the month before the baby's born. If you have any influence…"

"I don't," Mick hastened to say. "She'd just dig in harder if I say anything. It's the Callen stubborn trait. I recognize it well." He grinned to lighten the mood. "So, what can I do to help get this addition shipshape for guests? Marlee said you'll earmark one room for Rose and the second for the midwife, in case she has to bunk over."

"Right. She owns a snowmobile, but in the event of a blizzard, she'll have to wait it out. I'll finish laying the wood flooring in the smaller room if you'll start painting these walls. If I don't get them painted soon, Marlee will be out here wielding a roller herself."

"Bring on the supplies." Mick ran a hand over the smooth wallboard. "I don't mind staying here tomorrow. I can easily finish a second coat while you're at your potluck."

"No, you don't. I never have been gung-ho on company potlucks. In the past, too many well-meaning friends dragged over women they dug up God knows where. This time I'm actually looking forward to showing off my wife and family, but until you phoned, Marlee had jitters."

"She never said there might be single women at this shindig. Is that why my sister's so keen on dragging me along? She's always pestering me to get out and find a nice person of the opposite sex."

Wylie, who rarely laughed out loud, did so, and thumped Mick's back. "You'd rather we fixed you up with somebody of the same sex?"

"Ha, ha," Mick said. "I like women fine. Better than fine. But I'm picky. The woman I like best of the ones I've met in Montana so far, is kinda—well, probably attached to another guy. So it's obviously not going to pan out. And since it's not, don't you dare spill a word of this to Marlee. She'll be on my case until she worms out of me who it is. Then she won't let up."

The ranger smiled in sympathy for his younger brother-in-law's plight. "I won't say a word. How about I bring in the paint and rollers, while you spread that canvas sheeting."

Mick brushed aside thoughts of Hana Egan and bent to the task of making sure the canvas covered all corners. Wylie had done a great job installing tongue and groove hardwood. Mick forced himself to focus on the room. His house could stand renovation. Rather than head for sun and surf this winter, maybe he ought to stick around and spruce up the old place.

If he did that, he wouldn't have an opportunity to meet a suitable prospect for the position of Mrs. Mick Callen. Not that marriage was at the top of his list. Yet he envied what Marlee and Wylie had. And it was lonely rattling around that big, empty house.

He cleared his mind until Wylie returned to pour warm butterscotch paint into Mick's roller pan. Each stroke he made on the wall unfortunately reminded him of Hana Egan's eyes. He hurried around the walls so he could move on to the pale yellow of the smallest room, which made him think only of Stella's homemade banana cream pie.

Mick was primed for eating by the time they were called for supper. After the meal Marlee opened all the baby gifts Mick had bought and cried over each one.

He shrugged off her thanks, grateful when Wylie asked if he wanted to stay up late to hang the flower-sprigged wallpaper down to the wainscoting in the bathroom.

Marlee and the kids came out shortly after to say goodnight. "Mick, I made up the bed in Dean's room for you."

"Thanks. I'll be quiet going in. I know you said we need to get an early start in the morning."

Later, he tiptoed into the dark room. Piston and Wingman

had already found his bed, and Mick shooed the disgruntled dogs off. As he listened to the wind howl outside, Mick stepped to the window to see if it'd started to snow. Deciduous trees were bare, but their fallen leaves rustled around their trunks. Fir and pine boughs swayed in the wind, and the silver moon shone cold and crisp. Turning away, he climbed between sheets heated by the dogs' bodies and lay a moment, wondering if Hana and her pal, Jess, were sharing a sleeping bag for warmth on a wind-swept mountain that would be colder than it was here. Flopping on his stomach, he rubbed an achy hip that surely meant a change in weather was coming. He forced his breathing to slow so he could fall asleep.

IN THE MORNING, with everyone trying to use one bathroom to get ready, the house was pure chaos. Wylie didn't want anyone showering in the new bathroom yet, although the paint was dry. Mick was relieved to see the wallpaper hadn't slid off the walls overnight. Hey, maybe he *could* spiff up his house.

Marlee blew in with red cheeks after taking the dogs out. "Brr. It's beginning to snow."

Excited, Dean and Jo Beth crowded together at the door and looked outside.

"In or out!" Wylie bellowed. "Dean, you know enough not to let heat out."

The phone rang. Marlee answered. She frowned and hung up. "That was Ellen Russell. It's snowing and blowing at the potluck site. They're moving to the education room at headquarters."

Wylie stroked a fresh-shaven chin. "Four rangers from the outposts will have to fly in then. Makes for a crowded runway."

"Yesterday you suggested taking the chopper. I don't mind doing the flying," Mick said.

"I did bring it up, but later I started thinking the chopper will be a bumpier ride than the Merlin. I'm not keen on Marlee flying at seven months, let alone in the Huey."

She reached past her basketball belly to hug her husband. "Don't coddle me, Wylie. My great-great-grandmother had great-grandpa Callen on a wagon train somewhere along the Oregon Trail. I'll be fine. Taking the Huey makes sense. You and the kids and the dogs can sit on the pull-down canvas litters in back. I'll pretend I'm copilot. But, the wrath of a pregnant woman will be on you if either of those dogs eats my pies or the lasagna."

Laughing, they decided to load up. Soon after, Mick lifted off into pearl-gray clouds laden with snow.

At the main ranger station, the kids snapped leashes on the dogs, hopped down and were soon surrounded by other rangers' children. Dean introduced Jo Beth. Wylie did the same for Marlee and Mick.

Thanks to Ellen Russell, Marlee was absorbed into the circle of women bustling about the central meeting room, where someone had already set up folding tables and chairs in anticipation of moving the potluck indoors.

Ever observant, Mick noticed two female rangers didn't seem to mix with the gaggle of wives, nor did they hang with the men, who'd gone out back under a freestanding roof to pitch horseshoes. The younger of the two women had been introduced as Natalie Sweeney. She made eye contact with Mick. She had rosy cheeks and sandy hair. Pleasant enough looks, but her flirting didn't have much effect on Mick. He escaped by detouring outside to bring the dogs in.

It'd been a while since he'd spent time in the company of a bunch of guys who liked bullshitting with buddies the way the rangers were doing. Mick laughed at their tales about campers who should never have taken up that hobby. City guys who couldn't build a fire or even set up a tent.

Shortly after 1:00 p.m. the women called everyone in to partake of the food that had been tantalizing Mick for an hour. Everything smelled so good.

More emboldened once the married men joined their families, leaving Mick momentarily on his own, Natalie slipped between two people to reach him. "Hi, I work a couple of areas away from your brother-in-law. It's very remote. I'd love a chance to talk with somebody who's been out in the real world." She twisted a lock of hair around a blunt finger. "After you fill your plate, join me? I staked out two spots in a quiet corner, away from the kids."

Mick glanced down the line of people filling plates. Marlee and Wylie were deep in conversation with another couple. "Uh, sure," he told Natalie.

"Great. Here, let me refill your coffee cup and set it at my table…unless you want to switch to beer."

He debated, but finally shook his head and handed Natalie his empty mug.

"Everything looks so good," he joked with the ranger ahead of him, "I either need two plates or a sideboard."

"Forget sideboards, friend, you need armor. A word of advice…Pat Delveccio talked me into dating Natalie once. She's got a one-track mind focused on becoming Mrs. Somebody. If you don't believe me, wait. She's got a list of things she wants in a husband. You won't get two words in before she'll start grilling you about what you do, if you smoke, whether you go to church, how much you have in the bank. When she got to how many kids I thought I'd like to have, I ended the date real fast."

Mick loaded up his plate, unsure whether to join her or not. Maybe she wouldn't feel so free since they'd barely met and in no way were on a date.

Stopping behind his sister, Mick leaned down as she scooted over to make room for him. He murmured in her ear, "I got roped into eating with Natalie Sweeney. If you see me signaling frantically, come rescue me before dessert."

"Don't signal me, Mick. You need to socialize more."

"Thanks heaps." Well, he could always tell Natalie he was in a serious relationship—with a smoke jumper. As he made his way across the room, he noticed it was snowing harder, and his mind skipped to Hana and her pals. Had they already turned back? Undoubtedly, weather on the mountain would be far worse than it was here.

Mick sat, and had no more than dipped a fork into his meal when Natalie hit him with question number one.

"My friend Pat said you own a freight flying service. That's cool." As he chewed, he thought, Marlee's lasagna's not bad. "She also said you're on navy disability. That must provide you a nice nest egg."

She smiled, but the lasagna stuck in Mick's throat. He coughed and stuffed more food in his mouth.

By the time Natalie had worked her way to question number three, Mick's eyes were glazed. The park radio crackling to life saved him. Trudy Morgenthal had set it to take Park area emergency calls here. Talk instantly ground to a halt.

Mick heard enough of a frantic, garbled transmission to deduce that the hiking party of smoke jumpers had turned back, but not soon enough. They'd met with trouble.

He bounded out of his seat and crowded around the radio with the rangers.

"I outfitted that party," he said. "I know several team members. What happened?"

Trudy shushed him and turned to her boss. "It seems that last night they disagreed over whether to forge on to the peak or turn back. They went farther up the face before pitching tents. Today they decided to call it quits. But the first team roping down the ridge slipped and plunged into a crevasse. The guy on the radio knows they have injuries, and he's afraid some may be dead."

The captain scowled. "Damned crazy smoke-eaters. Who in hell issued them permits this time of year?"

"I did," said a ranger standing behind Mick. "I issued it last month. They delayed going twice because of fall fires. But I mean, I expected them to have common sense."

"Yeah, well, apparently they don't," the captain muttered. He scanned his men. "How many of you are sober enough to head out on a rescue climb?"

Several hands, including Mick's, shot up.

The radio stuttered to life again. "I'm getting word from the crevasse," a disembodied voice said. "Two women seem to be hurt bad. The most coherent one claims there's been no response from our guide. He fell first, but he's our most experienced climber. Can you send a rescue plane? I'm afraid if we don't get the injured out ASAP they'll die."

Mick wanted so badly to ask names and particulars. But a larger part of him was afraid to know who had fallen.

"We can't send either of our helicopters out in this wind. They're small and it's too risky," the captain said.

"I flew here in a Huey." Mick elbowed his way forward. "Trudy, ask if there's a clearing near them large enough for me to land away from trees."

"Mick, no!" Marlee squeezed past two burly rangers. "Have you looked outside? It's almost a whiteout."

Mick's solemn eyes found her in the crowd. "If not me, sis, who?"

CHAPTER THREE

RANGER WIVES CLOSED RANKS around Marlee Ames, because not only did her brother volunteer for the dangerous rescue mission, her husband did as well. Once it was ascertained there were three uninjured hikers, all ill-equipped for snow, Mick was elected to concentrate on the injured. Wylie was one of a hiking rescue party comprised of six rangers.

The meeting room where they'd gathered for the end of season feast doubled as a chart and map room. The captain pulled down a map and a blowup of the mountain region. Those slated to go crowded in to get a fix on coordinates and check the most direct access route.

Anxious, Mick wanted to race out and take off straight away because the longer they delayed the more they risked worsening weather. But he knew the value of good planning and coordination, so as Wylie slipped away to have a private word with Marlee, Mick crossed his arms and listened to everything that was being said. Two rangers far more familiar with the terrain pointed out potential trouble areas.

"It's one-thirty. If I don't spot the climbers on my first pass I may have to return to base and wait for first light. I don't want to get caught trying to lift off from the mountain after dark. Especially if temperatures drop and it starts to freeze," Mick said.

A ranger ran a finger over the topographical map. "They

probably left their vehicles here. We can drive about three miles farther using the fire road."

"One vehicle," Mick said. "They all piled into a big jeep. I saw them head out."

Wylie's friend Bud Russell pulled the ring tab and let the map roll up. "Pack lights and climbing gear in a toboggan. I estimate we won't reach them until eleven, or could be nearer midnight. We'll take sandwiches, thermoses of coffee, and thermal blankets. Damn weather's been practically balmy up until today. Their contact said they weren't prepared for bad weather except for a few who wore long johns. He said they're exposed to the storm."

"They can't be more than a mile on either side from a tree line," one of the older rangers said. "I know he said his radio battery is running low, but shouldn't we raise him again and suggest they leave the crevasse and hike to shelter?"

"I did suggest that while you guys were assembling volunteers," Trudy said. "They vetoed splitting up. They're worried about the snow obliterating the tree boughs they've cut and stuck in the ground to mark the crevasse. If their makeshift markers blow away, it's as good as writing off those who fell."

Mick shrugged into his jacket. "I'll reach the site long before you guys. Give me the bulk of the blankets and hot drinks. Depending on how many injured we're talking, and how severely they're hurt, I can maybe get off the ground with three. Two, if they require stretchers. One additional if ambulatory," Mick said. "If it comes down to a choice between flying out injured or dead, I'll focus on those who need doctors and leave you to handle the rest."

He could tell from the ring of stony faces that nobody wanted to think about dead bodies. Yet rangers were realistic. They all nodded grimly.

"Sounds like a plan," the captain said. "What if you can't

set down up there?" He posed the question lurking at the back of Mick's own mind, because the hiker on the radio hadn't been sure the clearing was large enough to land a big chopper.

"If I can't land, I can still drop supplies. I'll stack blankets and food in the copilot's seat. I volunteer with Angel Fleet, so my aircraft are all stocked with first aid kits."

"Do you want a ranger EMT to ride shotgun with you?"

"That would be nice, but I'm concerned about wind drag. I saw clips of that rescue on Mount Rainier in Washington state that went into the toilet because of wind shears and weight. I don't want a repeat of that. Can someone impress on the guy who radioed in that I have to grab the injured and get out? Even then it'll be tricky getting to Kalispell before all hell breaks loose with this storm. Tell him to use the climbing ropes to pull the climbers out of the crevasse and patch up injuries as best he can for transport."

Once Mick saw Trudy flipping switches on the radio to relay his message, he shoved open the door and stepped out onto the plank porch. Even under the overhang he got hit by quarter-sized snowflakes that seemed to be blowing in circles. "Damn them," he growled, thinking aloud about smoke jumpers who should have better sense.

"They're hotshots," Bud said from over Mick's shoulder.

"Yeah, but we work closely with Len Martin's crews," the ranger captain said as he hunched against the wind ripping away his words. "Len does get some green recruits. Kids who still think they're invincible."

"Three in this party are seasoned," Mick said. "One's a five-year veteran. Another, a woman I know, has spent three summers with Martin's crew."

Wylie jogged up to walk alongside Mick, as if he'd heard something more in his brother-in-law's words. He drew Mick aside when the others split up to ready a vehicle and their gear.

"One of those climbers wouldn't be the woman you mentioned at the house last night? The gal you're interested in who's involved with another guy?"

"What if it is?" Mick's steps didn't slow, but his jaw tightened.

Wylie hesitated, seeming to weigh his next comment. "Marlee thinks you haven't been yourself since Pappy died. She's worried you might do something…rash today."

Mick pulled up short in the shadow of the bird. He scowled as he dug a pair of leather gloves out of the cockpit. "What the hell does that mean, Wylie?"

"Just that this is a ranger call. I have to know if you're depressed enough, or personally involved enough, to get reckless with your life. If so, I'll have to order you to stand down. If need be, I'll handcuff you to one of the damned fence posts."

Surprise passed through Mick's lean frame, and then he found Wylie's swashbuckling attempt comical. Wiping a hand across his face to dust off the snowflakes stuck to his eyelashes, he laughed. "Are you seriously suggesting that if Hana doesn't make it, I'm gonna fly into the side of the mountain?"

"Put that way, it does sound extreme."

"Damned right. Tell Marlee my head's screwed on straight."

His hip objected to the shift in weather, making it difficult for Mick to hoist himself into the cold cockpit. Neither man spoke again, but their eyes met. Blowing snow cast a muted golden halo over the camp. All sound seemed muffled except for the ropes clanking against the flagpole that marked the entrance to the ranger station. The U.S. flag, the Montana state flag, and the forestry flag, all attached below a snow-covered brass ball, flapped wildly in the stiff wind.

Wylie gave in first and raised a hand for Mick to clasp. "Fire her up. I see Bill coming with the supplies. I'll toss extra

pillows and blankets in the hatch and lock her down." Several
heartbeats passed, then he shouted to be heard over the first
whir of the rotors, "Good luck, Mick."

A lump rose in Mick's throat, so he busied himself arrang-
ing the blankets and food Bill handed him, firmly in the
copilot's seat. Then he donned his earphones. That done, he
was in control of his feelings enough to flash his brother-in-
law a thumbs-up.

He felt the chopper rock as the men buttoned up the back,
but waited until he saw them bend over and run clear before
he lifted off.

Mick's thoughts threatened to turn into worry for Hana. He
refused to let that happen. Instead, he concentrated on the landscape fanned out below. As he climbed steadily, flying got
dicier. Crosswinds alone could be wicked for rotors. Add
blowing snow to the equation and bad conditions increased
tenfold. The saving grace, if there was one, was that the snow
was still dry. It blew off the Huey's blades instead of weighing
them down.

Below him, trudging slowly in single file down a steep
ravine, were three bighorn sheep. They had grown shaggy
winter coats and their brown hair was dusted white with snow.
Any other time, he'd linger over the rare sight. The fact that
the sheep knew to prepare for winter so soon lent an urgency
to Mick's mission. The jagged peaks he'd admired from home
yesterday cast shadows across neighboring slopes—slopes he
needed to see so he could land. First, though, he needed
enough light to spot the stranded hikers.

Higher up into the foothills, fog drifted in in deep pockets.
Yet another element against him. The snow and fog mix was
beginning to hide the terrain below.

Mick turned up the heat inside the Huey, hoping to melt the
flakes beginning to stick on the clear part of the bubble. Still,

he had to use his glove to wipe off the condensation building up inside the plastic.

He'd been in the air forty minutes when a hole opened and he saw a red light winking atop a radio tower. The first of three point markers Wylie's captain said he'd come across. Mick's stomach unknotted. He hadn't realized until then how tense he'd become.

It shouldn't be long now before he'd see where the hiker said they'd staked tree boughs in the shape of an arrow. He wondered how far up the mountain Wylie and the other volunteers were. He knew they had radios and would try to stay in contact with the hikers. Mick cursed himself for not having asked for their frequency so he, too, could keep tabs. He fiddled with the dials, but got only static.

The arrow.

He adjusted his speed, brought the Huey lower and hovered above the marker. People came into view. One motionless body was propped against a fair size rock that was being used as a wind break. It was impossible to tell if the figure was a man or a woman, since a jacket was draped around the shoulders and another tented his or her whole head.

To the left of the rock, Mick identified three more figures lying flat around a dark gash in the hillside. The crevasse. *Damn.* By the look of things he'd arrived before the crew had complied with his request to have all of the injured ready to be flown off the mountain.

Although the wind didn't seem quite so erratic now, Mick wondered whether he'd be able to lift off again once he'd landed. He quickly calculated the area, angle of descent and wind velocity. Wind, unfortunately, was unpredictable.

Where the climbers were more or less dictated that he had to perch on an incline. Would the weight of the Huey cause it to slide down the slick slope and keep sliding until it crashed into the line of trees below?

One of the figures at the crevasse hopped up and waved frantically. Mick wanted to yell at the foolish hiker and say, "Forget about me. Get those folks out of the hole."

But as fast as his anger flared it fizzled. He knew what it was like to be in need of rescue. He felt his palms sweat as he remembered getting the hell shot out of his F/A-18. Falling. His chute jerking open. Floating down as gunfire rained around him. His heart slamming against his chest as he hauled in his chute and detached it from his hips, one of which ran red with his blood. He'd dragged himself into underbrush, scared he'd die on unfriendly soil.

But he hadn't died. Six Black Hawks had shown up. Five fended off the enemy as one landed and rescued him.

Gritting his teeth, Mick wrestled the whirlybird onto a snowy perch. He hadn't fully shut down before opening his door and tumbling out in a crouch. His first aid kit in hand, he ran bent over to the person slumped against the boulder.

Kari Dombroski, he discovered. She was the one who'd brought Mick the money the hikers had collected to pay for the climbing supplies Jess had ordered. Mick still had the money wadded in his jeans pocket, where he'd stuffed it yesterday.

"Kari, it's Mick Callen." He touched her shoulder lightly and stared into eyes filled with pain. "I'm here to fly you to a doctor. You and others who've been hurt." He flipped open the metal lid of his first aid kit, still unable to make out the identity of those working feverishly to rope another climber out of the yawning crevasse.

"Can you walk?" he asked Kari.

Rousing, she shook her head. "Three of us lost our footing on snowy pine needles. We bounced off sharp rocks before we finally landed in the crevasse."

"Has anyone checked your injuries?"

"Norm Whitman said my right arm's broken in a couple of places. He didn't know if he should tape it to my side or not. It's swelling. My right leg is either broken, or I tore a ligament. I can't bear weight on it." Tears began sliding down her face.

Mick made a sling for her arm. She yelped when he placed her arm in it. "I have two litters in the chopper. But if I put you on one and your fellow climbers have worse injuries, I may need to leave someone behind. No matter where I put you, on a stretcher or in the copilot seat, it's going to hurt like hell."

"That's okay. I'll sit wherever you say, Mick. Please, you need to check on Hana and Jess. I'm afraid…" She broke off and her damp eyes spoke her fears more succinctly than words.

"Shh, I'll carry you to the chopper so you'll be out of the wind." Mick braced himself to lift her. She wasn't big, but his phony hip socket objected all the same.

As he stumbled toward the Huey, Kari blubbered through tears, "Jess's feet came out from under him first. He disappeared over what I thought was a ridge. Hana and I were dragged along 'cause we were roped to him. When I stopped falling, I rolled, and called to them, but I didn't get an answer." She sobbed against Mick's shoulder. "I thought we'd all die."

He set her down gently inside the Huey and focused on splinting her leg. He tore off the tape and got up, noticing her face had been scraped. Mick carefully rubbed on an antibiotic cream.

"We shouldn't have gone higher toward the peak," she said, trying but failing with her one good hand to hang on to the blanket Mick draped around her. He adjusted it for her and closed the lid on his kit. Keeping an eye on the storm outside, he poured Kari a cup of black coffee and wrapped her uninjured hand around the plastic cup.

"We should've turned back as soon as it started snowing

hard. Jess egged us on." Tears rimmed her lower eyelids and tracked over the welts on her cheek.

"Time to sort out blame later," Mick said gruffly. "Hang in there, Kari. I'll go see what's happening at the crevasse." A knot fisted in his chest as he slid out of the chopper. He'd known what Kari was afraid to say—that Hana and Jess didn't make noise because maybe they'd been killed in the fall.

He slogged uphill through worsening weather to where the others were just rolling a body out of the hole. Mick tried to muster anger at Jess Hargitay for being so irresponsible, but only panic filled his throat. Especially when he saw Chuck Hutton and Norm Whitman bent over a form too slender to be Hargitay.

A third man, the shortest of the three, faced the blowing snow. He wore a ball cap pulled so low Mick couldn't tell who he was. Not that it made a difference. He just needed to marshal his jumpy nerves and make himself look at Hana.

Chuck got to his feet. "She's alive," he told Mick, relief clear in his voice. "She screamed when we tightened the rope to hoist her out, over the rim. Then I suppose she blacked out again. She's gotta be hurt bad. My guess is internal. I don't feel broken bones. But I'm afraid to touch her much."

"And Jess?" Mick asked through clenched teeth as he knelt.

Chuck averted his eyes. "There's been no response from him. Roger's about to climb down to see. We were able to get Kari to disconnect her and Hana's ropes from Jess. The lot of them lost their footing and sailed past us so fast there wasn't time to grab their ropes, or even tell the women to hit their release clips."

"Why were both women connected to Jess— Forget it—it doesn't matter. I have a stretcher we'll use for Hana. I'll need your help carrying her to the chopper."

"You'll take us all, right?" Chuck shouted to be heard over

the howling wind. His teeth chattered and his face was already chapped from the cold.

"Wish I could, Chuck, but no. A hiking party from the ranger station is on its way up the mountain. I'll leave blankets, food and coffee. You can pitch a tent and wait, or you can hike down and meet the rescue team."

"Without Jess, we'd never find the route. This snow has made getting our bearings impossible. Jess was the one with the mountain climbing experience."

Mick didn't want to point out they were all dumb-asses for setting out with a storm forecast. He only said, "Kari's in a lot of pain. And I'm half afraid to move Hana." He glanced at the Huey, then at the inert woman. "I'll anchor litters to each side of the chopper wall for these two."

"What about Jess?"

"I can take three wounded if one's up to sitting in the copilot's seat. Everything—and everyone—in the body of the craft has to be lashed down. It's a matter of weight distribution, taking off in this wind. If anyone slid or rolled, it could throw me into a spin."

In fact, the wind had begun to cut through Mick's jeans. The snow had intensified, and the flakes were getting wetter. That was bad. His tracks to and from the Huey were already covered. He wore boots, but now noticed snow had soaked the bottom edges of his jeans.

Mick left Chuck and trekked back for a litter. He gathered as many blankets as he could carry and slung packs filled with sandwiches and coffee over both shoulders. Before leaving base camp, he'd taken time to line the interior walls where he'd strap the litters as best he could with blankets and pillows to make a sick bay for the most badly injured.

Kari was still crying, although more quietly.

"This stretcher is for Hana." Mick wanted to give her added

hope. "They have her out of the crevasse. She's unconscious, but she's alive."

"Please just hurry. I hurt worse with every passing second."

He promised to do his best then returned to the crevasse. Hana's face looked as pale as the snow. Instead of insulating her from the cold, Chuck had rolled her out onto the ground. She might already have suffered frostbite. Mick curbed his frustration, recognizing that they were all working under a strain. The uninjured climbers had done the best they could in crappy circumstances.

He shoved blankets and a thermos bag at Norm Whitman. "Bundle up and drink something warm," he ordered the man, whose fingers were turning blue.

Mick unrolled the canvas stretcher and shook out two thermal blankets. He eased Hana onto one, then moved her on her side so he could brush snow off her back.

She cried out sharply and her eyelids shot open. "Jess," she gasped in a breathy sob. "Stop. Stop! Oh, God, help. My back's in spasms."

Mick's fingers stilled instantly. He shrugged off the way she'd mistaken him for Jess, and did his best to treat her more gently as he placed her flat on her back. She let out another ragged cry as her eyes went back in her head. She'd blacked out again. He rolled two additional blankets lengthwise to stabilize her hips, then covered her from neck to toe with another. Though his own hands ached with the cold, he looped straps around her waist, hips and ankles, and buckled her firmly on the litter. Mick glanced up as the man in the ball cap, Roger, hoisted himself over the ledge of the crevasse with a lot of help from Chuck Hutton. Roger swayed unsteadily and suddenly bent at the waist and vomited all over the snow.

Rising, and ignoring the stab to his bad hip, Mick tripped

over Norm as together they converged on the pair standing next to the crevasse.

Roger managed a shaky, "Jess is d…de…dead. I think he br…broke his neck in the fall." With a cry, Roger grabbed the front of Chuck's jacket. "I told him two hours out that we should pack it in and go home. But no, the macho asshole called me a wimp. It could've been you, or me, or any of us dead at the bottom of that hole!"

Mick sensed Roger was a blip on the radar away from hysteria. He'd seen it in combat with men forced to face their own mortality. Roughly, he broke Roger's grip on Chuck, who shot Mick a grateful, ashen-faced nod.

"We've got to bring him up," Mick commanded, fighting his reeling thoughts. He knew he sounded harsh and unfeeling as he called upon his military training. "I've got a tarp in the aircraft we can wrap him in. I'll have to leave…uh…the body with you. The rangers are bringing a toboggan." Mick broke off. "We've gotta work fast. I have two injured women needing medical attention. Norm and Chuck, help me carry Hana to the Huey. If she wakes up and asks, don't say a word about Jess."

The men moved like zombies. Mick reminded Chuck, "I'll leave blankets and hot coffee. Pitch a tent and crawl inside out of the weather until the rangers arrive. Keep a light on so they can spot you in the dark. They estimated reaching here between eleven and midnight."

"I'm not waiting with any dead body. You can fly us all out." Roger latched on to Mick's throat. "I've seen war movies. A chopper the size of yours can haul a platoon. You're not leaving us here to freeze and die like Jess."

Up close, Mick could see how young Roger was—eighteen or nineteen. Which didn't make him less of a threat. In his current state of mind, the kid could easily do something stupid that would permanently ground the Huey.

Mick tried to reason with him. "Under normal circumstances the Huey could carry that kind of a payload. Mine's been renovated to haul freight. In this weather, the extra weight puts me in danger of crashing and killing us all."

"I'm not staying here." Roger tightened his choke hold on Mick. Norm dropped his coffee, splashing hot liquid across the snow as he leaped forward to pull Roger off Mick. But the younger man wasn't easily dislodged.

Mick gagged as they struggled. He tried, but was unable to gain solid footing in the slippery snow. He'd seen men go temporarily insane under fire. To Roger, this mountain was the enemy, and Mick's helicopter represented safe passage out.

Norm hooked Roger under both arms, breaking his grip, as Chuck hauled back and decked the kid with a roundhouse punch. As quickly as he'd attacked Mick, Roger sagged to his knees, leaving Norm grappling with his dead weight.

"Jeez, Chuck, why'd you hit him so hard? He's out cold," Norm yelled.

Chuck began to look wild-eyed himself. "I just reacted, man." He flexed his hands nervously.

Mick rubbed his throat. "He'll be okay. I owe you guys. I wish I could take everyone, but I think I'll be lucky to get the injured out." Mick relieved Norm of the young man, and deposited Roger's limp body on a soft pile of blankets. "He'll be woozy for a while after he wakes up. Listen, the rangers will rescue you. And if you care at all about Hana and Kari, help me get Hana into the chopper and out of this weather. Then…I'll lend a hand with…uh…Jess."

As they lifted the litter Hana began to thrash about and talk nonsense. Although he hated having to leave Kari alone with her, Mick felt obligated to help with Jess.

No one wanted to go into the pit again, but because Norm was the lightest, he was chosen to be roped down. Mick and

Chuck lowered him in silence. Bringing up a body wasn't a chore any of them wanted. But it had to be done. The process took longer than Mick had judged, because he had to keep prodding Chuck to pull on his rope. Once they had the body up, Chuck and Norm were so rattled, erecting the tents fell to Mick. The other men didn't understand why Mick demanded two of their tents, and he wasn't about to spell out for them that Jess needed to be under cover because of wolves and other predators.

Long shadows had slipped across the eerily silent clearing by the time Mick finished and flatly declared, "Look, I've gotta take off." Mick shook hands with first Norm then Chuck. As he left the site, the men dragged Roger, who had begun to stir, into the larger of the two tents. Mick knew they didn't want him to leave, but it was now or never.

Kari was gritting her teeth in pain, and Hana looked like death waiting in the wings.

Mick hadn't totally shut down the rotors, hoping to keep them from freezing up. Still, as he tried to lift off, the escalating wind was determined to drive him back into the hillside. He waged a battle of determination in his head while steadily increasing power to the rotors.

Sweat popped out on his brow and several drops slid down his nose as the tail rotor caught the downdraft and the main body of the aircraft bucked and pitched. He thought he was a goner.

Both women screamed, nearly bursting Mick's eardrums. He'd outfitted them with headsets to minimize the chopper noise, and also as a means to communicate with them if they panicked. Kari had resisted being buckled on a stretcher, but she couldn't get up to sit in the copilot's seat, so Mick had insisted on strapping her in. Because Hana had thrashed about earlier, Mick worried she'd break her restraints now or in flight.

He recognized that this wasn't the safest way to carry injured passengers on a two-hour flight. But he'd come this far, and Hana was alive. She'd said something the other day that stuck with Mick. Or rather, it was something she'd implied—a lot of people in Hana Egan's life had let her down. By damn, he didn't intend to be another person who failed her.

A giant sucking sound rent the air. The big helicopter popped loose from the stranglehold of the downdrafts and shot up and away from the side hill like a cork exploding from a champagne bottle. Mick's lungs eased as he let out a breath.

"Mick?" Kari's voice spoke urgently in his ear. "I felt the wall behind me rattle. What's wrong? Are we going down?" Fear made her voice shrill.

"Relax, Kari. Everything's fine," he said, hoping she couldn't see him shake out a handkerchief and mop his forehead. "How did Hana deal with liftoff?"

"Fine, I guess. God, I hurt everywhere from all the shaking."

"Sorry. I wish I had more pillows."

She said nothing, which was okay with Mick. He wanted to radio the ranger station and let someone there know his passengers' names and his destination. He'd also like them to alert Wylie's rescue party as to what they'd find at the end of their trek, but that wasn't the way Kari and Hana should learn what happened to Jess.

Trudy Morgenthal, the regular dispatcher, picked up Mick's call to headquarters. "Nice of you to touch base at long last, Callen. You've got everyone in a tizzy. And in Marlee's condition, a tizzy's the last thing she needs."

"You haven't heard from Wylie?"

"Wylie and Bill have called in a dozen times asking for updates from you."

"Yeah, well, I had my hands full."

Not free to say much more, Mick kept his transmission to Trudy short. He clicked off after asking her to tell Marlee he'd touch base after he reached Kalispell.

He felt a shimmer of guilt for leaving Marlee and the kids stranded. He could, he supposed, be back to ranger headquarters by 4:00 a.m. or so. All he was obligated to do was wait for an ambulance. Once the smoke jumpers were on their way to the hospital, he could return and take the Ames family home. He could. But Mick already knew he was going to tag along to the hospital.

His headset crackled. Kari asked shakily when they'd land.

"In about ninety minutes. I'll radio ahead for an ambulance when we're fifteen minutes out."

"I need to phone my boyfriend," she said.

"He wasn't on the climb?" Mick glanced back into the dim interior.

"He's not a smoke jumper. His name is Joe. He didn't want me to make this climb. He said I wouldn't get home in time to celebrate his mom's birthday. Now I'll definitely miss it," she sobbed. "And I'll probably have to ask him to come up here and drive me home."

"Where do you live? Southern California, like Hana?"

"No," she sniffed. "Denver. This was my last year as a smoke jumper. That's why I wanted to make this trek with the crew."

With Jess gone, Mick wondered who Hana would call. Did she have anyone?

"Is Hana awake?" Mick knew she could hear him if she was conscious.

He heard her ragged whisper. "I'm awake. I'm in a lot of pain, mostly in my lower back. And I can't feel my toes."

That didn't sound good to Mick, who'd taken advanced first aid courses in order to fly for Angel Fleet. He figured from

Hana's torn and bloody jeans that she'd bounced over rocks before landing in the crevasse. Chuck, Norm and Roger hadn't gone to any extra effort to support her back before pulling her out. But then, Mick had rolled her onto the stretcher. Chills swept his spine as he considered that he might have done her more harm than good in brushing snow off her back.

The last thing he wanted to do was transmit his panic to her. "I strapped you on the stretcher pretty tight. Listen, ladies, we're coming into some turbulence. It'll probably hurt but we should get through it quickly."

He hit an air pocket and dropped, then shot up almost as fast. Someone cried out sharply, and then both moaned in what must have been agony. Mick hated hearing them in pain and knowing he could do nothing to help.

He'd hoped for a break in the weather before he came within radio range of the Kalispell airpark. But no such luck. This storm seemed determined to beat Montana up on all sides.

"It won't be long until you get real medical attention," he told them ten minutes later. "I'm going to call now to ask for an ambulance. The paramedics will come onboard and give you something for pain before they move you."

Kari answered for the two of them with a weak, "Thanks, Mick."

He switched dials and made the request. Time was wasted as Mick had to explain to the dispatcher that this call wasn't in conjunction with Angel Fleet. Moments later, he was in the approach pattern to the airpark, when the tower imparted more bad news.

"It's been snowing hard and steady. We have no clear runway. Advise you to divert to a major airport."

"I have injured onboard," Mick informed the air controller. "Request permission to land. I don't have enough fuel to go to International."

When a voice finally agreed to let him land, Mick had little doubt his request would've been refused if he'd been flying any aircraft other than the Huey. Of course, had he been flying either of his light planes, or Wylie's, he couldn't have set down on the mountain.

It was just now eleven, which meant the rangers hiking up to rescue the stranded may have arrived. No telling how long it'd take them to trek out.

He rolled his head to ease the tension building between his shoulder blades, and listened to the controller issue directions for landing. Mick could barely make out the tower lights. Wind slammed him one way and just as fast jerked him back the other direction. He had to cut more power to fight a spin.

There wasn't a peep from the back, though some offensive language certainly left his mouth. Old habits formed in the military died hard.

It seemed to take a long time, but at last he corrected the spin. However, he was very near the ground. So near he was blinded by flashing lights from the emergency vehicle mere seconds before the Huey's runners smacked the snowy tarmac.

A sigh of relief rushed from his lungs. Mick had rarely had such a bad landing.

He shut down the rotors and jumped from the cockpit, grimacing from the pain that clutched his bad hip. His limp was so pronounced, one of the emergency crew assumed he was one of the injured. "Old war wound," Mick muttered, opening the door to give the medics access to the real patients.

The women didn't look good. Even in the diffused light flickering sporadically through whorls of blowing snow, Mick saw tracks from their tears marring their cheeks.

The medics got the women out and onto gurneys. Mick felt relief knowing a qualified attendant was caring for Hana and Kari.

Once the emergency vehicle had disappeared through the main gate, he hobbled to the office and left orders to refuel the Huey. "I won't be flying out again tonight," he told the clerk. He needed to know the extent of Hana's injuries. And whether or not in his zeal to rescue her he'd caused more damage.

CHAPTER FOUR

ON THE SHORT WALK to the lot where he kept Pappy's old Cadillac for just such trips to town, Mick opened his cell to call his twin.

Marlee answered so fast, Mick knew she must've been holding her phone. "Mick! I'm so relieved. You can't imagine how much worse the weather's gotten here—and on the mountain, according to Wylie."

"I'm sorry to leave you stuck there. Are you okay? How about the kids and the dogs?"

"We're fine. The dogs, too. We're all bunking with Ellen Russell. Wylie's decided to borrow one of the park's four-wheel SUVs tomorrow and drive home. Forecasters predict this storm's going to hang around. Wylie said there's no sense for you to risk your neck flying back up here. Sorry as I am to cut your visit short, I agree. I guess you know Dean's happy enough to keep Wingman."

"Did he mention I asked him to dog-sit while I go on vacation?"

"He did. But if you change your mind, we'd still love to have you come for the holidays."

"I know. I'll give it some thought. Right now I have other things on my mind. I'm on my way to the hospital to check on the climbers I brought in."

"Trudy said you were transporting two women. She said they had multiple injuries."

"Yeah." He was hesitant to tell his pregnant sister about Jess. On the other hand, he needed her to contact Wylie and let him know the situation.

"What aren't you telling me, Mick?"

Marlee had always had a sixth sense when it came to things he didn't want to spill. "One man died in the fall," he said. "Another, a young guy, went ballistic when he found out I couldn't carry everyone out. Chuck Hutton decked him. The kid's liable to try to cause trouble for Chuck and me. Will you alert Wylie?"

"I'll get him on the radio right now. Oh, Mick, I'm so sorry. How well did you know the man who died?" Her voice dropped in sympathy.

"We weren't friends. He's worked for Len Martin the longest, though. The thing is, I think he and one of the injured women were more than coworkers." Linking Hana and Jess left Mick with a sinking feeling. "Uh, Hana doesn't know Jess didn't make it out. I'm probably going to have to break the news to her."

WHY DID THE NAME HANA *sound familiar?* Marlee couldn't place it. "You sound… Mick, it hasn't been that long since you found Pappy Jack dead in his bed. Has this triggered post-traumatic stress?"

"I'm fine. I'm sick for Hana. As soon as the doctors get her pain under control, I know she'll start thinking straight and she'll be asking about Jess."

"Shouldn't you phone Captain Martin and let him handle telling her? I realize this climb was something his crew did on their own, but since they all worked for him, isn't he the logical one to notify next of kin?"

"I suppose he should be told. They were all set to leave Montana for the winter…" Mick hesitated again. "Hana doesn't have family anywhere."

"Mick," his sister said slowly, "am I missing something? Lord knows nobody has a bigger, softer heart than you, but…this injured woman who's just lost her boyfriend must have other friends. Closer friends."

"I didn't say Jess Hargitay was her boyfriend."

"No, but you did say they were *more than* coworkers."

"Listen, Marlee, I want to get to the hospital. So, I'll talk to you later. You just need to get on the two-way and tell Wylie what went on with the kid. His name's Roger Dorn."

"All right," she said. "But we're not done with this conversation. Call me tomorrow."

"So you can find a dozen more ways to call me a pushover?"

"I didn't. Mick, why are you so touchy?"

He heaved a sigh. "It's been a stressful day. Bye, Marlee." He hung up.

As HE LEFT THE AIRPARK, Mick shut off his phone and tucked it in his pocket. Marlee wasn't his mother or his conscience. She *was* two or three minutes older. And since the age of nine, when they'd learned this fact, she'd reminded him of it.

He exited the freeway and soon pulled into a snow-covered hospital parking lot. It looked like a Christmas card, with snow slanting past the brightly lit building. This was where he'd had his surgery last year. Mick remembered it had rained the day Marlee had checked him out.

As he approached the reception desk to ask about Hana, his mind flashed over the good times and bad ones he and Marlee had weathered together. Even before he asked the whereabouts of Hana and Kari, Mick's annoyance with his sister had begun to fade. She worried about the people she loved. She worried about him.

"And are you related to Hana Egan or Kari Dombroski?"

The middle-aged woman behind the desk pulled down a pair of half glasses and studied Mick.

He flipped out his ID, which included his volunteer pilot status with Angel Fleet. He knew that would gain him entry even though the organization wasn't involved. "I rescued the women off a mountaintop, and I'd like an update on their conditions."

Impressed, the clerk flipped through a set of cards that hadn't yet been filed. "They've both gone to the orthopedic floor for evaluation. Are you familiar with the hospital?" She set a map on the counter.

"Yes, thank you." Mick collected his ID and put his wallet away. He took off, not bothering to respond to the receptionist's casual comment about how grateful Hana and Kari must be. *Kari, maybe. Hana, not necessarily.*

He passed a brightly lit gift shop with a glass vase filled with greenery and miniature yellow roses in the window. Mick stopped and pushed open the etched-glass door.

A woman about his age glanced up. "May I help you?"

"Those vase thingies in your window. How much are they?"

Smiling, she picked up the vase and gave a figure. "Visiting hours are over, but we offer in-house delivery at no charge, sir. All I need is the patient's name and room number."

"Actually, this patient was just admitted." He gave Hana's name. As he did so, he remembered Kari. It wouldn't be right to buy flowers for one and not the other. In a case behind the counter he saw a vase full of fall foliage and red flowers. "Uh, that bouquet, could you send it upstairs, too?" Mick supplied Kari's name, hoping he'd spelled Dombroski right.

The clerk lifted an eyebrow. "What a shame that two of your lady friends were hospitalized at the same time." She wrote instructions on a delivery tag, but watched Mick from under her lashes. Apparently he'd interested her.

He could've put an end to her curiosity, but didn't. He swiped his credit card, signed the bill and pocketed the receipt. Mick walked out and went straight to the elevator.

He'd spent a week on this same ward, he realized when he stepped off the car. He hated confinement, and hadn't been the most cheerful patient, even though he'd received plenty of extra attention from several nurses. Especially Tammy Skidmore, who had slipped him her home phone number the day he'd checked out. Marlee had met Tammy several times. His sister liked the nurse and still bugged him periodically to ask Tammy for a date. Which Mick had not done.

Tonight, he found himself hoping she wasn't on duty. She was nice enough, but she hadn't shot up his interest antennae. Not like Hana did.

Mick scanned the nurses' station. Four of them sat at the L-shaped desk in the glassed enclosure. Mick recognized one. Rosemary Dubuque. Privately, Mick had dubbed her Rosie the Riveter, because she was the one who most often delivered his nightly pain medication, and popped him with a needle in his butt none too gently. And all too gleefully, it seemed to Mick.

She looked up when Mick strolled to the counter. "Well, if it isn't our pretty boy pilot. Don't tell me you've finally come hunting for Tammy after going off and breaking her heart?"

That comment had the other nurses giving Mick the once-over.

"Actually, Rosemary, I flew two fallen climbers off a Glacier peak. I'd like to see how they're getting along. I want to be sure they've been able to reach their relatives." Mick wrote their names on the visitors' sign-in sheet. "Frankly, I doubt my not calling Tammy broke her up all that much."

"You're right. In fact, if you're interested," she said, getting out of her chair to turn the clipboard around so she could read the names, "our Tammy no longer works here. She met a long-haul trucker and quit her job a month ago. They're traveling the States in his eighteen-wheeler."

That surprised Mick, but he was relieved. "Good for her. If you talk to her sometime, give her my best."

"Humph! These two you're asking about are still with doctors. Nothing's come down to us yet except their admitting forms. No way to tell how long they'll be tied up." That was a broad hint for Mick to leave.

A delivery man from the gift shop strode up to the desk and plunked down the two vases of flowers Mick had purchased. Rosemary broke off, taking time out to sign for the bouquets. She inspected the cards stuck on plastic posts. "Well, aren't you the Casanova? I must say, you do spread your charm around." She set the vases behind the counter. "Someone will see that your ladies get these as soon as they're assigned rooms. As I was about to say, if I were you, I wouldn't hang around and wait."

"You aren't me. I'll be in the waiting room. Please have someone notify me when Hana gets to a room. And Kari," he added a half beat later.

Nurse Rosie might not have responded except that Mick didn't budge from his spot until she nodded her assent.

He made his way to the visitor's lounge at the end of the hall and chose a seat in full view of any comings and goings. Mick knew Rosemary had never approved of the younger nurses like Tammy smuggling in forbidden food during his sojourn. Since there was no love lost between him and the night supervisor, he intended to look out for his own interests and keep watch.

He picked up an outdated magazine, and though he read a lot and usually enjoyed catching up on world news, he couldn't concentrate. The slightest noise in the hall drew his attention away from the article. Then his thoughts would stray to Hana, and he would wonder what was taking so long. Mick didn't want to consider all that could go wrong with her slender back. She was small-boned and probably not more than five-two in hiking boots. She was a natural strawberry blond who never seemed to fuss over her looks. For her coloring, she tanned well, he'd noticed. Spunky, she was quick to debate without holding a grudge. He also knew she listened well, and he loved her bell-like laugh. Hana just came in a great package.

What kept Mick glued to the uncomfortable chair in the waiting room was the clear memory of pain turning her whiskey-gold eyes to a shadowy amber. Pain he'd made worse by rolling her over.

Mick heard the squeak of a wheelchair, and rose when he saw an orderly wheeling Kari Dombroski down the hall. Two nurses joined them, and the four disappeared into a room directly across from the nursing station. He set aside the magazine and paced, knowing the staff wouldn't like it if he barged into the room before they got Kari settled.

He saw the orderly back out with the wheelchair. Mick prepared to leave the waiting area, but a door on the side wall of the waiting room swished open and a gray-haired doctor wearing surgical scrubs approached Mick with purpose.

"I'm Dr. Black. Royce Black." He consulted a chart clipped to a board. "A nurse said you were waiting, Mr....Egan." He went on before Mick could raise an objection. "I won't mince words. It may be weeks before your wife will walk again. Between my assistant and myself, we managed to relieve the pressure on her spinal cord, and we pieced her pelvis together. She suffered lateral compression and minimal vertical shear injuries to the entire pelvic ring."

"Hana?" Mick said. Everything seemed to move in slow motion.

The doctor shut the chart and nodded tersely. "That's right."

"I'm...I'm not Hana's husband."

"But," Black said, "you're the father of her baby?"

Mick felt his jaw drop. "Hana...is...pregnant?" Against his will, Mick's mind conjured up a vision of Jess Hargitay lying lifeless beside the crevasse. Mick's stomach roiled. He looked at the doctor. "I'm the pilot who rescued her today from Glacier Park. Mick Callen. Not Hana's boyfriend."

"Goodness, I'm sorry—I shouldn't have said anything." The stooped man began to turn away from Mick.

Mick plowed through the fog in his mind. "Wait, please, Doctor. I've known Hana for a couple of years. She doesn't have any family."

The doctor consulted the chart. Sighing, he confirmed that with a nod. "When she comes out of Recovery, Ob/Gyn will do a detailed history."

"There's something Hana doesn't know. One of the climbers in her party died today. They worked, uh, closely together. They were...very...good friends. Her doctor should be told."

The surgeon stopped his attempted retreat. "I see. This may impact her recovery. You should inform her attending OB, Dr. Lansing."

"Is he in the hospital? I need to know if I should tell Hana about Jess."

Black began to leave. "I'll see if I can find him. Why don't you go for coffee in our cafeteria downstairs. I'll have Dr. Lansing find you there."

Mick was halfway through his third cup of black coffee and his nerves were beginning to fray when a tall man with graying sideburns came in. He wore creased jeans and pointed-toed boots, which gave him the look of a gentleman cowboy. He glanced around the nearly empty room and headed straight for Mick's table.

The doctor thrust out a hand, which Mick pumped twice.

"I'm Felix Lansing, the on-call obstetrician. I've seen Ms. Egan, but she's still too groggy from anesthetic to give me a comprehensive history." The doctor sat and extracted a small notebook from his pocket. "I think Hana's pregnancy is sixteen to eighteen weeks along, so she's likely already seen an OB. If he or she is on our staff, I'll turn her charts over," he said, glancing expectantly at Mick.

"Dr. Black must've neglected to mention why I wanted to talk to you." Mick again outlined what he knew about Hana. Which obviously wasn't much, given that he'd been clueless about her condition. He tapped his fingertips together. "The man who died in the fall worked with Hana and was quite possessive of her. I don't know if they were involved. Another smoke jumper was admitted with a broken arm and leg. Kari Dombroski. She may know more. I don't even know where in California Hana lives or if there's anyone you can contact for her." Mick stopped tapping his fingers. "Is it safe for Hana to be told Jess died at the scene of their accident?" Meeting the doctor's intense blue gaze, Mick murmured, "Should I leave that to you, Dr. Lansing?"

"No, actually." Lansing clicked his ballpoint pen closed. "News of that nature should come from someone she knows. You wouldn't be here talking to me if you weren't concerned about her. So…you suspect there's a good possibility the man who died is the father of your friend's child."

Mick's heart bucked with each word the doctor spoke. When all was said and done, there was no denying that no matter how he wished it wasn't so, it probably was. But, dammit, from Mick's perspective, Jess had all the charm of a cobra. Yet, in the three summers Hana had spent at the smoke jumpers' camp, Mick had never seen her with anyone else. He hadn't witnessed any kissy-face between them, either. But every time Mick so much as started a conversation with Hana, Jess showed up, and he found reasons to touch Hana's hair, or her arm—which sure left the impression something was going on.

"It's possible," Mick admitted slowly. "Hana's been at the camp since mid-April. It's almost November. I heard that Jess went after all of the unattached women at the camp." Straightening, he shoved his now cold coffee aside. "If I tell her about Jess, I expect she'll admit if he fathered her baby. She's a straight shooter."

The doctor opened a silver case and extracted a business card. "Call my service if you find out." He unfolded his long body from the chair, forcing Mick to rise as well. The two walked to the door together, where they parted. Dr. Lansing shrugged into his khaki topcoat and pulled out his car keys. Mick strode to the nearest elevator.

Snow blew in as Lansing left. Plainly, as his sister had said, this storm gave every indication of hanging around. He could drive down the road and book a room at the nearest motel. Hooking his thumbs in his back pockets, Mick gnawed on his lower lip.

He got in the elevator and punched the number of the orthopedic floor. Mick vividly recalled what it'd been like to wake up from surgery in a field hospital surrounded by strangers. He wanted Hana to see a familiar face. Orderlies were bringing her down from Recovery as Mick exited the elevator, and he trailed behind the stretcher. She looked small and fragile, but had more color than she'd had when he'd brought her in. Now, like then, her eyes were closed.

To kill time and let the staff finish with Hana, Mick sauntered down the hall and stuck his head into Kari's room. She was just hanging up the bedside phone and glanced up as his shadow fell across her leg, which was casted and suspended from the ceiling by ropes and pulleys. She struggled to sit up farther against the pillows.

"Hey, Mick." She pointed to the vase of flowers. "Thanks! They were a nice surprise."

"You're welcome. I sent Hana some, too. Because you're both so far from home."

"Yeah. It's a nice gesture. You caught me saying goodbye to my boyfriend. Joe's plenty peeved that I went on the climb." Oddly, Kari grinned. "He's on his way here, though. Maybe seeing flowers from another guy will get Joe off his duff and make him pop the big *M* question. He says he wants a committed relationship, but he won't ask me to marry him. Anyway, you probably don't want to hear about the sad state of my love life. How's Hana?"

"She had surgery on a pelvic fracture. They just brought her from Recovery. I'll check on her next." He didn't mention Hana's second condition, but gestured to Kari's elevated leg. "They sure have you trussed up. Were your injuries more extensive than we thought? I hope nothing I did in binding your arm and leg made things worse."

"No, in fact the doctor said it helped that you splinted my knee and made me lie on the stretcher with my foot elevated. My arm has a clean break, but in two places. Honestly, Mick, my brains were scrambled earlier. I didn't ask about the rest of the crew. Jess, especially."

"Chuck, Norm and Roger get all the credit for pulling you and Hana out of the crevasse. But, uh, Kari, I have bad news about Jess. He was…killed in the fall." Mick spoke softly, not sure if she would burst into tears or fly into hysterics.

Color leached from her face. "I knew he was too quiet. God, I'm sorry, but Jess was so determined on that climb. When it started snowing hard, the rest of us wanted to turn back. He belittled the guys so badly they agreed to go on, but then Hana refused to go another step. She told Jess we weren't outfitted for snow, and we weren't. Even then, he went all Rambo on us, because we sided with Hana. He roped me and Hana to him like that was safer but he yanked us both down the trail. I'm sure that's why we all fell."

"I guess that would explain his choosing the mountain face rather than an easier path that would've taken longer to descend."

"Is that what he did? It'd be so like him to punish Hana by making the going more difficult for everyone. I know they argued. I was back too far to hear what all was said."

"So, were Jess and Hana unofficially engaged or something?"

"Heck, no. On the hike, Hana and I shared a tent. The night after Jess acted like a total ass, she told me she loved working for Captain Martin, but that she was going to request a new post next summer. Because of Jess."

Mick was surprised—and confused—by that. Then he had another thought. "Did Hana seriously date any other member of your crew?"

Kari grimaced. "Jess would've made that pretty impossible. He staked his claim on her every summer. Like, he made sure they were assigned to cover the same section at fires. But in her spare time, Hana either kept her nose in a book or fiddled with spit-polishing our gear. Why the personal questions?"

"No reason. Other than she led me to believe she has no family. I thought she and Jess might have had a thing going. Since they didn't, I wondered if I needed to try to contact a boyfriend or ah…anyone else significant."

"Obviously you know more about her than I do, Mick. I thought she must have family in California. Only, now that you mention it, the rest of us women were always on the phone to family or boyfriends. Not Hana. And she was the one most dedicated to the job. Me, I was passing time until I could convince Joe to get married. Hana considered forestry her career."

That didn't surprise Mick. But before Kari got suspicious and started remembering how he'd made a habit of seeking Hana out whenever he flew in supplies, he should probably leave. "It's long past visiting hours, Kari. They probably haven't run me out because I volunteer with Angel Fleet and the night nurses are used to seeing me wandering around. Make them take care of you, okay?"

"I'll only be here until Joe shows up and springs me sometime tomorrow. His sister is a nurse. I can bunk at her house until these casts can come off."

"Oh. Well, good luck." Mick waved, and hurried from the room. He wasn't at all sure the nurses would let him stay much longer, but before he left he intended to visit Hana. He wanted to look at her, touch her, know she was alive.

The hall was empty, the ward winding down for the night. Mick stopped in front of Hana's door. Shoving a hand nervously through his hair, he realized he probably looked terrible. His shirt had rips from where a tent stake that blew loose in the wind had lashed across his chest. His boots were muddy. And he hadn't shaved since early morning. But the need to see Hana overrode the fact that maybe he ought to defer his visit until morning.

Pushing open the door, Mick advanced as quietly as possible toward her bed. Hana was little more than a twig beneath a woven white spread. He didn't see how she could be four months pregnant, she was so skinny.

A small light burned above the bed, and an emergency call-cord had been clipped to one edge of her pillow. Her red-gold curls fanned out over a white pillow like a welcoming beacon in an otherwise sterile environment. Mick paused at the foot of the bed and absorbed the peaceful picture she made lying there, her chest rising and falling normally.

Her thick, sooty eyelashes lifted and fluttered shut again, then her eyes opened wide. Her breathing turned ragged. She'd obviously seen his dark silhouette looming but hadn't known it was him. He moved into the light.

"Hana, it's okay. It's Mick…Callen," he added for good measure.

"Oh, Mick. Wha-at time is it? What are you doing here? Where am I?"

"The hospital. You fell on the mountain. Shh. It's late. I'm grounded for the night. I talked to the doctor who fixed your back, but I wanted to see for myself that you got through surgery okay."

"Surgery?" She blinked a few times, but instead of chatting up a storm like Kari had, Hana turned to face the wall. Between it and her bed stood a square metal table that held Mick's flowers. She gestured feebly at the roses.

He shifted to the balls of his feet, unsure if he should stay or go. But dammit all, she faced an uncertain future at best. And she'd face it without Jess. "I just wanted to provide a familiar face, Hana. I went through months of recovery myself, so I sort of understand what you're going through."

She shifted her head toward him and stared with gold eyes awash in misery. Edging closer, he covered her fidgety fingers with his larger hand. "I'm here as a friend. But, Hana, your surgeon mistook me for a relative. So…I'm aware that in addition to your injuries, you're pr-pregnant."

She jerked free of his hand and curved hers over her stomach. "The doctor said my baby survived the accident." For several tense minutes, Hana's mind stalled. She'd guarded that secret for months. She shouldn't have gone on that outing. One mishap and it was a secret no more.

"Life's final irony," she mumbled through dry, cracked lips.

Spotting a straight-backed chair, Mick dragged it over to Hana's bed. He sat, cleared his throat and avoided looking at her for a time. "I can't tell you how sorry I am about the outcome of your climb. There's something…you aren't aware of…that I hate like hell to tell you. Hana, Jess, uh, died in the fall that injured you and Kari." The words poured out, and he held his breath.

Hana gasped and attempted to lean up on her elbows. Failing that, she whipped her head back and forth. "The climb." She moaned. "Jess got pissed at me and the others. We knew we shouldn't go farther." Tears bubbled along the lower rim of her eyes. "I woke up freezing. I remember Kari telling me you were flying us to Kalispell. How is she?"

Again Mick covered Hana's shaking hand. "She's down the hall. She broke her arm and a leg, but she says they're releasing her tomorrow to a friend from Denver."

"Her boyfriend, Joe. I'm glad he's coming for her."

Mick's hold on Hana tightened. "You don't have to avoid talking about Jess, Hana. It's healthier to let out your feelings. I'm guessing you never told him about the baby. I don't imagine he would've organized the climb if he'd known. He'd have been setting up a summer wedding instead, and you wouldn't be going off to college classes."

Hana squeezed her eyes shut as Mick finished. "You think Jess and I… Oh." Her fingers jerked involuntarily. "No, Mick, I'd never have wanted things to turn out this way. But I hadn't planned on telling Jess about the baby. That probably sounds selfish. But two wrongs don't make a right. Please, I'd rather not talk about this now."

She worked her hand from beneath his and curled it over her flat belly. In a whisper, she said, "Jess is…uh…was a perpetual good-time Charlie." Her sad expression met Mick's briefly. "My father was exactly like that. Take it from me, any kid deserves better. Even one who's getting a crummy start in life." Her lips turned down. Deliberately she rolled her head to face the wall again.

Her acknowledgment of her pregnancy, plus her renunciation of Jess, shocked Mick. It wasn't at all what he'd expected. Maybe the pain medication loosened her tongue. In any event, her body language dismissed him, although it took Mick a minute to process that. He found the air in the room suddenly stifling, and climbed shakily to his feet. "It's late," he muttered, "and I need to see about booking a room in town tonight. I don't know when I'll have more supplies to pick up in Kalispell. If something does come up in the next week or so, I'll drop by to see how you're doing."

He replaced the chair and moved to the door. His hand was on the knob when Hana's raspy voice stopped him. "Mick, a nurse said you sent the roses. Under other circumstances... Well, I'm sorry these aren't other circumstances. But thank you."

Mick glanced back and saw the tears trickling down her cheeks. "You're welcome," he said, then left, eager for some fresh air.

Outside, he rubbed a hand over his unshaven jaw. So Hana Egan was nowhere near being the tough cookie she'd tried to make others believe she was. Digesting that, Mick concentrated on buttoning his bomber jacket as he made his way off the ward.

He rounded a corner at the elevator, and narrowly missed bumping into a trio of weary doctors. Mick identified Dr. Chapman, the surgeon who'd replaced his hip socket. They made eye contact and exchanged meaningless nods. The elevator had dinged its arrival by the time recognition dawned on the doctor. "Mick," Dr. Chapman called. "Mick Callen? My colleagues here have spent twenty minutes on the line with Angel Fleet trying to find a plane and pilot. Last year, if I recall, you and your sister were involved in mercy flights? Are either of you still volunteering?"

"I fly for Angel Fleet." Mick's hand automatically went to his cell. "I've been here for several hours. Dispatch wouldn't have been able to reach me. When I flew in, there was a heck of a snowstorm. Has it let up enough to get a plane in the air?"

"I'm not sure. Dr. Dodd here has a liver waiting in Great Falls. And fifty units of AB negative blood. His team's got a three-year-old girl upstairs in desperate need of both. If he can't get this shipment by tomorrow night or the next morning at the latest..." Chapman shrugged and the other fatigued doctors studied Mick hopefully.

A surge of adrenaline brought new life to his tired bones. "Give me the info. I'll check the weather, then phone Angel Fleet's dispatch. If both airports open up by early morning, I'll make your run. Frankly, saving a life would go a long way toward balancing a mountain rescue gone sour today."

The youngest of the three doctors lifted his head. "I heard about a climbing accident on the eleven o'clock news. Smoke jumpers. So, you're a park ranger? The reporter said a team of you guys had just started down the mountain with three survivors. One person was killed in a fall."

Mick swallowed. "I'm not a ranger. I own a freight flying service." That was the best he could manage, because he couldn't stop thinking about the fourth and fifth survivors who lay upstairs. Mainly the fifth—Hana—who, in addition to a severe pelvic fracture was pregnant with the dead man's baby.

Mick grieved for her, which must have shown, because further discussion of the accident waned, for which he was thankful. He accepted the paper Dodd had scribbled information on. The men shook hands, and Mick left with purpose now. Having a new mission made it easier to put Hana Egan out of his mind.

CHAPTER FIVE

HANA WATCHED THE DOOR CLOSE on Mick Callen's heels.
Once it was clear that he was well and truly gone, she let go
of the tears she'd been holding back. She cried for Jess,
arrogant jerk that he was. He'd convinced her they were both
going to die in the early July fire that had cut them off from
the rest of the crew. And he was totally without remorse about
spiking their adrenaline to the fever pitch that ended in unpro-
tected sex. She'd felt like killing him over his juvenile trick at
the time but she'd long since accepted responsibility for her
foolish part in sex that meant nothing to either of them.
Besides, he couldn't help the crap in his background that made
him who he was any more than she could. Never had she
wished him dead.

Now, everything had changed.

She cried for herself, too, because she was afraid and she
hated being afraid. Because she probably needed help and it'd
been a long time since she'd had to rely on anyone but herself.

And while she was wasting time on useless tears, she shed
a few for Mick Callen—the nicest man she'd met in—well,
maybe ever. She'd known it would be hard to leave him permanently. When she'd heard Jess phone Mick, asking to have
supplies delivered for the climb, she'd changed her mind and
agreed to go with the others. Dammit, she should've skipped
the chance to see him one last time.

Hana dried her eyes. Tears never solved problems. That was why she hadn't indulged in them in years. She'd been sixteen the last time. Now she was thirty. Old enough and wise enough to know better.

OUTSIDE, THE STORM SEEMED to have slackened. Mick couldn't tell if the snow swirling in the air was falling from the sky or blowing off the hospital roof. He craned his neck, hoping to see a break in the clouds. Flying to Great Falls to collect a donor organ depended solely on the weather. Airpark personnel had access to the latest state-wide weather forecast. Those reports would help him decide whether it was feasible to fly out tomorrow.

From the parking lot he caught glimpses of an indigo sky. The first sign that he might be able to fly tonight. Although, if so, he'd go home, grab a few hours' sleep, and trade the Huey for a plane that wouldn't be as bone-jarring.

The heavy body of Pappy Jack's old Cadillac crunched over the snow of the hospital parking lot. Traffic had pretty much cleared the highway, leaving only borders of white on both sides. Another positive sign that pointed to getting airborne.

Mick arrived at the airpark and was encouraged by activity at the hangars. On his way to the office he heard the drone of an engine overhead. That meant the tower, which had been closed, was up and running.

The clerk told him that navigational weather service said the storm had blown through Montana faster than expected, although it managed to dump several feet of snow in the mountains.

Mick considered the report, briefly thinking how Hana's and Jess's lives might have gone had the storm not passed through Montana. But he of all people knew it didn't help to play the if-only game.

Before filing a flight plan, he phoned Angel Fleet dispatch. "Alicia, it's Mick Callen. I'm in Kalispell. I ran into Dr. Dodd. Did you locate anyone to pick up blood and an organ for him in Great Falls?"

Alicia Vickers was a retired nurse. She and her doctor husband, John, had founded Angel Fleet because Alicia's brother had lost his wife and unborn daughter when a downed tree blocked the only road leading to a rural medical facility. Mick knew Alicia and John still worked tirelessly to recruit pilots into the program. And whenever a flight involved helping a child, Alicia begged, pleaded or badgered listed pilots until the job got done.

"Mick, you have no idea how welcome your call is. The storm has grounded every pilot I've called. An hour ago John told me to give up. I couldn't. I've been praying for a miracle. You're that miracle, Mick."

"Well, truth is, the storm blew out. I'm probably just the first pilot to check in."

"Oh, you. Mick Callen, you never accept the credit you deserve. Because of your good heart, little Katie Felton might live."

"Let's hope so. Dr. Dodd has the tough job. I don't envy him." Mick shared a bit of his rough day, then said, "I'm heading home to grab a couple hours of shut-eye. As long as there's no shift in the weather, I'll fly out at first light."

"Goodness, are you sure you're okay to make a Great Falls run so soon after that rescue?"

"I wouldn't have phoned in if I didn't think so, Alicia. You work your magic getting the cargo from the hospital to the airport. I'll touch base again after I take possession."

"Right. You fly, Mick, I'll cut red tape. Radio me before

you land in Kalispell tomorrow. I'll make sure there's a courier waiting."

Mick had always been impressed with how efficiently the Angel Fleet network operated. He thought they could move mountains if need be.

Mick was in the air before it struck him that he'd be returning to Kalispell tomorrow. Way sooner than he'd led Hana to believe. But his promise to check on her had been loose. Really, there was no reason for him to make the drive to the hospital.

Except that he wanted to see Hana again.

Mick adjusted his headphones. He imagined he could hear Marlee giving him a lecture about not getting involved with a woman who had Hana's problems. But how involved was he if he offered her only friendship?

Even an hour later, after Mick had staggered out of his shower and fallen across his bed, his exhausted brain told him he wanted more than mere friendship with Hana Egan.

He successfully closed out those thoughts, but still went to sleep with a very clear image of her tear-filled eyes. She'd looked so small and vulnerable as he walked out on her.

Mick's alarm blared at three-fifty. Groaning, he tried to blot out the sound by burying his head under his pillow. But the buzz was relentless. He rose on one elbow and cursed. With eyes at half mast, he sleepily scanned the room in search of Wingman before recalling that he'd left his dog with Dean.

Then Mick remembered he had a mission. All at once, the previous night's events steamrollered over him.

He shut off the nagging, now intermittent, bleat and flung off his covers. While stifling a yawn, he rubbed his prickly, unshaven jaw. The beginnings of his beard always grew in darker than his flax-colored hair. Hair that was too long and stuck up all over. God, he must look a fright.

He made short work of shaving, taming his wild hair and

finding clean jeans, then rummaged in the kitchen for something easy to eat.

Bless Stella Gibson. She'd stocked his fridge with orange
juice and a couple of homemade muffins. Pumpkin and
zucchini, Mick discovered after biting into both. He needed
to give Stella a raise, he decided as he enjoyed the muffin. Last
time he tried, she'd hugged him and thanked him for employ-
ing her and for allowing her to feel a part of the family. Stella
and Wade never had children. Since she'd been an only child,
and Wade's family lived on the east coast, she'd loved being
needed by Pappy, then by Mick and for a short time, Marlee.

Mick left a note on the kitchen counter, praising her baking
and letting her know about today's run for Angel Fleet. Halting
briefly, he scribbled, "Don't expect me home until late
tonight." He hadn't decided yet, but he might stop in to visit
Hana.

The flight to Great Falls was uneventful. Fanned out below
his plane, a patchwork landscape of melting snow defined the
path of the storm. The Arrow purred like a well-fed kitten.
Mick landed with time to spare.

He called Marlee as he waited for a courier to bring the
organ receptacle and units of blood. Because planes were
landing and taking off with noisy regularity, Mick hunched
over his cell, pressing a finger to one ear so he could hear
better.

Marlee had been worried. "We've been home for over an
hour. I tried calling the house repeatedly. And your cell. What
gives? I finally reached Stella in the office. She said the Huey's
back. I sent her to knock on the kitchen door, but there was no
answer. I asked her to go in, but she didn't want to wake you
if you were sleeping in."

"I left Stella a note in the kitchen. When Pappy was alive
she always stopped at the house first to make sure his medi-

cines were laid out. Now that it's just me, she has the idea that I need my privacy. Why, I have no idea." He sighed. "She must not have noticed the Arrow gone from its bay. Jeez, and I'm counting on her to watch my place this winter."

"You made a delivery she doesn't know about? Mick, how do you expect Stella to bill customers if you leave her out of the loop? You and Pappy were both guilty of that. Do you know how hard it is to deal with your gentlemen's agreements? Besides, that's no way to run a business. You need a paper trail."

"I'm flying for Angel Fleet," Mick told her when he could get a word in. "I'll call and set Stella straight. I phoned you to make sure Wylie and crew made it down the mountain okay with the rest of the smoke jumpers."

"Ah, so you didn't call for sisterly lecture number 102?" Marlee laughed. "The guys got back shortly before 3:00 a.m. Wylie said the trek down the mountain took half the time climbing up did. For one thing, the weather had improved. He and the others were plenty beat, though. I drove the company vehicle home, so Wylie could sleep. He and the kids have just gone to feed Dean's patients. Last week they found a half-grown elk who got tangled up in some rolled wire. The elk is skittish of Piston. So it's just me and the two dogs at home."

"Okay. Tell Wylie I'll check with him later. I wondered if he or any of his men spoke to Captain Martin about Jess Hargitay."

"Wylie's captain contacted Len. Someone from the hospital had already phoned him about the two women. Mick, were they not aware one of their friends had died up there? Wylie said the news shocked Captain Martin."

"I don't know if Hana or Kari got in touch with Len. They both suffered injuries. Probably hospital admitting needed to check on their insurance or something. Huh, so if Martin didn't know about Jess, it stands to reason he likely doesn't know when or where he'll be buried. God, I hate this. It's just…I have to deliver a liver to Kalispell. I thought if there were plans under way for Jess's service, I should let Hana and Kari know. Although Kari may be gone by the time I land."

"I had the impression you didn't know Jess very well. The smoke jumpers told Wylie how much you did to help them. I know it's like you to go the extra mile, but perhaps you should step back from this one. I mean, Wylie and I think you're still grieving for Pappy. We're afraid you're going to prolong those feelings."

Mick decided to say nothing further. "Marlee, I see the crew have loaded my cargo. I've gotta split. There's a sick little girl in Kalispell who's counting on me to get this liver there as fast as possible."

"Ew. I'm glad I never got orders to transport organs when I filled in for you with Angel Fleet. I know it's a needed service, but the practice seems…well, macabre."

"I focus on the fact that these organs can save a life."

"I know they do. You fly safe, Mick. We'll talk later."

He stowed his phone, jogged to the Arrow and signed the form for the liver. While he was taxiing down the runway, it finally became clear to Mick what he needed to do for Hana. He had a big house and a guest cottage. As soon as he reached Kalispell and turned over this shipment to the courier, he needed to contact Dr. Lansing's answering service. Or if Lansing had turned Hana's case over to her regular OB, then he'd talk to that doctor. It should relieve their minds to hear Hana had a place to stay while she recovered from her broken pelvis.

SHORTLY AFTER NOON on Monday Mick entered Dr. Lansing's office. Half the chairs in the small but cheery waiting room were filled by women in various stages of pregnancy. Only one other man sat there, bouncing what was surely a newborn in his arms. The man, little more than a boy, darted nervous glances toward a door that led from the room. A row of sliding glass windows separated the room from the doctor's staff, and Mick made his way there.

An attractive woman with cocoa skin opened a window. "May I help you?" she asked, and smiled.

"Are you Dr. Lansing's secretary?"

"No. That would be Marsha." She turned aside. "Is Marsha back from lunch?"

A second woman glanced up from her computer screen. "I heard her come in the back door a minute ago. Did you buzz her on the intercom?"

The first woman lifted her phone and punched in two numbers. "Marsha, it's Shandra. There's a man here asking for you. Well, he asked for Dr. Felix's secretary." She covered the mouthpiece. "Are you a new detail man? Marsha only schedules drug reps to see the doctor on Tuesdays."

Mick hadn't even known what a detail man was. "Uh, I met Dr. Lansing at the hospital the other night. We discussed a friend of mine, Hana Egan. He told me to speak with his secretary if I had further information. I don't, but, oh, hell, it's complicated. I'd really like to see the doctor, please."

The phone rang and Shandra put the secretary on hold. She reached up to slide the window closed, forcing Mick, who was leaning on the counter, to jump back. It was clear from the way Shandra never took her eyes off him that she considered him a nut.

Heaving a sigh, Mick again glanced around the room. Obviously the other women weren't all too sure about him, either. Only the nervous young man paid no attention because the bundle in his arms had begun to cry.

About then the inner door opened. A smiling young woman was being escorted out by Dr. Lansing himself. She dashed over and relieved the man of the crying baby, and carried the wiggling infant back to the doctor, who grinned as he peeled back the blanket to inspect the wrinkled red face. The girl beamed. Dr. Lansing wished her well and started to return inside but happened to glance up and see Mick.

"Ah, young fellow. Mick, right? I visited Ms. Egan on my morning rounds. I was actually hoping to catch you there. I'm afraid she did nothing to fill in the blank spaces on my chart." The doctor checked his watch and slid a glance around the room. "Come, I'll introduce you to my secretary. As you see, I'm behind, but Marsha will take down any information you can supply."

Mick followed Dr. Lansing. "Doctor, please, could I have a moment of your time? I realize you don't have any reason to discuss Hana's prognosis with me. But after speaking to her coworker, I'm doubly convinced Hana has no one to turn to. Since others on her crew have left or are set to leave the smoke jumpers' camp for the winter, I may well be Hana's only friend still here. It occurred to me that if Hana needs someplace to recover, I'd offer mine. It's big. I employ a neighbor, a nice woman, to keep house and assist in my office. And, I'd be available to fly Hana to Kalispell whenever you want to check her. Or until she recovers enough to provide for herself…and…and…the baby." That last sounded strained.

Dr. Lansing studied him. "All laudable goals, Mr.…ah…Mick." The doctor gestured to a private office. After following Mick in, Lansing shut the door. "I shouldn't discuss her without her permission, but I can see you have Ms. Egan's interests at heart. I'll be blunt. Due to the nature of her pelvic injury, and the fact that she's more than sixteen weeks pregnant, ideally she needs to be near a medical facility that offers top-notch orthopedic care and a neonatal unit capable of handling the smallest premature infant. Dr. Black, who pieced Ms. Egan's pelvis together, doubts she can bring a baby to full term. If she does, a normal delivery would be impossible with her weak lumbar vertebrae and pelvic bones."

"Then how will she deliver?"

"Cesarean, which entails an even longer recovery." The doctor pushed back the cuff of his lab jacket and looked at his watch again. "Listen, I sense you truly want to help Ms. Egan. I'm sharing this information so you'll understand the serious position she's in. If you have any influence, my advice is not to waste it offering temporary housing, but rather get her to consider going home to L.A. where I know at least one hospital has the staff and equipment she needs."

"Look, Doctor, I'm no stranger to worst-case warnings. I spent weeks in a military field hospital hearing all the gloom-and-doom predictions. I've recovered. I prefer to believe Hana can do anything she sets her mind to."

The slightly stooped, kindly doctor shook his head. "She needs to be closely observed at a progressive facility that has the specialties I mentioned, plus more. Even then, there's no guarantee her lower back or pelvis will ever be strong enough to carry her baby to the point of a safe delivery. Frankly, she could miscarry any day."

No matter how softly that was said, the message jolted Mick. He stepped back and rubbed his chest where it felt as if he'd taken a physical blow. He blinked several times, unable to erase the image of Hana's hand sneaking out and protectively covering her abdomen. Yes, she'd admitted that conceiving the baby had been a huge mistake, but Mick instinctively knew that it'd be harder for her if she lost her child.

"L.A. has the right stuff? Who else? Will it be easy to get into a hospital out there?" Mick fired off questions.

"Down the hall, second door on your right, you'll find Marsha McGill." The doctor pulled a prescription pad out of his pocket, ripped off a sheet and wrote several things. Handing it to Mick, he said, "Give that to Marsha. She has a computer program listing all hospitals in the U.S. and the disciplines they specialize in. She can get a contact person at each facility." The doctor went out, walked a few steps, and turned to look at Mick behind him. "Good luck. Ms. Egan's a lucky woman to have someone like you for a friend."

Mick wasn't comfortable fielding personal compliments. He shuffled from foot to foot and stared at the paper in his hand until the doctor plucked a chart from a door holder and disappeared into the room. Mick didn't know what exactly he was letting himself in for; he just knew something inside him said Hana needed help. And who would help her if not him?

He found the secretary's office. Her door was open and she was busy at work behind her desk. He cleared his throat to get her attention.

The silver-haired woman removed a pair of half glasses and let them fall the extent of the chain circling her neck. She started to rise, but Mick waved her back into her chair. "I just spoke with Dr. Lansing. He said you can help me locate hospitals where my friend could get the kind of care she needs." Mick set the paper in front of the secretary.

She put her glasses on. "Oh, you're Mr. Callen. Dr. Felix left a message on my answering machine letting me know you might call." She looked over the doctor's note and shook her head. "That man asks the near impossible. A state-of-the-art orthopedic hospital that has a top neonatal unit and social services to boot. This will take a while. You might as well sit, Mr. Callen."

"Mick. Call me Mick." He perched on the edge of a straight-backed chair. "Dr. Lansing didn't mention social services to me. Does that mean Hana has no insurance? I figured she'd have some coverage as a smoke jumper. I think they're part of the forestry service." He started to crack his knuckles, but as the woman scowled, Mick linked his hands in his lap instead.

"I'm not at liberty to discuss a patient's finances. You'll have to ask Ms. Egan."

He nodded, but said, "Hana's closed-mouthed about most anything to do with her private life. She hasn't been forthcoming with Dr. Lansing. How can I help her if I don't know what she needs?" Marsha gave him a look that brought an end to the subject of Hana's finances.

She turned to her computer and began tapping keys. Every once in a while she stopped, scrolled down, and a few times jotted something on a yellow legal pad.

Mick thought about his circumstances. He had savings. He wasn't rich by any means, but he'd used only a portion of his military disability to breathe life into Cloud Chasers. When his sister came onboard for nearly a year, she'd collected on many of the company's outstanding accounts. The main issue would be getting strong-willed Hana to accept monetary aid. Mick had spoken with her enough during discussions about various books and articles to have a fair idea of where she stood on people taking handouts. She was dead set against anything that smacked of government welfare. But maybe a loan from a friend, extended until she got back on her feet, would be a different matter.

"All right. Here are your choices," Marsha said, rolling her chair forward. "There are more than I would've imagined. L.A., Denver and Seattle if you want to stay west of the Mississippi. East of there you're looking at New York, Miami and Chicago."

Winter was just around the corner. Mick imagined Denver

had as much snow as Montana, and Seattle would have both rain and snow. Smelly, smoggy L.A. probably had sun if it could burn through the pollution. Only Miami fit his earlier plan for spending his winter on a white sandy beach. Because it was at the opposite end of the country and would mean hours of travel time for Hana, Mick squelched his hankering for sun and sand.

"I'm thinking, since Hana planned to enroll in college classes in L.A. this winter, it's the best of the ones you listed. How do I contact them? Do you have names and phone numbers of people who'll help me get Hana admitted? After I leave here, I'm going by the hospital to see her. I'd like to go armed with as much information as possible to try to convince her this is in her best interests."

"Try the gentle approach. I know it's hard for men who are prone to laying out just the facts." Marsha smiled as she jotted down names. "And another thing, men always want to think they're in control of everything, that they know what's best. Not that you asked for my advice, but I wouldn't recommend charging into her room like the cavalry at the ready. Start by telling her how much better she looks, and ease gradually into discussing what Hana thinks she'll do next week or the week after." Marsha ripped off the sheet and passed it to Mick.

"Uh, thanks. For everything." He folded both pages she'd given him and tucked them in his shirt pocket. "I'll try to keep what you said in mind. I have a twin sister who'd tell you I fit squarely into the group of guys charging through life like bulls in dish shops or whatever that saying is." He stood and made sure the chair was exactly as he'd found it before he left the office.

Which might have been what prompted Marsha to call out, "If I can be of any further assistance, or help you navigate channels to get Ms. Egan financial aid, please call. If I'm away from my desk, leave a number where you can be reached."

"Thanks. I may not have much success convincing Hana, but I'm sure going to try."

Later, backing out of the doctor's parking lot, Mick rehearsed a few possible lead-ins. He took the long way to the hospital to give himself extra time. The route took him past a shop he recognized, where Stella had referred him several weeks ago to buy gifts for Marlee and Wylie's baby.

Mick didn't want to picture Hana pregnant with Jess Hargitay's baby. Maybe you shouldn't think ill of the dead, but it was a fact that he and Jess had disliked each other. Nevertheless, it was also true that if a woman had a soft spot, it was babies—especially her own. He pulled to the curb before he could talk himself out of it, and wedged the old Caddy between two newer cars.

The store owner recognized Mick the minute he walked in. "Hello again. I wouldn't have expected you back so soon, considering how much you bought the last time."

"I need something for a friend." Mick reached for a soft white teddy bear that had drawn his attention before. He'd ended up buying a more realistic brown one for Marlee, thinking about the grizzly cub Dean and Wylie had rescued and nursed back to health. Mick squeezed the white bear and liked the feel of its soft fur. "This will do." He set the toy on the counter. "No need to wrap it. I'm on my way to visit her now. If you remove the price tag, I'll take it as is."

"This is my favorite toy. I can't keep enough of them in stock. New moms love them. He's just so huggable." She removed the tag and rang up Mick's purchase.

It'd been precisely his thought—that Hana could hug this bear. With her injuries making her condition iffy, it would give her something to hold on to.

Satisfied, Mick climbed into his car feeling better about going to visit Hana. Yes, he intended to discuss her future, but why rush? First, he ought to establish himself as a friend she could count on in good times or bad. Once he crossed that bridge and became more than a mere acquaintance, he could get serious about her long-term plans.

Revved, he bounded up the hospital steps. In the lobby, he took the bear from the bag and stuffed the sack in the trash. As he boarded the elevator, a bevy of nurses of all ages cooed and oohed over the cute bear.

Mick got out on Hana's floor and entered her room still wearing a smile. It fled when simply seeing her partially reclining, with her pale face scrubbed clean and her red-gold curls clipped back, landed a sucker punch to his gut. He'd always thought her beautiful, but never delicate. Not like now.

"Hey, how's it going?"

"Mick?" Tiny lines emerged between her eyebrows. "I didn't expect you to be back so soon." A hand fluttered to the ties holding a hospital gown closed at her throat.

He barely managed to recover from the tender feelings rushing through him. God, he had to get a handle on this sappiness or she'd think he was a babbling fool.

"I looked in on you yesterday, but you were asleep." He gestured with the bear. "Saturday night on my way out I ran into a doctor I know. He'd been trying to find an Angel Fleet pilot to fly a donor organ in from Great Falls today. I think we talked about mercy flights once."

"Yes, we did." She glanced away, a bleak expression on her face. "At the time I considered myself indestructible. The last thing I ever expected was that I'd be on the receiving end of one of them. But…I suppose…do most people thank you for flying in to save them?"

Mick wasn't sure what her words implied—that Hana

would rather he'd left her to die with Jess? Had he misread things? Had she been in love with Jess all along?

He crossed to the bed and wrapped her tan, fine-boned hand around the soft toy. He felt how cold her fingers were, but resisted rubbing them warm. "The last thing *I* ever expected was to hear Hana Egan feeling sorry for herself. A risk-taker like you? I watched you train once—saw you parachute out of a diving plane. You executed a landing roll, followed by heavy cargo retrieval as good as any I've seen in the military." He smiled to soften his words. "Snap out of it, Egan. Give Smoky the Bear a hug. He needs one."

Unable to help herself, she glanced down and giggled. "Smoky the Bear isn't white. Honestly, Mick, you can't chew me out one minute and do something so sweet the next." Still, she hugged the stuffed toy and stroked its fur. "You're making me one of your do-gooder projects, are you? You already sent me flowers."

Spinning a visitor's chair around, Mick straddled it. "I've spent my share of hours staring at hospital ceilings. Friends brought me stuff. I hope I never gave the impression that I didn't appreciate them or their gifts."

Her gaze flew to meet his. "I didn't mean... It's..."

Mick stayed quiet, waiting for her to complete a sentence. He hoped it'd reveal more about Hana Egan.

"It's just…that I hunted long and hard to find a career where they taught self-reliance. Today, a doctor who poked and prodded me said I likely won't return to that career soon…if ever." She fondled the bear's ears. "So, yeah, you caught me whining. Thanks for the swift kick. It's what I needed. Gifts bring me to my knees, though, so don't show up here with any more, okay? I've gotta toughen up so I can face what's down the road."

Letting his chin drop, Mick cursed silently. Rather than

soften her up so she'd accept his help, the damned bear had had the opposite effect. Then again, she *was* hugging the animal instead of throwing it at him.

"I used to bring you books at camp."

"Oh, I'd love something to read." Her face lit up, then a frown moved in. "Right now they won't let me out of bed even to use the bathroom. Reading may take my mind off what happens next."

"What does happen next?" he asked casually.

She shrugged. "Can we just talk about books I might like?"

He pursed his lips, tempted to force her to discuss a future she clearly wanted to avoid facing. Her eyes pleading, she stared at him. With a sigh, he gave a nod, signifying agreement with whatever her heart desired.

CHAPTER SIX

MICK FUMBLED THROUGH his pockets for a paper on which to write Hana's requests. All he found was the information Marsha McGill had given him on hospitals offering services Hana would need. He quickly tucked it back in his pocket.

"There's a pad by the phone, if you want something to write on."

"Uh, thanks." He got the paper, then returned to his chair. "Okay, shoot. What'll it be? I recommend something light. At least, I had a hard time concentrating on anything too weighty between doses of pain meds."

She eyed the three drip lines running into her arm. "Yeah, I doze on and off until the pain in my back wakes me up. I remember you mentioned having several surgeries. Did your doctors pry into every aspect of your life? Did it bother you?"

"In the military your life is already laid bare on some form somewhere. What are they asking that you object to?"

"Things like, who should they call? And when I'm released, where do I plan to go for rehab? Oh, and a lot more personal stuff about how I plan to care for myself…and a baby. Can't they see my whole life's been turned upside down?"

She'd provided Mick with the opening, but her agitation was so palpable he elected to hold off pressing her. "Want me to find you a book on home-based businesses? About all it takes is a computer and imagination."

The laugh she uttered was dry as sand. "I don't have a home *or* a computer. Everything I own I carry in two duffle bags. Well, and a metal case filled with firefighting equipment." She leaned back her head and blinked at the ceiling.

Hell, he was going to have to dive in headfirst after all. "Did I dream that you told me you were enrolled in college classes this winter? Where did you plan to live? And how do you type college papers without a computer?"

"I rent a room that's walking distance from the campus, and the money I earn fighting fires pays for that and books and tuition. Libraries have computers. I won't be going back to school, though," she said. "Winters I've worked part-time delivering pizza, and…oh, now even that's impossible. And why finish my degree in forestry? I'd planned to work in reforestation. That's a physical job." She'd tucked the bear in the crook of one arm; her free hand restlessly rubbed her belly.

Clearly her mind was on the baby. But Mick wasn't ready to talk about Jess Hargitay's kid.

Hana's hand grew still. Gnawing her upper lip, she said, "Len Martin phoned. He'll store my gear until I can pick it up. He said…Jess's parents arranged to ship his body home. Would you have guessed Jess was the family black sheep? All the Hargitays, even his sister, are high mucky-muck San Francisco lawyers."

"I didn't know. I guess you'd like to attend his service. And shouldn't you tell Jess's parents about the baby?"

"Are you kidding? Jess called them tyrants. I never told him. Why would I tell them? I know you have questions, Mick. Just…don't." She closed her eyes.

"Back to the books you want," Mick muttered in a gravelly voice.

"Oh, I guess anything new by politicians. That'll take my mind off my troubles and is guaranteed to light a fire in my blood."

Mick couldn't help but laugh. He recalled the lively political debates he and Hana had had over the two summers they'd swapped books. "Okay. I've also been meaning to pass along a book of Michael Crichton's I finally read. *State of Fear.* It's fact-based fiction. It'll get you riled up and make you think twice about what environmental activist groups you might want to get involved with."

"That sounds like a book I'd like. Maybe just bring that one, Mick. The doctor who visited this morning, Dr. Lansing, made it sound as if I won't be here long." She glanced away again. "I didn't take in half of what he said, but I gather I need treatment not available in Kalispell. I have no idea where I'll go, or how. Wouldn't you think one hospital would be pretty much like another?"

"Some specialize." Mick fingered the pocket holding the paper with her options. No, first he'd talk to the person Marsha McGill said could help with Hana's admission. He wanted everything lined up before he presented his suggestions to her. "I have the book at home. I'll bring it tomorrow." He rose and righted the chair. "You're beginning to get droopy eyes. I don't want to tire you out. Is there anything else you can think of you'd like me to pick up? A robe? Slippers? I can fly up to Martin's camp and collect your gear if you'd like."

She laughed, but broke off abruptly as it obviously hurt her. "Sorry, smoke jumpers don't do warm woolies. When we're out we sleep in full fire gear, including steel-toed boots if we sleep at all. At base camp it's so hot in the cabins we make do with the thinnest, rattiest, oversize T-shirts available."

Mick, who didn't blush easily, felt heat climbing his neck just imagining Hana in nothing but a thin T-shirt. "Well, you're not at camp now. The other day Stella packed up some clothes my sister left in our guest house. I'll see if there's a robe. If I know hospitals, someone will be getting you up and moving soon. Hospital gowns do nothing for a person's modesty."

"Stella? I don't know why I've never thought to ask if you had a significant other."

"Stella's close to sixty. Pappy hired her to clean house and cook decent meals. She still does that for me, plus works half days in my office."

"Sorry. I didn't mean to be nosy. It's none of my business if you keep a harem."

"You have my permission to get nosy." His eyes as they roamed her face soon had Hana burying bright pink cheeks in the bear's fur.

He watched her pull herself together. "On second thought, forget bringing me any books, Mick. You're too nice a guy. It's best all around if we say goodbye."

"That's not going to happen unless you plan to order the nurses to bar me from your room."

Hana plucked absently at the plush bear's bright eyes, her own growing misty. "Why now, Mick? When my life is more screwed up than it's ever been."

"Don't know, but I'll be sure and ask the next fortune-teller I run across."

"Mick Callen, I swear! You make me laugh, you make me cry, and right now it hurts to do either."

"I'm sorry." He turned suddenly serious again. "Hurting you is the very last thing I want to do, Hana. I hated bouncing you around on the flight from the mountain to here. If anything I did, rolling you over, loading you on the stretcher, or anything else compounded your injuries, I'm sorry."

"Oh, Mick, don't blame yourself. My injuries came from the fall. I've tried, but I don't remember everything that happened after Jess got mad and took off downhill. Kari and I saw his feet fly up, then he started sliding and couldn't stop. Kari confirmed that. Oh, by the way, she checked out about an hour ago. She had a nurse wheel her in for a minute. Her boyfriend, Joe, came, too. What a guy. He drove for two days to get here, he was so worried about her. From the way she used to rave, I thought he'd be really hot." Hana's nose wrinkled prettily. "Definitely not! Not my idea of hot, anyway."

Mick was afraid he was the exact opposite of her idea of "hot"—fit, dark-haired, muscle-bound Jess. He decided not to comment, however, and merely completed his trek to the door. "Rest easy, Hana. I'll drop in tomorrow. Right now I want to see how the surgery is going on the little girl I brought the slice of liver for."

"Ugh, Mick, that sounds gross."

"Actually it's great. Some doctor discovered kids can survive with only a section of an adult liver. They can save way more kids now than before."

"That *is* good. So, you like kids?"

"Yeah, and dogs, but I guess you probably knew that."

"Your dog's a rascal. A friendly rascal." She smiled and rested her chin on the bear.

Mick wanted to take with him the memory of Hana smiling. So even though the air was thick with the possibility of finding out more about her, he tossed off a two-fingered salute and slipped out, closing the door softly.

In the hallway, he stopped to take in a deep breath. Marsha McGill said to include Hana, not plan for her. But Marsha didn't know how stubborn Hana Egan could be.

HANA STUDIED THE BEAR for a long time after Mick left. She shouldn't have been so wishy-washy about sending him away. *For his own good.* A year ago she'd guessed he was interested in her. Oddly, he was the first man she—well—whose feelings she returned.

For most of her life in the foster care system she'd kept boys and then, later, men at a distance. That she'd let Jess, who embodied all the things she didn't like about men, breach her defenses, was the irony of it all.

But she needed to quit thinking about Jess and about Mick, and get serious about deciding her future. Maybe she could get her tuition money back. And the room she rented every year was on the ground floor so she'd be able to stay there.

She couldn't let Mick's gifts of this bear and the flowers, and his offer to bring her books and his sister's robe make her vulnerable. She knew women who'd see his kindness as an opportunity to cozy up and get him to take care of them. It wouldn't be honest, but some women were shameless about such things. Well, not her. Hana had always lived by her wits. And she'd continue doing that. First she had to determine her options.

She set the bear aside and reached for the nurse call button. The best place to start would be to get that doctor to repeat what he'd said during morning rounds when she'd been too groggy to listen.

MICK NEEDED to figure out exactly how to go about convincing everyone he was doing the right thing for the right reasons, some of which were moderately obscure to him. For now, he left Hana's ward and headed to pediatric surgery to check on Katie Felton.

Mick found the ward clerk. "Hi, I'm Mick Callen, the Angel Fleet pilot who delivered an organ yesterday. I met Katie Felton's doctor the other night. If it's not against the rules I'd like to find out how her surgery went, or is going."

"It nice to meet you, Mr. Callen. We're all so grateful to volunteers like you." The woman lowered her voice. "One of the surgical residents came out a minute ago and updated the

Feltons on Katie's progress. Her deterioration has been so hard on her parents. She was losing ground day by day, so this liver is truly a gift of hope."

Mick rattled the loose change in his pocket. "How much longer do you think she'll be in surgery? When will they know if the transplant took?"

"If the liver is working Dr. Dodd will know before he closes. But with transplants, the first few weeks are crucial because of a possibility of the body rejecting the organ, or of allergic reactions to the rejection medications."

"I'll keep my fingers crossed. And I'll probably check back. I'll be around anyway. I have a friend who is a patient upstairs."

"I'm sure it'll be fine to update you. After all, you are Katie's angel of mercy."

"I don't know about that." He ducked his head and tugged on an ear.

"I do," she said simply.

Mick left the hospital feeling good about his role in helping kids like Katie. Earlier he'd apologized to Hana for giving her such a rough flight. But had he not risked flying that day, it was possible more people than Jess would've died. Thinking beyond that, Mick liked helping people and being needed. No one had really needed him since Pappy died.

His phone rang the minute he turned it on. "Hey, Stella. I'm on my way to the airpark. Do I need to pick up supplies for anyone?"

"As a matter of fact, Porter Weaver lost shingles off two of his cottages in the storm. I wasn't sure you'd have room in the Arrow to carry four rolls of tar paper and ten bundles of composition shingles. I promised Porter I'd ask, though. He's willing to pay double your normal delivery fee."

"Double, wow! Oh, heck, money doesn't matter. He's in a

bind. Sure, I'll fly out his order. For the usual rate. Who has his merchandise? Don Morrison?"

"Yes. Just a minute. Don gave me the gross weight." Mick heard Stella rummaging through papers, and then she came back and named a figure.

"That's well within my payload. Will you phone Don and have his warehouse deliver the goods to the airpark ASAP?"

"You're going to fly out now? In your message, it sounded as if you were staying in town late."

"Then, I thought I might. Now, I have another agenda. I'm considering a change in my vacation plans. Depending on what time I land tonight, I'd like us to sit down and take a good look at my books to see how long I can afford to be away. I may wrap up so I can leave next week or shortly thereafter."

"Then you *are* going to leave Montana? Marlee's going to be sick with disappointment. I know she hoped you'd stick around for the holidays."

"Yeah, she's a hurdle I'll have to tackle."

"How long are you planning on being away? I figured you'd be back to start flights again in late February or early March. That's what I told Angel Fleet."

"What if it's not until early April?" The end date Mick had calculated brought him to Hana's due date, even though he knew Dr. Lansing said that it was unlikely she'd carry her baby to term.

"That's some getaway," Stella mused aloud. "If you're gone that long, you'd better locate a pilot to fill in after spring thaw. The lodges will be crying for supplies."

"I know. I'm making a list of things I need to see to. Listen, I'm heading onto the freeway. I've got to hang up. Let me know if Morrison can't deliver Porter's roofing material today."

They hung up and Mick's next call after he arrived at the

airpark was to Dr. Lansing's secretary. "Ms. McGill, it's Mick Callen. I've just come from visiting Hana. I still think L.A. is best. I wonder, could you arrange a phone appointment with Lucy Steel, the hospital coordinator there?"

"I'll be glad to set up a call. And Dr. Felix will be happy to hear you convinced Ms. Egan this quickly."

"Uh, Hana doesn't know...yet. But if everything's all arranged, why would she balk?"

"Hmm. Were you able to get particulars on her insurance coverage? We may be able to arrange aid. Getting her accepted will be easier if we can show funds going in."

Mick swallowed hard, then blurted out an idea he'd been batting around. "I'll talk to Captain Martin. He's Hana's last boss. If her insurance ran out at the end of the fire season, have the coordinator list me as the person responsible for paying Hana's bills."

"Mr. Callen!" The secretary sucked in a breath. "Are you aware of how costs mount for critical or ongoing care?"

"You cut the red tape so they'll take Hana. I'll come up with the money."

There was silence for several seconds. "I'll see what I can do," she said determinedly, as if she'd just made up her mind to help. "Can you phone back around four-thirty? I'll nab Dr. Felix between patients. I believe he has a former colleague who's in charge of the high-risk pregnancy department at that particular hospital. I'll try that route. You'll need accommodations near the facility. It's less expensive than in-patient or a nursing home. Hana will need physical therapy to keep her muscles toned, too...." Her voice trailed off.

"Whatever it takes," Mick said with conviction.

"Well, if you haven't run yet, then you *are* serious. I'll talk to you at four-thirty, Mr. Callen. I hope we can work this out."

Mick hung up after mumbling he hoped so, too. Suddenly,

he had doubts. Then he went straight back to being convinced that this was best for Hana.

The roofing supplies he was to fly to the Weavers' lodge were waiting. Fortunately, the smoke jumpers' camp was on his return flight path.

A COLD WIND BLEW off the lake and hit Mick broadside as he disembarked at Porter's place. The nearly white-haired man pumped Mick's hand. "I can't thank you enough for bringing me this order so fast. The almanac says we're in for a bad winter. Hopefully my son and I can get a jump on repairing my cottages before the next storm rips through here. I hear there's another one brewing north of the border."

"Another storm?" Mick had been so busy he hadn't been vigilant about staying aware of the weather forecast. It felt cold enough to snow again tonight.

"Yeah, and a few lodge owners are getting edgy. Especially the ones who have guests scheduled through Thanksgiving. Some years our weather's mild enough for backcountry travel in late fall. This year, cancellations will probably shoot profits all to hell."

"In a business like mine, a guy figures on posting profits only eight or nine months each year. I'm in the process of winding down now. Looking at heading for sunshine. Last season, Pappy refused to budge. I can't help wondering if his health would've held out longer if I'd tried harder to talk him into going south."

"Mick, you can't beat yourself up over something like that. We old-timers are part of the wilderness. We develop the instincts of wild animals. I'll wager Pappy sensed it was nearing his time." Weaver clapped Mick's back. "The way I see it, a man who dies in his sleep is a man who's at peace forevermore."

Deep in thought, Mick nodded absently. "I hope so. Come to think of it, the last week before Pappy died he had less dementia. He seemed happy."

"There, ya see? Rest your mind, Mick. Well, I'd better call my boys and get cracking on those roofs. How long are you gonna to continue to fly in case I find more damage than we estimated?"

Mick scanned the sky. "A week, maybe. It'll depend on the front. Then I'll take off to a warmer clime."

"Good for you. The warnings could fizzle out and be nothing."

"Let's hope. I flew in the last snow and it's not my idea of fun."

"That's right. I heard you took part in a daring rescue."

"Hmm. I guess at one point, when I lifted off the mountain, I prayed for all I was worth."

"I would've thought smoke jumpers had more sense than to climb that peak this time of year. With losing a man, I'm sure they're all regretting it now."

"Which reminds me, I'm stopping to collect one of the climbers' gear from Captain Martin. So I'd better get going."

"Pass on my condolences to Len, will you? He and Lorna never had kids. All of those young people who work for him get treated like family."

Mick returned to the Arrow, hoping that was true. If so, maybe the captain would extend Hana's insurance benefits.

He lifted off. Below, he identified two elk cows, followed by a massive bull. The elk sniffed the air before leading his group to drink at the lake. Their coats were long and shaggy, a surefire indicator that sub-zero temperatures were just around the corner.

Twenty minutes later, Mick landed at an almost deserted forest firefighters' camp. A direct contrast to his last visit when the smoke jumpers were eagerly preparing for their end-of-fire-season climb.

The captain himself emerged from an equipment shed. He pulled a rag from his back pocket, and, eyeing Mick's approach, he wiped grease off his hands.

"Mick Callen. I couldn't figure out who'd be flying in. I wasn't expecting anyone."

The men met at the gate and shook hands. Martin, a graying, square-jawed man, was stockier than Mick and a head shorter. "I was hoping for a chance to thank you personally for everything you did the other day to help my crew."

Len was always a slow talker, but even more so today. The accident had taken its toll.

"No thanks necessary, Captain."

"I eventually wormed the whole story out of Chuck and Norm. They were scared I'd write them all up in a report that would negatively impact on their service records. Given all they went through, I wouldn't have even if they weren't technically finished here for the year."

"How does that work? Their contracts?" He shuffled his feet, shifting his weight from his bad hip. "As you know, Hana Egan was injured. She's still in the Kalispell hospital. Do you know anything about her insurance, Len? She's going to need specialists. I stopped to get her gear." Again Mick was careful to avoid any mention of Hana's secondary condition.

"She that bad? Never let on a thing when we talked. But that's our Hana." The two men fell silent for a bit. Martin roused himself first. "Her gear is still in the women's bunkhouse. Walk over with me to get it. I'll have you sign a release form."

"No problem. About her insurance…?"

"Some of the crew qualify for year-round coverage. Mostly the ones assigned to natural resource projects during times of fire inactivity. Chuck, for example. When he left here he was headed to help control a beetle infestation in Colorado."

"Hana was signed up to take college classes this winter."

"That's right. She did last winter, too. If I recall, she went off the Forestry roster until the start of a new season. Smoke jumpers are an independent lot, Mick. I wouldn't be surprised if Hana felt no need for insurance over the winter."

That was no more or less than Mick expected. He followed Martin into the rustic bunkhouse. Hana's things were stacked in a corner. As she'd told him, her worldly possessions were zipped into two duffle bags and a metal case that held her fire ax, equipment belt, worn leather gloves and safety goggles.

Mick signed a receipt and gathered up the whole of Hana's life in a single armload. He found that unsettling. As he stowed the items in his cargo compartment, her lack of possessions hit him hard. He quickly closed and locked the door.

The captain moved aside and tucked the tips of his gnarled fingers under his belt. "Please give Hana me and my wife's best wishes for a speedy recovery, Mick. I'm always concerned about sending crews out to fight fire. I worry they'll be cut off from roads, or be trapped and overcome by smoke. Hana and Jess had a real close call our first blaze of the year. A doozy. We nearly lost them both, Jess told me later. It's unbelievable that with all they go through at work tragedy happened on a fun outing." Len shook his head. "Lorna and I fly out tomorrow to attend Jess's funeral. I felt someone should pay respects."

Mick tried to appear concerned, but everyone knew there was no love lost between him and Hargitay. Mick wasn't one to offer lip service for the sake of making himself seem like a better guy. "Have a safe trip," he said instead. "I probably won't see you till spring. Cloud Chasers is closed for the winter."

It wasn't until Mick was in the air and the whole sad debacle began to prey on his mind that he decided to make an unscheduled side trip to see his twin. He had to tell her about his plans. Something said *do it today.* Maybe it was the stillness gripping the smoke jumpers' camp, or the fact that Hana's insurance had run out. And Marlee was all the family he had left in this world.

Crosswinds contributed to a bumpy landing. Mick swept off his earphones and shut down the Arrow's engine, thankful he hadn't radioed ahead. He'd hate for Marlee to witness the way he crow-hopped the plane down Wylie's newly asphalted runway.

In the wilderness, the arrival of a plane drew everyone within hearing distance. Mick hadn't finished notifying Stella of his unscheduled stop before Wylie, Marlee, the kids and dogs all appeared at the end of the path that led to the house.

Mick stored his phone and opened his door. His feet had barely touched the landing strip when he was inundated by laughing kids and barking dogs.

"To what do we owe this surprise visit?" his sister called.

"I'll bet Mick smelled your chicken and dumplings," Wylie said, trying to keep a straight face. Mick, as a rule, made disparaging comments about his sister's dumplings doubling as hockey pucks. Today, he said nothing.

He knelt and let the kids hug his neck and the dogs lick his face. The normalcy of it all filled the yawning hole that had opened in his chest after he'd collected Hana's few belongings.

Rising, Mick flung an arm around his twin. "I happened to be in the neighborhood," he said, hoping she'd let it go at that.

She always saw through him, and wore a look that said she did now, too, but was willing to bide her time.

"Uncle Mick, we picked the rest of our pumpkins today," Jo Beth exclaimed, skipping alongside her uncle's longer stride.

"First frost on the pumpkins was when Pappy said it was time to pick 'em for making Thanksgiving pies," Mick told her.

They trooped into the house, warmed by a wood fire. Kids and dogs soon tired of the attention lavished on them by the new arrival and ran off to play in another room. Marlee poured hot cider and cleared places for the three adults at the breakfast table. "Okay, Mick. I know you weren't just in the neighborhood. I spoke to Stella less than an hour ago. You've put her in a snit, but she's loyal to a fault. No matter how much I tried, I couldn't get her to rat you out." Marlee stirred her cider with a cinnamon stick, eyeing her brother as she licked it off.

"Hana Egan, the woman hurt worst in the climbing accident, grew up in foster care. She has no family." Mick cupped his mug and wore a brooding expression.

"And this affects you, how?" Marlee kept her tone light.

"She needs specialists. What she needs can be gotten in L.A. I've decided to fly her down there. Probably next week."

Wylie sipped from his drink. "That'll take you three or four days. So then you'll fly back?"

"I'm not planning on returning to Montana until spring. Late spring," Mick stressed. "Her doctor's secretary is checking on houses to rent near the hospital. Oh, and Hana's insurance lapsed before her accident. So…I'll…uh…be visiting Carl Bledsoe at the bank tomorrow. I'm thinking a mortgage on the main house and land. It's free and clear. I'll exclude the guest house, of course, since Pappy left it to you, Marlee."

She choked and spewed cider across the oak table. Wylie curved one hand around her arm. With the other, he mopped up the cider with a hastily grabbed napkin.

"Mick Callen, that's the dumbest idea you've ever had! Who is this woman that you're willing to stake your entire future on her? I want to understand. Give me reasons," she said.

Her brother sat stubbornly mute. She fixed him with a hurt stare. "Why, Mick? She's virtually a stranger. We...I...want you here for Christmas."

"Hana fractured her pelvis in the fall. And..."

"And what?" Marlee saw the opening and pounced.

"And...she's pregnant," he blurted. "I already told you Hana's alone in the world. The doctor says she's at risk of losing the baby."

Marlee and Wylie exchanged bewildered expressions. "Are you saying it's your child, Mick?" his sister asked softly.

"No. Not mine." He wished to hell it *was* his kid. Mick stared into his mug.

Marlee whirled around and frantically appealed to her husband. "Wylie, you talk sense into him. Tell him getting tangled up in a mess like this is insane. It may even spell bankruptcy."

Wylie, a man who never rushed his thoughts, darted a worried glance from his wife to his brother-in-law. Finally, he rested his broad back against the nook wall. "Let him be, sweetheart. Can't you see Mick's mind is made up?"

Marlee laced her hands across her swollen belly and chewed her lower lip. "I don't pretend to understand any of this, Mick," she said brokenly. "Lord knows we've had our share of heartache over the past few years."

"Yes, but we've had each other."

"That's what I was going to say. Understand it or not, like it or not, we'll stand by you. Cloud Chasers belongs to you, as does the house. Pappy wanted that. Just don't ask me not to worry."

Mick raised his head and their eyes so like mirror images met, and for a moment both pairs glittered with unshed tears. He turned aside first, ducked his head and discreetly wiped his away. Wylie handed Marlee a clean napkin, since he'd used hers to wipe up her cider spill.

After dabbing her eyes, she grasped her cup. Instead of drinking, Marlee ran her thumbs around the rim of the crockery mug. "You'll stay the night, won't you, Mick?"

He shook his head. "I have a lot to iron out. I promised the doctor's secretary I'd get back to her about Hana's insurance situation. Stella and I need to take a hard look at my ledgers. And according to Porter Weaver, another storm is hung up at the border. Thanks all the same for the offer of a bed, but time's pressing in on Hana." Mick rose and set his cup in the sink. Bending, he dropped a light kiss on his sister's temple.

"Smoke jumpers are part of the forestry family," Wylie said. "Rangers donate to a slush fund set up to help our brothers and sisters in need. Tomorrow I'll do some checking and see if maybe your friend falls under that umbrella. If not, I'm on a committee that puts together fund-raisers for guys who, say, have lost a house in a fire. With all the rangers' wives who make crafts or jams and jellies for the county fair, I'd think there's time before the holidays to hold a major bake sale, too."

"Wylie," Marlee said, clapping gleefully. "That's a great idea. We could earmark funds specifically for Hana. That way Mick won't have to sign away so much."

"All I want is for Hana to have the care she needs to get on her feet and get back to a semblance of her normal life."

Mick prepared to leave.

Wylie followed, talking additional possibilities for raising funds.

Marlee rounded up the kids to tell their uncle goodbye.

"Why aren't you staying for dinner?" Dean asked. "Gosh, you aren't going to take Wingman home, are you, Uncle Mick?" The boy's fingers tangled in the dog's fur.

"We made a deal, Dean. I'm paying you to take care of Wingman until I open for business again next spring."

Marlee studied her twin with faint distress.

Mick intercepted her look. "What?"

She rushed up to hug him as tightly as she was able to, given the mound of her stomach that got in the way. "I came home to Montana so we could be closer to each other. I'm afraid you're going off to California and we'll lose you for good to Hana. We don't know her, Mick. I hope you really do. What kind of woman lets a man she hardly knows take over her life?"

Wylie eased his wife back, holding her to his chest. He kneaded the taut muscles along her shoulders. "Remember, Mick, women having babies go through a lot of highs and lows. Your sister's extra-emotional right now. Good luck, and we'll be in touch."

Having pulled his jacket off the hook, Mick patted the dogs, ruffled the kids' hair and shared a final look of understanding with Wylie. To his twin he said, "Montana's in my blood. I promise you'll see me after spring thaw. Anyway, it's not like California's on another planet. We'll keep in touch by phone. I'll expect to be the first person outside this house to hear whether Santa brings me a new niece or a nephew." Mick gently brushed his fist over her jaw, then ducked out of the house and loped along the trail to the Arrow. A twinge in his hip reminded him that he'd pushed too hard during the past few days.

His chest remained tight even after he soared off into the gathering clouds. Mick knew his twin didn't understand why he was doing this. He couldn't put it into words, either. But, like breathing, giving Hana every chance was something he had to do.

CHAPTER SEVEN

"Ms. Egan." A thin woman wearing a plain blue suit, brown hair pulled into a tight bun, entered Hana's room. She cross-checked the name on the end of the bed with what was on the clipboard she carried. "I'm Pat Stevens, hospital social services counselor."

"I don't need that." Hana, who had a long, unhappy history with social service counselors, found herself looking about for an escape. Of course, in her condition, that was impossible. She crossed her arms over her stomach. Her lower back ached more than yesterday, the pain becoming sharp with her slightest move.

"I have a request from Marsha McGill at Dr. Lansing's office. She's working with Mick Callen. They've asked our office to evaluate you for monies allotted to needy California residents for hospital care. If you qualify, it should speed your transfer to a facility that's better equipped to handle your care long-term."

"I'm not needy. I have a job. Well, I had one. I'm a smoke jumper."

The woman gave Hana a pitying look. "Our records show that was a summer job. What insurance you had was terminated. It says here you're a part-time college student as well. I've taken the liberty of running a financial check. Frankly, Ms. Egan, your bank balance *may* have gotten you through a term at UCLA, but considering the length of time your doctors say you'll need specialized care and the fact that the funds in your bank won't cover the bills you've accumulated here, I looked into what options you have. I recommend filling out these welfare forms today. The welfare office in your home county assures me they'll expedite the paperwork so you'll be fully approved by the time Ms. McGill works out your transfer."

The pains shooting up Hana's back and across her abdomen stole her breath. The possibility of going on welfare for any reason burned through Hana, making her too dizzy to understand everything the Stevens woman implied.

As she looked down on the patient, Pat Stevens frowned. "Ms. Egan, if this is a bad time, I can come back tomorrow morning."

Hana tried to nod, but a tearing pain had her crying out. She made three stabs at her call button. Each time, the plastic slipped out of her sweaty hand.

"Here, let me call your nurse. Better yet, I'll go out and find one." She gestured toward the door, then seeing Hana knotting her sheet between her hands, the counselor literally ran from the room, calling for help.

SHORTLY BEFORE NOON, Mick walked out of the bank with a spring in his step. With the exception of a few heated moments, when Carl Bledsoe had outright tried to make a deal to buy Mick's land instead of extending a mortgage, negotiations went far better than he'd imagined they might. The figures Carl bandied about concerning his property's worth astounded Mick. And he'd had a hard time making clear to the banker that he wasn't interested in becoming an aimless millionaire. Whitepine was home. Mick loved flying charters. He liked having elbow room. As usual, he was cash poor, but all he wanted was to lay hands on enough money to help Hana.

Now it was accomplished. The loan check was signed and deposited to Mick's account. Marsha McGill said she had Lucy Steel searching for physical therapists. And last night Mick had reached a workable agreement with Stella. All that remained was bringing Hana on board with his plan.

Driving to the hospital, he passed stores that enticed him to stop and buy Hana another gift. He thought of her meager possessions sitting in the Arrow's cargo hold. A display of sweaters drew a second glance. He'd like to buy Hana a soft, pretty one. She deserved pretty things.

The Caddy idled at the stoplight. Hana had instructed him to not buy her any more presents. Besides, were L.A. winters cold enough to warrant sweaters?

The light changed to green and Mick left the stores behind. He saw a lingerie shop. If she slept in a ratty T-shirt, she needed sleepwear. But what did he know about buying that?

Mick continued past the lingerie shop and others. Flowers. Candy. And one called The Jewelry Box. Hana's earlobes were pierced. Sometimes she wore small gold or silver studs. Never anything Mick would call fancy.

Hmm. If he waltzed in with earrings, she'd toss him out. He'd better stick with the Crichton book. It lay on the passenger seat. When he parked at the hospital, he had nothing but the book, and no speech rehearsed to convince her to accept his help.

The woman at the reception desk recognized Mick and motioned him over. "Are you here to see your friend, Ms. Egan?"

"Yes. I'm taking her a book." Mick lifted it and started past the desk.

"I wanted to tell you that a few minutes ago I filed a room change for Ms. Egan."

"Hana? Are you sure?" Mick retraced his steps to the counter.

The woman returned a card to its holder. "She's been moved down the hall to ICU. Intensive care," she elaborated, though she appeared uncertain in the face of Mick's sudden, ferocious scowl.

He smacked his free hand flat on the counter, then set off for the elevators at a near run. *What had happened?* Not half an hour ago he'd spoken to Marsha McGill. Wouldn't she have told him if—if— Mick's mind refused to complete the sentence.

Breath coming in spurts and fear eating at his frayed nerves, Mick impatiently hit the up elevator button six times. In his haste to board the car, he almost mowed down three interns who were getting off in the lobby.

He bolted out on Hana's floor before the doors were fully open and dodged nurses and an orderly pushing a creaking gurney.

Mick recognized the doctor who'd mistaken him for Hana's husband. Dr. Black stood at the nursing station writing on a chart. Was he reporting on Hana? In Mick's concerned state, he jostled the doctor's elbow, forcing him to glance up. Something—not quite recognition—flashed in his eyes.

"Dr. Black, I'm sorry to bother you. I'm Mick Callen, remember? We spoke the other night about Hana Egan. Downstairs they said she's been moved to Intensive Care. I'm not a relative, but I'm pretty much the only person here for her. I've been working with Dr. Lansing on moving Hana to a California hospital. Please, if something to do with her condition has changed, can you tell me?"

Royce Black closed the chart and returned it to the hanging file. He took in Mick's rattled appearance. "Hana has numerous superficial lacerations, we assume from being dragged over rocks. She's developed a secondary infection. ICU is a precautionary measure. Dr. Lansing and I plan to treat her vigorously with antibiotics to keep the infection from doing damage to her surgery site."

"So, it's not too serious?"

"It could turn serious. It'd help if the patient had a desire to be healed."

"Hana's no quitter," Mick insisted.

The surgeon slid gold-wire glasses up his nose. "You have that on good authority?"

Mick shrugged in response to the brusque question. "No, sir. I expect Hana has a lot weighing on her mind. I'm doing my best to try to ease some of her concerns. In all honesty, I'm not sure she'll agree to accept help from me."

"How's your staying power?"

"Pardon me?"

The doctor's bushy eyebrows merged over an eagle-beak nose. "Put bluntly, will you let her run you off if she yells at you? Because I suspect she will. Near as I can tell, that little lady has a big chip on her shoulder."

"Everyone in her past let her down. I won't."

"Ah, that's the spirit. But when the going gets tough remember this conversation. Ginny," the doctor said to a nurse on her way by, "I'm authorizing Mr. Callen to visit our patient in bed one. Felix Lansing wants her moved out of our fresh Montana air into smoggy L.A. This may be the person who can get Hana to consent to a transfer. Give him ready access, and we'll see."

Ginny was an apple-cheeked woman as wide as she was high who moved at the speed of light, Mick discovered. She latched on to his arm and swept him down the hall before he managed to thank Dr. Black.

Whereas the last time Mick saw her Hana had three IVs running in her pale, blue wrist veins, today two lines dripped fluid in each arm. She looked even smaller in here, surrounded by beeping, flashing intensive-care trappings.

She must've sensed someone in the room. Her eyes opened a crack. Then grew wider, reflecting vague distrust as she watched Mick's progress into the room. "Go away. Nurse, I left word at the station that I don't want to see anyone."

"Now, now, is that any way to treat a handsome visitor?" Ginny checked the bags of liquid pumping into Hana. She straightened her patient's sheet, pulled the white bear out from under the light throw, and clucked a bit as she shoved the stuffed toy in a drawer of the pedestal table. With a wry quirk of her lips, Ginny bustled out, leaving Mick to deal with his fate.

"I brought you that book."

"I don't want to read." Hana shut her eyes.

"No time?" Propping a foot on the lower bed rail, Mick set the book within reach of her right hand.

Her eyes opened a slit. "Let me see if I can put this in terms you can understand. Get lost, Mick. Quit meddling in my life."

"Bringing you a book is meddling in your life?"

"You know you've done more." She thrashed restlessly. "This morning I was visited by a hospital social services counselor who said you and Dr. Lansing's secretary are apparently discussing me behind my back. How dare you?"

That stung. Mick thought Dr. Black knew what he was talking about when he'd mentioned Hana yelling. "So, sue me. I admit I nagged Marsha McGill into putting herself out for you."

"I want both of you to *butt out*. Just who do you think you are?"

"I have a better question. Who are you? Or more to the point, who have you become? The Hana I admired had common sense. And guts. Today, you can't manage to be civil to someone who wants to see you get well." Mick wheeled and grabbed for the door his nurse escort had shut. He was out and the door was closing on its own when Hana called his name. He wavered. *Go, or turn back?* Sighing, Mick slowly went back inside. However, he made no move to return to her bedside.

Hana echoed his sigh. "Mick, this is so hard for me. I hate feeling dependent. What can I say?" She tried to wave a hand, but the lines taped to her arms resisted.

"'Thanks' might be a good start."

"For what? Proving yet again that I need to be shuttled into a state system I thought I'd escaped for good? The hospital counselor said your Marsha McGill is signing me up for welfare." Hana's eyes shone with tears she did her best to blink away. "I know how welfare folks operate. I'd have no say about…anything. I'd rather die than let people who don't give a damn get their grubby paws on any child of mine. That's what'll happen, you know. I have no home, no job, no means of support. It's a short step to saying I'm an unfit mother!"

Nothing got to Mick the way Hana's tears did. He slowly walked to her bed. "Hana, I don't know the person who talked to you. I swear, I told Ms. McGill welfare funding was out. My brother-in-law, the ranger, came up with a plan." Mick filled Hana in on the Forestry Service special fund and Wylie's offer to initiate a holiday fund-raiser. "Will you let us work out details? You just sign the form requesting transfer to the California hospital."

"I can't go as long as I have this infection."

"Dr. Black thinks antibiotics will take care of it."

A shaky sigh trickled out. "I suppose. But you don't know L.A. like I do. Everything there is massive, hectic and impersonal. I take college classes there only because I'm a resident and I can attend UCLA without paying out-of-state tuition. If I'd ever tried to set foot on campus without any means of support, I'm afraid I would've been swallowed by the system again."

"Hana, I won't let that happen." Mick bracketed her face with both hands and made her focus her restless eyes on him. He hoped he could convey reassurance.

She chewed a trembling lower lip. "If only they'd wait until I was walking first. Then I'd feel I had some control."

Mick straightened. "We'll find a physical therapist to work with you in L.A."

"Just like that?" She tried to snap her fingers, but they didn't snap. "And we *who?*"

Mick realized he'd hit D-day. Disclosure day. "Hana, remember what I said when I delivered supplies for the climb?" He didn't give her time to search her memory, but plowed forward. "I said I planned to spend this winter someplace warm. I've decided that someplace can be Los Angeles."

"Why? To hold my hand? I can't let you waste your vacation like that, Mick."

Hearing her reaction, he was glad he hadn't told her he'd wired a deposit to hold a single story, two-bedroom, older home that a friend of Dr. Lansing's had found a half block from the hospital. Mick had taken a virtual computer tour of the home and area. He thought Hana would like the tree-lined street, and the quiet older neighborhood, within walking distance of a grocery store and pharmacy. The price seemed reasonable for L.A. Hana would probably freak, though, if she knew what it cost.

"Where I go doesn't matter. Southern Cal has plenty of sun. And you'll be there." He could dole out particulars to Hana in small increments. Especially as her mouth fell open at what he'd already revealed.

But for a time it seemed to Mick that she'd let the subject drop. Seconds before he claimed victory in round one, she started shaking her head. "Since the day I turned sixteen and emancipated myself from the California Foster Placement system, I've had one rule, Mick. Never be beholden to anyone. You told me you planned to spend the winter on the beach of some tropical island. By no stretch of the imagination does L.A. fit. I won't let you rearrange your life on my account."

"If I was the type, I'd toss you over my shoulder like a cave man, Hana, and just fly you off to California."

"You and whose army?" Still, she laughed at the image, and he saw a dimple.

"If you had a telephone in here I'd call my sister. She'd tell you to give up now, because eventually I'll wear you down."

"Okay, Mick. I'll agree, providing you answer one question honestly."

He cocked a finger and said, "Shoot. I'm ready for both barrels."

"What do you get for your time and trouble? I've quit asking *why.* You always dodge that bullet."

"I get a change of scenery. My business slows down to nothing in the winter. Marlee moved. Pappy passed away." He shook his head. "And I hate seeing you uncomfortable. I liked who you were when you were healthy and whole."

"Whole would be nice. I'm having real pain right now." Her pinched face attested to her statement. She fidgeted with the white cotton coverlet.

Mick became concerned enough to press her call button.

A nurse, not Ginny, but another one, dashed into the room carrying a small paper cup. "What are you doing here?" she demanded. "This is ICU. Visitors are restricted."

"Dr. Black okayed my visits. Will those pills take away her pain? She looks feverish."

The nurse reached up and yanked a white curtain around Hana's bed. "I think you should go now, sir. I have to examine the patient."

"Need help? Just kidding. Please make her better." Mick offered the sour-faced nurse his best smile, one that had stood him in good stead with women of all ages since he was a kid.

It had the desired effect. "By all means, I'll do everything within my power to make her well, young man. So, shoo."

Mick waved to Hana. "See you later. On my way out I'll tell the social services counselor you'll sign the transfer." With that, he left.

Nurse Ginny was sailing past Hana's room and heard his "Phew!"

"You struck out?" She braked to a stop.

"What? No, I think I succeeded. Well, semi-succeeded," he admitted under Ginny's scrutiny. "Helping Hana is going to be a process of three steps forward and two steps back."

"That's how medicine usually works," Ginny said, falling in beside Mick as he traveled down the hall. "Patients can be their own worst enemy."

"That's the truth. I've been on both sides of that fence. I remember my sister accusing me of being too stubborn for my own good. Stubborn because I wanted to be healed instantly. Hana's like that. But she's not feeling so hot right now. May I leave you my number, in case she gets worse? As I keep telling the staff here, she has no family."

Ginny pulled Hana's record and wrote Mick's cell number in the blank space under *person to be notified* of changes in Hana's condition.

He left the ward planning to visit her again the next day. At the elevator, a small group of doctors were engaged in earnest conversation. That reminded Mick he needed to check on Katie Felton. As he changed elevators to get to Pediatrics, he realized he was becoming comfortable with the layout of the Kalispell hospital. He thought about the sprawling L.A. complex he'd looked up on the Internet. Dr. Lansing's secretary said Hana would want to remain as an outpatient for as long as possible. Not only would it be cheaper, but the woman suggested Hana would be more comfortable in a home environment. Cheaper or not, Hana wouldn't be happy with any price, if she wasn't paying for it.

He probably should've leveled with her about that, Mick thought as he stepped out on the pediatric surgical floor. One of two nurses writing in charts glanced up when Mick's shadow fell across the desk. A tall, red-haired nurse recognized his name when he gave it. "Ah, the night clerk said you'd pop in again for an update on Katie. I was skeptical. Angel Fleet generally does phone follow-ups. I've never seen a volunteer pilot drop by."

"I have a friend hospitalized upstairs. I trust Katie's news is good, or I doubt you'd be so cheerful."

"It's like we're seeing a brand-new kid. Before the transplant, her skin, and even the whites of her eyes, were yellow. This morning she's pink. It's a fine thing you did, and in a storm. Once it started snowing hard, we all gave up hope of her getting that liver."

"The storm eased up," Mick muttered. "I'm happy to hear that so far she's good. I understand it'll be some weeks before she's totally out of the woods."

"True. Still, most reject in the first hours following surgery. Dr. Dodd was smiling when he came out of Katie's room after morning rounds. That's the most significant sign that things are going well. If it's bad, he's poker-faced."

"I hope it's easy from here on out. This time of year a kid her age should be looking forward to a visit from Saint Nick in a couple of months."

A nurse twittered. "Dr. Dodd said something similar. Only, he said Katie already received the best possible present delivered by Saint *Mick*."

"Whoa! Dr. Dodd has a warped sense of humor." Mick joined the nurses who laughed.

As Mick left the hospital, he wished Hana would treat him a little like a saint—or at least trust him. Although, if she could read his mind and see how often and how prominently she used to appear in his nightly dreams, it'd be goodbye to any trust he'd built.

Mick stopped with his car key in the door. He'd only just realized that since her accident, he no longer had erotic dreams about Hana. Had that changed because he now saw himself as her rescuer?

He climbed into the Caddy and ground the motor. And realized the dreams ceased the night Dr. Black announced that Hana was pregnant.

THE NURSE EXAMINING Hana checked her temperature. "That young man was right. You have a fever. Who's your doctor?" She reached for Hana's chart.

"Dr. Black's taking care of me post-surgery," she murmured, looking at the nurse with glazed eyes. "I am hot. How high is my temperature?"

"One hundred and three point six." The nurse sponged Hana's face with a cool cloth. "The antibiotic he's put you on probably needs more time to take hold."

"Should my lower back hurt worse than the day they pulled me out of a crevasse? I'm not sure about taking pain pills." Hana cupped both hands across her abdomen. "On a scale of one to ten, with ten being the most excruciating, I'm at nine. Is there a safe pain medication? For my baby? Poor kid didn't ask for a mom who went mountain climbing and fell in a hole."

The nurse tucked a new disposable thermometer under Hana's tongue. Almost instantly the meter flashed a hundred and four point two. Dumping it in the trash, the woman stripped off her gloves, raised and locked the side rails on Hana's bed and headed for the door. "I'll ask Dr. Black about pain meds. Breathe through your mouth, and that'll help you get through the worst, Ms. Egan."

Hana saw three nurses in the doorway—no, two nurses. What were they saying about breathing? What did it mean? Steeped in a fog that seemed to shroud her brain, she remembered a girl from one of her group homes, one of the pregnant teens, reading to them from a maternity manual. Something about panting like a puppy to ride out the contractions. Jeez, was *that* the source of her pain? Dr. Lansing hadn't minced words. He'd called her pregnancy high-risk. He recommended she end it, but she was too late to make that decision. He also said that if she went into labor they'd have to take the baby. And he hinted that many women walking in her shoes would welcome that outcome. Or had she imagined that was what he, and Mick, and everyone thought?

She stretched a hand through the side rails on her bed, opened the drawer and sighed with relief when her fingers closed over the white teddy bear. She brought him to her chest and hugged him tight. "I want my baby," Hana murmured, her tears dripping in the soft fur. "Maybe it's stupid and unrealistic, but I want my baby." *And come what may,* she thought, *my kid is going to be loved.*

SATISFIED AT HAVING convinced Hana to go to L.A., Mick stopped to give Dr. Lansing and his secretary the news.

Marsha received his announcement by rushing around her desk to close her office door. "When did you last see Hana, Mick? Not ten minutes ago, a nurse from ICU called to let Dr. Felix know Dr. Black is prepping Hana to go back into surgery."

"Now? Today?" Mick was stunned. "I left her room, visited Pediatrics for a few minutes, then drove straight here. It hasn't been more than fifteen or twenty minutes. Well, maybe half an hour. What is it? Is she…losing the baby?"

"Dr. Black doesn't think so. But he alerted Dr. Felix just in case. He told me it's common to miss a bone sliver in pelvic fractures. Her temp hit a hundred and five. The antibiotic isn't fighting the infection. A second look at her X-rays showed a spot, a bone chip that may be the irritant. Dr. Black plans to use a local anesthetic to minimize risk to her pregnancy."

"I'm going straight back to the hospital. Would you do me a favor and notify the folks in California that this might delay checking Hana into their program?"

"I will. And Mick, try to think positively for Hana's sake."

Mick tried to do that as he left Dr. Lansing's parking lot and merged onto the freeway. Reaching the hospital in record time, he parked and raced to ICU. He met Ginny leaving a patient's room. "Mr. Callen, I tried to reach you on your cell. I'm afraid I don't have good news to share."

"I know. I stopped at Dr. Lansing's office, so I know Hana's back in surgery."

"It's lucky Dr. Black was in-house, since her condition deteriorated rapidly."

"I thought she looked feverish. I hope my visit didn't cause her downhill slide."

"It has to do with her original injury. Do you know where the visitors' lounge is on this floor? If you'd like to wait, I'll have Dr. Black stop in for a word after he finishes."

Mick knew where to go, but he didn't know what to do with himself to pass the time alone in the big empty room. He paced the perimeter, but got tired of that and dropped into an uncomfortable chair. A beige phone sat on a squat lamp table.

Cell use wasn't permitted in the hospital. He did have a credit card that would work for the house phone.

Charging the call to his card, he punched in his sister's number. "Marlee, they've taken Hana in for more surgery. She developed a raging infection from a stray chip of bone or something. Sis, I'm scared. You know, I never worried about any of my surgeries. But this is…different."

"Surgery is always more difficult for the one who waits. You can't let your mind run amok, though."

"I was feeling good after visiting her. She agreed to transfer to the hospital in L.A. Now I wonder if I should've pressed her harder before this. L.A. has a whole host of specialists Dr. Lansing says she needs. Marlee, Hana could die right here." He hadn't realized it until the moment he said it.

"Mick, you've gotta stop thinking like that. As long as there's breath, there's hope. I've never met Hana, but any woman brave enough to be a smoke jumper has got to be tough. Plus, she's pregnant. She'll fight like a tiger to save her baby."

"Even if she's lost the baby's father? What if Hana cared more for Jess than she let on after the accident? Do people die of a broken heart?"

"Oh, Mick, why torture yourself this way? Listen, take Pappy Jack as an example. He loved Gram to distraction, but lost her to cancer, and Dad, his only son, to a car accident not long after. He lived for a whole lot of years. Partly, I think, because he had us. Hana has you in her corner, Mick."

"I don't know what to do to help her."

"You're helping her by being there. By the way, Wylie organized a forest ranger craft and bake sale for next weekend. Rain, sleet or snow, we're figuring on a good turnout. The flyer calls it Hana's slush fund. Appropriate, we thought, given the prediction of snow."

"You guys are the best. I hope you're not overdoing it, sis. You have a baby to worry about, too."

"I'm fine. I made the flyers. The kids helped me bake cookies. Dozens of them from recipes Rose sent. She used to host a cookie exchange at Christmas for the navy wives. Which reminds me of something she brought up yesterday. She said if you're going to be gone all winter why let your house and the guest cottage sit empty? She's apparently gotten involved again at the base. I gather there's a huge need for places of solitude to house war-weary reservists coming home from extended Gulf tours. Rose said most aren't ready to jump into their old jobs. The more she and I talked, the more I thought it'd be a great solution for you. Especially if you stay in California later into the spring, past when the charter business picks up. Rose thinks some of the pilots would fly a few freight runs in exchange for housing."

"That's brilliant. If Pappy hadn't had this house and business waiting for me, I would've been one of those guys not knowing which way to turn. How do we go about signing up for something like that?"

"Turn it over to Rose and Stella. Let them work out the schedule with Rose's veterans' group. Stella will be in touch with you. You can notify her when you expect to be back. Rose is confident she can negotiate some type of subsidy that'll more than pay for water, electricity and general upkeep."

"This sounds better and better, Marlee. And you know what? I feel better."

"Glad I could help."

"Everybody needs a sounding board. Or a pet. Hana has neither. I remember you asked why I'd get involved. She asked, too, but I botched the answer. It boils down to the fact that Hana doesn't have a single person she can count on."

"She has you. And you have a dog. Well, that's debatable.

Wingman has really taken to Dean and vice versa. By next spring, the bond they've forged may be too hard to break. I thought I should warn you."

"I have eyes, Marlee. I saw what was happening my last visit, brief though it was. I can always go back to the animal shelter. There are a lot of dogs who need good homes. If you're all right with me giving Dean my dog, we can consider it done."

"He'll be so happy! Dean rescued three kits from a gray fox who didn't come back to her lair. He has them in a dog bed here at the house. It's so cute. Wingman and Piston both let us know when the kits are hungry or crying."

"And you call me a softie. You've got yourself a stepson who's gonna be even worse about collecting strays."

As Marlee laughed, Mick saw Dr. Black walking toward the waiting room. "I see Hana's doctor. I need to catch him."

"Call me after you find out details. That's an order, Mick." She barely got it out before Mick disconnected.

He sprang out of his chair and met Dr. Black in the hall. "How's Hana?"

"I removed two bone chips, one of which was the culprit. It'd punctured a blood vessel. A small hemorrhage caused her spike in fever. She'll be much improved by this time tomorrow."

"Bone chips. Is that something we'll need to worry about down the road?"

The doctor gave a wry smile. "The aim in all my fancy surgery is to ensure that her pelvic ring knits. Normally in women Hana's age, bone regeneration is rapid. Were it not for the added stress of pregnancy, she'd be up walking in a matter of weeks."

"So, because she's pregnant does that mean she can't get up until after she has the baby? Sorry, but I'm not real savvy about her type of injury."

Dr. Black dug underneath his surgical frock and brought out a pad and pen. He made a few swift strokes, enough for Mick to see an interpretation of how the hip bones and pelvis connected to the pubis and sacroiliac, which the doctor identified for him. "Look at this and think of a Life Savers candy. I'm sure you've seen one break in the package. That's like Hana's pelvic ring." He drew three slashes, depicting the fractures. "I imagine Felix Lansing told you a normal delivery is out of the question. The baby exits here. Hana's ring won't be solid enough for years, if ever, to allow a natural birth. They make pelvic slings for muscle support. Hana's body will start to expand as the baby grows. Definitely, if today's surgery controls her fever, I'll want her up and moving about. She should get into the habit of putting on the corset, or sling, every time she so much as walks across the room."

Mick nodded thoughtfully. "I'll make a note to buy a couple of those slings. Dr. Lansing's secretary can probably point me in the direction of a medical supply outlet."

"Hana said you're flying her to a hospital in L.A. They'll set up a triple-track program for her. Orthopedic, obstetrics, pre- and post-natal tracks."

"Since you brought up the flight, any danger of that putting Hana at a greater risk? I've thought that maybe the way we hauled her out of the crevasse and then strapped her on a canvas litter worsened her injuries. Then we got bounced around in the weather. There's no guarantee it won't storm again for part of our trip. Should she consider booking on a commercial flight instead?"

"No. I'd want her to lie flat for travel. Will you have a nurse on board?"

"Do I need one? I could offer a short vacation to a nurse from here."

"Don't you dare. We're short-staffed as is. Buy a solid

foam pad, and put it on your litter. Ask Dr. Lansing to give Hana a mild sedative for the trip. He'll have something that won't depress the baby." Black pulled at a cuff and glanced at his watch, then thrust a hand at Mick. "I'm late to a meeting. If I don't see you before you leave, Mr. Callen, good luck."

Mick stood for a moment feeling at loose ends. Hana was the one who could use a bit of luck. But if he planned to be Hana's caretaker throughout the three programs the doctor mentioned, Mick realized he needed to read up on pelvic injuries. If others had beaten it, so could Hana.

He'd forgotten to ask when he could see her again. Before checking he called Marlee back and relayed everything he could remember of what the doctor had said.

"Learning more about her type of injury is a good plan, Mick. The bookstore in Kalispell probably has a health section. You might also want to buy a book that deals with pregnancy."

"What do I need to know about that?"

The phone line remained silent for so long Mick said, "Hello? Did I lose you?"

"No. I had to wrap my mind around what you said. If you're planning to act as Hana's nurse, every phase she goes through will affect you. It's Wylie who listens to my fears, gripes and concerns about the baby. It's Wylie who rubs my back every night when I ache so much I can't sleep. It's Wylie who has to try to run down weird food at midnight to satisfy my quirky cravings. When Hana hits those phases, Mick, that's going to be you."

His brain stumbled over the prospect of rubbing Hana's back. "No," he said, through clenched teeth. "Wylie does that because you guys are married and it's his baby. Listen, someone just came in, and I think they need this phone. We'll talk another day." As he hung up, he heard Marlee say, "But, Mick…"

CHAPTER EIGHT

NURSE GINNY RAN UP to Mick as he left the waiting room. "I'm glad I caught you. Ms. Egan is asking for you."

"Me?" He did a three-sixty, thinking maybe Dr. Black hadn't left yet.

"Yes, you. She's feeling cheerful. Of course…her anesthetic hasn't worn off yet." The nurse gave Mick the room number and peeled off down another corridor.

He opened the door of Hana's darkened room. "You get around," he joked. "Three addresses in one day. A dodge to try to ditch me, or avoid bill collectors."

Hana reached for his hand. Hers was cold; his, twice as warm. "Mick, I'm glad you waited. I heard a nurse tell Dr. Black you had. I…ah…am so sorry," she blurted.

"For what?" He chafed warmth into her cool skin.

"I was snarky earlier. And I'm ashamed. When they wheeled me into surgery I was so scared, thinking what if you gave up on me, too?"

In a move unexpected by both of them, Mick leaned down and kissed her. Feeling her mouth soften under his sent a curl of desire through him. Her response was the type that as a rule invited deepening a kiss.

Either his brain kicked in at the right moment, or else the noise Hana made in her throat sounded panicky enough to serve as a gut punch. Mick bolted upright immediately and

dropped her hand. "I thought we'd established we're friends."
He needed to see Hana relax from her state of shock. "Pals
hang together through fair weather or foul. Not just when the
going is easy."

Hana started to speak, but her voice sounded croaky until
she licked her lips. It was a sexy move that—if he had good
sense—would send him running.

"It seems like a one-sided friendship," she got out. "I asked
the nurse to find you because I don't know what got into me
earlier…or just now, for that matter."

"Blame it on terrible pain and a temperature of a hundred
and five."

She blinked several times in succession, and Mick teased
her about looking like a baby owl. That produced a genuine
smile that broke the strain between them since Mick's surprise
kiss.

"I want to start over. I'll try to be worthy of your friendship. But…bear in mind I'm pretty much used to operating in
an every-man-for-himself environment."

"Then we'll have to find you some new friends. Or a different job. Whichever is easier."

Hana had rolled to her side to take an ice chip. She rolled
back, all but choking on the piece. "You've got to stop making
me laugh, Mick. The shot they gave me is wearing off."

"In that case, it's a good time for me to get going. Shall I
tell a nurse you need something for pain?"

"No. The less pain meds I take, the better for the baby, Dr.
Lansing said."

Mick did leave on that note, but he wondered why no one
had been frank in telling Hana that her odds of actually having
the baby weren't good. Had anyone broached the subject of
terminating her pregnancy for the sake of her health? Mick
recalled that Dr. Lansing said something the first night about

Hana wanting her baby. Did she mean regardless of risk? It was probably a question that needed an answer before they went to L.A. Although it took Mick back to what he'd said to Marlee. Hana's pregnancy was a separate issue from the injuries she'd received in the fall.

As he left the hospital, Mick remembered that Marlee had recommended he get a book on pelvic injuries. He spent the next hour browsing the bookstore and walked out with a bag full of fiction and biographies. He figured he'd be hanging around clinics a lot waiting for Hana. As well, he bought a Merck Manual. A sales clerk showed him it had a chapter devoted to pelvis fractures. Mick skipped over a dozen shelves dedicated to birth and babies, although he'd leafed through one book titled *High-Risk Pregnancies*. He left without it.

Mick flew to Whitepine, where he spent the rest of the week preparing for an extended absence from his business.

Stella Gibson and Rose Stein arranged a three-month trial for Mick's home to be a navy R & R. If it went well, Stella could renew the contract from week to week for however long Mick remained in L.A. He hadn't actually considered what either he or Hana might do after she healed. That was a hurdle they'd worry about once she'd improved to that point.

Twice each day, he called her. "Guess what?" she said at the start of their Friday call. "Dr. Lansing and Dr. Black just left my room. They agree my infection's under control. And I do feel a hundred percent better. I can check out Monday, if you've arranged an evaluation in L.A. for inclusion in something Dr. Lansing called a teaching program. What exactly is that, Mick? Will I be a guinea pig?"

"Ouch. No. The way it was explained to me, the teaching program gives you cross-discipline treatment at a lower cost. Otherwise you'd have to go into a single discipline, such as orthopedic or ob/gyn, as a private patient."

"Shouldn't you have asked which I prefer?"

"I left it up to Dr. Lansing. Is something bugging you, Hana?"

"I don't know. No. Yes. All right, I'll tell you. It's the doctors, their staff and you all making arrangements for *me*."

"But you've been flat on your back and medicated up the wazoo."

"We've talked every day. My brain's not frozen, Mick."

He could hear her agitation. He'd hoped they could avoid this confrontation until they were already in L.A. and had her checked into the outpatient clinic program. Then it'd be too late for her to back out.

"What? No comment?"

"I only want what's best for you. What do you want?"

"Put like that, it makes me sound ungrateful," she said. "Did you know a nurse had to help me to the bathroom last night, and again this morning? It's a humbling experience not to be able to…uh…you know, take care of basic necessities."

Hearing her despondency sent panic through Mick. Why had he thought the two of them could manage on their own? Mick jotted himself another note. Initially, she'd need a visiting nurse. As it was Friday, and they were planning to leave Monday, he should get right on it.

"Hana, how about if I phone you later? I have some business I should wind down before things close for the weekend."

"Wait. Another thing. One of the nurses casually said you must be piling up some hefty expenses on my behalf. I won't take charity, Mick. Not even from…a friend."

"And…" he prompted when her statement trickled off.

"I want a tally. I don't know how or when, but I'll pay you back every cent."

Mick paced the length of his phone cord, and stared out the

window at the creek running through his woods. He had no clue how much smoke jumpers made. Already the bills were significant. "That's something we can settle later."

"No, I want it agreed now. If I have to volunteer in your business for however many weeks or months it takes, that's what I'll do. Years, even."

Years? That held a certain appeal. "You mean file invoices and stuff?"

"Anything. Fix meals, chop wood, whatever."

Mick studied the fire crackling in his oversize stone fireplace. With Hana's bad back, he doubted she'd be able to lift even one log. "Uh, sure. That sounds good. We'll work out a barter. Now I've really gotta go. We're set for Monday. Dr. Lansing arranged an ambulance for you to the airpark early enough so we can beat the storm."

"It's going to storm? Will the flight be as bumpy as before?"

"I hope not. I'm flying the Seneca, not the Huey."

"Oh. Okay, I'll shut up now. I'm placing my life in your capable hands, sir."

"Great. See you, Hana." Sheesh, that woman sure knew how to put a man on the spot.

He made a series of calls to Los Angeles to register Hana in the clinic. He arranged for a month of visiting nursing care and hoped that would be enough, combined with the already scheduled physical therapy.

Assured the transfer was almost complete, the last call Mick made later that night was to Marlee. "I'm taking Hana to California on Monday. I'm calling to wish you guys a happy early Thanksgiving and a merry Christmas."

"Oh, Mick. Darn. I promised myself I wouldn't cry, and here I am…. I hoped you could visit once more, at least. Can you fly up tomorrow? I'll thaw a turkey. We can pretend it's Thanksgiving."

"Thanks, but you know we both hate goodbyes. Besides, I have a checklist of things to do. Tomorrow I'm servicing all the planes. I'm taking the Seneca and leaving the Arrow and the Huey in case any of Rose's navy fliers takes one of my freight runs. Next year we'll get together for the holidays, sis."

"A year is a long time. After losing Cole and Pappy Jack, then Dean's brush with death, I've come to treasure family reunions, Mick."

"Think of Hana, who has no one."

"She has you, Mick. And she's a lucky woman. I hope she's aware of how lucky. I know you've felt…you had big boots to fill following in Dad's and Pappy Jack's footsteps. I just want to say I think you've filled them admirably."

Mick fought a knot swelling in his chest. No boy or man had ever tried harder to live up to the legacy of the men who'd shaped his future. Heroes, both of them. He cleared his throat several times before he was able to sound normal. "You tell that big galoot you married to knock the snow and ice off the phone lines regularly. And de-ice the damn cell tower. I expect to get my doses of home via phone calls between now and spring thaw." He closed with a whispered, "Love ya, twin."

SATURDAY MICK wore himself out servicing the planes. Sunday night he got up almost every hour to make sure the wind hadn't blown in the snow already accumulating at higher elevations. He'd considered spending the night in Kalispell. At the last minute, he'd decided he'd sleep better in his own bed. *Right!*

When the alarm did sound at 5:00 a.m., he was dead to the world. It took two cups of black coffee to jump-start his dragging butt. He taxied out of the bay, and smiled as his running lights glinted off the orange of the goldfish windsock bobbing at the end of the runway. Stella had bought Pappy a new one, for good luck, she'd said. And the two had argued over it until Pappy Jack capitulated and told Mick to replace the torn and ratty knitted sock that had marked the end of Cloud Chasers' runway for most of Mick's thirty-five years.

Today he turned and made a second pass. Never let it be said he'd argue with Lady Luck. He'd gotten in the habit of kissing his fingertips and pressing them to his window as he soared past the goldfish. Once for Hana and again for him.

The ambulance was scheduled to have her at the airpark by six-thirty. That way he'd be in the air by seven, and with luck, well past the Idaho Bitterroot range before the storm from Canada took hold.

Things went according to plan, except that snow began to fall before Mick helped an ambulance crew strap Hana to a cot he'd buckled between the double row of seats. Dr. Black's instructions were to make sure she could stretch out flat.

"I hope this doesn't hurt, Hana."

"It's fine. Dr. Lansing gave me a mild sedative. He assured me the sedative is safe for the…uh…you know, baby."

Mick nodded absently as he signed the receipt authorizing the ambulance company to bill him. He thanked the crew and watched them jump down into the swirling white flakes. Mick bolted the door, then affixed Hana's headset. "This is so you can talk to me. Anytime except when I'm on with the tower. If you're comfortable, I'll go settle in the cockpit and turn up the engines. Jeez, I hoped we'd be well ahead of this storm."

"I'm okay. Are we flying straight through?"

"Dr. Black said that's best. The hospital faxed your records to L.A. last night. That'll be home until you get back on your feet."

She didn't respond, but stared at him with eyes that said she was eager to go, but apprehensive, too. Mick brushed his knuckles across her chin—a jaunty, give-'em-hell gesture understood by military, park rangers and smoke jumpers.

As the snow began to slap his windshield, Mick thanked whatever insight made him prepare the piston-driven Seneca for this trip. It was a workhorse. He buckled his harness, donned earphones and listened to the engines purr before requesting clearance. He'd already pulled the latest weather news, mapped a route and filed a flight plan.

Once they were aloft and clear of air traffic control, Mick said, "Hana, you're free to talk now. We'll hit a little turbulence. It won't be anything like what we went through the day I brought you off Mount St. Nicholas in the Huey."

"That seems a lifetime ago."

"Have you heard from Kari, or Chuck and Norm?"

"Kari phoned one day when she was bored. She's going to physical therapy, all while planning her wedding. She said Roger's not going back to join the crew next year."

"That's probably good news for Len. That kid was a powder keg waiting to blow. I wouldn't want to be on a fire line with him if the going got tough."

"Finally something you and Jess would've agreed on. Jess and Roger were always at loggerheads." Hana waited a decent interval, then added, "I phoned Captain Martin yesterday to say goodbye. He and his wife were always good to me. He said you knew he was going to Jess's funeral. You never said anything to me."

"We weren't exactly close, me and Jess."

"Don't growl. It didn't take a genius to figure that out. What happened between you two? I always wondered if you'd clashed over a woman."

"No, that wasn't it. Let's just say Jess was a clone of every cocky bastard I ever met in the navy and let it go at that."

"Sorry. The captain said when it comes to arrogance, Jess's

dad and brothers made Jess look like a piker. He said it was the coldest funeral he's ever attended."

"That's too bad. I supposed a lot of the crew would go, but Len told me he and his wife were probably going to be the only forestry folks there."

"Not surprising. The temporary nature of the job throws complete strangers together for a summer or maybe two or three. It's hard to make friends."

A few moments passed, then Mick asked, "So, what possessed your group to climb Mt. St. Nicholas?"

"Jess. He and a few guys from Bigfork made the climb the year before. I thought it sounded like fun then. But my classes had started a week earlier. Since I didn't get to go then... Anyway, what does it matter now? They made it without mishap. We screwed up royally."

Mick tried changing the subject, but Hana gave one-word responses. After several attempts, he left her to her thoughts while he cursed himself for asking about the others. That had opened the door for Hana to start thinking about Jess. Mick constantly wondered what Hana saw in him. Well, she said he was like her dad, which hadn't sounded like a glowing character reference. However, at some point she must've... loved Jess enough to make a baby with him. Another hard-to-reconcile fact. Mick would have expected someone with Hana's street smarts to take responsibility for her own birth control.

Trying to piece that puzzle together could drive him crazy. He could ask Hana and be done with it. What kept him from doing that was the distinct possibility that he might not like her explanation.

"Hey," he called. "We lost the snow over Boise. Now we have rain trying to drown us and northern Nevada. With luck we'll hit sunshine over Tonopah."

His passenger mumbled something that sounded like "Good," and they fell into silence again.

Since flying was Mick's first love, his passion, doing so in peace and quiet wasn't a hardship. He continued flying due south. His predictions were right; they hit sun a few miles before Tonopah. That lifted his spirits.

He'd flown in and out of Long Beach numerous times, visiting buddies who were living or stationed on the coast. He decided to rent hangar space there, so that if he and Hana got sick of each other, or if she had day-long appointments, the plane would be near enough for him to pop down to San Diego or Del Mar. That way Hana couldn't accuse him of giving up his entire winter vacation to babysit her.

Around Bakersfield, he turned and flew along the coast. He was familiar with Vandenberg Air Force Base. Looking down on the rows of fighter jets, he felt a twinge of sadness for his lost career.

Not long thereafter, he said excitedly to Hana, "I see white-caps on the ocean. And surfers. Since you grew up in southern California, I guess you surfed."

"I didn't exactly hang with a surfing crowd. Hobbies cost too much. I considered it lucky if I landed with a family who stretched their funds far enough to put three squares a day on the table and shoes on my feet. Don't tell me a Montana boy surfs?"

"That was the highlight of being stationed in Hawaii. The military rented out all types of sports gear to us at decent rates."

"Hmm. I'd love to watch you someday. Oh, what am I saying? Chances of that are slim to none." Mick heard a quaver in Hana's voice.

"We'll be here for five or so months. Don't you think in that length of time the doctor will let you go for a car ride? It can't be more than a couple of miles from the hospital to the beach."

"Mick, I wouldn't count on me participating in much of anything. Between Dr. Lansing and Dr. Black, they didn't paint a very rosy picture."

"You said a nurse had you up on your feet."

"Right! A few steps to the bathroom. My current goal is to sit for ten to fifteen minutes in a chair on that air-filled donut thing. I'm already sick of doing nothing but lying in bed."

"Dr. Lansing said you'll be up and about using a walker."

"When? He said my baby's starting to gain weight. He or she is only going to put more stress on my pelvis."

"I know. But Dr. Black told me to buy a sling to help with support. I would've picked one up at a medical supply house in Kalispell, but I thought it'd be a month or so before you need it."

"You and Dr. Black discussed me…er…my pregnancy. When? And why?"

"Don't be mad. I want to understand everything you have to deal with so I know how to help."

"Then talk to *me* about it," she snapped.

Mick didn't have to see her face to know she was miffed. If she wanted, she could make trouble for Doctors Black and Lansing. Both had crossed the boundaries of patient privacy rights. "Hana, I'm going to get on the radio with the control tower. They'll be giving me landing instructions."

"We're there?" she said incredulously. "It doesn't seem that long since we left Montana. Flying sure beats hitching, or even taking the Greyhound."

"You hitchhiked? Don't you read newspapers? That's dangerous."

"I'm careful. Was…careful. My hitching days are no doubt over, too."

Mick saw red just imagining her accepting rides with who knew what kind of derelict stranger. He calmed down enough to radio the tower. Then he checked to be sure the ambulance he'd booked was there. It was.

By the time the Seneca's wheels met the runway, Mick knew he'd do everything humanly possible to make certain Hana never had to hitchhike again. "Wheels down," he said as he softly touched ground. "How did you weather the landing?" he called back.

"We're down? I didn't feel so much as a bump."

He removed his headset and leaned around the seat to where he could make eye contact with Hana, and flashed her a satisfied grin. "Damn, am I good or what?"

"Modest, too," she said.

"Hey, sunny California is working its magic already. It's nice to see you smile."

"That's not thanks to California. You make me smile, Mick."

She sounded so serious he had to work to conceal the warmth her words stirred in him. He hid his feelings by rubbing his hands briskly and saying, "Time to get this show on the road. I'm going to leave you for a minute while I talk to those ambulance guys."

Hana sobered. "Then I guess it's goodbye. When do you think you'll visit?" Her words poured out, uneven and pretty ragged.

"Uh, Hana. I hope you're not in a rush to boot me out. I plan on riding with you in the ambulance."

"You do? I thought you'd rent a car."

"Later. After I see you settled and we've met the hospital coordinator."

She seemed satisfied but said nothing.

Mick climbed out and signed for a plane hangar. He met the ambulance crew and tossed their duffles in the back.

He knew he'd soon have to lay out his plan to be her caretaker. He didn't know how she'd react.

They got stalled in snarled traffic, and it was an hour past the time Mick had thought they'd be at the rental house. As they pulled up in front of it, according to his watch, he had six minutes at most to get Hana inside and to blurt out his confession before Lucy Steel, the coordinator from the hospital, was due to arrive.

The residential street where the small rental sat, overshadowed by two-story older homes on both sides, was everything Mick imagined after taking the virtual online tour. Red maples and mulberry provided a shaded walkway. The wide front veranda on the small house had a screened porch running its full length. The small backyard had a covered patio with furniture, as well as two bird feeders and a birdbath.

Two streets south they'd passed a thriving business district. Just one block away, the hospital complex fanned out over two acres.

Mick directed the ambulance crew to bring Hana to the bedroom overlooking the grassy backyard. He'd prearranged for a hospital bed in that room.

He signed forms for the ambulance driver, but his eyes never strayed far from Hana. He noticed how she took in everything as the men rolled her gurney up the entrance ramp and through a compact, furnished living room.

"Thanks, guys." Mick let them find their own way out. "Do you want the head of the bed cranked up a bit?" he asked Hana. "Or were you bounced around so much coming in from the airport that it feels good to lie flat?"

Hana's hand shot out and latched on to Mick's sleeve. "Quit fussing. Tell me what's going on. This is no more a hospital than it's a rocket ship to Mars, Mick Callen."

The room had two chairs, a rocker and a ladder-backed chair with a thatched seat. Mick flopped down in the rocker and clasped his hands between his bent knees. "Here's the deal, Hana. Having you stay here for as long as you're able to, and working through the outpatient program costs a fifth as much as inpatient care."

"Okay, that sounds reasonable. But I don't know I can get up and around enough to take care of myself yet."

"You don't have to take care of yourself. Is that what you thought? I told you I was coming here anyway on my winter break. I'll be your go-fer guy as long as you need me. Me, and a visiting nurse for a while."

Hana's eyes became saucer-round. "Mick, I can't..." Her head thrashed from side to side and her hands plucked at the cotton throw an ambulance attendant had draped over her. "I'll try again. I'm not letting you ruin your vacation."

A loud bell echoed through the house. "The door," Mick announced inanely, bounding out of his chair. "That'll be the hospital coordinator." He fled the room. And despite the air conditioner being on, he wiped sweat from his forehead. Ms. Steel was here to get Hana's formal, final consent to be in the program, and he wasn't sure he hadn't already bungled this deal.

He opened the door after peering through the old-fashioned, oval etched glass. Mick determined that the sturdy woman standing on the porch holding a satchel briefcase had to be the hospital worker. Indeed, she thrust out her hand and said, "Mr. Callen? Lucy Steel. I trust the Bailey rental meets your approval." She bustled in, taking in everything at a glance as Mick shut the door behind her.

"We were tied up in traffic so we're not quite settled yet." Mick waved toward the back bedroom. "Hana's tired from the flight and a long ride from the airport. Come with me. I'll introduce you."

Hana didn't put on a welcoming face. Neither did she scowl rudely as Mick had seen her do on other occasions. He performed brief introductions, then backed to the door. "I'll leave you ladies to discuss details. The ambulance driver pointed out a car rental agency a few blocks from here. I'll go lease a car. If I have time, I'll pick up a few groceries to tide us over."

Hana might've thrown in her two cents, if she hadn't been occupied with figuring out which of three buttons raised the head of her bed. Lucy agreed for them both. "That's a fine plan, Mr. Callen. Acquaint yourself with the area. Ms. Egan and I will get to know each other. For the course of her treatment and care, I'll be her liaison with Dr. George, chief orthopedic resident, and Drs. Walsh and Mancuso, who'll be her obstetric and neonatal specialists."

"Hana?" Mick suffered a belated attack of conscience. "Does my plan work for you?"

She flashed Mick a wry smile. "Now you ask my opinion? It's fine, Mick. Everything is fine. Soup. Get soup and crackers, please."

"Anything special?"

She gave a weary shake of her head.

He tore out, determined to get back before Lucy Steel left. And he wasn't a block away before he wished he'd waited and booked Hana's admission interview for the next day.

Everything took longer than he'd allowed for. The car rental place practically fingerprinted him. He rented a Cadillac. Mostly for the large, comfortable interior. The car had plenty of leg room for when Hana was able to take a car ride. And Mick was used to driving one of the big boats, although this bronze edition was way newer and fancier than Pappy's old clunker.

Navigating a cart through a crowded chain grocery store was an experience Mick would have to get used to. There were more people in this one suburban store than lived in all of Whitepine, Montana. As time slipped away, Mick cut his list short. He raced around, hastily tossing in essentials like bread, milk, juice, fruit and an assortment of soup and crackers for Hana. He'd noticed a microwave in the kitchen, so as an afterthought grabbed several easy-to-fix microwaveable meals. Everything fit in two shopping bags.

Returning to the house, Mick was pleased to find that, while it didn't have a garage, there was a parking slab off the street on the south side. He grabbed the groceries and ran up the porch steps, whistling. The door had been locked when he'd left, but now pushed open. He noticed that the blue compact car that'd been parked at the curb had gone. He'd missed Lucy Steel's indoctrination.

Fumbling to return the door key to his pocket, Mick felt wary about how Hana would greet him. It was conceivable that he'd laid out all the up-front money for nothing. Because when it came down to the wire, Hana did have control. She could've sent Lucy Steel away.

"I'm home," he called loudly as he stepped inside, and grimaced thinking that he sounded like a husband.

Silence. He thought Hana might have fallen asleep. And that would be good for her. Mick went to the kitchen and put the milk, juice, butter and eggs in an already cold fridge. He even folded the bags and stored them under the sink before he told himself he'd dallied long enough.

Hana's bright curls stood out against the stark white of a pile of pillows. Glasses Mick had never seen her wear were perched on her nose. Papers lay strewn across the bed. Blue and yellow folders stuffed with more papers sat within her reach on a bedside table.

Mick leaned a shoulder against the door casing. "Anyone ever tell you that you look cute in specs? Like a schoolmarm?"

She gazed at him over the top of the glasses for a long moment, then pulled them off. "Mick, I'm scared. My first appointment's at four o'clock this afternoon. Did you see a wheelchair on the porch? Lucy said she'd have one delivered. It's not motorized. I think she expects you to push me to the hospital. How far is it, do you know? I can't have you waiting on me hand and foot."

"I volunteered for the job. Even at night you only have to call through this monitor." He pointed to a wireless baby monitor Lucy had wedged behind Hana's lamp.

Mick crossed the room and leaned down to press a warm kiss to her plump lips. "Now tell me what all these papers say," he said, smiling as he eased back, meeting her eyes.

"An appointment schedule," she said, busily shuffling papers as she dragged her eyes away from his. "Emergency numbers. Lucy said they need to be peeled off and stuck on every phone in the house. A ten-page diet." Hana made a face. "Oh, and the blue and gold packet is from the physical therapist. She starts tomorrow. Her name is Danika Olsen." Hana fell back against the pillows; the movement ruffled the papers. "There are rules, reams of them. And finance forms."

Mick gathered those up and quickly read a few. "I didn't see the wheelchair, but if it's there, I'll bring it in. You have an hour until you need to be at the hospital. Why don't I fix a can of the soup I bought? While it heats, you should try to rest." He made a neat stack of papers on the table. At the door, he turned back. "I didn't think to ask if you need assistance…uh…going to the bathroom. I don't know the visiting nurse's schedule." His face felt hot, and he was afraid he was blushing.

"Lucy already handled that. She's very efficient." Hana lifted her arm, showing him a plastic coated bracelet. "I'm officially an outpatient. She brought three nightgowns, two robes and two pair of slippers." She paused. "Mick, we need to talk."

"About what?" He detoured to the window and adjusted the blinds to shade the room. Then he fiddled with the thermostat.

"About all of this." She waved her hand impatiently to take in the room.

"You don't like the house?"

"I love it." She burst into tears. Mick rushed to her side, but she held him off. "My whole life I've never lived anyplace this nice. Not ever."

Mick didn't know what to say. He rubbed a hand over his face. "I wish you were here under better circumstances," he mumbled. He gave the foot of her bed a pat. "I'd better go heat the soup."

Passing through the living area, he hunched his shoulders and wiped first one eye, then the other on his shirtsleeve. The wheelchair had been tucked behind a large flowerpot. He dragged it into the foyer. Talk about old—the chair was positively rickety. Flimsy seat. He wouldn't trust it to hold Hana. Removing his cell phone, he stepped into the kitchen and called to arrange for an ambulance.

He took her a cup of tomato soup. "Where's yours?" she asked as he turned to leave.

"I still have things to put away in the kitchen." He didn't, but neither did he think he could handle it if she decided to share details about places she used to live. She acted as if she didn't deserve this, when she deserved far better!

She finished the soup. Even though she knew he was no more than a couple of rooms away, she felt starkly alone. That shouldn't be anything new for her. Half her life had been spent by herself. Ordinarily she didn't mind. This was new and different and yes, a little scary. She munched a cracker Mick had left on the side of the saucer. Since she'd started attending college part-time six years ago, she'd had a life plan that she'd gone about fulfilling. Now, she needed a new life plan.

She wished Mick had come to eat with her. If he was serious about bartering her help in his office for— Hana stopped to really examine this room. Beautiful inlaid parquet floors. Flowered fabric on the walls. Except for the bed, furniture that looked like it cost a mint. She was injured, not brain damaged. Mick needed to level with her about what he was spending on this house, and everything else. She hadn't owned much in her life, but she hadn't ever been in debt either. Hana Egan paid her way. Mick needed to know he had to be realistic. She couldn't live beyond her means.

He came and collected her cup, but dashed out again without giving her a chance to bring up finances. Then another ambulance crew barged in. She tried to make Mick listen.

"What happened with the wheelchair?"

"It's broken down. It's not safe. I'll rent a sturdy one with a motor tomorrow."

"Lucy said it's a hop, skip and jump to the hospital. Mick, aren't ambulances expensive?" she whispered as an attendant slid her out of the vehicle a few minutes later.

Mick dropped back and let the attendant wheel Hana into the clinic where her first appointment was to be. She didn't let up on him. "I started adding up in my head what I owe you. I'm going to be indebted to Cloud Chasers for the rest of my life."

Ignoring her, Mick got in line to hand over her appointment card at the desk.

"Ms. Egan will begin by seeing Dr. George. He'll call for her soon," he was told.

Dr. George did just that. Fresh-faced and roly-poly, the doctor shook hands with Mick, who wheeled Hana into the room. Bending, Mick said, "I'll be out in the waiting room. Have someone tell me when you're finished."

Panic rolled over her as Mick walked off. Dr. George turned out to be kind, soft-spoken and thoroughly professional. "Your orthopedist in Kalispell did a good job," he said after his exam.

"Our X-rays show the pelvic ring is knitting." He held up still-wet films from the portable machine so she could see the new calcified ridges. "The majority of your care from now on will be in the hands of Hugh Walsh and Rebecca Mancuso." Glancing toward the door, he said, "And here they are, right on schedule."

Hana's head spun as Dr. Walsh began to press on her belly, pausing to write copious notes, and Dr. Mancuso, introduced as the neonatal specialist, looked on. "I take over after you deliver," she said. "My job is to ultimately hand you a healthy bambino. Or bambina," she added.

Dr. Walsh pulled off his gloves. "I'll try to get you through as many weeks as possible, Hana. I have a strict regimen for you to follow. We'll go over it before you leave. I also want a sonogram soon."

"Uh, I have a friend in the waiting room. I'd like him to hear this part. His name's Mick Callen. Could someone get him?"

"Is he your baby's father?"

Hana's eyes widened. "No. The baby's father is…dead."

The doctors exchanged low words. Dr. Mancuso slipped from the room, and returned with Mick. After introductions, Dr. Walsh delivered orders for a high-protein diet and biweekly physical therapy sessions to strengthen Hana's back. "You'll need to see she doesn't shirk," Walsh told Mick.

"I'm no stranger to PT," Mick said. "I had a hip socket replaced last year, and surgeries on my side and leg before that."

Hana had opened her mouth to tell the doctor she could manage her own PT, but the news of Mick's multiple surgeries had her studying him instead. Obviously she didn't really know the man she'd seen as a welcome diversion in camp. Mick's visits allowed her an escape from coworkers with whom she had only firefighting in common. Mick read widely, and debated current events heatedly. Hana realized she'd instinctively felt he had more substance than any of the men in camp. Now as she watched him listen carefully to Dr. Walsh's instructions, Hana wished she'd had her lapse of good sense with Mick and not Jess. But a lapse was a lapse, and after-the-fact wishes were useless. At the thought, she heard echoes of one foster mother's favorite phrase. The old witch had repeatedly slapped Hana as she shouted, *If wishes were horses, kid, dirty little beggars like you would ride like a queen.*

Not much had changed. Hana still felt like a dirty beggar girl.

CHAPTER NINE

MICK DID HIS BEST to look interested, but tuned out the doctor who droned on and on about Hana's pregnancy. He did hear, though, Dr. Walsh underscore the strain Hana's soon to be expanding abdomen would place on her slight stature and bones already weakened by multiple fractures of her pelvis and cracks in her lumbar vertebrae. As the doctor carried on, Mick slunk into the background, gravitating to a window that overlooked the hospital parking lot.

He didn't want to think about Hana growing big with Hargitay's baby. These feelings weren't something he was proud of. *Damn!* Mick planted both elbows on the sill and pressed his forehead to the cool glass but felt more tension when a team of nurses streamed in to prepare Hana for a fetal ultrasound.

What the hell was he doing here? He should have listened to Marlee's initial skepticism.

"Mick?" Hana's quavery voice drew him instantly from his grim thoughts. She was afraid, the fear of trying to overcome this alone flickering deep in her eyes. Mick guessed she was concerned about the test. It was plain she wasn't sure about asking him to stay with her, though, probably because of the churlish way he was acting.

Seeing her small hands nervously digging nails into her palms, Mick decided then and there that he had to divorce these feelings he had about her pregnancy from his desire to help Hana.

Mustering an encouraging smile, Mick thought he sounded semicheerful as he moved into the circle around Hana. "I'm right here. You're gonna be just fine."

She reached for him, but Mick had again backed out of the group.

In the X-ray room one of the nurses pushed a metal chair nearer Hana's bed. Smiling at Mick, the nurse patted the chair. He had no choice but to move in closer. He swung the chair around to face Hana and thus block out the attendants peeling back her blanket and hitching up her gown. But Mick didn't move fast enough. He found himself staring at Hana's pearly white belly, and was at once fascinated and shocked to see a rounded bulge not visible when she was covered. Slightly woozy, Mick sat quickly and clasped Hana's hand tight, more for his reassurance than hers.

Relaxed, she obviously didn't sense anything amiss. She burrowed into the pillow, and offered up one of her sweet smiles. Mick felt like a jerk for giving the false impression of happy supporter.

The technician to his right told Hana, "I'm going to rub a jelly-like substance on your abdomen. It'll be cold."

Her aide wheeled a TV monitor on a stand up next to the bed. After wiping the jelly off her hands, the technician picked up a small wand attached to a cord that was plugged into the monitor. "This is the transducer," she said, and began moving the wand over the area beneath Hana's slightly protruding belly button. Oceanlike waves began undulating in circles across the black TV screen. Dr. Walsh, who'd left the room, returned and stepped up to better see the monitor. He pointed to something amid the waves.

Hana had tucked her free arm behind her head. She turned

to follow the doctor's finger. Her cry of delight had Mick leaning toward the machine to see what everyone was twittering about. To his surprise, he identified the outline of a fetus. The boxing motion of tiny arms galvanized Mick. He was looking at Hana's baby. Emotions swelled his chest— emotions unlike anything he'd ever experienced.

Dr. Walsh took a gadget from his jacket pocket and measured Hana's stomach. "I think you're at maybe seventeen or eighteen weeks gestation. Is that right?" Walsh asked Hana.

"What did Dr. Lansing estimate?"

The doctor picked up her chart and shuffled the papers clipped to it. "This report from Dr. Black indicates twelve weeks when you were first admitted." He frowned at Hana and back at the monitor. "The baby's crown-rump length suggests you're further along. My guess is full term is more like late March. Maybe early April."

A flush crept up Hana's neck and fanned over her cheeks. "There's only one possible date I could have gotten pregnant," she muttered. "If I had a calendar I'd be able to give it to you. It was when the Great Bear Wilderness fire was at its peak." She sent an uneasy glance toward Mick, as if expecting him to corroborate the statement.

"That was a bad fire," he said, not really attuned to the significance. "The worst of the summer," he added, even though his mind had stalled on what she'd said about there being only one possible day she could've gotten pregnant. Did that mean she and Jess didn't sleep together again after that time she'd told him about? Or just that every other time they'd used protection?

"I see Dr. Lansing's estimate is nearer mine than Dr. Black's. Can you phone me with the precise date?" Walsh continued with his measurements, jotting his findings on a clean sheet in Hana's chart. "I'll repeat the ultrasound next week.

We can't afford to miscalculate. I'm sure Dr. Lansing impressed upon you the importance of not allowing fetal stress to weaken your partially healed pelvic ring. I'll be juggling the maximum birth weight advisable to hopefully ensure the baby's health and yours. You do understand there's little chance that we'll allow you to go full term?"

Hana blinked and nodded.

"Good. Balancing our predictions is a bit like knowing when to fold a poker hand. We want the fetus at optimum size for survival, but we still have grave concerns about your starting labor prematurely. That's the prime reason for having you undergo low-impact physical therapy. To get your abdominal muscles in the best shape possible."

Hana swallowed repeatedly and darted worried glances between the monitor and Mick.

He cleared his throat. "Doctor, will Hana be confined to bed until she…until you take the baby?"

"I hope not. Hana, you'll be coming here for regular appointments with both Dr. Mancuso and me. Today I see you came by ambulance. Next week or the week after I hope to see you out and about in a wheelchair. Soon thereafter, walking with a walker. You won't run foot races for a few years," he said, smiling as Dr. Mancuso printed a copy of the picture on the monitor.

Once the neonatal specialist placed the print in Hana's hands, Hana couldn't seem to stop staring at it. Mick noticed her thumb softly brush over and around the oval center, where the baby's image was clear.

"I'll go call for the ambulance," he murmured, eager to escape Hana's beatific expression. She had eyes only for the grainy picture.

Heading for the door, he couldn't stop imagining how Hana might look if she were to become as pregnant as Marlee the last time he'd seen her. Marlee's baby was due sometime around Christmas but she was almost Mick's height. Hana was a head shorter. Once her baby got bigger, it'd have nowhere to go but out. He imagined Hana with a basketball stomach.

Gazing after him, Hana frowned. The technician wiping the gel off Hana's belly paused to pat her patient's hand. "He's a man, honey. Cut him some slack. There's something about the ultrasound validation that makes a lot of men skittish."

"Mick's just a friend. It's not his baby." Not for the first time, Hana caught herself wishing that wasn't the case. Wishing she and Mick were having this baby together. But maybe he wouldn't be any happier about that. Hana restlessly rubbed the spots where the nurse had removed the electrodes.

"I thought I saw more than friendly connection there. Humph. In that case, probably the less you talk to him about the baby, the better. Bachelors are even more squeamish than prospective dads."

Hana held her breath until the nurse restored her clothing. It saddened her to think she couldn't share her thoughts and feelings about the baby with Mick, who truly was her only friend. Then again, who said he'd stay the course? In her limited experience, men didn't stick around when the going got tough.

She took a last lingering look at the sketchy image before tucking the ultrasound photo in the pocket of the thin robe Lucy Steel had given her to wear.

Her baby. *Her* pregnancy. It had nothing to do with Mick.

The man filling her thoughts stuck his head around the door. "Are you ready to go, Hana? The ambulance just pulled up out front."

"She's ready as ready can be," one of the nurses said. She dug in the pocket of her uniform and handed Hana a wrapped candy. "A little sugar never failed to perk me up when I was pregnant," the young woman whispered.

Aware that she was feeling blue, Hana opened the mint and popped it in her mouth. It wasn't until an ambulance attendant wheeled her to the van and Mick, seeming detached and aloof, guided her rolling bed down the ramp, that Hana vowed to take his presence in her life day by day. The best thing for her would be to get out of this funk and throw herself body and soul into becoming self-sufficient as quickly as possible.

The ride to the house was short. Feeling drained, Hana welcomed the solitude of the bedroom after the ambulance crew shifted her from their gurney to her bed. The men didn't close the door, so as Mick handed over his credit card and signed the receipt for the trip, she was reminded of her mounting debt.

She saw him then rip up his copy and toss it in what must be a waste can sitting beneath the small cherrywood desk Hana remembered seeing. "Mick, don't tear that up," she called.

He came to her door. "Do you need something? I thought you'd prefer to take a nap between now and suppertime."

As if his words were a catalyst, Hana yawned. "Gracious." She covered her mouth. "Oh, the power of suggestion." She smiled sheepishly at him while attempting to shift higher on her stack of pillows.

Mick rushed to her bedside. "Do you need to get up? Don't try unless I'm here, Hana. Dr. Walsh made clear the precautions you need to take with moving around."

She waved away his smothering. "I'm not getting up, Mick. Will you relax? I just wanted a serious word with you. I saw you tear up the receipt. Shouldn't you keep them? Or at least make me a copy?"

"I get a monthly statement."

"Oh. I've never had a credit card."

"What? Never?"

She shook her head. "When I filed for emancipation, the welfare worker warned me against falling into the credit card trap. She said if I couldn't manage my expenses I'd land back in the system. So I quickly learned to live within my means. Old habits die hard, I guess. Even after I got in with the forestry service, I stuck rigidly to a budget. Now I think it's a good thing. At least I didn't come into this mess with a bunch of unpaid bills. Especially since they're piling up fast. Which is what I want to talk to you about. I'll need an account of every penny you spend on me. Since you'll have to file your statements, is it possible to set up some kind of journal where you list expenses month by month? We can go over them. That way if I have questions about any expense you can clear it up while it's fresh in your mind."

Mick snorted in disbelief. "You think I'm going to pad your bill?"

"Of course not! I trust you. Still, I'd like some up-to-date documentation so I'll have it in case you leave."

"Leave?" Mick pulled the ladder-backed chair up to her bed. He sat and leaned forward, trying to keep from raising his voice in irritation. "If you're annoyed about something, just spit it out."

She flopped back on the pillows. Not looking at him, she chewed at a fingernail.

"Well…I'm waiting."

"You asked for it. I hurt my *back* in the fall. There's not a thing wrong with my eyesight. At the clinic today, you gave off plenty of signals, all of which said you'd rather be anywhere but in that room. That was my first exam of many. Dr. Walsh and Dr. Mancuso outlined a lot more of the same boring kind of tests. I figure it's only a matter of time before you realize you made a mistake, pack your bags and go on your way. So I need to know the financial score."

Mick sprang from the chair and ran a hand through the air. "Oh, you figured that, did you? Well, you're wrong. Don't judge me based on what other guys have done to you, Hana."

"What's that supposed to mean?"

"The boyfriends who mistreated you."

"Boyfriends? Oh, I suppose you think I'm a slut because I'm pregnant."

"Jeez, I don't think you're a slut!" Mick raked the hair out of his eyes. His tone softened. "It's been a long day for both of us." He adjusted Hana's cotton spread. "You look exhausted. Rest. I'll go set up a spreadsheet on my laptop. I'll print us each a copy at the end of every month. It's not that big a deal to me, Hana, but I can tell it's important to you."

Tears leaked from under her half-closed lids. She brushed them away. "I never used to cry. Dammit, I hate bawling women."

Mick took her hand. "Hana, what did I say now?" His voice was gruff. He sat awkwardly on the edge of her bed and patted her arm. When she only sobbed harder, Mick leaned closer and slipped his arms around her. His chest pressed against her torso, and he felt her heart leap. It kicked his into high gear.

"I hate it when I'm bitchy and you're so darned nice to me, Mick." Hana wiped her wet eyes on his shirt. She made a fist, and smacked halfheartedly at his broad, solid shoulder.

"Hey, now you're beating me up? No wonder you think I won't hang around if all I get is abuse." This time, Mick's words were laced with laughter.

Hana stopped crying and made an attempt at a smile.

It was probably going to be another mistake, but Mick couldn't help it. He placed both hands on the back of Hana's head and kissed her the way he used to dream about. Doing that had been on Mick's mind a lot since he'd taken that first taste. This kiss began with a different feel. No friendly peck, this one.

When Hana didn't push him away, or slug him harder, Mick was emboldened. That he felt Hana kissing him back with equal fervor set off a mad fluttering of need in Mick. A need he'd kept in tight check for too long.

He freed a hand and combed his fingers through her satiny hair. She tasted of mint. Mick recalled a nurse handing her a candy after the ultrasound.

More than mint, though, Hana tasted of a passionate, desirable woman. Mick parted her lips and let his tongue explore her mouth.

Hana didn't know how, in the space of minutes, they'd gone from a heated argument to heat of a whole different kind. She wasn't all that practiced at kissing, but it didn't take a genius to recognize that Mick no longer had building a spreadsheet on his mind. She now lay flat against the bed. His big body curved over her—gently at first, but then harder. She was aware of a change in his breathing. It came in hot, rapid spurts as he kissed her neck, the hollow of her throat, her ear....

She grew breathless, too. A hunger in no way connected with food clawed its way into her belly, shooting shivers along partially paralyzed nerve endings. Mick's tongue had again invaded her mouth. Hana wanted more.

Mick made a noise in his throat. As much as he wanted to press his body into hers, he wasn't so far gone that something didn't warn against relaxing and letting Hana take his full weight.

A sharp pop had Hana gasping, and Mick whirling. A few gray feathers were stuck to the window. A bird had flown into the glass.

He turned to Hana, and their eyes met.

"Oh, the poor bird. Mick...?" One of Hana's hands clasped Mick's bicep, which was still rock-hard. She brought the other to her lips.

He unfolded his tense body, releasing hers. "I'll check on the patio." Mick crossed to the window and pushed his face against the glass to peer straight down. "Dazed, but not dead. A dove, I think. They're hardy. I'm betting she'll be good as new within ten minutes."

"How did that happen?"

"The sun's going down. It turns the window into a mirror. She probably saw the reflection of the trees."

Hana threw back her covers. "I want to see for myself that she's all right. I couldn't bear it if she's not."

Mick spun around and saw Hana struggling to get out of bed. "Whoa." He made a giant stride and grabbed her under the arms.

She instantly went still and felt heat streak up her neck. Hana shrugged off his hands. She avoided looking at him as she rubbed the feel of him from her arms.

"Hana? Should I apologize?"

Guilt stung her cheeks.

Mick leaned his head to one side. "I won't lie. I wanted to kiss you."

"But we went so fast from arguing to…to…well, one extreme to the other. That matches what Dr. Walsh said about pregnancy causing mood swings. Wide swings, he said. Hormonal. Oh, I know you weren't listening then." Hana swung her legs over the edge of the bed and slid into a shaky stand, both hands propped on the mattress.

Light exploded behind Mick's eyes. Hana figured she'd kissed him that feverishly only because she was pregnant with Jess Hargitay's kid? "No way, Hana. No way in hell! I'll grant you hormones were involved. But I kissed you and you kissed me back because we're healthy adults, and I'm me and you're you."

Seeing her sway unsteadily while she attempted to tie the

sash to her robe, Mick swore, scooped up her light body and set her carefully on the bed.

"Relax, dammit. I'm not going to jump you, Hana. In fact, there'll be no more kissing until you're the instigator. I'm going outside to check on your bird."

Hana heard the back door slam. Her breath escaped in a stream.

There was the muffled sound of a phone ringing somewhere below her window. She heard Mick's voice in a low rumble that soon faded. Obviously he was on his cell and he'd left the patio.

She tugged the sheet up to her waist. Leaning back with a sigh, Hana touched two fingers to her lips. She wondered why Mick had kissed her in the first place. She wasn't exactly on the A-list of available single women. He'd said they were both healthy adults. Mick certainly fit that description, but Hana couldn't be placed in that category. Still, broken though she might be in parts, other areas were functioning as designed. But that wasn't true either. The *will* functioned. Lovemaking itself was out of the question.

While at the hospital, she'd idly flipped through a packet of information the doctors had given her and noticed a line in boldface type that said women with high-risk pregnancies had to "be creative" when making love with their partners since normal lovemaking was dangerous for mother and child.

The mental images the idea of getting creative conjured up had Hana fanning herself with her robe. Not that she'd have to concern herself with that paragraph. Since she didn't have *that* kind of partner.

The back door slammed again, breaking her reverie. Hana lay still, listening to Mick's heavy tread coming her way. A tiny spark deep inside died from regret as she spared a moment to imagine what creative lovemaking with Mick Callen would be like.

By the time he appeared in her doorway, she'd managed to get back under the covers and successfully wipe out her inappropriate thoughts.

"The bird survived," he announced. "She, if it was a she, walked across the patio and then took off. It's really nice outside," he added. "Enough sun to warm the patio. A far cry from Montana weather. Tomorrow, I'll rent a good wheelchair. Maybe we can get you up and out for a while. It shouldn't do you any harm to catch a few rays."

"That sounds fantastic, Mick. Why tomorrow? What's wrong with now?"

"I should've mentioned it earlier. I just heard from Danika Olsen, your physical therapist. She'll be here in ten or fifteen minutes."

"So soon?" Hana's shoulders jerked and she began to fidget. "I thought Dr. Walsh said the sessions would start later this week."

"Ms. Olsen apparently works through a home health-care service. She needs to do an initial evaluation to file with her office supervisor. She said it wouldn't take long to do the paperwork."

"Why can't she see Dr. Walsh's evaluation? I've been prodded and examined quite enough for one day," Hana said petulantly. Then she wrinkled her nose. "Jeez, Mick, tell me to shut up, why don't you? I can't believe I sounded like such a crybaby."

Mick felt bad for her. "I've been in your shoes. I remember times I felt the whole world was out to get me. but I got over being mad at the world. So will you."

"I wish I had your faith."

The doorbell rang in three distinct tones.

"Ding dong, the witch is here," warbled Hana.

"Isn't that *the witch is dead?*" Mick corrected, striding out of the bedroom.

"Yeah, but if I said that you'd probably have me committed," Hana called to his disappearing back. *A nice back the man had, too.* Mick Callen was built like a—well, he was plenty to drool over. Everyone at the smoke jumpers' camp had seen that she'd noticed. It'd irked Jess. Between Mick's deliveries, he'd harassed her about her interest in the pilot. Jess had a terrible temper, and the mindset of a mongoose. He'd latch on to anything that pissed him off and never let it go.

Hana sighed. She probably deserved to pay and pay again for her stupidity. Especially since Jess was the last man she'd ever have hooked up with permanently.

Mick ushered a statuesque, suntanned goddess into Hana's room. "Hana, this is Danika Olsen, your PT. Danika, your patient, Hana Egan."

Hana had to consciously tell herself to close her mouth. The PT had thick, dandelion blond hair pulled casually back in a ponytail. She wore hot-pink short shorts and a spandex tank pulled tight over Double-D boobs Hana would kill to have. Well, at one time she would have. When kids in her high school had teased her about being flat-chested.

The woman dropped a pink-and-black duffle just inside the door, crossed the room and held out a hand to Hana. Danika bit her nails, too. Hana grinned. At least they had something in common.

"Sorry for coming on such short notice," the blonde said. "This is really more of a get-acquainted visit."

"How long do you plan to stay?" Mick's deep voice interrupted the women's study of each other.

Danika glanced over one model-perfect shoulder. "Not more than fifteen or twenty minutes. Is that going to be a problem?"

"Not at all. When we left the hospital I saw a medical supply store. This might be a good time to pick up the back brace Dr. Walsh wants you to have, Hana. And I'll see if they have the cream Dr. Mancuso suggested you use after showering."

"Cocoa butter," Danika inserted quickly. "It's the best thing to keep from getting stretch marks," she said, turning back to Hana. Seeing Hana grimace, Danika added, "Believe me, the little bugger you're carrying doesn't care if you have perfect skin. He eats, he grows and he'll leave you a mess. Or she will. Do you know which you're having?"

"I have no idea. But that reminds me, I need to look at a calendar and phone Dr. Walsh with a date."

"If you don't want to know your baby's sex, be sure to tell the ultrasound technicians. Some women like knowing, others don't. Me, I wanted to plan in advance what color to paint my nursery."

"You have kids?" Hana knew she was gaping again.

"One of each. A boy, five, a girl, three," she said as she pulled a notebook and pen from her bag. "Okay, tell hubby he can run along."

Hana blurted, "Mick's not my husband."

"No?" The PT did another once-over of the man lingering on the threshold. "Sorry for the mistake."

Hana shook her head. She didn't know how to explain Mick's role to this beautiful woman who said she had two children, but wore no wedding ring, and openly showed her appreciation of Mick's physique.

"If you need to pin me with a title," Mick said, "put me down as Hana's caregiver."

"No kidding?" The blonde's ponytail whipped back and forth as she examined Mick, then Hana.

He bolted, leaving Hana to merely shrug when Danika gave a low, sexy whistle. "I get it. He's gay, right? Gotta be. That man's built like no caregiver I've ever seen."

The PT's proclamation forced Hana to recall the steamy kisses she'd just shared with her now so-named caregiver. Although if Mick Callen wasn't straight, that might explain why he'd willingly tie himself to her and step out of the market for however long he intended to stick around. Still, Hana knew better.

"Mick's a pilot," she felt compelled to say. "Formerly in the navy. His plane was shot down over Afghanistan. We met in Montana."

"I see. That explains his slight limp. I saw it, but only because I'm trained to see such things. So really you're like roommates if both of you are in recovery mode."

"I am. Mick says he's fully recovered."

"He looks fully something."

Hana cleared her throat. "My goal is to get just as fully recovered, which I believe is why you're here. What do I have to do to strengthen my lower back?"

"You had quite a tumble. Three breaks in the pelvic ring, and two cracked vertebrae. Levels L4 and L5, it says here." Danika had unfolded a letter, obviously from one of Hana's doctors.

"How long do you think it'll be before I get back on my feet?"

"To do what?" The blonde arched a pencilled brow.

"Everything," Hana declared. "I'm used to independence. I want that back."

"Today I'm only filling out your history and a preliminary physical report. I never make predictions of the sort you're asking for, Hana. Every patient is different. We all heal at different rates. Drs. Walsh and Mancuso requested I work with you two hours a day, twice a week."

"For how many weeks? That should give me some idea of how they think I'll progress."

"Sorry, the order is open-ended. I like that you're eager to get to work. But there's danger in being overly eager. Asking too much of injured tissue and bone is as detrimental as doing nothing."

Danika turned a page in her book. She asked questions, and jotted answers. Hana had heard them all before. When Danika asked how many weeks pregnant she was, Hana hesitated. "My doctors in Kalispell each came up with a different estimate. Dr. Walsh believes I'm about seventeen weeks along. If I had a calendar I could pinpoint the day, the hour and probably the minute I conceived." Hana rolled her eyes.

The therapist laughed as she removed a calendar from her day planner and passed it to Hana.

"I landed in camp at the end of May. We had lots of small fires." Hana flipped through the weeks. "In July, right around the fourth—it was a Tuesday—a camper accidentally started a fire in old-growth timber that quickly got out of hand. Tree sap was exploding all over the place. I'd never fought a fire like it." Hana stared at the calendar, but she was remembering and reliving the event.

"You had sex during a forest fire?"

Hana shook off bad memories. "I… You wouldn't understand. The fire cut my partner and me off from the rest of our crew. A rolling blaze chased us until we fell into a cave. Oh, what does that matter now?" She put a finger on the calendar. "Tuesday, July fourth, that's the day I got pregnant. Some Independence Day!"

"Thirty-nine weeks puts you at mid-April. You don't look it, Hana. With both of my pregnancies I looked like I'd hidden a watermelon under my shirt from sixteen weeks on."

Hana let her gaze roam over Danika's flat stomach. "How long did it take you to get back in shape afterward?"

"I worked at it, so a couple of months. My husband is a

former dentist who started a dental supply company that's gone international. We entertain his clients frequently. I refused to look like a blimp stuffed in a sequined dress."

"You're married then?" Hana's gaze shifted to Danika's ringless left hand. "No wedding band. I actually hoped you'd be a resource for single-motherhood tips."

"I do massage along with physical therapy. Rings can be hard on a patient. I was always taking them off when a patient needed massage therapy. After I lost the third set, Tom, my husband, said he wasn't calling our insurance company again. If you haven't had much experience with babies I can recommend a couple of good books." She tore a page out of her day planner and scribbled down two titles and handed it to Hana.

"Thanks. As a kid I used to have to help care for kids of foster families. No babies, though." Hana lay back, feeling her tension escalate. "The OB in Montana didn't hold out much hope of my having this baby. Everyone thinks I'll lose it."

"With your problems, did you consider termination?"

"Well, I lived in denial that I could even *be* pregnant until the accident, and by then I was borderline too late. Anyway, I'd have refused. I'm afraid, though. I want to do right by her…or him."

Danika closed her notebook and stood. "Woman to woman, I don't believe fear or denial got you this far, Hana. You knew, and you want this baby. I'll do everything I can to help you prepare your body. We'll start tomorrow. I'll bring a booklet of exercises you can do daily, even confined to bed. You've got guts. I like that."

"Funny, Mick said the same thing about me. Since the two of you see something in me I don't, I'll trust your instincts. And I'll work hard."

The therapist stowed her notes, zipped her gym bag and slung it over her shoulder. "Will you be okay alone until your…until Mick returns? I've got another appointment." As she was checking a watch hanging on a gold chain around her neck, the front door opened, and the object of their discussion blew in. He carried a bag and a handful of brown-eyed daisies.

"Phew, glad I made it back before you left. The medical supply store sent me to another place four blocks up the street." He held up the sack. "Success, but pelvic slings, or OB corsets, as they're apparently called, aren't plentiful. You okay, Hana? I probably shouldn't have stopped to buy flowers, but I thought they'd brighten your room. Since you're stuck there night and day for a while."

Danika turned and winked at Hana before she slipped past Mick. "Friend, caregiver, whatever you call him, he's a keeper. Tomorrow. Two o'clock." She left, closing the door softly.

"What was that about? Were you two talking about me?"

A secretive smile lifted Hana's lips up. "Girls talk about a lot of things. Men think all we do is sit around and discuss them."

As it always did, Hana's rare smile hit Mick in the gut. But he sensed a change in her attitude. "Looks like you got along well with the blond bombshell. I worried that you might throw her out."

"She's married. Has two kids."

"So?"

"So nothing. In case you had designs on her."

"I didn't bring Danika Olsen daisies, Hana."

"No. No, you didn't." Her smile widened.

For Mick the banter was over. He felt himself falling, and didn't know where he'd land.

CHAPTER TEN

HANA'S NEWFOUND determination to get back on her feet allowed them to forge a routine. One afternoon, several weeks later, she insisted on going over the spreadsheet Mick had set up. Hana nearly fainted when she saw the figures. "Mick, I'll have to do more than file for you to pay back everything I owe. We have to cut expenses. Also, I want to learn bookkeeping. You're doing everything else, I should help with this."

"Okay. But right now you have enough to keep you busy between PT and doctors' appointments. I'm not worried. The navy's leasing my house. Stella—remember I told you about her?—said the rehab program is going great and paying its way."

"All the same. Cancel the visiting nurse. That's a huge expense."

"In a few weeks."

He'd seen Hana blanch at the bottom line even after he'd fudged everywhere possible. Mick had padded the amount Wylie's group had raised at their fall bake sale. He'd inflated the funds made available to her from the forestry department's slush fund. Damn, he hadn't wanted to get into this. Now that she was up and around more, it was hard enough beating her to the mail delivery every day. Dr. Lansing's secretary had been dead-on about how fast medical costs added up.

"Tell you what. I'll set up a few dummy spreadsheets for you to practice on."

"Perfect." She beamed at him. "I need to feel like I'm contributing."

"Yeah. I felt like that when I had my last surgery and Marlee pulled my load *and* hers."

He set up a practice sheet for her that night, and she worked on it diligently.

Three weeks slid by with Mick shopping for groceries, cooking and doing laundry. Between the visiting nurse and Danika, Hana's private needs, such as showers, hair care and nightgown changes, were taken care of.

Mick liked early mornings best. He'd help Hana into her wheelchair, and the two of them would eat breakfast on the back patio. They often lingered a while to read and soak up the morning sun.

One morning Hana said, "I'm so sick of wearing these cotton hospital gowns and robes day after day, night after night."

Mick marked his place in the military thriller he'd been reading and glanced up. "The duffle bag with your clothes is in the hall closet. Want me to dig it out?"

She laughed. "I doubt I could button any of my old shirts across my middle. And I'd never be able to zip up my jeans. Haven't you noticed one part of me is getting to be as big as a house?"

Mick had noticed, but he went out of his way to ignore Hana's expanding waistline. He tended to focus his attention on her face and hair. Studying her now, he recalled the day he'd flown supplies to Marlee, and how she'd gleefully pounced on the package of maternity outfits she'd ordered online. She'd gone into her bedroom, then she'd come out wearing a loose, girly-looking top over twill pants. She'd pulled up the top to show Wylie an inset of stretchy fabric, and insisted she finally felt comfortable *and* stylish.

"Do you know of a store in this area that carries those pants that expand?" He made stretching motions. "Order what you want and have them shipped to the house, or I'll go pick them up."

"I always buy clothes at a discount store." Hana's hands circled her softly rounded abdomen. "I have no idea who carries maternity stuff. Would I order bigger than my normal size, do you think?"

"You're asking the wrong person. I told you my twin sister's expecting. She ordered clothes online. I'll get her on the phone, and you can ask her where she got her stuff."

"But she doesn't know me."

"Sure she does." Mick paused. "Marlee knows you were injured. It's her husband's fellow rangers who raised money to help you. I talk to her about once a week. Usually when you're working with Danika."

"Is that because you haven't wanted me to hear your conversations?"

He laughed. "No. It's more so you can sweat and swear in private."

Hana's mouth flopped open. "How do you know I swear when I exercise?"

Mick grinned. "Because *I* did. I think all PTs are part sadist."

"You're so right. So...what exactly have you told your sister about me, Mick? She must think I'm a horrible person." Hana's hands stilled.

"Marlee doesn't—" Mick broke off, shoved a bookmark in his book and set it aside. "Honestly? At first she thought I'd taken leave of my senses." He closed his left hand, cracked his knuckles with his right hand.

"Stop. You do that too often. You have nice hands, Mick, and you're going to wreck them."

He immediately stopped and rubbed his palms over his knees. "Sorry, it's a nervous habit I developed waiting to fly night missions in Afghanistan."

"Do I make you nervous?"

"Sometimes, yeah."

"I'm sorry." She paused, seeming at a loss for words. "You were saying about your sister?"

"Just that she sometimes tries to be my mother."

"I suppose if she can recommend an online store, that'll save me time. Okay. I'll talk to her."

Mick called Marlee. After the preliminaries, he handed the phone to Hana. Rising, he grabbed his book. "I'll be back in a few minutes," he mouthed.

Initially Hana felt awkward talking to someone she'd never met. It was plain that Mick's sister knew more about her than vice versa. As well, Hana found out, Marlee Ames was insatiably curious. But Hana wasn't about to spill her guts to a stranger.

"Mick has fair taste, but I wouldn't trust him to buy maternity clothes. When it comes to that, men are obtuse." She supplied Hana with Web sites. "You're lucky," she added, "if you haven't had morning sickness. With both of my pregnancies I barfed every morning for three solid months. But then, I recall Mick saying you were past your first trimester at the time of the accident."

"I…yes, that's right. I wish my pregnancy was normal," Hana said, sounding wistful. "Every time I see these doctors, they fuss, measure and worry I'll go into premature labor and miscarry."

"That must be rough. I hope you'll prove them wrong." She then recommended the same book Danika had. Supposedly the authors, who were pediatricians, covered every possible baby problem from birth to six years. "Do you know if you're having a boy or a girl?"

"I begged them not to show me ultrasound photos that'll reveal my baby's sex."

"I'm the same. Wylie has a son and I have a daughter. We'll love either a boy or girl. Did Mick tell you he practically bought out a baby store? He came in with everything in green or yellow, to cover all the bases, he said."

Hana's voice fell. "He hasn't said much about your baby, and he never brings up mine. Either he talks around the subject, or avoids saying the word *baby* like it was a curse or something."

"That's interesting. For a guy, my brother's amazingly intuitive and sympathetic. Have you tried to involve him? Maybe he feels left out."

"I don't think so. I can't explain, but there's this detached look that crosses his face whenever anyone talks about the baby."

"Huh. That doesn't sound like Mick. He's great with my daughter and my stepson. Ask him point-blank. Hana, I hear Wylie and the kids coming in from feeding Dean's wild-animal menagerie. They'll want to warm up. It's been in the teens every day and drops to zero at night. Wylie thinks we'll have snow soon. Maybe tomorrow. And it's supposed to keep snowing until Thanksgiving. Ask me if I envy you and Mick all that California sun."

"I won't tell you I'm sitting on the patio, then. And a thermometer Mick bought to hang out here says seventy-seven."

"Rub it in. But there's a lot to be said for Montana winters. Makes for good snuggling on icy nights."

Hana didn't respond. She tried to picture a pregnant woman in bed with a man. She didn't make a habit of spending the night with men. Jess had been her first in a long time, and the hard cave floor had served them, however briefly. She'd recognized her mistake moments after the fire had raged past.

"Are you still there, Hana? Sorry, that was insensitive of me. Mick, of course, told me about losing your baby's father."

It surprised Hana that Mick had shared something so personal. But she wondered why he'd stopped at that, and let Marlee think condolences were in order. She thought she'd made it clear there hadn't been that kind of relationship between her and Jess. "Don't let me keep you," she said, hoping she didn't sound curt. "Or wait. Do you want to speak with Mick again? Here he is. I have to get ready for my physical therapy appointment."

"Tell Mick we'll yak later. It was nice talking girl talk with you. Call any time. Wylie's afraid I'll slip on ice outside, so he wants me to stay in until the baby's born. I humor him." She laughed. "Bye for now."

Hana said goodbye and quickly hung up. Though as a rule she wasn't the jealous type, she recognized the stab when it struck. Did she envy Mick's sister a husband who loved her and pampered her? Damned right she did. And that was a revelation.

Mick approached, tapping a finger to his watch. "You two must've gotten along well. I hated to interrupt, but it's almost time for Danika to get here." Mick circled Hana and began wheeling her toward the door. Her chair had a motor, but as often as not, he moved her from place to place.

It dawned on Hana how much care Mick gave her. Was it significant? Oh, sure, he'd kissed her a couple of times. That didn't add up to love. While she couldn't fault his attentiveness, much of the time they were like two strangers sharing a house.

"You're quiet, Hana. Marlee didn't say anything to upset you, did she?"

"She was very helpful. She told me about a couple of online stores that have maternity clothes. If I can use your laptop, I'll price some stuff, and see what I can afford."

"Don't skimp." He might have said more, but the doorbell rang just as he wheeled Hana into her bedroom.

"That'll be Danika. I'll go let her in." Mick set the chair brake and disappeared.

Hana heard their mingled voices in the next room as they laughed and joked. She was poignantly reminded of how far she still had to go to be independent.

Danika entered Hana's room, followed by Mick. He jingled his car keys. "I asked Danika to direct me to the nearest bookstore. We've read everything I brought from home. Do you have any requests?"

She rattled off the title of the child-rearing manual. "Will you also get me a book of baby names? Marlee said they have one, and are in the process of picking names for either a boy or girl."

Mick's gaze slid away. "Uh, sure. Anything else?"

"*Bookkeeping for Dummies* if they have it. I'm serious, Mick, about working off my debt to you by helping out in your office next year."

Usually he shrugged when she brought that up. He didn't this time.

The more he thought about it, the more he liked the idea. If she worked for him, he could give her a place to live and watch out for her. They hadn't discussed anything after her—after—well, after. But a man took care of the people he lov—whoa—

"I'll try to be back in two hours," he called, hurrying through the house and out to the car. He moved into his seat and realized he was sweating, and his hands were shaking.

As he started the car, he mulled over what had just happened. If Hana was requesting a book of baby names, did that mean Dr. Walsh thought she wasn't going to lose the baby? Or had Marlee filled Hana's head full of unrealistic dreams?

Mick had no problem locating the store. To his surprise, there were so many baby name books, it took half an hour to pick one. Who would've thought choosing a kid's name would be so hard? He tucked it under his arm and went in search of fiction. He loved bookstores and tended to go overboard. Today was no exception. Running late, he returned to their street and saw that Danika's car was no longer parked in front of the house.

Collecting the two bags of books from the backseat, he went inside and headed straight to Hana's room. An apology sat on the tip of his tongue—where it stayed.

Hana sat up in bed, one arm looped around the white bear he'd given her in Kalispell. Her fiery hair had been brushed into a mass of curls. Sun streamed in the window, gilding her skin. She no longer wore the drab cotton robe provided by Lucy Steel. Instead she was draped in shiny satin. Sea-green satin.

"Look what Danika bought me." Hana stroked a hand over the nightgown, and Mick could only think the PT deserved a bonus, because the whole sexy package drove the breath from his lungs.

"I was worried when you didn't phone. Did you run into traffic? Danika stayed as late as she could."

He popped open the top button on his shirt, needing room to breathe. "I always lose track of time in a bookstore."

"Were you able to find the books I asked for?"

He moved closer and passed her one bag.

As she unpacked it and studied the baby name book he'd selected, a stray thought hit Mick. He hoped and prayed Hana's baby looked like her rather than Jess. Not that Jess was unattractive or anything. It was just that it'd be an awful—and constant—reminder for Hana.

"These are all perfect. Thanks. I can't wait to dig into the lot. I'll start with the book of names." She reached for a steno pad and pencil lying on her nightstand.

"I'll go get supper on. You're probably starved."

"Actually, no. Danika whipped us up a fabulous berry and yogurt smoothie." She pointed to his sack. "Did you buy out the store?" she teased. "I know you're probably dying to get into a new book. I'm okay with eating later."

"Fine with me. I found two new airplane magazines. I never can resist them. I got the next in the spy chronicles, too. But I shouldn't start it until I finish the book I'm reading. Maybe I'll flake out on the sofa for a while and look through the aeronautical magazines."

The living room couch was well within Hana's view. Despite telling Mick she planned to start with the name book, she leafed through the bookkeeping manual first. After she opened the name book, her gaze kept moving to Mick's lean body stretched uncomfortably on the short chintz couch.

Kari Dombroski once called Mick ordinary. Hana hadn't contradicted her coworker at the time because she leaned toward dark-haired guys. Fair-haired Mick was quite dashing, however. He had long legs, a nice butt and a decent amount of muscles. Their mornings in the sun had given him a tan that set off his pale hair and blue eyes. Blue-green. Aquamarine.

The object of her interest raised his head, catching Hana staring intently, and she flushed.

"Do you need something?"

"I'm lonely, I guess. And stumped. Would you come and help me pick out possible names for my baby?"

Heat chased a cold chill up Mick's spine and back down again. He opened his mouth to refuse. But she looked so adorable, he couldn't refuse her anything. "Sure. Not that I'm any authority." Dropping his magazine on the coffee table, Mick stood. In a way he was pleased to think Hana valued his suggestions.

Hitching up his beltless, low-riding jeans, he ambled to her bedside and straddled the chair he spun away from the wall. "Read some of the names in your book."

She opened it to the list of boys' names starting with *A* and wrinkled her nose. "Aloysius, Ambrose, Argus..."

"Whoa! Time out." Mick rent the air with a whistle and made a *T* with his hands. "I hope you're joking."

"Of course. By the way, is your real name Michael?"

"Mick's the name on my birth certificate. Why?"

"No reason. I like Mick. I just assumed it was a nickname."

"Nope. I was named after my mother's father."

"That's nice." Hana nibbled on the pencil eraser. "Maybe I could borrow your other grandpa's name. Jack, wasn't it?" she murmured. "Jack is a solid name for a boy. That's what I want, a name that's strong and rock-solid."

"Pappy would be flattered. Uh, me, too. Hey, my dad's name was Shane. He was strong and reliable."

"Oh, I like that a lot." She thumbed several pages. "Huh, Shane means, the Lord is gracious, the same as it says for Jack."

"Really? What does Mick mean?"

"Um, this book has Michael and Mickey. No Mick. Mickey is enthusiastic."

He grimaced. "So not me. What about for a girl? Look up Hana. What does it mean?"

She paged backward. "Oh, this book says Hana is Japanese and means flower. The Biblical spelling, with a second *n* and an *h* at the end, stands for grace. Maybe we should forget meanings. They seem more meaningless if you ask me."

"I'm partial to Heather. Scottish, and hey, maybe she'll have your red hair."

"Perish the thought, the poor kid. Heather's...okay," she

said, not wanting to offend Mick. "I favor Cassidy, I think. It says here, Cassidy means clever girl."

"I wonder who comes up with name meanings. Who cares? Well, maybe a kid's mother does. My sister was named for a childhood friend of our mom's. She used to say Mick and Marlee flowed well with our last name, too."

"These all sound fine with Egan." Hana set her notebook aside. "Monday is my next ultrasound. I'm also scheduled to see Dr. Mancuso. I'll ask her advice, and maybe the nurses'. They must hear interesting names every day."

"Good idea. Make a list of all the ones you like now, and see how you feel about them after the little squirt arrives. Did my sister happen to say what names she and Wylie are considering?"

"Sorry, no. Oh, maybe she has dibs on Shane or Jack."

"I doubt it. I'll ask her next time I phone."

"Please. Wow, would you look at how late it's gotten. I've wasted two hours poring over this name book and all I have to show for it is possibly three, not counting Heather. It's okay. A bit overused though."

"You just started, Hana. There's plenty of time, right?"

She moved restlessly and smoothed the blanket covering her growing stomach. "I hope I have plenty of time. The thought of having a preemie scares me, Mick."

"So? Why dwell on the possibility? You're holding up well. Aren't you? I mean, I haven't gone in for your last two appointments with Dr. Walsh. Come to think of it, why are you seeing Dr. Mancuso? I thought she takes over after you deliver."

"She has a formula for calculating the baby's weight. They're all worried about weight. Too much, not enough. It's their biggest concern."

"You're following their orders to the letter. That's all you can do."

"Oh, guess what? I can't believe I forgot to tell you when you got home, Mick. I'm so excited. Danika let me use the walker today. Come and help me out of bed. I'll put on my robe and walk with you to the kitchen. I can tear lettuce for a salad while you cut up the rest of the roast chicken we had last night. Chicken Caesar salads will make a light, healthy supper."

"Suits me." Getting up, he bumped her bed. Her list of names fell on the floor. Mick started to hand it back. "Uh…Hana, it's great that you're thinking of giving your kid one of my family names if it's a boy. But I don't want you doing it because you, ah, mistakenly feel obligated to me. Know what I mean?"

She met his eyes as he helped her stand. She had to tilt her head back quite a way, but her gaze never wavered. "I do owe you more than I can ever repay, Mick. If I had family I cared about, but…I don't. I like *Jack* and *Shane*. If you'd rather I not use them, tell me."

"Hell, no. I meant it when I said Pappy and Dad would be flattered to have a namesake."

Hana tied the robe he held for her, and inched the walker toward the kitchen. Mick gave her three cheers and that made her smile.

At the counter, they worked side by side preparing salads. Mick melted cheddar and herbs over crisp flatbread. As they sat down to eat, Hana asked Mick what he'd found interesting in his airplane magazines. He told her at great length. Neither brought up the subject of naming her baby again.

"It's still nice out. After we clear the plates, can we take a short walk down the street?"

"You want to get dressed again?"

"My robe covers more than if I wore shorts like most everyone does here. I'd like to see something beyond our fence. I'm not used to being tied down, you know."

He rinsed the dishes without comment. Finally he fixed her with a faint frown. "Is that wise, Hana? Today's the first time you've been on your feet in a while."

"Please. I feel really good."

"How much did Danika say you should walk each day?"

Hana tried to shrug away his nagging. "It's my body, Mick. Since I dismissed the visiting nurse, I need to start being more self-reliant."

"I know it's your body. It's a weird position for me. Marlee said I pushed too hard. I felt I didn't push myself enough. Turned out she was right. I fell. It set my recovery back several weeks. You have more than your recovery to worry about if you fall."

"I'm not asking to walk a mile. To the end of the block and back is all, I promise."

He slammed the dishwasher door.

"You aren't my keeper, Mick Callen. I'm in charge of my life. I'll go without you," she said, her chin at a stubborn angle.

"Dammit, Hana. I'm not about to let you go out alone." He heaved a sigh, and she knew he was giving in.

She smiled and linked arms with him. "Thanks, Mick. You must know that for someone as active as I've always been, even walking down the block is liberating."

"I do know. I care what happens to you." He led her to the side door so she wouldn't have to contend with the porch steps.

"That's sweet. I don't deserve you."

"Yes, you do," he said fiercely.

The sun hadn't quite set. It glowed red-orange through the trees and cast long shadows over the cars parked along the street. Neighbors were coming home from work. As Mick and Hana strolled the street, lights popped on in a few homes. Turkey and pilgrim cut-outs graced a few windows.

"I've lost track of time," Hana murmured. "When's Thanksgiving?"

"A week. Well, a week and two days." Mick sniffed the air. "Back home I'd be snowed in by now. I might even be cussing as I thawed water pipes. Hard to believe we're only a few states away and basking in sixty-degree evenings."

"Until I became a smoke jumper, I'd never seen snow," Hana murmured. "My first year on the job we fought a fire in Idaho's Sawtooth range in a foot of snow. I couldn't understand how trees could burn when we were freezing our buns off."

"If it was a dry season, the sap would be like tinder."

She nodded, seeming to have slowed down. Mick noticed. "Time to turn back?"

"I think so. Gosh, who'd guess walking less than a block could be so exhausting? At least I ought to sleep like a log."

"I hope."

"With all this extra exercise and fresh air, I'm sure I will."

In the early dusk, her gold eyes had turned lively, and she'd begun to remind him of the old Hana. He didn't have the heart to tell her of the many nights he'd spent in agony because he'd asked too much of spent muscles.

"Speaking of fresh air, the breeze is bringing in the scent of the ocean. Or is it my imagination?"

She paused, then shook her head, making her curls bounce. "Going to the beach is the next thing on my list, Mick. Monday I'll ask Dr. Mancuso or Dr. Walsh if it'll hurt me to ride in the car and maybe walk a bit on the wet sand. It can't be more than a twenty-minute car ride."

"Half an hour in traffic. Traffic is what would keep me from living here permanently. A quick trip to the grocery store can end up being an hour or more, what with the crush of people."

Hana laughed, her hold on Mick's arm tightening. "You're

such a country boy. This is nothing compared to inner-city L.A."

As they slowly made their way home, Mick cautiously introduced a subject he'd been afraid to broach. "The way time's flying, Hana, have you given thought to what you might do after...uh...after the doctors release you?"

He felt her stiffen, but he held on instead of letting her pull away. "It's nothing you need to decide ASAP. But it's better to plan. To have a couple of alternatives."

"A couple? Mick, I don't even have one idea. Well, not beyond doing some work at your place until I pay you back. Except, when I think about that, I have no clue how it'll be possible. What on earth will I do with a baby in an office?"

"My mom raised twins working in that office. My grandfather had the office built with an alcove Mom used for a nursery. Of course, over the years the alcove's become a storage place, but it could be cleaned out without much work."

"I'd have to buy a car that would get me back and forth to Whitepine, to the pediatrician and all." She laughed sarcastically. "A car's expensive. I can't afford rent, let alone a car. It's depressing. That's why I don't look beyond today." She turned up the walkway leading to the side door.

"I have a big house, Hana. Or, my sis owns the smaller guest house that sits on Cloud Chasers property. Pappy and Grandma lived in it until she died. Shortly after she passed away, my folks were killed at an unmarked train crossing. Pappy moved to the main house to care for me and Marlee. I call the cottage small, but there are two bedrooms. Like I said, it belongs to Marlee, or I'd offer it to you rent-free."

Inside, Mick flipped on the kitchen light he'd turned off when they left the house. Hana blinked in the sudden bright light. "I said I'm taking one day at a time. I'm afraid to make plans, Mick. Nothing's for sure yet. I could still...lose the baby." She cradled her stomach. Her eyes looked bruised.

She didn't come right out and admit she was afraid of that outcome, but Mick could tell that she was. "We have lots of time," he said. "The last thing I want is to pressure you. You've had a busy day. Need a hand getting into bed?"

Her face drawn, she nodded. "See how dumb it is for me to talk about doing your filing or anything else, Mick? I can't even get in and out of bed on my own."

He let her lead the way to her room. He crossed it to turn on the antique lamp on her nightstand. The low light bathed the room and Hana in a soft yellow glow. Mick helped her slip off her robe. His fingers itched to massage the bare shoulders she rolled forward as if to ward off tension. Gritting his teeth, he took her elbow impersonally and guided her into bed.

"Wait. I need to go brush my teeth and…uh…well, do you have something you could do in the living room for a minute?"

"No problem. I'll go check to see all the doors and windows are locked."

Mick made a circuit of the house. When he got back, she stood beside the too-high hospital bed looking lost.

"Wow, you were speedy. Why didn't you holler?"

"Having to ask for help is the part I hate most about this whole ordeal."

"Hana, everyone needs a helping hand sometime in life. Maybe you're out of sorts because you've pushed yourself today. Listen, I'm probably going to stay up for a while and read. If you need anything, call me. I can hear you with that wireless gadget Lucy Steel provided."

"It's a baby monitor. She said I can put it in my nursery and hear the baby from any room in the house if I take the speaker with me." Mick got her up on the bed and Hana slid between the sheets, fell back and closed her eyes, clearly done in.

He pulled up the rail and locked it in place.

"These stupid rails make me feel like a two-year-old," she muttered.

Mick chuckled. "Patience is a virtue, Hana. You're so much like I remember being, it's uncanny. If you continue to progress with walking, after a few days there's no reason we can't leave the rails down. Once you're steady on your feet you'll be able to get up and down without help. Before you know it, I'll be dispensable."

Her eyes plumbed the depths of his. "I hope I haven't grown too accustomed to having you around."

He stilled. "Would that be so bad?"

"Yes. Yes, Mick, it would."

Unsure what to say, Mick reached over to shut off the light. Plunging them into darkness, he walked out. He knew his heart had taken a hit. When she hadn't even brought up the possibility of naming a boy after Jess or anyone in his family, Mick had read something into that—too much, obviously.

In his room, he kicked off his boots and flopped on his bed. It was a big four-poster. Mr. Bailey, the owner, had a thing for antiques. This bed, though, was one that would be better shared.

Forget it, man.

Sitting up, he shrugged out of his shirt. He retrieved the book he'd been reading; as restless as he felt, he was sure he'd finish it. His part of the baby monitor allowed him to hear the softest of sounds in Hana's room. He knew the minute she quit thrashing around and he heard her breathing grow even as she finally fell asleep.

He read until well after midnight. He reached the last page of his military thriller, satisfied that he'd figured out the villain less than halfway through the book. He closed it and set it aside, then stifled a yawn as he rose to peel off his jeans.

Mick realized noises were coming from the monitor. He bent nearer. *A moan. Was she having a nightmare?* Rezipping his jeans, Mick made up his mind to check.

Without taking the time to put on a T-shirt, he left his room and hurried through the house, coming to a stop outside her door. He hauled in a deep breath before tapping. After all, if he was wrong about the nightmare he'd feel dumb barging in.

"Mick?" she asked in a shaky voice.

"Are you okay?" He cracked the door an inch.

"I'm fine. Oh, hell! No, I'm not. Come on in and say I told you so. I…think I overdid the walking. I have major charley horses in both legs. Owwww," she yelped. "Damn, damn, damn. There's another one. Hurts like hell."

"Pull up your gown."

"What?"

"I'm going to wet a towel with hot water. I know cramps are a bitch," he said. "Hot packs and massages helped mine."

Mick spread a towel under her calves and ran hot water into a basin he found under the sink in the kitchen. He wrung the wet towels out as best he could and eased them around the backs of her legs.

"I can see every time your muscles spasm. You did overdo it today, Hana. Is this helping at all?" he asked nearly half an hour later.

"Much better." She tried to reach down to rub the back of her right leg. Her fingers tangled with Mick's. They both jerked back, and between them tipped over the basin of hot water.

"Holy shit!" Mick yanked Hana and the white bear up and away from the spreading puddle.

She grabbed on to his neck. Dumbfounded, for a minute they both stared as water soaked through the towel, her sheets, and probably the quilted mattress pad.

"Hana, I'm sorry. I'll give you my bed. I'll take the couch."

"Forget it! I saw earlier how your legs hung off that puny thing. It's no bigger than a love seat. You wouldn't sleep a wink."

"This is totally my fault. I'll mop up, then sleep here in the rocker."

"Is your bed a single?"

"It's colossal. An antique. I doubt they had queens when that bed was built, but it's gotta be an oversize double."

"Then we'll share."

"Hana, I don't think that's such a good idea." Even now Mick felt the tantalizing skin along her arms and back heat his bare chest.

"Like in my shape we'd even be tempted to…do anything but sleep."

Mick's heart slammed erratically as he stalked through the dark house to his room. He gently set Hana down on the side he hadn't rumpled. "Sleep," he ordered. "I'll be back after I strip your bed."

He took his time and was glad to hear sleep sounds coming from her side when he returned. He sat gingerly on his half of the bed, holding his breath as he eased down, still wearing his jeans. *Man, yes, he was tempted.* He wasn't a monk.

Mick could tell it was going to be one long, tortured night. Thankfully, the rhythmic rise and fall of Hana's breathing helped him relax. Before his mind could play too many tricks, he fell asleep.

CHAPTER ELEVEN

MORNING SUN SLANTING through half-closed miniblinds high-lighted fuzzy dust motes, Mick saw as he woke with a start. *What the...?* His arms circled a warm, lush woman. It took a few minutes for him to wake up enough to recognize the throb below his waist. An erection the size of California.

The memory of dumping hot water on Hana's bed last night returned in a rush. Like a shot, Mick released the woman he was spooned around. His jeans got tangled in the sheet as he tried to vault out of bed. God, had the zipper that was killing him left an imprint on Hana's soft body?

Seeing Hana, he realized they'd been sleeping nose to nose, and the softness had been her pumpkin-round belly. "Jeez!" Pumping his legs wildly, he unwound his feet from the con-fining bedclothes, and bolted.

Hana's eyes flickered open to the sight of a man dancing around beside the bed. She sprang up and clutched folds of the dark blue sheet up to her neck.

"It's all right," he said, teeth clenched. "I'm off to shower." He reached into his closet and tore clean clothes willy-nilly off hangers, determined to hobble out of sight before Hana saw how she'd affected him. His next thought as he slammed the bathroom door—could the way he'd wrapped his bigger body around her hurt the baby?

For the first time since arriving in California, Mick longed for an icy Montana shower. Water that came from the pipes here just didn't cut it. "Damn!" He kept spinning the cold water faucet and grit his teeth waiting for it to get cold enough. Crap, he hoped Hana didn't wonder why he took so long in the bathroom. He'd be here all day if he didn't stop remembering how desirable and inviting she looked sleeping in his bed. All flushed and disheveled.

He had it bad, Mick finally admitted. Hana looked desirable and inviting all the time, even pregnant with another man's kid.

There it was, the rock bottom truth he'd refused to admit before now. Bracing his arms against the shower wall, Mick stuck his whole head under the cool, stinging stream. He'd tried to ignore his real reason for helping Hana when he'd talked to Dr. Lansing in Kalispell, and also to Marlee and Stella. He hadn't been truthful with anyone, least of all himself. He'd rationalized that this jaunt was tantamount to going the extra mile, as he would for Angel Fleet.

He wrenched off the water, stepped out and buried his face in a towel. He was anything but altruistic. He wanted Hana.

He didn't want her baby. Well, he didn't want any offspring of Jess Hargitay—the asshole jerk.

So, what did that say about the kind of man he was? That he was a jerk, too?

It was easier to live with himself if he didn't answer that, Mick thought, vigorously toweling dry so he could dress.

After he tucked a black T-shirt into clean jeans, he wrapped his dirty ones in the wet towel and strolled into his bedroom, expecting Hana to be gone. She sat on the edge of his bed, her bare feet dangling a foot off the floor. Her hands were folded serenely in her lap.

"What are you waiting for?"

"I...I'm not supposed to walk without help or using the

walker." She sounded apologetic, although her eyes told him she was shocked and hurt.

"Of course. Hana, I didn't mean anything."

"It's all right." She held up a hand as if to ward him off. "I'm a mess. I know it." Her fingers plucked at the rumpled satin nightgown. "Danika thought this would lift my spirits. But pretty trappings don't change the way you look at me."

Mick measured the distance to the door and moved past her. "How's that?"

"With disgust, that's how."

Floored by her one-two punch, he nearly laughed. "Yeah…right!"

She shrugged a bare shoulder negligently. "Then with disapproval. Nearly the same thing. What I can't figure out is why you saddled yourself at all when I know for a fact you intended to spend your winter on some sandy beach."

"Hana, I don't feel saddled."

"You do. You are. Bring my walker, please. Then I want you to go. Go spend the day at the beach."

"And leave you alone?"

"You smother me. I hate it. I've always taken care of myself and I can do it now. And before you leave, phone Lucy Steel and tell her to send someone to pick up that damned hospital bed. I slept fine last night in a regular bed. I want one that I can get in and out of by myself."

She was miserable, and that was why she lashed out at Mick. Couldn't he tell she *didn't* want him to go off and leave her? If he went, she'd know he really wanted out. Well, she wouldn't be an anchor around his—or anyone's—neck.

MICK KNEW AN ERUPTION brewing when he saw one. Hana was well on her way. If she wanted him to stop smothering her and go to the damned beach, then so be it. Maybe there was such a thing as too much togetherness. A break from each other might be exactly what they both needed.

He went to the laundry room, where he tossed his bundle in an overflowing basket filled with Hana's sheets and other items belonging to her. "Right." Mick snorted. "Like she's in any condition to cook, clean house or do laundry on her own. *Ms. I-don't-need-your-help.*"

He pulled out his cell and called the hospital coordinator on his way to get Hana's walker. "It's Mick Callen. Who do I speak with to have Hana Egan's hospital bed removed? She wants it replaced with a regular bed." He was still talking to Lucy as he handed Hana her walker.

She didn't stick around to hear the rest of Mick's call.

He stared after her stiff, departing back, thinking it probably caused her pain to march out in a huff like that. *Damn stubborn woman.*

He heard her shower go on as, one-handed, he flung a beach towel and sunscreen into a sports bag. He hopped around as he shed his jeans and put on swim trunks, then again struggled to pull the jeans on over his suit. He fiddled with the sunglasses he'd picked up off his dresser.

"Thanks, Ms. Steel, I'll tell Hana."

Damn! He couldn't go off and leave Hana showering. What if she slipped and fell?

He messed around, making his bed and even reading a few pages of the spy chronicles until he heard the water shut off. Mick tossed the book in his bag, and didn't have to think twice before pulling out his cell again and punching in Danika Olsen's number.

"I know you're not scheduled to work with Hana today," he began after preliminary chitchat. "I wondered if you'd have a spare couple of hours today to fit her in. I'll pay triple time."

"I have an opening, Mick, but I don't know if it's wise to

work in another session. This is her request, right? She's got a crazy notion she should be like Wonder Woman."

"Actually it's my idea. I'll pay you just to come hang out with her. She says I'm getting on her nerves, so she's throwing me out for the day. I don't think she's ready to go it alone. So, I'd appreciate if you'd keep this call between us."

"I'll be blunt because you obviously need to hear this. You get on her nerves because Hana has the hots for you."

Mick couldn't quell a strangled laugh. "What've *you* been smoking?"

"I swear, men are so blind."

"Hana's either still grieving over Jess, or I'm just not her type. Period."

"Is that what you think? Wake up and smell the coffee, Callen. She made a mistake. A big goof with that guy. And she's a smart chick, but she's constantly beating herself up over it. I see it breaking down her self-esteem."

"Is that why you dolled her up yesterday?"

"Dolled her…oh, the naughty nightgown?" Danika laughed devilishly. "Caught your attention, did it, Mickey?"

"Mick. Just plain Mick. Yes, I'd have to be a eunuch not to notice." He heard his back teeth grate together and hoped she hadn't.

"So, I'm right." She sounded triumphant. "You do have feelings beyond friendship for Hana."

"You're stirring up trouble here, Danika. You should remember your patient's condition."

"Mickey, Mickey, Mickey. Hana's pregnant. It's not a communicable disease."

"I'm hanging up. Will you come and see her today or not?"

"I will, but when I met you, Mick, I thought you were so noble."

"I'm not. And Hana's not just pregnant. A broken pelvis knocks her out of any bed sport."

"The paraplegics I work with wouldn't like to hear you say that. If you're a caring partner there are ma-any ways to get mutual satisfaction."

"This isn't what I called you for. Goodbye, Danika."

"Wait! Don't go off in a huff. I'll swing past and fix lunch for Hana. You know, Callen, you're a selfish bastard. Expect that triple-time charge."

She beat him, and hung up first. That woman had some damned nerve taking a hunk out of his hide.

Plenty hot under the collar, Mick zipped his bag shut in one mighty tug and stalked through the house, barely pausing outside Hana's open door. "I'm outta here," he yelled. "Lucy Steel is sending someone to switch your bed with a regular one. Don't wait up for me. I may kill a six-pack or two and crash at a beach hotel tonight."

Mick didn't know if Hana responded or not. He wasted no time stomping out of the house. He threw his bag in the Cadillac, jumped in, rammed on his sunglasses, started the engine and took off with a squeal. He rolled all the windows down, wanting to feel the wind on his face.

A block away, he ended up in heavy traffic. At the first red light, he had time to cool off. His fingers tapped the wheel impatiently. Damn, but he'd acted like a dumb-ass teenager.

Traffic crawled on the coast highway, too. Pulling out his cell phone, he dialed his twin. "Am I a selfish bastard?" he asked right after Marlee said hello.

"You should know better than to give a sibling that kind of opening. How long do we have? Let me count the ways."

BACK AT THE HOUSE, Hana clung to the bathroom sink for support. She'd been brushing her wet hair when Mick delivered his goodbye, sounding more irritated than she'd ever heard him. She'd been toying with making peace, too. She wanted to clear the air between them.

The outer door slammed and the brush slid from her limp fingers. And it'd have to stay on the floor until someone came along who could bend over and pick it up. "Blast!"

She grabbed her walker and in a fit of frustration, kicked the dropped brush through the door into her bedroom. Slowly, she made her way to the chair, sat and got weepy. Damn, she hated women who cried over men. And she'd been guilty of that very thing more times since the accident than in her entire life.

The house felt empty and lonely with Mick gone. What was wrong with her? He'd been gone only ten minutes, for crying out loud.

But she knew what was wrong. Three or four times during the night she'd woken up and leaned on an elbow to watch Mick sleep. He had a cowlick that parted crisp blond hair he must gel into submission during waking hours. And a little scar just below the center of his right cheek. It left a tiny dimple when he was asleep. His lips—well, Hana hadn't wanted to think about it. Still didn't. Mick's lips were…inviting.

She ought to be a man-hater. Only she wasn't. What'd happened with Jess in that cave had been almost as much her fault as his. While she wished she hadn't been so impulsive, she wouldn't put all the blame on Jess, or curse the outcome.

She stroked her belly, already supported by the maternity sling Mick had thoughtfully bought for her. Today she was back to wearing one of the utility cotton gowns. Funny how satin had lifted her spirits. She'd felt like a princess when she'd glanced up and seen Mick standing in her bedroom door looking bedazzled.

Considering the way he'd acted on finding her in his bed,

the earlier reaction must have been just appreciation for the sexy nightie, not for the woman wearing it.

Why did she care? She'd never given two hoots about men. Not until one summer day, her first year in Montana, when Mick dropped out of the sky and she saw he had more than a man's lecherous thoughts in his head. So why was she annoyed now that he displayed no signs of lascivious urges toward her?

Because she wanted him to think she was special. Not pleased to be spending so much time mooning over Mick Callen, Hana made her way out to the patio. It wasn't easy to use the walker and carry the heavy book on parenting, too. Determined, she eventually managed. All that effort and the book was dry reading. Maybe it'd make more sense after she had the baby.

If she had the baby. She hadn't let on to Mick how concerned she was when Dr. Walsh said he wanted Rebecca Mancuso to see her Monday. The nurse who'd set up the appointment had casually reiterated that Dr. Mancuso was the staff neonatalogist who specialized in very premature infants. Hana had asked to see a preemie and the nurse had wheeled her down the hall to the Infant ICU nursery. Hana had seen dolls bigger than the babies in those isolettes. The littlest ones, no bigger than a man's hand, had tubes taped to their tiny ankles and chests. All wore eye patches. To ward off retinal blindness, her escort said. She also said retina damage was common among preemies.

What mother didn't want her child to be healthy and whole? Hana shut the book. Her parents hadn't wanted her, period. Even though she'd been born healthy.

She wanted this baby despite the way he or she had been conceived. She'd never had so much as a kitten or puppy to care for, or to care for her. Suppose she turned out to be a lousy mother? In an effort to erase that from her mind, she turned her thoughts to Mick. Again…

He made mornings interesting by simply sharing a table, and looking so adorable when he got involved in his reading. Whatever possessed her to send him off to a place hopping with beach bunnies? She knew the type of California girls who hung out at the beach. Luscious, leggy, suntanned goddesses. A man like Mick would be a ten on their radar screens, and probably they on his.

Lonely and bored, she made her way back inside. The doorbell sidetracked her. She set her book down. Guessing her caller was Lucy Steel's emissary sent to exchange beds, Hana shuffled to the door.

Danika Olsen breezed in carrying a great-smelling bag stamped with the name of a local Chinese restaurant.

"I was in the neighborhood," the PT said. "This restaurant doesn't use MSG. I should've phoned to ask your preference. I lived dangerously and bought a variety. I get overzealous. I have enough here to feed an army."

Hana frowned. "I sent Mick away."

"Forever?"

"No. No, of course not. At least, I hope not." She felt stricken at the thought.

Danika hugged her. "He'll be back, hon. Bad penny and all, you know."

"Mick's not a bad penny." Hana broke down. "Danika, I don't know what got into me. I acted like a…like a two-headed viper. All Mick's ever done is treat me like a queen. And maybe that's my problem. I'm not used to that. I expect the worst. Especially of men."

"Girl, you're a sad case. I don't know the guy well. I think you've fallen for him, though." Danika took plates out of the cupboard, and rummaged for silverware and napkins. "Sit.

Let's eat before this feast gets cold. We can verbally dissect your 'caregiver' over lunch."

Hana pulled out the chair where Mick had put one of her three air-filled pillow rings. She pointed it out to Danika. "See, this is what I mean. Wouldn't most men buy one of these and expect a woman to drag it from spot to spot? Not Mick. He said that didn't make sense. He bought one for the patio, one for the kitchen and another for the living room. I haven't used that one yet." She sank down, propped her elbow on the table and rested her chin in her hand. "I don't understand why he's so nice."

"You want a spoonful of everything?"

"It all looks good. Sure, I guess," she said listlessly. "Danika, you said you think I've fallen for Mick. I have and it scares me to death."

"Why?" The therapist set down two plates. She spooned out Moo Shu pork, lo mein, tofu mushrooms, and topped off each plate with an egg roll.

"Why? Mick's been too attentive. I know he'll change." Hana nibbled on the egg roll, paused and poured on hot mustard sauce. "He'll get bored and restless, and tired of me. He'll move on. It's how men are."

"Not all men," Danika said pragmatically. "My mom and dad just celebrated their fiftieth. My guy's still sticking around after ten years of marriage."

Preoccupied with smearing the sauce on her egg roll, Hana said pensively, "I can't fathom what that kind of stability's like. It seems unnatural."

"Because you came from a broken home?"

"Make that no home. No roots. Mick's parents died when he was in high school. But his grandfather stepped in and gave Mick and his twin sister an extension of what they'd always had. I have nothing to compare that with. I've pretty much always lived out of a suitcase. Being here—" she waved a fork around "—with Mick, has a fairy-tale quality to it. I feel as though any minute it'll all go poof and disappear."

"Ah, like Cinderella's gown and coach, you mean?"

"Modern-day, but yeah." Hana bent her head and got serious about eating.

Danika forked through her lo mein and picked out the mushrooms. "I'm beginning to understand why you kicked Mick out today. Ordering him off to the beach puts you in control. So if he gets restless and bored, and does leave, you can say it was bound to happen. You can survive, because you saw it coming. More than that, you actually engineered being left behind."

Hana's head snapped up. "How do you know I sent Mick to the beach?"

"Uh-oh! Darn it, I opened my mouth and stuck my big foot in it. Hana, honey, Mick phoned and offered to pay me triple time if I'd add on a PT appointment for you today. I can't have you exercising that much. I said I'd drop in for lunch."

"So, you weren't in the neighborhood at all?" Hana dropped her napkin over her plate and struggled to stand. "Mick's paying you to…like…babysit me? Get out." She pointed to the door with a shaking finger.

Danika fell back in her chair and sighed. "Serves me right for taking a personal interest in the private life of a patient. Listen, Hana, I let Mick think I was going to charge him. I'm not. Each of you slinks around, mooning over the other. I prodded him and he came this close to admitting he's crazy about you." She brought her thumb to her forefinger. "You're such a cute couple."

Hana's knuckles were white where they gripped her walker. "They teach matchmaking in PT school? I thought I could trust you."

"Can I help it if you're both too stubborn to see what you've got in each other?" She got up and started removing serving spoons and closing food cartons.

"Mick really called and asked you to spend time with me today?"

"He really did." Danika put the cartons in the fridge and rinsed their plates. "Not something a man getting ready to take a hike would do, huh?"

Hana frowned. "But…he more or less said he didn't plan to come home…uh…come back here tonight."

Danika leaned a shoulder against the refrigerator. "Male posturing. He probably wanted you to beg him to stay. It's not too late. He has a cell phone. Call and say you miss him. Say you wish he'd come home."

"Beg? I can't do that." Hana shivered.

"I suspect many a love's been lost when a couple lets pride get in the way."

Hana leaned heavily on her walker. "You have so much, Danika. You probably can't understand. Right now all I've got left is my pride. If Mick cares about me at all, he'll come home so I won't be alone tonight. Without me asking."

Pushing off from the fridge, Danika said, "I've gotta run. I'll leave you to your daydreams, Hana. I stored the leftovers in the fridge. At least you won't have to knock yourself out trying to cook tonight." She slung her handbag over one shoulder and headed for front door.

Slower to get under way, Hana trailed behind. "No matter what brought you here, thanks for coming. And, Danika—" she sighed "—I'm my own worst enemy. I do trust you."

"No problem. Listen, don't let that stubborn pride stand in the way of calling me if, for any reason, something goes wrong and you need help."

Hana caught up to her, and bent awkwardly over her walker

to give Danika a hug. "I have a phone in every room. Mick taped a label with the hospital emergency numbers on each receiver."

"That man does have a lot of redeeming qualities." Danika wrenched open the door, still grinning as the man under discussion wheeled in and parked the rented Cadillac beside her jaunty sports car.

The women standing in the doorway looked at each other. "Well, well, well," Danika murmured. "I definitely predict that one's a keeper." She nudged Hana, skipped down the porch steps and turned to shoot her a parting grin.

If Mick heard anything being said on the porch, he paid no attention. He got out of the car, popped the trunk lid, and proceeded to unload his sports bag and several shopping bags.

"Hey, Danika." He stopped, all smiles. "I hoped I'd get here before you left."

She waggled her fingers at him in a little wave and slipped into her small car. Revving the powerful motor, she pulled out onto the street without glancing back.

Mick didn't know what to expect from Hana. He'd halfway counted on Danika serving as a buffer in case he was still in Hana's doghouse. Rubbing his chin, he discovered he'd gone off that morning without shaving. That wouldn't earn him any points. But perhaps she wouldn't mind the unkempt Hollywood look.

In the doorway, Hana watched Mick fiddle around. Maybe he didn't want to come in with her standing there. Too bad. He'd just have to deal with her. Even if he planned to leave, she intended to have her say. In spite of the terrible pain in her heart, Hana stood her ground.

Mick hesitated on the bottom step, well below where she leaned on her walker. He gradually raised his eyes to hers. "I'd ask how everything's going. But," he noted, "I have to say you did okay without me."

She let a few seconds tick past while she struggled with the deadly sin of pride. Recalling Danika's lecture, she chewed on her lip. "Not really, Mick. I missed you."

His silly, cockeyed grin soon had Hana grinning back. And prompted her to blurt out, "I'm sorry I acted like a witch this morning. I can't even remember why I picked a fight."

"You didn't. It was my fault." Mick would have apologized further, but a maintenance crew from the hospital pulled up just then and wedged their pickup into the spot where Danika's car had been. Two men got out and one hollered up to Mick.

"This the house that needs to send back a hospital bed?"

"It is," Hana answered as the man approached. "I hope you're also going to put back the double bed. It was wrapped in plastic and put in the storage shed out back."

The burlier of the two men unfolded his order sheet. "Yep, says here that's our order."

They charged past Mick and one held the screen door while the other workman helped Hana turn her walker to go back inside. The three disappeared down the hall, leaving Mick unamused and feeling expendable. Then he thought about how many times Hana had insisted she could take care of herself. Translated, he guessed that meant she *wanted* control. He remembered he'd felt pretty much helpless when he first arrived home after military surgeons had taken him apart and put him back together. Later, as Pappy Jack's dementia worsened, Mick had been forced to get off his duff.

Hana had gotten off her duff. Mick squelched his hurt feelings and whistled as he carried his purchases into his bedroom.

The men spent two hours at their task. Mick stayed out of the way.

He came out of hiding when he heard Hana at the door, thanking the workers and telling them goodbye.

"All done to your satisfaction?" he asked.

She eased her walker around. "Where have you been? I thought you'd gone off again. They had a terrible time hauling that heavy bed up the back stairs and through the house. You might have offered to help."

Mick had showered and shaved. He hadn't, however, pulled on his boots. He stood in the kitchen arch, hands on hips, idly rubbing one bare foot over the other. "I didn't think you wanted me to interfere."

After a brief silence, she said, "I deserve that."

Mick noticed how drawn she looked. And she kept taking one hand off the walker to rub her abdomen. "You seem especially tired. If they have your bed set up, maybe you should lie down and rest for a while."

"They set the bed up and piled the mattress on top of the box spring. Their contract doesn't cover putting on sheets and blankets. I…ah…hate to ask, but frankly, I'm not sure I can manage making up a bed."

"Dammit, Hana, why do you hate to ask? I don't know when to offer help and when not to. We need to clarify something now. Have I ever, in all the weeks we've been here, given you reason to think I wouldn't happily do anything you asked?"

"No, but please don't shout at me. You've…you just don't know what it's like. Every day I wake up thinking, well, today is the day you'll get fed up."

Mick listened, and read between the lines. "Let's sit down. I want to understand all of this."

They stared at each other, neither moving. Finally, Hana relented. She shuffled over and sat in the chair that held one of her pillows. She leaned back and closed her eyes.

"On second thought, let's skip it. I don't—I've never wanted a showdown." Mick's voice gentled. "I went shopping today. Want to see what I bought?"

Her eyes opened a slit. "Shopping? At the beach, you mean?"

"The beach was windy and crowded. I walked a bit, and talked to a couple of old-timers fishing off a dock. Then I left. Just a minute. I'll bring out the bags. I saved the receipts and didn't remove any tags. We can return anything, or everything."

"We?" The word wobbled out, sounding feeble. Mick left the room so abruptly he obviously hadn't heard her. She tried to imagine what he might've bought that he'd need or want her approval on.

He came back with two big shopping bags, and sank down cross-legged at her feet.

Hana couldn't help it. What woman alive didn't feel a ripple of excitement at the prospect of a surprise? She sat up straighter before bending slightly, her arms supported by the upholstered chair arms.

Mick took out a tissue-wrapped bundle and set it on her lap. "Open it," he urged when several moments passed without her moving.

She broke the gold seal with her thumb and folded back the layers of thin paper. "Oh, oh! Oh, my," she crooned, and gently pulled out a tiny white drawstring baby gown. Blue lambs on fluffy clouds were etched on the fabric and matching cap. A tag said it was designed for preemie babies.

Hana slipped one hand out from under the gown and surreptitiously wiped her damp eyes. Her quiet thank-you was ragged.

Mick decided she didn't want him to see, so he pretended he didn't. Instead, he removed another, similarly wrapped gift from the larger bag, and set it on top of the box with the gown.

This time Hana exposed a soft, hand-knit, cashmere baby afghan of pale yellow. The tassels were yellow alternated with white. She held it to her cheek and sighed.

"Here," he mumbled, heaping another, larger package on her lap. He took back the other items to allow her room to unwrap this one. It was a tower of three boxes, tied together with a white satin ribbon. The manufacturer's tag declared it to be a complete layette. There were mint green and white receiving blankets, a terry towel and washcloth, a bassinet sheet, and three sleepers. In the center of the top box was a squeaky toy shaped like an airplane.

It was the plane that made it real to Hana. "Oh Mick, an airplane. I can't believe you found something so perfect." She smiled, and licked at salty tears that had reached her lips.

Shifting to his knees, Mick used his thumbs to swab them away. "Hey, none of that. You seemed worried about the appointment with Dr. Mancuso. I wanted you to have some…uh…reason to believe…in miracles."

Her throat was so constricted, all she could do was nod and hug the boxes.

Mick gently tugged them away. "Dry your eyes, please? I'm not through. I have another bag. This one's for you."

He shook out a white maternity blouse and a burgundy jumper, followed by a dress with tiny pleats down the front. It was navy with a white collar.

She'd barely had time to tell him how much she loved the dresses, when Mick hauled out three pairs of knit maternity pants in different colors, each with a matching cotton top. All were made for the balmy California weather.

Hana wrapped her arms around Mick's neck. Even though the stack of clothes acted as a buffer between them, her full breasts brushed his chest. Mick thought for a minute his heart would stop beating.

Hana kept repeating brokenly, "Thank you, thank you, thank you."

Closing his eyes, Mick hesitated, then rubbed his hands up and down her back. Again he knew it wasn't her thanks he wanted. He wanted Hana's love.

CHAPTER TWELVE

ON SUNDAY, Wylie phoned. "Hey, Mick, you son-of-a-gun. Weatherman says you're basking in eighty degrees. I measured out back—we have six feet of snow."

"I sympathize, buddy. You have a plane. Let Marlee fly the four of you down here for Thanksgiving. I'll even cook a turkey. Or we can pack a picnic and go to the beach. The kids would love that."

"Marlee wants to hit you. She says she's too fat to fit behind the plane's steering column. I'll attest to that. Ow, ow! She's smacking me with the dishtowel. Husband abuse," Wylie teased through laughter. Sobering, he said, "Travel is out, Mick. Kidding aside, she's way too pregnant to fly."

"But…everything's okay with the baby?"

"That's why I'm calling. The midwife rode over on her snowmobile yesterday. She swears Santa and the baby will arrive together. Jo Beth and Dean are bouncing off the walls, they're so excited. How's your…uh…how's Hana? Marlee thought she'd phone again, but she hasn't."

Mick and Hana sat on the patio, he on his cell phone, she attempting to learn to knit baby booties without much success. He got up and paced to a flower bed across the yard on the pretext of inspecting a butterfly. Once there, he lowered his voice. "Tomorrow Hana's seeing a doctor, a specialist in babies who come early. This is real early. The hell of it is she's scared, and that can't be good for her. Her primary care doc watches her blood pressure, and reminds her at every visit that she's high risk."

"High risk for what? Losing the baby? Or having it arrive early?"

Mick shut his eyes and rubbed the bridge of his nose. "Either/or."

"How does either/or sit with you? Maybe I'm talking out of turn, but a few weeks ago I got the impression you'd like to forget about the baby."

Mick dug his toe in the flower bed, scattering the butterflies. He made indistinguishable noises, clearing his throat.

Wylie didn't let up. "Hana told Marlee you go out of your way to avoid talking with her about the baby. Are you hoping she'll miscarry?"

"How can you ask that? Hell, Wylie, I want to do the right thing. I'm trying. I went over names with her. I bought a few gifts for the baby. But…"

"Yeah? But what, Mick? I can't believe you'd resent an innocent baby."

"Dammit! Not the baby. I resent the kid's father." Mick couldn't catch his breath for a second. It sounded petty even to his own ears.

And it must have to Wylie, too. His disgusted snort made Mick defensive. "It's easy for you and Marlee to preach. My situation is different."

"I've walked the walk, Mick. I can tell you I don't give a damn who fathered Dean. He's my son in every way that matters. And I love Jo Beth. The heart's expandable, you know. There's room for a lot of loving in it."

Mick saw Hana watching him. He could tell she knew something wasn't right with his phone call, and she was starting to look worried. "You didn't *know* Dean's real dad. Or Jo Beth's for that matter."

"If it matters that much to you, Mick, why are you hanging around down there?"

"For Hana. I can't…don't want to abandon her."

"Ah, then you're in love with Hana? I see. You thinking about marrying her, Mick? And then what? Ask her to give up her baby?"

Mick hit the end conversation button and thought he'd feel better. He didn't. He swore, kicked a rock, and didn't give a damn that pain shot through his foot. He stuffed his phone back in its case. It rang again. He knew it would be Marlee, so he didn't pick up. Instead, he stomped around the side of the house, and didn't come back until he felt more in control of the raw guilt Wylie had stirred up.

"Was that your sister?" Hana asked when he returned and picked up his book.

He didn't want to get drawn into idle conversation. He wanted to escape. He would have, too, had he not glanced down at the misshapen mess of yarn that was supposed to be a baby bootie. Hana held it as carefully and reverently as if it were a national treasure. A twisting wrench under his ribs, followed by a slow, agonizing tearing, forced Mick to flop down in the lawn chair. "It was Wylie. They're buried in six feet of snow."

"I heard you invite them down for the holiday." She dropped a stitch and painstakingly picked it up again.

Mick's body reacted involuntarily to the way Hana flicked out her tongue as she worked diligently on a second bootie for the baby. Her baby.

"Well, are they?"

"Sorry, I spaced out. No. Marlee's too pregnant to fly." Mick used his hands around his middle to show how big she must be.

Hana unconsciously ran a hand over her belly. She wore

one of the new smocks Mick had bought. "She must be way bigger than me." Lines appeared on her forehead. "She's due around Christmas. Dr. Walsh estimates April for me. I'm not big at all. Maybe something's wrong. Do you think the baby's stopped growing?"

The concern in her voice forced Mick to examine her shape. He recalled trying once to picture how she'd look pregnant. "Well, in a few weeks you've gone from flat to looking like you're hiding a cantaloupe under your shirt." He smiled, because he detected other subtle changes in her—changes only a man would notice.

Another jolt ran through Mick. He jerked his eyes away from her breasts, and concentrated on her belly. The material of her smock was so thin, it showed a slight protrusion of Hana's navel. His fingers itched to feel the bump. And yet he didn't want to endanger her baby.

He tried to imagine how all those changes in her body felt to Hana. All the questions sweeping through his mind had him blurting, "Hana, does it hurt when your skin's stretched?"

"When he moves and kicks, you mean?"

"He?" Mick's chin shot up.

"Or she. I don't know the baby's sex. It seems insensitive somehow to always refer to an unborn baby as *it*."

"Oh, I wondered if one of the nurses slipped up and said something at your last visit. You had another ultrasound, didn't you?"

"Yes. Once Dr. Walsh settled on a target date for full term, he increased the number of ultrasounds to one a week. Checking for signs of early labor—echoes, they call them. Gosh, he just did a somersault, the little acrobat. Come, feel right here."

Mick stiffened imperceptibly. "Uh, my hands are way bigger than yours. I don't want to cause any…damage."

"Don't be silly. You can't do any harm by cupping your hand just above the sling." She ran both hands over the spot, then grabbed Mick's hand. "Feel this bulge. I can't decide if it's a foot or a rump. What do you think?"

Mick's curiosity got the better of him. Letting her drag his hand across the table, he slid out of the chair and went down on one knee beside her.

"There. Feel that?" She smiled directly into Mick's eyes.

"I don't... Wait, yes I do feel...something." He knelt there longer than he'd expected to. A horde of emotions stormed through him.

Mick got up awkwardly.

"What's wrong?"

"My hip locked," he said, scrabbling for the first excuse that came to mind. Really, a host of ambivalent feelings swirled inside him. He'd undergone similar panicky pangs when Dr. Black had mistakenly thought he was Hana's husband, and revealed that she was pregnant.

"It's me. I'm wrong, Hana. The wrong man. I'm going inside to make some business calls. Then I'm going out for a while. There's a gym a few blocks over I've been meaning to check out. My PT said I need regular workouts to keep this hip from stiffening up."

"Oh," she said quietly, not meeting his eyes. "All right. I've said all along I don't want you to feel you have to babysit me, Mick."

"Good." He grabbed his book and left the patio without looking back.

Hana sat very still, fighting tears, although she was on the verge. Mick's sudden unrest vibrated in his wake. She'd told Danika he wouldn't stick around. That day last week he'd surprised her and come back. Then, she thought he might have staying power. Hana fingered the pretty blouse, one of the gifts he'd lavished on her. Mick gave material things generously. He was miserly when it came to what she wanted. Emotional support, but on equal footing.

This wasn't the first time Hana had been cut adrift. But it hurt more—because she'd come to expect more from Mick. With him she'd had a sense of belonging, a sense of family. Or maybe she'd been blindsided by the fact that he'd been so darned good to her. Hana wasn't immune to that, especially since the holiday season stoked old, bad memories. Like when stores brought out Christmas decorations, she was reminded of one foster family who had, at Christmas, used the state money they'd received for taking her in to give their own two kids stacks of toys. Hana had got one ill-fitting cotton dress. No one had even bothered to wrap the gift.

So, she'd been exceptionally touched when Mick bought presents for her baby. "Things are nice to have," she told her baby, rubbing her belly as if it were a crystal ball. "But more importantly, you'll have my love forever."

She shook off the lethargy she'd felt when Mick left the patio. By the time the front door slammed, she'd pulled herself together. The old Hana relied on herself.

Mick had mentioned that the forest rangers banded together to help employees who'd fallen on hard times. She wondered if their help extended to retraining forestry workers who'd been hurt and could no longer do their old job. Wylie Ames might know.

Hana went inside and pulled a chair up to the phone. She ran her finger down the list of numbers Mick had compiled, and called his sister.

"Hana! Where's that rat fink brother of mine?"

"Out. He said he was going to the gym."

"Good, he feels guilty for hanging up on Wylie."

"He hung up on your husband? Why?"

"Because Mick's being a jerk. How are you? I can't see my

feet. I've long since given up wearing shoes. Do you feel like you've been pregnant a year? I do."

"I spend more time concerned with staying pregnant long enough to give my baby a good start in life."

"Sorry, Hana. I know your situation's different from mine. You're doing okay, aren't you?"

"So far. But Marlee, I need to… Look, I have to be self-sufficient. Mick said the forestry service slush fund paid ten thousand dollars of my hospital bill. I wondered if they make loans, say for schooling to retrain for a different career within forestry. I know I'll have a C-section whether the baby comes on time or is early. And with my injuries I'll never be a smoke jumper again. I could learn to be a dispatcher. Would you ask Wylie if the fund might pay interim living expenses or something until I can get back to college?"

Marlee mumbled in the background. She must have covered the receiver and was probably talking to Wylie.

"Hana, Wylie said you must've misunderstood Mick. The fund sent a thousand dollars and we raised another thousand at our craft sale. Wylie said our fund is local. The long and the short of it is, they don't make loans. But I don't understand. Mick said when he mortgaged Cloud Chasers—well, the property—that you wouldn't have any money worries."

Hana gasped. Mick had lied to her about what she owed.

"Did you two have a fight?"

"A fight? No." Hana rubbed her head where it had started to throb. "I think he's close to bolting."

"It's the baby. He's getting panicky. At least that's the impression Wylie got today."

"That's what I thought. I…hoped I was wrong. No matter how indebted to him I am, if he doesn't like kids, there's no way I can do what we talked about—work in his office. Children can sense when they're not liked or wanted."

"It's not that Mick doesn't like kids, Hana. He loves them. I wish you could see him with my daughter and Wylie's son."

"What, then?" Her hand flew to her stomach. It was *her* baby. Mick had virtually taken off at a dead run after feeling her baby move.

"I don't know," Marlee said unhappily. "I honestly don't know why he's acting like such a jerk. I wish you wouldn't give up on him, Hana."

"I have to," she said, tears clogging her throat. "I need to get my life in order. And if the fund didn't pay ten thousand dollars, I must owe Mick nine thousand on top of the huge debt I already had. Please, Marlee, I'd rather you didn't tell him we had this talk."

"I want to tell him and shake him up, Hana. He shouldn't worry you like this. That's not what you need. What I'd really like to do is pop him upside the head."

"All the words in the world won't make him change the way he feels about my baby. Even if Mick splits, will you call me after you have your baby?"

"Sure. Same goes for you, Hana. I always wanted a sister. We can be pretend siblings."

Hana was near tears. Mick was too close to his family for what Marlee proposed; it just wasn't feasible. But her whole life, Hana had longed for a sibling. "Pretend sisters works for me," she lied.

"Take care, okay? And the offer to smack my brother stands. Although it may have to wait. Wylie says I move too slow to catch anyone at the moment."

That picture helped dry Hana's tears. It was nice to think about a make-believe sister who would be in her corner come what may.

Mick waltzed in a short time later wearing a muscle shirt and shorts.

Hana sat at the kitchen table. She'd gone back to her knitting. She glanced up and followed Mick's progress down the hall. The baby kicked, reminding her of what brought about his earlier departure. An involuntary clenching of her muscles had probably disturbed the little rascal. It was a darned shame Mick had the fine-toned body Hana liked a man to have. There were many things she liked about Mick Callen, and only a few she didn't.

"Did you have lunch?" he asked when he reappeared after showering. He'd changed into casual slacks and a knit shirt.

"Yes." Hana didn't take her eyes off her project, although her hands shook, making it hard to pick up stitches. So, were they going back to being civil?

"I talked to your sister. You lied to me about the amount the forestry fund paid. Why, Mick?

"If you knew I'd paid most of it, would you be here?"

She stared at him with accusing eyes and trembling lips.

"I rest my case." Mick rummaged in the fridge, slapped together a cheese sandwich, and left the room.

Several hours later, he reappeared and began preparing the evening meal. By then Hana was rigid with tension. They ate tuna and tomato salads in absolute silence. Mick sat on a stool at the counter, leaving Hana alone at the table.

She picked at her salad. A bunch of ways to start a conversation flitted through her mind. She didn't try any of them. Her heart felt like a lead weight. She'd barely eaten anything, but she'd had enough of Mick's silence. Rising, she fumbled for her walker. If she didn't go to her room she'd start a fight she'd probably regret.

"Your appointment tomorrow with Dr. Mancuso is at nine? Do you want to walk over, or should we take the wheelchair?"

"I'll walk. You don't have to go. It's a waste of your time."

"Nonsense. You have no idea what she's going to do.

Besides, I think you're a long way from walking that far by yourself. Even with the walker."

"How will I know unless I do it?" She stopped under the arch. "Oh, suit yourself, Mick. You will anyway."

She punctuated her statement with a sigh. Mick knew he was the cause of that sigh. He should say something to make amends. Except that Wylie's barbs, coupled with the sensation of the baby's movement, left him feeling inept, and a bit of a heel. As he'd put his body through a vigorous physical workout, he'd settled on the source of his problem. Jess Hargitay. Granted, the jerk, know-it-all S.O.B. was out of the picture. A million times a day, Mick asked himself why Hana would go to bed with a guy like Jess. Someone even *she* said had no substance. He was no nearer answers tonight than he was the day Hana had admitted Jess had fathered her baby.

It was a wonder Mick didn't break their supper dishes the way he slammed them into the dishwasher.

The next morning, he overslept and was running late when he tapped on Hana's bedroom door and told her she needed to hurry and come eat.

"I'm too nervous about today's appointment to eat," she called through the door.

Mick rested his fingers on the knob. "You think Dr. Mancuso's going to have bad news?"

"I don't know." Hana pulled open her door, nearly making Mick tumble inside. She was fully dressed, but dark circles ringed her eyes. "Last time, Dr. Walsh spent too much time listening to the baby with his stethoscope. Maybe there's a heart problem, or some other reason they'll need to take the baby early."

"Did you ask him what he heard?"

"I didn't think about it being too long until last night."

He nodded. "Still, you should eat *something*. Those diet

papers the doctor gave you stress the importance of dividing your calories between three meals and two snacks a day."

"What good will it do to eat if I have such a nervous stomach I throw it all up?"

"You've got a point. Okay. No food now. We'll eat at the hospital cafeteria after your appointment."

"Mick, I'll eat if it feels right. Give me credit for having *some* brains."

"Jeez, I do. If you're ready, let's go."

The walk seemed endless. Mick had difficulty matching his long stride to Hana's slow progress with the walker up the long incline to the clinic.

"You always check me in, Mick. I'll do it today. I need to start handling this kind of thing."

This was a wing of the hospital clinic they hadn't been to before. Mick hunted for Dr. Mancuso's waiting area while Hana went to the desk. He spied the doctor's name on a door, and across from the office, a row of chairs under a bank of windows. He hadn't yet taken a seat when Dr. Mancuso rushed down the hall, the tails of her lab coat flapping. She recognized Mick and detoured. "Mick, I'm so glad you came with Hana today. I meant to have my secretary phone and suggest you sit in on the appointment."

He darted a furtive glance toward where Hana still stood in line. "She...uh...said she didn't sleep well, and she's touchy. I'd hate to intrude."

The doctor waved Mick's mumbled excuse aside. "I'm not conducting an examination. We're just sitting down to talk."

Hana turned and saw them together. She gave the receptionist her name, then with a heavy heart, moved her walker toward them. What were they discussing so earnestly?

Hearing Hana approach, Dr. Mancuso glanced up and saw the tension lining Hana's face. "I was explaining to Mick that today's visit isn't the sort where you need to put on a hospital gown. I've asked him to join us."

It would be impossible, Mick thought, for Hana to grow whiter. Her gorgeous eyes managed to appear weary and sad at the same time. "Okay," she finally said, a shade above a whisper.

"Then let's get to it." The doctor led them into her compact office. "I had a nurse bring in a donut cushion, Hana. It's in the wing-backed chair. But you pick whichever chair feels most comfortable."

Hana pressed a hand to each seat and ended up choosing the chair that was highest from the floor. "It's harder to get up from soft, squishy chairs." Looking at the doctor, she asked, "How long will I have to use a donut cushion?"

"We'll do another pelvic X-ray after you deliver. I don't have to tell you our goal is to minimize problems for the fetus. You've already had to undergo more X-rays than I like for anyone who's pregnant." She tented her hands. "You won't be able to have any of the spinal-type anesthetics for your C-section. Resorting to a general anesthetic would depress an infant's vitals. And with any premature birth, depression of vital signs is worrisome."

"I didn't go on that mountain climb with the intention of falling in a crevasse and potentially causing harm to my baby."

"We know, Hana. It was an accident." Dr. Mancuso flipped open Hana's chart and focused her attention on the history page. "You're at our facility because we can offer you the best possible care for both your injury and your baby's birth. When Dr. Walsh received the initial request from Dr. Lansing to include you in our program, they discussed bare bones medical stats and possible outcomes."

Hana raised her head. "What else is there?"

The doctor glanced at Mick. "A large part of this program's

success rate, my portion in particular, which is about ensuring that our preemies thrive, depends on the involvement of a mother's extended family."

Mick immediately recognized the ramifications of the doctor's words. He shifted uncomfortably in the larger chair. The back fanned out, and he had to shift to see Hana. It'd become her habit to lock her hands defensively over her rounded abdomen at the slightest confrontation. She did so now.

"Are you insinuating that my baby's at greater risk of not thriving since I'm an orphan?"

The doctor turned the page on the chart. "That's one factor. There are others to consider." She didn't flinch under Hana's glare.

"Name the others." Hana half rose out of her chair, causing Mick to move closer and grasp one of her flailing hands.

"Hana, that's the purpose of this meeting. I know, we all know, you want the very best for your baby. That means making sound decisions."

Hana eased back down onto the cushion. Her dark pupils, enlarged and haunted, tracked Dr. Mancuso's every move.

"I'll get right to it. According to Dr. Lansing's notes, terminating the pregnancy was not a viable option when he examined you. There's no mention anywhere that you were ever briefed on the possibility of adopting out your child."

"Adopting out?"

Mick felt Hana's pulse leap. His did, too, as he recalled Wylie flinging that at him. Then he turned again to look at Hana and saw her horror, misery and suffering rolling at him in waves. And he heard Danika Olsen calling him a selfish bastard, along with Wylie's accusations that Mick had a too-small heart.

Damned if he did. He leapt up. "Is that the reason for this

meeting, Doctor?" Hana's damp, shaking hand added to the anger he felt. "Hana may not have biological family to support her, but she has me. And I have family who are one hundred percent behind her. Write down that Hana won't be giving her baby to any strangers."

The doctor rocked back in her swivel chair. "Hana, one last chance. We have foster parents who specialize in taking in preemies. Single parenthood is hard enough when you're healthy and the baby's healthy. You have no home, no job and no prospects as near as I can tell from what you've told us."

Mick started to refute that statement, but knew in his gut that rebuttal had to come from Hana. He squeezed her hand. She blinked at him and it was as if a force moved through her. "Mick owns a charter flying service in Montana. Once I have the baby, and as soon as we're all able to travel, I'll be renting a guest house on his land, and working full-time in his office."

Rebecca Mancuso studied one, then the other, and calmly shut Hana's chart. "Then it's settled. Enjoy your Thanksgiving holiday. Hana, I'll pop in on your regular appointment with Dr. Walsh next week."

CHAPTER THIRTEEN

As THEY LEFT the clinic having received no bad news, Mick expected Hana to be in better spirits. Instead, her steps dragged, and she seemed distant. At the house, she went straight to her room.

Mick lingered at the door and watched her stop at the dresser. Whether she'd decided to move the vase of spent daisies or was planning to throw the dead flowers away, he didn't know, but the vase slipped from her grasp, hit the floor and shattered. Hana buried her face in her hands.

Mick ran to her side. "It's okay, Hana. Here, let me lift you out of the glass. You sit on the bed. I'll go get a broom and dustpan."

"Stop…being so helpful. I need to clean up my own mess." She batted at his hands, but as she turned, glass crunched under her feet.

"Hana, what is it? If you're pissed off because I butted in with Dr. Mancuso, I'm sorry. She asked me to be there and I wasn't going to stay silent and let her attack you."

"It's not that. What if she's right? Look at me." She flung out her arms. "I can't take care of myself, let alone a baby. I'm a leech. I've be…become my mother." Soundlessly tears coursed down her face, dampening the front of the new jumper she'd worn for the all-important doctor's appointment.

Mick wasn't following her train of thought, but it was as if having her fears voiced had dealt Hana a final blow. "Honey, no!" Mick felt as wretched as Hana looked. "There are professional nannies. Or we'll pay Stella to babysit. She doted on Jo Beth when Marlee lived with Pappy and me."

Mick swung Hana up into his arms. Rather than deposit her on the bed, he sat with her in the rocker. The chair runners crunched glass. Mick paid no attention, and concentrated instead on supporting Hana's injured spine.

"I don't want to be a loser like my mother, Mick. She dumped me with a friend and took off with some sugar daddy. Her friend told me she went from one guy to another—with whoever kept her in booze, cigarettes and shoes. The note she left said I was a liability. Boyfriends wouldn't shell out for somebody else's kid. I swore if I ever found myself in her situation I'd move mountains to keep my child." Hana hid her wet face in Mick's warm neck. "But…I can't. I'm like her after all."

Mick's stomach pitched. Did she see a parallel between him and her mother's boyfriends? He did, and hated what that said about the kind of man he'd become. He wasn't like that, dammit.

He missed part of what Hana said, but he tried to catch up as she continued talking. "My mother's friend called social services, who put me in foster care because she didn't have the means to care for me. Like Dr. Mancuso said, I have no money and no job. It's a matter of time until Welfare steps in to shuffle my baby from stranger to stranger. It's history repeating itself—just like one of my foster moms predicted."

Mick pieced together what she said and some of what she didn't. "Listen, Hana. You'll keep your baby. I'll make sure of it."

She tried to stand. "You don't want my baby, either, Mick."

"I want you, Hana." He kissed Hana. To take her fears away. To make *her* feel loved, and wanted.

Mick's caress felt good. In the back of Hana's mind, though, she knew his heart wasn't in that promise. But emotionally, she was spent. And—she liked kissing Mick. He made the sun shine in her heart.

He lavished kisses on her eyes, ears and neck, until she moaned and relaxed as he covered her lips. In time her tears dried, and Hana forgot she'd been crying.

Soon though, kissing wasn't enough. Pulling back, she captured Mick's face and held it still. "More, Mick, I want…more," she panted.

He struggled out of the unsteady rocker, taking care not to jar her back. His blood felt sluggish, hot and thick. Mick didn't have a nerve in his body that wasn't vibrating as he stumbled through broken glass toward her new bed.

Laying her down, Mick gazed lovingly at Hana's flushed face. He pressed his forehead to hers. "We can't do this," he said, his voice ragged.

"We can't?"

Mick knew she wouldn't be the one to stop them. The sharp staccato of the doorbell saved him from refusing her again.

Hana stiffened. "What time is it? Almost one, yikes! That'll be Danika." Hana tried to sit up. "I must look a mess."

Rallying his thoughts wasn't easy. It was Hana shoving at his chest, along with a second burst from the doorbell, that succeeded in moving Mick.

He set Hana on her feet. "Go tidy up. I'll let Danika in. While she gets set up, I'll find that broom." Plucking Hana's walker away from the worst of the glass, Mick wrapped her hands around the metal handles before he rushed from the room.

He yanked the front door open as the physical therapist was turning to leave.

She spun back. Ever observant, she took in Mick's flustered appearance. Grinning, she dug an elbow into his ribs. "Am I interrupting something, you sly devil?"

"A vase. Hana broke one," he stammered. "I need to sweep up the glass. We just got back from the visit with Dr. Mancuso." Mick broke off as Danika entered the house.

"How did that go?" She stood aside while he shut the door.

Hana answered from her bedroom door. "Dr. Mancuso listed the reasons I'm not mommy material. She believes I should consider adoption. Or maybe let someone foster my baby. Someone better equipped." Hana pressed a hand to her stomach.

"You're kidding? This doctor lives in L.A. County where our welfare system is bursting at the seams with crack babies?"

"Mick came to my rescue. He told Dr. Mancuso no one's going to take away my baby." Hana shot him a grateful glance, but Mick averted his eyes.

Danika patted him on the back. "Bravo, Mickey! I take back what I said the other day. You have got the right stuff."

Hana had joined them by then, but clearly felt outside their banter.

"Danika called me a selfish bastard," Mick told Hana. But, as he recalled more of their conversation, he grew embarrassed thinking of other comments she'd made—she'd flatly stated there were ways to satisfy a partner sexually, even if normal lovemaking wasn't possible. Considering the clinch Danika's arrival had broken up, he really didn't want to explain this to Hana. Regardless, Mick began picturing the ways.

"Glass," he said, to redirect his mind. "We left it spread all over Hana's floor. Gotta find a broom." He hurried off, afraid to stay in case Danika recounted their phone conversation. Fortunately, he hadn't experimented, or her leaning on the doorbell would've really been an interruption.

In Hana's room again, Mick swept up splintered glass and broken stems and carried them outside to the trash bin. Still restless, he scrubbed her floor. Not even physical exertion took his mind off inventive methods of making love with Hana. He knew his way around a woman's landscape well enough. In the navy he'd had no end of women impressed with his job as a fighter pilot. Any bedroom experience he had didn't extend to pregnant women, however. Experimentation with Hana—well, even imagining it got him hard again.

Which Mick did not need. He squeezed out the mop and dumped the dirty water, deciding he had to get out of the house to take his mind off her.

"I'm going out for half an hour or so," he said, poking his head into the room where Hana was exercising. "What time are you set to finish your workout?"

"I have forty more minutes." Hana spoke from a prone position on the mat. "Will you come in for a second before you take off?"

He slipped through the door.

"Danika has invited us to spend Thanksgiving with her family. They live in the Manhattan Beach area. Do you think it's okay for me to ride in a car for that long?"

"She's the medical professional. What does she think?"

Hana's lips pulled to one side. "Um…Danika said I should probably ask Dr. Walsh. This was my way of trying to find out if *you'd* like to go, Mick. I heard you tell Wylie you planned to cook a turkey."

"Then why beat around the bush? The truth is," he said, "I've never fixed a bird in my life. Stella prepared most meals for me and Pappy Jack."

"Why'd you tell Wylie you'd do a turkey, then? What are your holiday plans, since they decided not to visit?"

"I said I'd fix a traditional Thanksgiving dinner to sweeten the pot. I hoped it might entice them to come. Since they're not, I figured I'd pick up a ready-made meal somewhere for the two of us."

Danika broke in. "My husband, Tom, is smoking a turkey in a fancy new smoker he couldn't resist spending a fortune on. We'll keep side dishes simple. Keegan, that's my five-year-old, will eat anything we put in front of him. Holly's three. She'll insist on yogurt. Let this be fair warning—if you spend a day with my little angels, you may wish you could opt out of having this baby, Hana."

"You don't mean that." Hana groped her bulging abdomen protectively.

"Oh, you're absolutely right. I love them to pieces. Holly's at that stage, though, where sometimes I could wring her neck."

"The parenting book said two is the hardest stage."

"Yeah, well, not all kids follow the book. That's something no one ever tells you. Then you bring an out-of-step kid into the world, and every day is trial and error."

Mick studied his watch impatiently. "You can take notes on Thursday, Hana. Danika, if Walsh okays Hana going, is there something we can bring? Wine? Do you and Tom have a favorite?"

"Bring rolls. Hana can't drink. Tom and I don't. His younger brother died an alcoholic. Joe ruined more family holidays than Tom or I care to remember."

"That's sad," Hana said.

"I can take alcohol or leave it," Mick said. "Hana, you should ask Dr. Walsh about a car trip before we say yes to Danika."

"I want to go Thursday. It's my body."

"I know," Mick said. "But why do something reckless at this stage of the game?"

Hana tossed her head. "Danika shouldn't have to wait until Wednesday, which is when I have my next appointment, to plan for extra guests. Besides, I'm tired of living by someone else's rules."

Mick chewed on his lip. Hana's comment sounded like a challenge.

Danika recognized it, too. "Listen, you two. We're fixing a bird anyway. Hana, I have to back Mick this time. Call me after you see the doctor. I'll keep my fingers crossed that he says it's okay."

WEDNESDAY, HANA couldn't wait for her appointment. "I'm going to Danika's whether or not Dr. Walsh says I can," she warned Mick. "If you don't want to drive me, I'll call a cab."

Mick saw she was determined. But he worried about everything. Holiday traffic, and was it risky for Hana to use a seat belt? What if he had to slam on the brakes? Would it reinjure her fractured pelvis? And what about the baby? But that was silly. His sister had driven home from the ranger station when she was more pregnant than Hana. "If you're going, I'm driving, Hana."

"Really? But…you still think I should ask the doctor."

Mick felt torn. The last thing he wanted was to see her disappointed.

But an hour later, Hana emerged from her appointment wearing a big grin.

Mick set aside the magazine he was reading. "Let me guess. Dr. Walsh said you could go to Danika's?"

"Yes. Give me your phone. I'll call her now to see if we're still on."

They were. Mick accepted the phone Hana handed back to him. "After I walk you home, I'll go buy rolls. Is there anything else you'd like to take? A hostess gift?"

"Gosh, what's appropriate? I typically worked on holidays because I got paid double time. Or if I had a holiday off, I studied."

Mick stored that tidbit about Hana. Her life must've been lonely. "Well, as a rule I take wine or candy. They don't drink. Candy's probably not good. Danika's into health food."

"Flowers?" Hana ventured.

Mick snapped his fingers. "Great idea." Hana looked pleased at his response.

Later, as he waited in a long line to check out at the grocery store, Mick called his twin to wish her happy Thanksgiving.

And then, Stella.

"Same to you, Mick. We have two airmen here. I offered to cook them dinner, and they're delighted. When you arrived home to recover, I'm afraid I didn't fully appreciate what you were going through. Sometimes these boys wander out to the office to talk. Occasionally they say things I'm sure they didn't intend to let slip about the horrors of war."

"I'm glad you're there to listen, Stella. I had Pappy Jack. He'd seen as bad or worse. God, I miss him."

"Me, too. Is everything okay with you, Mick? Marlee worries that you'll invest so much of your life in this young woman, you'll be crushed if she gets through her ordeal and up and goes her own way."

"Invest…you mean…money? I'm keeping track. I'm not overspending."

"I meant invest too much of yourself, Mick."

"It may be too late for that, Stella. You could say I'm pretty invested. In fact, I'll probably bring Hana home when I come back in the spring. She's determined to pay back what I've spent on her. Of course, she doesn't know how much that is. It'd freak her out."

"Oh, Mick. Relationships built on half truths start out with three strikes against them."

"Hana's lived her whole life with three strikes against her. I want to show her there's a better life."

"You're an old softie. But we women like to do things for ourselves. And a single mom has other considerations. Are you thinking about that, Mick?"

"I hoped you might give Hana a hand with her baby, Stella."

"*Her* baby? So, you won't be bringing her home as Mrs. Mick Callen?"

"Sorry, Stella, gotta go. I've reached the grocery checkout. It's a zoo here today, what with all the Thanksgiving shoppers."

"It's easy to hang up and ignore me. I don't think it'll be so easy to do that with your conscience. You have more in common with your grandfather than I thought. Did you know I would've married that old coot if he hadn't been hung up on the fact that he was my husband's best friend? Now they're both gone. I'm left here by myself to think about all the time we lost."

She clicked off before Mick had recovered from her sneak attack. He shoved the phone in his pocket.

He could picture his life with Hana; he'd thought about little else. When it came to adding in a baby—Jess Hargitay's baby—the picture developed a hole in the center. But the hole was growing smaller....

At home some forty minutes later, Mick set on the counter the wheat rolls he'd bought along with a centerpiece he got for the Olsens. Then he went in search of Hana. He'd brought her mums, a mix of dark red, brown and gold. The stems were tucked in a swirl of fall leaves. A few acorns glued to the ends of spikes added a woodsy effect. The green glass vase was tied with a bow the color of Hana's eyes.

She reclined on her bed, deep in the book of baby names. "Mick, that bouquet is beautiful," she said when his movement caught her eye. "Danika will love it."

"Hers is in the kitchen. I bought a table centerpiece. These are to replace your daisies."

"I can't believe you'd trust me with another vase."

"Accidents happen. If I'd noticed the daisies were dying, I'd have replaced them before this."

"I've never known a man who buys as many flowers as you. Did a girlfriend train you well?"

"Um…my dad used to bring Mom flowers once a week. Her eyes always lit up. So do yours."

Hana's cheeks flamed. "Mick, stop it. I can't handle it when you say things like that."

He set the vase on her chest of drawers, then tucked his fingertips in the back pockets of his jeans. "You don't like compliments?"

"Not…not really," she stammered.

"Why?"

"Because."

"Give me one reason."

"Flattery makes me uncomfortable. I wonder what's behind it. Like, what does he *really* want from me?"

Mick stiffened, feeling the sting. Given all he'd done since her accident, the last thing that would've occurred to him was that she'd think he had an ulterior motive.

"I know your life was no bowl of cherries." He frowned. "If flattery bothers you so much, how come you fell in bed with an asshole like Jess Hargitay?" Mick hadn't intended to blurt that out. And from the shock on her face it was clear Hana hadn't expected it, either.

She had a temper, too. "So that's it? I knew something's been eating you, Mick. You know what? At least Jess was consistent. He was an arrogant asshole seven days a week. You, though. One day you shovel sweet nothings at me. The next you kiss me blind. A few days later you treat me like a leper, and then run off to sulk, giving me no clue what I've done."

Mick had reasons. He'd fallen for Hana. He'd fallen hard a long time ago. Only—she was having another man's baby and she made no excuse for that, gave no explanation.

The air in the room almost crackled. Mick's hands were now out of his pockets and clenched into fists.

Hana clutched her swollen abdomen, but her chest heaved with each heated breath.

Mick would've liked nothing better than to continue this shouting match. Oh, he could spill his guts about the things he'd heard about Jess. What if he told Hana another female smoke jumper had considered charging Jess with harassment? She didn't; she'd just left the forestry service. Yeah, Mick wanted to throw all that and more at Hana. Then they'd see how she defended the weasel.

Except, she shook like a leaf and was plainly mad as hell.

Mick had heard her doctors repeatedly say not to let her get upset. They said excessive stress could bring on premature labor. Mick's feelings for Hana ran so deep that he wouldn't gamble with endangering her life, or her baby's for that matter. Not even to ease the pain in his gut.

Getting a grip, Mick fought to level his voice. "I don't want to fight with you, Hana. You should probably try to sleep. If traffic's as heavy as I expect, it could be thirty minutes each way. And you haven't ridden in a car yet. You're used to our house being quiet, and you're able to grab naps. Tomorrow you won't get to nap."

"Right, turn the tables. Make this about my condition."

"What are you talking about?" He paused in her open door.

"Mr. Butter-melts-in-your-mouth—I-didn't-come-here-to-fight-with-you,-Hana," she said in a falsetto. "Well, dammit, we used to argue over books, politics, the environment, just to name a few things. Suddenly, you're all patient, calm and reasonable, and I'm someone in need of a nap?"

"Good night, Hana."

"Go to hell! First and foremost, I'm human, you know." She raised her voice because he'd left. "You never finish anything, Mick. The other day you kissed me into frustration, then stopped cold. Two times you've provoked an argument, then let it hang. Maybe I'm tired of being sent to bed like a naughty child. I'm a woman, Mick. A grown woman."

Slam. Mick shut the door with more force than he'd intended. Her accusation stoked a not-quite-dormant fire to life.

DAMN. Hana wished she'd just told Mick the truth. Why hadn't she told him what'd happened that day of the fire?

Mad at Jess, mad at Mick, even madder at herself, Hana closed the book of baby names and heaved it at the door.

OUTSIDE HANA'S ROOM, Mick paused to calm down. He heard something hit the door with a thud. She must've thrown the book of baby names.

Mick debated whether or not to open the door and retrieve the missile. She shouldn't climb out of bed, or bend to pick it up.

Her bed squeaked. Mick's hand tightened on the knob. The

light shining from under the door disappeared. Hana must've shifted and turned off the lamp.

Quietly, Mick took his sweaty hand from the knob. He moved away from her door, careful not to step on areas of the living room floor that he knew creaked.

He reached his room, stripped and lay seminaked on top of his sheets. Only then did Mick allow himself to mull over everything Hana had said in her fit of temper. She'd been frustrated by his kisses. She wanted him to see her as a woman. Was she extending an invitation?

Mick pounded his pillow into a wad. It didn't calm him any.

THEY BOTH SLEPT IN, and appeared at the same late hour in the kitchen. Shortly before it was time to leave for Danika's.

"You look nice," Mick said. Hana wore one of the sleeveless tops and a pair of maternity capris he'd bought. "That's not flattery," he added quickly.

She ignored his last remark. "Thanks, but I've gotten pale as a ghost. I used to have a nice tan."

"Hmm. I'd better toss sunscreen in the bag." He disappeared, and came back carrying a tube. He also handed Hana her sunglasses.

"How did you get to be so thoughtful?"

"Don't start on me again, Hana. Can we go and act like we're having a good time? Can we try to be civil to each other today?"

"I meant that in a nice sense, Mick. I'm sorry, I don't have much experience when it comes to social graces."

"You should take a sweater," he said. "It'll be cool near the water after the sun goes down. Wait here, I'll get one from your closet."

"The black one," she called as he started off. "It's the only one that still fits."

He put the sweater in the bag and thought about how empty Hana's closet looked. "You're going to need more than sweaters when we go back to Montana in the spring."

"I was going to say I have my Forestry jacket, then I remembered it got shredded on rocks when I slid into the crevasse."

She looked so sad, Mick cursed himself for having brought up something that would remind her of the accident.

He helped Hana into the car. He laid a pillow across her stomach before he latched her seat belt.

"At the risk of you biting my head off, the pillow is further proof of how considerate you are, Mick." She smiled innocently at him.

"Common sense." He started the car. "Hana, didn't any of your foster moms like you?"

"One. I wasn't very old, maybe five. They wanted to adopt me, but her husband died suddenly of a heart attack. I heard later I was considered unadoptable because my mom never relinquished her parental rights. You can't be adopted if there's a chance a real parent may show up and want you back. And the truth is, most couples want infants. Are you having second thoughts about what you told Dr. Mancuso?"

"No, Hana, I'm trying to learn more about you. Where was your dad in all of this?"

"The friend of my mom's? She was a stripper. She said my dad was married and had grown kids. I told you I hated my mom for dumping me like trash. But I used to make excuses for her. Like, maybe she'd been in a car wreck, or she'd come back and found her friend had moved. But a year ago, that friend still lived in the same place." She sighed. "I was three weeks old when my mother took off. She never looked back."

"Who named you?"

"Hana Lee was the name the friend gave the social worker. She said my mother was Hanalore. Would you believe the friend never knew my mom's last name? They worked at the same strip club. A judge picked Egan. Technically I'm a nobody."

Mick objected to that.

Hana sloughed him off. They fell silent until they reached the Olsen home. A beautiful house set behind privacy gates, it offered a view of the beach and ocean below.

Tom Olsen was a surprise. He was nearly a foot shorter than his beautiful, athletic wife. He had a receding hairline and wore glasses. It was soon evident by every word and action how much in love they were. And he had a great sense of humor.

Their daughter, Holly, was shy. She clung to her mother's tanned leg. Danika, as always, wore shorts.

Keegan Olsen talked a mile a minute. His mother had told him Mick was a pilot. The boy immediately dragged Mick upstairs to see his toy plane collection. When he came back, Mick said, "I would've given my eyeteeth at his age to have that collection."

Danika raised her head. She, Hana and Holly sat on a sofa going through an album. "Tom's parents overindulge him. First and only grandson, you know."

The boy ran off to follow his dad, who'd said he was going to check the smoker. "What are you three so engrossed in?" Mick asked, stepping up behind them.

Hana showed him. "This is Holly's baby book. It's filled with photos of her from birth to now. There's room for two more years. It's so great she'll have this record, Danika."

"A friend gave me the book at my shower. It's the most comprehensive I've seen," Danika said. "I'll jot down the brand. I'm sure you can buy one like it in town."

"I don't even own a camera," Hana said as she turned to the last page.

"Mick can buy a pack of disposables." Danika flipped back to the start and held it out to Mick. "You only have one opportunity to get shots like this in the delivery room."

He took the album, and he scanned picture after picture of a squalling, wrinkly, red infant. The baby in the photograph didn't at all resemble the chubby brown-haired girl seated on the couch.

He flipped a page and was surprised to find himself envying the smiling dad holding the swaddled bundle. There were other pictures of Tom leaning over Danika's hospital bed. She appeared tired, but happy. Tom wore a constant expression of love and wonderment. Something moved in Mick's chest, and squeezed his heart. He recalled how empty his house had felt without family around. *Family comes first. All else comes after.* Pappy used to say that. Mick imagined his house with another family. His and Hana's.

He passed the album back to Hana. For the rest of the day he couldn't shake the image of the beautiful family. He blinked when the picture in his mind became Hana, him and a wrinkled baby, not wrinkled but a doll-like infant with strawberry-blond fuzz covering a perfectly shaped head. Dr. Walsh had said the upside of Hana having a cesarean was that her baby would have a nice-shaped head.

Mick shook off the images and wandered outside to find Tom and Keegan. The three tossed around a football amid the smoke puffing out of the smoker.

Inside, the women put aside the album. Danika, who already had the table set on the patio, popped the rolls in the oven. She carried side dishes out, letting Hana carry only an empty plate for the turkey.

Dinner was great. Everyone teased Hana about how much turkey and dressing she put away. Holly, as Danika had predicted, asked for yogurt. Tom managed to talk her into trying some mashed potatoes and gravy.

A soft breeze carried the smell of the ocean. Whenever they fell silent, they heard seagulls squawking, and the incoming tide.

The men cleared the table, suggesting the women relax on the lounge chairs. "Be sure to use sunscreen," Mick called to Hana.

"Thanks, it would've slipped my mind. What would I do without you?"

Danika winked at Mick and Tom nudged him. "Go help her slather it on," he murmured. "She shouldn't bend to do her legs."

Mick followed her to the lounger. He made her hold her hair back while he spread cream on her face. She leaned her head back so he could better reach her neck. The *V* of her top gaped a bit, enough for Mick to see the swell of her breasts. They were pale with webs of tiny blue veins. He made sure to cover the exposed flesh with sunscreen. He wouldn't have guessed he could get so easily turned on, yet it was obvious that not all the heat he was feeling came from the sun.

He enjoyed the task, and lingered over it. Before it was time to cap the tube, Mick saw Hana watching his every move. It was apparent that his touch affected her, too. If they'd been home, and she'd looked at him like that, Mick wouldn't have stopped there. Because their day was only half over, he felt compelled to lean down and mutter, "Later."

All afternoon, every time his eyes cut to Hana, hers were tracking him. If he and Tom hadn't taken the kids for a walk on the beach to hunt for seashells midday, Mick thought he would have exploded.

Even though he had a great time, and they made plans to get together again in the near future, Mick was ready to leave by six, when the sun sank out of sight over the ocean. He had more than driving home on his mind.

As he pulled out of the Olsens' driveway, Hana stretched. "What a marvelous day. I hate for it to end."

"Who says it has to? We have a patio. It's a warm, starry night. I'd suggest a nightcap, but it'll have to be lemonade."

"Is that what you meant when you said *later?*"

"At the time I was dreaming of you and me necking in the hammock."

"Mick." His name didn't come out shocked so much as coy.

"I didn't read you wrong, Hana. You had the same thoughts."

"I admit it. I did. Now that we're almost home, I worry that the anticipation will lead to a letdown."

"You think I can't deliver?"

Hana's dark eyelashes dropped. "I have no doubt you can. But, Mick, I owe you honesty."

He exited the freeway two blocks from their house. "Don't ruin the day. All I'm asking you for is tonight. Forget that either of us has a past." He pulled into the drive, shut off the motor, and stepped out. He thought he'd needed to know the details of her life leading up to the accident. Now he understood that was baloney.

She'd released her seat belt and sat very still, frowning as if she had a weighty argument going with herself.

Mick lifted her out and shut the door with one hip. He could have put her down and guided her along the walk. But he didn't. He carried her through the side gate, into the backyard, where solar-powered lights dotting the flower beds cast a soft golden glow over the patio and the huge canvas hammock.

He'd waited almost eight hours to kiss her. She'd been waiting, too, so their coming together was like a cataclysmic explosion.

No matter how involved he was in kissing Hana, he was ever mindful of her fragile state. He settled in the hammock first, and eased her down beside him so that his body supported her trunk and the unbalanced weight of her pregnant belly.

She sighed the moment he released the hooks that held her maternity corset. They kissed frequently, and grew emboldened enough to explore the secret places that made him a man and her a woman.

"I feel awkward," she whispered, ducking her head.

Mick lifted her face to the light and kissed her over and over. "Don't," he admonished, his voice deep and husky with emotion. "I've imagined you naked in my arms for more than a year. I promise, you don't disappoint."

For a time they said no more. Passion led them to new, shivering heights, an experience that left them damp and shaking.

"This is not fair to you, Mick. I can't…can't."

"You can. You did. Sweetheart, I knew this was going to be make-do. It won't always be this way." Too filled with emotion to say more, Mick tucked her head under his chin and rubbed her hair softly while he collected his fractured thoughts. "I've been trying to get this out for weeks. I love you, Hana. I'd be honored if you'd consent to be the most important person in my life. I know you don't feel the same way about me and I don't have a ring to give you, but I can get one…we can buy one tomorrow. Today I started thinking how you don't have family, and I don't have a lot of family…"

Hana froze. She sat up and patted around them for her displaced clothing. Her eyes were huge in the dim light, her movements almost spasmodic.

"Hana, wait, let me help so you don't hurt yourself."

She swung her legs off the hammock, and held her maternity top to her breasts. "No, Mick. My answer, it's no!" Her voice cracked. "Please, I want—I *need*—to go to my room. Take me now!"

CHAPTER FOURTEEN

HANA COULDN'T TALK to Mick. He couldn't have chosen a sneakier, more hurtful trump card to lay down when she was still reeling from his unselfish lovemaking. Her bone-deep desire to have a real family was and always had been her Achilles' heel. She wasn't doubting that Mick wanted her. It was evident in his eyes, in his touch, and in everything he'd done for her. But he didn't want her baby. Hana felt that in her soul. And she knew what it was like to grow up in households with people who pretended to care about her. She wouldn't subject her child to that. Not even for the comforts Mick could provide her. Not for anything.

In her room, Mick tried repeatedly to get Hana to tell him what he'd done wrong. She closed herself off. He finally gave up and went to bed. Not to sleep, but to go over in his mind how something that had started out so fine had ended up so bad.

The next two days weren't any better. Hana stayed holed up in her room. Mick took her food. She thanked him politely. So politely she sounded like a robot.

At loose ends, Mick wandered around like a lost puppy.

When he turned the calendar to December first, he decided to phone his sister for her family's Christmas list. If nothing else, he could put the shopping—which he generally left to the last minute—behind him.

"Marlee, it's Mick. It's a sunny eighty degrees. Puts me in the mood for Christmas. I thought I'd get a jump on shopping."

"Are you crazy?" His twin laughed. "It snowed all night here. I know because I was up with Braxton-Hicks."

"With who?"

"Not who—well, they were two doctors. I think. That's what they call contractions that are false labor. When I was pregnant with Jo Beth, I panicked. A navy nurse explained it's a time the baby is turning and preparing to drop for the hard work of real labor. And you couldn't care less about this, right?" She laughed again.

"I care. If the baby's not due till Christmas, it's a bummer you have to suffer so early. Are you overdoing it, maybe?"

"Rose is here. She insists that the midwife's wrong. She predicts I'll deliver in the next couple of weeks. She could be right. Second babies can come early."

"If it's snowing hard, will your midwife make it in time?"

"We're prepared. Wylie's sticking close to home. Rose's neighbor, Emmett Nelson, is pitching in to help with chores. What about you? How's Hana?"

Mick told her about their Thanksgiving with Danika's family. Of course he bypassed what had happened after they got home. He did say, "Hana's been in a foul mood the past week. She wants to be left alone."

"Speaking from experience, Mick, I recommend giving her space. Men don't understand. Pregnancy alters a woman's body and emotions. Which also explains why you want to get out of the house, even if it means going Christmas shopping." She named a few things the kids wanted. "There's really nothing Wylie and I need. We have each other and we're all in good health. We miss you, Mick. Gathering family around a Christmas tree means more than gifts. Promise you'll spend Easter with us?"

"Easter is a long way off. I'll probably be home by then.

Did Stella tell you the guy currently renting your cottage, Kent Mackey, expressed an interest in staying on and flying for Cloud Chasers? It sounds like his wife—he's been married a couple of years—is all for it. Suzette is her name. Apparently, she does computer consulting, so she can work anywhere. She's okay even with Kent working part-time."

"Stella told me Kent liked the idea of volunteering with Angel Fleet, too. Oh, hey, I almost forgot, Stella heard from an old friend of yours. I wrote his name down. Here. Paul Sheldon was in Bozeman on business. He works for Lockheed and lives near where you're staying. Irvine. Know it? Here's his cell number. He said to give him a call."

"Paul's an old flying buddy. We used to play golf together. Thanks. I may call him after we hang up. If we figure out a time to meet, it'll give me an excuse to put off Christmas shopping."

"If you wait long enough maybe you can buy gender-specific gifts for my baby."

"If that's important, you could've asked the baby's sex at the ultrasound."

"Did Hana cave? You said she was holding out."

"Far as I know, what she's having is still up in the air."

"Far as you know? Mick, are you still keeping yourself out of that part of Hana's life? As a rule I don't meddle…"

Mick snorted, but Marlee went on. "A woman and her unborn child are a unit. You've heard the old saying, love me, love my dog? That's a hundred times more true for love me, love my kid. Get the message?"

"I do. I see us as a family, Marlee. It's not so easy convincing Hana. Jess doesn't matter anymore. Hey, is that Wylie I hear in the background? Tell him hello, and that I'll expect a call from him when the new Ames baby shows up." They wound down and said goodbye. Feeling melancholy, Mick didn't wait to think about it, but instead, phoned his friend.

"Hey, buddy. Long time no see. Golf?" Paul Sheldon responded. "I don't play anymore. I've developed other interests since I got married. Your sister said you're in my neck of the woods. I have an idea, Mick. My wife wants a certain antique mirror. I just found one at an antique store near Huntington Beach. If you don't mind tagging along while I poke through a musty old attic, we can grab a deli sandwich afterward at a little place I know and get caught up."

"Suits me. Give me directions. I'm at loose ends today, so this is perfect." They nailed down particulars, and Mick pocketed his note.

"Hana," he called on his way to her room. "I've arranged to go meet an old navy buddy. I'll be out most of the afternoon. Is there anything you need before I take off?"

"No. I heard you on the phone. I thought you were talking to your sister."

"I was. My friend contacted Stella, and she gave his name to Marlee. She's having what she called false labor. Her baby may come before Christmas."

"Really? Is she worried?"

"Didn't sound it." He let silence hang there for a beat or two, then said, "Are you, Hana? Is that what's wrong? Or is it more that if something happens and you, say, lose your baby, it'd be a drag to be tied down to me?"

"What an awful thing to say!"

She looked so horrified Mick immediately felt contrite. "I'm sorry, Hana. God, I shouldn't have even implied that anything might happen to the baby." Mick went down on one knee beside the rocking chair. "Can you forgive me?"

"It's okay. I've thought about our situation a lot, Mick. I've gotta admit, if our roles were reversed, I'd probably feel the same as you."

He reached for her hand, but she snatched it away.

"Dammit," he said, jumping to his feet to pace back and forth. "Not long ago, what you're saying would've been true. Not now. I can't explain it, but when we were looking at the Olsens' baby album, at first I pictured us. You and me. But the baby was a blank. Then, like that—" Mick snapped his fingers "—I pictured us with a real baby, yours, and we were happy."

"Mick, you don't have to try so hard. It's okay. In Kalispell you said I needed a friend. I did. I still do."

"Now I want more, Hana. I think I always did."

"Mick, you don't want to keep your navy buddy waiting." Hana picked up the paperback she'd been reading and opened it, plainly dismissing him.

Frustrated, Mick clenched his hands. "I don't know what it'll take to make you see me as I am, not as I was." He found Hana's silence harder to bear than if she'd put up an argument. "I'm trying my best here to prove my love," he said desperately.

She kept her eyes on the book.

Giving up for the time being, yet determined to find a way to break the barrier she'd put up, Mick strode to the door. "You have my cell number if you need me. I plan to be back before dark. I may try to get in some Christmas shopping since I'm already going to be out and about."

Her unwillingness to acknowledge him was irritating. Mick stormed out of the house and drove off in a huff.

He easily found the parking garage where Paul had said to meet, and Mick recognized his old friend from his long, lanky build. He was shocked to see an empty sleeve where Paul's left arm ought to be. No wonder he quit golfing.

They shook hands. The grip of Paul's right hand was strong. "Might as well get the bad news out of the way. Two months after your accident, I had to bail out on a routine reconnaissance flight. Nothing the docs could do to reattach my arm.

I've had eight plastic surgeries on the left side of my face. You remember I was engaged to my high-school girlfriend. That's the best news. Nicole stuck by me. We've been married three years. She wanted to get married the day I got home. I balked at saddling her with the face looking back from my mirror. Anyway, our love's stronger because of everything we've been through. You, Mick? Are you hitched?"

"Nah. I went home to recover at my granddad's. His cargo flight business was in shambles. Plus, he had hardening of the arteries. I pulled the business back from the brink. Then Pappy Jack died," Mick said abruptly. "He left me the business and all the property, except for a house he gave my twin sister."

"Your housekeeper said you flew a woman to California, and that you're hanging with her until she gets well?" Paul posed it as a question while motioning that they had to cross the street to the strip mall.

"Long story, buddy. Hana's a smoke jumper who fell in a crevasse while she was on a mountain climbing expedition that wasn't for work. She hurt her back. Her career's gone." Shrugging, Mick said, "She's got an added complication. She's pregnant."

Paul's right eyebrow rose almost to his hairline. The fact that his left didn't move reiterated the extent of his facial injuries. "Your kid?"

"No, but I sure as hell wish it was." He paused. "It can still be mine, you know."

"That says a lot. Hey, this is the shop where Nicole's girlfriend claims she saw the mirror. Nicole got me hooked on antiques. I like seeing if I can get a real bargain. The trick is to not act like you want the item you're dying to buy. Get my drift?"

"I think so. I'll poke about while you dicker."

The shop had three floors. The men were soon separated

amid old dishes and furniture. Mick tripped, glanced down and saw a curved rocker foot attached to a walnut baby cradle. Crouching, he ran his hand over finely milled spindles. There was something unique about this cradle that Mick liked—it had a woven bonnet that pivoted. Presumably to keep drafts off the baby. What a dunce he'd been, buying clothes and nothing else. He remembered thinking during the virtual tour of the house that the alcove in the bedroom that became Hana's would make a great temporary nursery.

"Find something you like?" Paul said from above Mick's head.

"Hana's never mentioned if she'd like a crib, bassinet or cradle." Mick's hand never stopped stroking the woodwork.

"If the price is right, why not buy it. If…Hana, that's her name? If she wants something different, you can always sell this piece for what you put into it."

"Hmm." Mick rose and dusted his hands together. "Find your mirror?"

"I made an offer. The owner said no. I'm giving him time to reconsider. Bring the cradle. If he thinks he may lose two sales, maybe he'll be more willing to come down on the mirror."

The men were successful. They crossed the street, each awkwardly struggling with his treasure.

"Let's lock these in our cars, then we can go eat. Nothing like a good bargaining session to stoke my appetite." Paul grinned, and again Mick noted how one side of his friend's mouth moved, but the other remained stationary.

"I've never looked into plastic surgery," Mick said. "I took a butt load of shrapnel and my thigh was riddled. I have a titanium hip socket."

"And we're the lucky ones," Paul murmured, pausing to set the mirror against his car so he could hit the remote to open his trunk. "We didn't come home in a body bag," he elaborated, hoisting the mirror one-handed with some difficulty into his trunk.

"That's the truth," Mick agreed. He had to haul the cradle up to the next parking level. "I only limp now when it gets cold or the humidity goes up."

"And you choose to live in Montana?" Paul shook his head.

"It's home." A faraway look came into Mick's eyes as he jockeyed the cradle to fit in his rented Caddy's trunk.

"Is Montana Hana's home, too?"

"Uh, no. She's a California girl." Mick slammed his trunk lid and turned. "Any suggestions on how to make her a convert?"

Paul mused as they walked to the deli he'd mentioned, "How about buying her a five-carat diamond set in platinum? That, and some old-fashioned begging."

Mick considered his friend's suggestion throughout lunch. Even without golf, the men had a lot in common. When it came time to part, they agreed not to let so much time pass before meeting again. "I know!" Paul said, jingling his car keys. "Maybe you'll invite Nicole and me to your wedding."

Hopefulness lodged in Mick's chest, even though he said, "Don't hold your breath. Hana thinks I'm not keen on being a dad to her baby."

"That cradle should add a few hash marks in your favor."

Mick had his doubts. But, for added insurance, he drove along side streets until he saw a nice jewelry store.

He discovered it was easier to choose a cradle than a ring. The clerk kept asking what his fiancée liked. "Does she favor wearing an engagement ring and adding a wedding band? Or does she prefer you to have matching bands? These come etched, or in mixed gold and white gold. We also have a nice selection of bands that have three or four diamonds inset across the top."

"Uh, we haven't really discussed rings."

"Oh." Clearly that confused the clerk. "Men do select bridal sets to surprise their prospective bride. Sometimes *they're* the ones who are surprised."

Mick frowned at the woman.

"Yes, I meant unpleasantly surprised. It's common for women to know from quite a young age what dress they wish to walk down the aisle in and the exact ring they want on their finger. I assume you've heard the phrase *diamonds are forever.*"

Mick stared at the rings. "Maybe the divorce rate wouldn't be so high if that phrase was changed to *marriage* is forever."

"Indeed. Why don't you look around some more. If something catches your eye, I'll be glad to give you the price."

He wandered from case to case, picturing Hana's small-boned hand. He'd always liked her hands. She kept her nails short, but polished, and took care to use cream often. Now, he pictured those hands feeding a baby and changing diapers.

How would he be at that? He got along okay with kids the age of his niece and Wylie's son, Dean. Or even Danika's son. He hadn't been as much of a hit with three-year-old Holly, though. Mick knew guys in the navy who were plain-spoken about separating men's duties from women's. Mick's parents never had those hard-and-fast rules. He thought he'd follow their example of share and share alike.

Now that he was warming to the idea of being a dad himself, he was determined to be a good one. A hands-on father.

"You're smiling," the clerk noted from her perch in the middle of the store. "Have you seen something you like?"

"Maybe. I'm partial to this set of three rings."

The clerk pulled a key out of the drawer. As she approached, her eyes took in the set beneath the glass Mick tapped on. "Platinum. You certainly have good taste. The pink diamond is two carat. Nearly flawless." She removed the rings, turned a tag and announced the price.

Mick mentally patted himself on the back for not blinking an eye. That, at least, seemed to please the elegantly appointed clerk. His approval rating shot up several notches higher when he took out his debit card. "I think, hope, Hana will be pleased."

"If she's not, you should seriously examine your relationship."

Mick almost laughed at the clerk's quick switch in allegiance.

"This will take a minute to go through the system, as it is a sizeable amount."

"That's fine. I'm not in a rush." Mick used the time to study the other customers. Two men in suits and a woman already dripping in gems. He realized why the clerk had had doubts about him. His jeans, while clean, weren't new, and his T-shirt was faded. Mick was very glad he'd worn his least run-down boots.

This had simply been the first jewelry store he'd seen. He should've considered the fact the store sat in the center of tony Fountain Valley.

"We're all set," she said, sashaying back to where Mick waited, "except for sizing. We can fit your ring today. Your fiancée's will have to wait, unless you know her ring size."

He picked up the solitaire. "This looks about right. Although, I heard her say to a friend on Thanksgiving that her hands are swollen. Water weight," he murmured. "She's going on six months pregnant."

The clerk dropped the rings into Mick's outstretched hand. *Idiot!* he thought. The woman's eyes clearly conveyed what she was thinking, that Mick should've been buying a wedding ring long before now.

"I'll take these as is if you'll box them. If they need altering, I'll bring them back."

The woman boxed Hana's set separate from his. She put both in a gold-flecked bag and cinched the satin cord handles tight before handing it over.

Mick escaped as quickly as he could. His watch read nearly four-thirty. He'd spent far more time looking at rings than he'd intended.

He took out his cell phone and punched in the house number. He didn't want Hana worrying, although he'd indicated he might go Christmas shopping. But he hadn't bought a single gift.

The phone was busy. His heart turned handsprings. *She was calling to check on him.* He hung up and waited. *Nothing.* She and Danika were likely gabbing.

Mick wasn't that far from home, although he got snarled in rush-hour traffic. He pulled in at five-fifteen, folded the gold bag as small as it would go and stuffed it in his pocket. A tight fit. The darned thing bulged at one end and poked at his appendix with a sharp edge at the other.

He'd use the cradle as a cover. Whistling, he hauled out his surprise and wobbled up the steps. "Hana, I'm home," he yelled and knocked the cradle against the door casing. "Come see what I found today."

He kicked the door shut, then came to a halt when Hana appeared in front of him.

"A cradle. Oh, Mick, no!" The last word wrenched out in a sob as she burst into tears.

He dropped the bulky piece of furniture and pulled Hana into his empty arms as she stood there with her walker.

She flung her own arms around his neck, crying harder.

"I can sell the cradle, sweetheart. I swear, it's no big deal. I didn't ask what you want the baby to sleep in."

"It's not the cradle, it's beaut…beautiful. It's… Mick, I'm spotting."

"Spotting what?" He pulled a hand free to scrape wet hair out of her even wetter eyes.

"Blood. I'm spotting blood. That's the first sign of miscarriage. It…just…happened. I tried to phone you and your line was busy, so I called Danika. She's coming to get me to take me to the hospital. Dr. Walsh said if that ever happened, I should go in straight away without an appointment."

Mick's heart twisted. He thought he might throw up. Think. He had to think.

"Traffic's a nightmare, Hana. We're not waiting for Danika. I'll write her a note and tape it to the door. Why are you on your feet? I'll carry you to the car. No, to the clinic. It'd take longer finding a parking place."

"I'm so scared, Mick."

He was, too. And the first thing that came to his mind was that this was his fault. Their creative lovemaking had triggered this…spotting.

Hana didn't recall Danika's cell number offhand, so Mick wrote a note and put the PT's name on it. He couldn't find tape. Ultimately, he thumbtacked it to the door.

"Won't that ruin the wood?"

"I don't care." He lifted her carefully after locking the house. "I shouldn't have gone to meet Paul today."

"There's nothing you could've changed if you'd stayed home."

"I would've been here, and you'd be seeing Walsh right now."

"It only just started, Mick. I don't know what I did."

"Hana, I manhandled you last week. Thanksgiving night. I'll bet that did it."

"Mick, slow down. You're going to collapse and drop me. As for that night…we didn't really do *anything*."

"We were both plenty…you know…excited."

Hana ducked her head under his chin. "That's true. Still, I don't think anything that felt so good could be bad for me."

Mick's steps faltered. "You say that now, but that night you were p.o'd. Because I said I loved you, or because I asked you to marry me? Or both?"

"Neither. It's not your fault. I wanted more, Mick. I wanted you to love and accept my baby, too. Now," she said, breaking down again, "it's probably…not going to matter."

"Sweetheart, love… I do." Mick struggled to walk fast, breathe and talk all at the same time. "Dr. Walsh is the best doctor to deal with high-risk pregnancies."

"It's probably my fault because I want everything to be right for this baby."

"If that's the case, it's more mine—for acting like a jerk over its being Jess's baby. As I told you this morning, I had a real epiphany seeing Danika's baby album."

"You have every right to be unhappy with me, Mick. At first I was so mad at Jess I couldn't see straight. Then I was madder at myself. I need you to try to understand. I only had sex with Jess because I thought we were going to die. He let me think it."

Mick stopped walking. "Say that again?"

"It's true. Do you remember how bad the Great Bear Wilderness blaze was?" She didn't wait for Mick to answer. He'd started uphill to the clinic, so she kept pouring out her heart. "The fire cut Jess and me off from the rest of the crew. We dug a trench, but the blaze leaped it. We lit a backfire, and it crowned and raced through the tops of the trees, driving us farther from help. Fire singed my hair. My back was so hot I was afraid I'd fry. I'd never been so afraid of dying."

"Hana, you don't have to say any more. I don't care why you slept with Jess. He's gone. I love you, no matter how it happened."

"No. There'd always be questions lurking in your mind. I'm telling you, we both thought we were goners. It was dumb luck that Jess stumbled and literally fell headfirst into a cave. The fire was all around us. Jess had been trying to get in my pants since the day I started with Captain Martin's crew. I can't swear Jess knew we'd get out, but I know my life flashed before my eyes. He said we could suffocate. When the cave filled with smoke, I remember Jess said, *this is it, angel eyes, we're about to die.* My mind went numb. He began kissing me, and one thing led to another. About all I remember thinking was that I'd been alone all my life. And I didn't want to die alone."

"But you didn't die."

"No, and Jess, the creep, knew the cave. He knew there was a catacomb of rooms and a back way out that would land us in an area that'd already been burned. After he got what he'd wanted from me, he thought it was funny that I believed we'd bought the farm. That's what I meant when I told you in Kalispell that Jess was so irresponsible I'd never want him to be in my child's life. By the time I realized I'd missed three periods, I'd made up my mind to leave Martin's crew. I should never have gone mountain climbing. I did it because, well, that crew was the closest thing I had to a family."

"Don't stress about it, Hana. I've heard enough."

"I need to tell you everything. Up there, Jess got mad. He was so arrogant he thought I'd sleep with him again, if you can imagine. On the climb, he kept after me. We had a huge fight. Jess hated being told no. Inadvertently I guess I caused the fall. He took off because he was furious at me. Kari and I couldn't keep up. Then…I don't know…Jess slipped on ice. And…and you know the rest. He was an ass, but I should've been smarter. And mad as I was, I'd never have wished for him to die."

Mick clasped her tighter. "That story fits with the Jess I heard about. I'm glad you told me, Hana. I honestly couldn't reconcile the person I knew you to be with…well, with you having Jess Hargitay's baby."

"*My* baby. I don't want anything to happen to the baby."

"No. And we're here now. Stop beating yourself up. When Marlee and Wylie thought his son, Dean, might die from the same kind of cancer that killed Marlee's first husband, she said the doctor told them medicine works best amid positive thoughts and expectations. I'm going to park you in a chair, and have them page Dr. Walsh or Dr. Mancuso. While I'm doing that, you concentrate on positive thoughts."

Danika got there before Hana's doctor, who was handling a difficult delivery, arrived on the scene. However, Walsh had instructed the nursing staff to admit Hana, and they were in the process.

"You're shaking in your shoes, Hana," her friend said, squeezing her hand. "People spot in routine pregnancies, too. It's often nothing."

Hana made a face. "Maybe if mine was a routine pregnancy, I'd be less worried."

The nurses prepared to whisk Hana away. "No visitors until after the doctor examines her." A nurse Mick recognized from their many clinic visits issued the directive. Hana objected, but the nurse refused to budge. So Mick joined Danika outside the room. A pain in his left groin had him shifting and stretching out his leg.

Then it dawned on him that the pain was caused by the ring box. He dug out the package. "I bought something today.

Maybe you wouldn't mind giving me an opinion." He pulled out the larger of the two velvet boxes, and popped the top.

"Holy Sisters of Guadalupe." Danika's eyes widened.

"Is that a vote in favor? Will Hana like it?"

"I wish you hadn't waited this long to give it to her."

Mick glanced away. The stone winked in the harsh overhead light. "Because you think she may not accept it if, God forbid, she loses the baby?" He shut the box, threw away the bag and stuffed one box in each front pocket.

"Give the man a Kewpie doll."

Mick slumped, cracking the knuckles on one hand.

"Hana tells you to stop that. It's not helping her plight or yours, Mick."

"Her plight *is* mine." He leaned forward and rubbed his hands over his face. "I bought an antique cradle today. I carried it into the house, but then she hit me with the spotting thing. Rotten timing, huh?"

"It's a sweet gesture, if it's real."

"What do you mean *if?* Damn tootin' it's real."

"You haven't hidden your feelings well, Mick. You separated the fact that Hana's going to have a baby from any love you have for her."

"I did have reservations, but I've gotten past them."

"Good. What I told her about spotting being no big deal may be a stretch of the truth. The doctors can't let her go into labor. She's early. Too early."

"Tell me something I don't know."

"Can you cope if the baby's so premature it develops other problems? Possible blindness, or cerebral palsy. Failure to thrive, or immature lungs. Are you prepared to stay in California for weeks, or months if needed to get the baby's weight up?"

"Are you painting gloomy pictures in an attempt to drive

me off? It's not going to work. I love Hana. I'm in for the long haul."

She stood and slapped Mick's back heartily. "That's the spirit. Listen, I have an appointment in Oxnard at seven o'clock. I need to go." She pulled a business card out of her sports bag. "Here. Call my cell and let me know the doc's verdict. I'll say a prayer on the drive across town."

Mick took the card. "Thanks. Your lecture got me doing plenty of praying. You're a damn fine lecturer—like my twin."

"Tom says I do get on my soapbox. I rarely involve myself in a client's problems. There's just something about Hana...."

"Yes, there is. She's good to the bone. Life's given her too many hard knocks as it is, but I have my fingers crossed that her luck's ready to turn."

"Let's hope. See you, Mick."

Once again he was left the only person in a waiting room. And time dragged by so slowly.

At last Dr. Walsh stepped out of the room. Mick ran to meet him. "How's Hana? And the baby?"

"According to the fetal monitor she's having low-grade contractions now and then. They're not regular, which is good."

"What about the blood? The spotting?"

"We have her lower body elevated. For the time being, it seems the bleeding's stopped. I'm going to keep her overnight. She may have to stay longer. Possibly until we're forced to take the baby."

Mick massaged a nasty ache in his temples. "When might that be?"

"Son, when it comes to babies, there's simply no predicting what they'll do. I've put in a call for Rebecca, er...Dr. Mancuso. A precautionary measure to put her on alert."

"May I visit Hana?"

"By all means. My number one rule—keep a patient happy.

She's champing at the bit to see you. As I've said before, don't do anything to upset her."

"I bought her an engagement ring today. Do you think my giving it to her will fall in the upsetting category?"

The doctor studied Mick's strained features. "I'm remembering back to when I asked my wife—only she wasn't my wife then. She was relieved I'd finally wised up enough to pop the question. You have my permission. Ask loudly enough and with assurance enough that the little guy hears. I think babies are far more astute in the womb than many of my colleagues believe."

Walsh left and Mick beat a path to Hana's door. "Hi." He crossed the room, bent over the bed and kissed her lazily but thoroughly.

"Hi, yourself," she murmured. "You made a liar out of me, Mick. I told the team of nurses you were probably buying out the hospital gift shop. I expected bouquets and stuffed animals at least."

He straightened partially, dug in his pocket and came out with the ring box. "This didn't come from the gift shop. Will it do?" He opened the lid. The light over her bed brought out the rosy hue of the pink diamond.

All color drained from Hana's face. "Is that...real?"

"It better be." He took the ring from its slot and grasped her limp left hand. "I'm asking again. Will you marry me?" He slid the ring over her knuckle and breathed a sigh over the perfect fit. "I'm asking for better or for worse. In sickness and in health. Through this baby and maybe a few more. And everything in between this hour and when our hearts stop beating, Hana."

She lifted the hand that wasn't connected to drip lines. It wasn't her ring hand. She stroked Mick's hollow, stubbly cheek. "When I get out of here I wouldn't object to a simple service at the house before Christmas. You, me, a minister. Danika and Tom can witness."

"It's a date," he said, feeling tears push at the backs of his eyes. To hell if anyone saw and thought him unmanly. Letting them fall, he brushed her hair back, and kissed her softly and seriously.

CHAPTER FIFTEEN

A TOUCH-AND-GO WEEK that had Mick on edge worrying about Hana went by. On Wednesday of the second week of her forced bed rest, Dr. Walsh eased the flat-on-her-back restriction. Nurses got Hana up to walk around the room.

Mick brought her a fifteen-inch Christmas tree in a pot to celebrate.

"I love it." Hana walked over to inspect the decorations.

"Since you're doing better, I ought to run out and get busy on my Christmas shopping. I've left it so late I'll have to ship the presents for Marlee's family to my place and see if Kent Mackey can find a good enough day to fly them up to Wylie's."

"You shouldn't have hung out here all day every day. The children will be disappointed if your gifts don't arrive on time."

"I'm going to sign both our names on the tags. Is that all right?"

"I'd be pleased, but Mick, they don't know me."

"They're going to know you," he said, pulling a set of forms from his pocket. "Fill these out, and I'll get someone in Admissions to notarize your signature. If I take these to the courthouse, they'll give me our marriage license."

She held out her left hand and used her little finger to adjust her engagement ring. "I still have a hard time believing I didn't suddenly wake up in a dream. I keep hoping I'll improve enough for them to let me go home. Dr. Walsh said maybe tomorrow or the next day. I'd love it if we could be married before Christmas." She touched the star at the top of the little tree.

After she'd filled out the forms, she murmured, "Christmas is a holiday for families. But I've spent most Christmases alone."

That broke Mick's heart. He was determined this holiday and all holidays to come would be better for Hana.

"Don't overdo it while I'm out playing Santa." He tenderly gathered her close, and put his whole heart into a goodbye kiss.

Hana's eyes glowed when he released her. "I also dream of the day when I can be a real wife to you. A wife in every way, Mick."

He brushed a thumb across her lips. "I just want you well. We're not rushing…anything. From the day we say *I do,* we start a new life. We start our family."

She curved a palm around Mick's cheek. "I'm so afraid."

"Of what?" He clasped her hand and pressed a kiss to the center of her palm.

"That I'll wake up and find everything gone. You, the baby, all evaporated." She shivered even though Mick did his best to wrap his arms around her.

"Take a deep breath and relax. Everything's going to be smooth flying from here."

He left to go shopping, but reluctantly. And not before he stopped and talked to one of the nurses he knew. "I'm spending the day out, Jan. I'm going to try to make a dent in holiday shopping. Hana seems sort of down. Do you think you can check on her more often than usual?"

"No problem, Mick. I wish I could get my husband to handle our holiday buying. Don't worry about Hana. She's at that stage in pregnancy where emotions are a roller coaster. It's normal. Go on, get outta here."

Mick had his list. And once he hit one of the huge, three-level malls, he was like a horse headed to the barn after a hard day's ride. He bought the newest Barbie and accessories for Jo Beth, a cool train set for Dean, and clothes and household items for Wylie and Marlee. He found a sweater for Stella. What to get Rose Stein and her friend Emmett Nelson, who were spending the holidays at the Ames house? Rose loved to cook. Finally he decided on a holiday cookbook. A winter hat and gloves for Emmett. He could probably use them, being a San Diegan in snowy Montana.

Mick didn't forget small gifts for Danika's family.

Hana was the most difficult to buy for. He wanted to shower her with every nice thing he saw. He pared it down to a few items. A dainty watch to replace the clunky all-weather one she'd worn for work. He also bought an album, white with gold lettering that said Our Family.

A digital camera was next. There were so many to choose from, and all the special features boggled his mind. He eventually shut his eyes and picked one of the top three according to the salesman, a kid who had both ears, his lips and his tongue pierced. But he knew legions more about cameras than Mick.

He'd had the stores wrap everything, which saved him a lot of grief.

A call to Stella confirmed that Kent Mackey was more than happy to fly gifts up to Wylie's place.

"Kent says the weather reports are calling for a clearing over the holiday through to New Year's," Stella said. "That'll give you plenty of time to send the gifts. How's Hana?"

"Better. That's why I'm racing around in a buying frenzy. I'll get these gifts shipped, and then I'm off to buy a Christmas tree and decorations. It's weird driving by Christmas tree lots and seeing trees that come from our neck of the woods."

They laughed.

"So, you think Hana will be home by Christmas?"

"I'm counting on it. If you, or anyone you know, has a pipeline to the Man upstairs, pray for her and the baby, please."

"I will, Mick. He should be getting used to hearing Hana's and Marlee's names. Oh, by the way, the midwife showed up. Her snowmobile broke down a mile from Wylie's. He put on snowshoes, took an extra pair for her and trekked out. If it was me, I wouldn't have known how to use the darn things. She apparently did fine."

"Good. Wylie said he bought a camera cell phone. He's promised to try to forward early shots of the baby. If he's not too nervous. He's rattled. Usually he's the cool, collected park ranger."

"Just you wait until Hana's set to deliver."

"I can wait. Well, *I* can. They'd like her to get into January at least. But when the time comes, I'll try not to embarrass you all by making a fool of myself." They talked a bit more, then Mick took his purchases to a place where they boxed them up and handled shipping.

He decided on a tree right away. A mountain white fir. Its pungent scent made him homesick. He almost bought out the store of decorations. Uppermost in his mind, however, was giving Hana a tree so glorious she'd never forget their first Christmas together.

After he'd hauled everything into the house, he phoned Hana's room to touch base and tell her he'd be there for evening visiting hours.

"Mr. Callen, this is Jan Baker. Hana's in the middle of an ultrasound. May I take a message?"

"Ultrasound? Is everything all right?"

"They just set up, so there aren't any results yet. I'll have her phone as soon as they're finished."

Mick thought about leaving the tree to decorate later. He could be at the hospital in five minutes. He'd lost track of what dates they ran routine tests. Maybe this was one.

The tree fit in the bay window. He didn't have to move the sofa or chair. Because he kept imagining Hana's excitement, he loaded the tree with decorations, after all. Last year, the focus at Christmas time had been Marlee and Wylie's wedding. They'd put up a small tree at Pappy Jack's urging for Jo Beth's and Dean's sake. Dean had been too sick to fly there, which took much of the joy out of the holiday for everyone.

Mick hung a last twirling ball, then set a lighted angel on top. He hoped this would be a happier Christmas. Unplugging the lights, he set out for the hospital.

As he neared Hana's room, a flurry of activity in and out of her door caused Mick a stab of anxiety. He jostled someone in the waiting area, and grabbed hold of a nurse he didn't recognize who was leaving Hana's room.

"What's going on? Is it Hana? Tell me. I'm Mick Callen. Hana and I, we're going to be married."

The nurse, who'd been frightened by him, relaxed. "Dr. Walsh and Dr. Mancuso are with Hana. There was something in the ultrasound. I believe they're discussing surgery with her right now."

"Surgery? You mean to take the baby? It's too soon." Mick's brain fogged as he tried to calculate just how early. Three months. More than... He let go of the nurse's arm and barged into the room, his heart pounding like a kettle drum.

Hana heard the disturbance at the door and stopped mopping her eyes with a crumpled tissue. "Mick, oh, Mick! It's time. But it's way too early. Dr. Mancuso left to go make preparations with infant ICU."

Dr. Walsh injected a calm voice into the hubbub around Hana's bed. "The baby's vitals aren't the greatest, Mick. There's growing fetal distress. We could wait and run more tests, but as I explained to Hana, since we have to give her a low dose of a general anesthesia, that further depresses the baby. So the question is do we wait and risk more problems? Waiting may buy us days. Or with extreme luck, a full week. I'm leaning toward not waiting."

"You know best," Mick muttered, forging his way to Hana's side. She squeezed his hand for dear life. It was her left one. The diamond he'd bought flashed mockingly.

Mick faced Dr. Walsh. "How long before you take her to surgery?"

"An hour. Right now all surgical suites are in use. You have time to change into scrubs, Mick. I know Hana wants you to be there."

"I want that, too. But…I also want us to be married before she has the baby."

"Mick, that's not possible." Hana tried to sit up, but a nurse pressed her back.

"Hana, listen to me. If we're married, the baby has my last name. The birth certificate will say *Callen.* Do you remember telling me how strangers picked your last name, and it has no meaning? It's important to me that this little sprout be ours. Yours and mine. No adoption process to juggle afterward. I'll be the one, the only, father."

Hana's tear-swollen eyes sought the doctor. "Is it crazy or is it possible? I'd like that…a lot." Her free hand covered her stomach.

Dr. Walsh rubbed his brow. "It's crazy, all right. You'd need a license and that takes time I'm not sure we have."

"We have our license. The day I gave Hana her ring, Lucy Steel notarized her signature and phoned a judge at the courthouse. They processed the license today. It's…uh…at the house."

"Then we can do it. Somebody find the hospital chaplain and get him up here on the double. Mick, you run home and get the license." Nurses scattered. Walsh shot Mick a stern look. "You'll have to make do. No time for fuss or bother. You probably won't even know your witnesses."

Mick slid his hand up to cradle the back of Hana's head. "I realize it's not what we planned—"

"Nothing from the start of this pregnancy has been planned, Mick. This is a huge step for you. What if the baby has weeks or months or years of health problems? Or doesn't survive," she said in a smaller, strained voice.

He stopped her ramblings with a kiss. "For better or worse, remember?"

She nodded because she was too choked up to say anything more.

He hurried out. In fifteen minutes he was back, out of breath and ripping open a package that held three disposable cameras. He handed them out, then gave Nurse Jan their license.

Shortly thereafter, a slightly flustered, rumpled man of the cloth bustled through the door. He pulled a well-thumbed Bible from his inner jacket pocket. "As a rule, I have questions I ask a prospective bride and groom. But I hear we're racing the clock, so I'll dispense with preliminaries. You both look old enough to know your minds. Names, please. Do I have two volunteers who'll stand up with this couple?"

"I should be running off to scrub for your surgery, Hana," said Dr. Walsh. "But if Reverend Porter can speed up his speech, I'll be happy to do the honors."

Jan Baker stepped up to the other side of Hana's bed. She was a nurse they both liked a lot. "Me. I want to witness. I'm so excited. I love you both. No two people belong together more."

The minister cleared his throat. "Well, if I needed a testimonial, Ms. Baker just provided one." He opened the Bible, but spoke from memory. "Dearly beloved…"

Seconds after the last word was spoken, Dr. Walsh instructed Mick, "Hurry, son, kiss your bride quickly." Flashes twinkled from the bystanders Mick had commandeered to take photos.

Walsh headed for the door. "Nurses, prep my patient. Richard," he said to the pastor, "sign the marriage documents and drop them by my office. This wedding is official, isn't it?" He looked askance at the hustle and bustle going on in the hospital room.

"It's official. Shall I stick around to christen the baby?"

Mick wore a sappy grin as he collected cameras. "Would you be so kind, Reverend? I'd like you to, if Hana agrees."

"Yes, all prayers are welcome." Her voice quavered as two orderlies wheeled her out the door.

Mick trailed behind, his knees knocking. He let himself be shoved in a room to don blue scrubs and blue socks over his boots. His hands shook so badly he found it nearly impossible to tie the mask. Then he paced in circles, worried about what came next.

An out-of-breath nurse stuck her head in the room and beckoned to Mick. "We're ready for you. I understand you have a camera."

"Three," Mick rasped. He grabbed them off the chair and clumsily dropped them all in a clatter. The nurse stooped to collect them.

"If you have a cell phone, turn it off, or put it on vibrate. No camera flash in the doctors' eyes. I've been instructed to tell you that after the baby is cleaned up, Dr. Mancuso will take charge. The baby will go directly into an isolette and while Hana, er, your wife is stitched up, you can either stay or watch what's going on with the baby from the window outside ICU."

Mick felt torn. "What does Hana want me to do?"

"She said you'd ask. She wants you to keep tabs on the baby."

His throat too constricted to speak, Mick nodded his head. His palms were so sweaty that, after pocketing a camera, he rubbed them repeatedly on the blue cotton.

He'd been in enough surgical suites that he should be an old hand. He considered himself a strong man. But from the first cut along Hana's stark white abdomen and the sight of red oozing along the thin line, Mick was sweating like a Missouri mule. He feared he'd disgrace himself and faint dead away.

He kept it together because Dr. Walsh and his team clamped off the bleeders in record time. Mick barely had time to wipe his forehead on his sleeve when the doctor had the baby out.

"Picture time," a nurse whispered, nudging Mick.

His heart was so filled with wonder and joy, he nearly couldn't snap the shot. The tiny red body did have reddish blond fuzz, just as Mick imagined that day at Danika's. Suddenly, other hands reached up and the baby disappeared from Mick's view. Dr. Walsh called for a needle to stitch Hana.

Around Mick, everyone looked strained until a thin, shrill cry rent the air.

Dr. Mancuso bobbed up briefly. "It's a boy. Weight, two pounds, six ounces. If I stretch him, fifteen inches. Apgar six."

It registered with Mick that they'd had a baby boy. "A boy, a boy," he shouted, grinning at no one, because Hana was out, of course. Mick couldn't have been prouder if he'd truly fathered the baby. He grinned and blubbered to anyone within earshot.

A different nurse than the one who'd led him to the operating room ushered him out. "Two pounds plus is good," she said. "The six Apgar isn't fantastic, but it's not bad for a six-month preemie."

"What's that mean, Apgar?"

"It's a scale by which we register the baby's heart rate, respirations and all other vitals." They stopped beside a clear glass window. Inside, a host of green-clad nurses ministered to Hana's baby. *His and Hana's baby.*

Mick rested his forehead against the glass. He sensed that the baby squalled, although not much sound penetrated the thick pane. Little arms and legs pumped. He counted ten fingers on red, wrinkled hands, and five toes on each flailing foot. He didn't move until a hand clasped his shoulder and squeezed. Mick jerked up. "Dr. Walsh. Oh…if you're here, then Hana's done. How…how is she?"

"Groggy, but fine. We'll keep her in Recovery a while. She'll drift in and out for the rest of today. You can see her as soon as she's settled in a room."

"Did you tell her she…uh…we have a beautiful boy?"

"I did. She needed to hear he came through fine. Dr. Mancuso will monitor him closely. He'll be with us for some time, Mick. His lungs aren't fully developed and his weight needs to come up a couple of pounds. He'll be on oxygen and hyperalimentation fluids. This won't be easy on you, but it'll be worse for Hana. She'll be healing from a cesarean, yet she'll want to spend hours here with the baby. It'd be good if she can pump breast milk once it comes in, and bring it over. That won't be fun." He took a quick breath. "He'll be confined to an isolette. However, we've found preemies do better if parents reach in and touch them, or slip their hands under the babies and rock them. You'll both have to wear masks and gowns at each and every visit."

"We'll do whatever you and Dr. Mancuso say. He's a gift. It's a miracle he's alive."

"You've had quite a miraculous day. A wedding, a baby— it's truly the Christmas season. Come by my office before you go home to collect your marriage certificate. Have you two named your son?"

"Uh, we batted a few names around. I'll defer to anything Hana wants."

"No need to rush. Staff will be around with forms. But I expect you'll want to notify your family soon." He slapped Mick on the back and sauntered off.

Family. Mick should phone Marlee. He should also let Stella know. And Danika. But he was feeling his way here. Shouting from the rooftop was Hana's right. Or they could make the calls together when she got to a room. Mick liked that idea best.

He tiptoed in to see her the minute a nurse said it was time. He expected to find her weak, or sleeping. She leaned up on an elbow and welcomed him with an undignified whoop. "You've seen him, Mick. How does he look? Gorgeous?"

"Handsome." Mick kissed her. "Boys are handsome, my love. And yes, he's all boy. He has your hair color. I didn't see his eyes. They put pads on to keep out the light. But a nurse told me that, for as little as he is, he's giving them hell."

She settled back against a pillow. "We'll be good parents, won't we, Mick?"

He pulled up a chair, took her hand and kissed her knuckles as he sat. "We'll be the best. We have to name him. Would you like me to go home and get your list?"

"If it's still okay with you, I'm set on Jack. It's simple and strong."

Mick had a hard time swallowing, so he kissed her hand again. "We could use your last name as his middle name."

"As I said, Egan's not really who I am. I never ran this past you, but I thought a lot about your nephew calling you Sky Knight. How does Jack Knight Callen suit you? You're my idea of a knight in or out of the sky. And it'll give our son another important tie to you. Maybe he'll follow in your footsteps if you teach him to fly. Then he can volunteer for Angel Fleet."

"I don't know what to say, Hana. You've already given me so much by marrying me and allowing me to share Jack. Letting me teach him to fly would be like…you can't know how I've imagined teaching a son to fly, like my dad and Pappy Jack taught me."

"Then it's settled. I'm dying to see him. They said maybe in a few hours, if I'm wheeled down. Will you take me?"

"Yes, but I have something for now. I took a few digital pictures on my cell phone. I thought we'd phone Marlee, Danika and a few others. I wanted photos to transfer."

She squealed. Together they fawned over the grainy shots before making their picks. Wylie answered at the Ames house. "Mick, you must have twin-radar. How did you know Marlee's an hour into honest-to-goodness labor?"

Mick and Hana shared private shock as they held the phone between them. "Uh, that's not why I called. Hana and I got married. Today. Not long before she had the baby. We beat you, buddy. We have a son. Tell Marlee we named him Jack. For Pappy. Hold on a minute and we'll transfer a photo. He's a little guy, but damn, Wylie, he's beautiful. And he'll grow."

Hana punched his arm. "You're silly. Have him tell Marlee we'll keep our fingers crossed that all goes well for her. They should call us as soon as they have the baby."

Wylie agreed. He said Rose was yelling for him and he had to go. Not before saying, though, that Jack was a charmer.

They worked through the rest of their calls. Danika screamed with delight. "How soon can you have visitors? Oh, wait, I need to buy a baby gift. A boy. And you're okay, Hana? C-sections can be rough."

Hana felt on top of the world. Within hours, she'd badgered nurses into letting her and Mick gown up to visit baby Jack.

Mick was afraid to touch him, he was so little. "He looked bigger through the window," he whispered. Without hesitation, Hana reached through the arm holes in the isolette. She didn't lift him, but stroked his back and tiny feet and hands. Mick decided he could do that, too.

Hana overtaxed herself. She was nodding off before they made it back to her room. Mick prepared to go home for the night when his cell vibrated. Wylie's number appeared on the readout.

"About time you called. What took Marlee so long? She said second babies came fast. Nine pounds?" Mick turned to Hana and they both gasped. "A girl. Bridget Eve. I like that. Eve is after our mom," Mick muttered in an aside to Hana. With Wylie again, Mick said, "So, we both got early Christmas gifts. Nine pounds, sheesh. Bridget makes four of Jack. We'll have to feed him a lot so he can catch up. I'm sure he'll be holding his own by the time we see you at Easter."

Hana took the phone. She and Marlee compared the virtues of their babies. A few minutes later, Mick took the phone. "I'll let you go, Marlee. You should rest, and so should Hana. I'd like her home by Christmas. Dr. Walsh said Jack will have to stay in the hospital a month or two, or more."

The siblings said their goodbyes.

"Do you need to get back to Montana before then?" Hana asked Mick.

"Honey, I'll stay here until you're both cleared to travel. Perhaps longer. You and I need time to learn how to be parents after Jack's released. I'm also not keen on taking a premature baby to Montana until the weather warms up. We'll shoot for getting home by Easter. We're invited to Wylie and Marlee's for that weekend."

A WEEK PASSED before Hana was discharged. Jack had gone down to one pound fourteen ounces. He faced a long, slow climb up to five pounds.

"I know how happy you are to be able to walk without holding a pillow over your incision, Hana. Please, though, let me carry you across the threshold. You got nothing else of the wedding you and Danika were planning." They both now wore matching wedding bands, and Hana had her solitaire.

She held up her arms and sank against him as he hoisted her up. "It's not the wedding frou-frou that matters, Mick. I love you so very much."

He kissed her as they crossed into the living room. When he set her down on her feet, the beautiful Christmas tree was the first thing she saw. Hana covered her trembling lips with one hand. "It's so beautiful. And all those gifts. Where did they come from?"

"My family, Danika's, and a couple from me."

Between the time she arrived home and Christmas Eve, Hana did little but sit and admire the tree. During the day, she pumped breast milk for Jack, and they made visits to the nursery.

Because Hana hadn't been able to get out and shop, the majority of the gifts were for her and Jack. She opened all of them. Mick was content to bask in her excited glow. She unwrapped a baby quilt that had appliqued airplanes on a blue background scattered with puffy white clouds, and lovingly placed it in the dark wood cradle.

"It's from…Rose. Mick, listen to her note. *Hana, we've never met. When I lost my husband and then my son, and Marlee went off to Montana with my only grandchild, I became*

*a bitter woman. Now I'm happy. I have my granddaughter
back. As well, I'm acting grandmother to Dean and little
Bridget. If you don't mind, I have enough love in my heart to
include Jack.*

"She's never met me. Yet she's willing to complete Jack's
extended family."

"Rose has come a long way. All I can say is don't swear
around her." He grinned. "But if you forget, my niece, Jo
Beth, will remind you."

"I can't wait to go home to Montana and meet your family."

"Your family, too."

She smiled, crossed the room and sat on his lap for a kiss.
"That's for Santa."

NEW YEAR'S DAY approached. They hadn't missed a day of
visiting Jack. They were relieved and happy to hear the nurses
talk about how much he'd improved. Alert, he appeared to
relish his parents' touch.

Mick floated on air—without a plane. Although he had
cajoled Hana into taking a short flight along the coast to San
Diego on New Year's Day—to shake out the kinks in his plane,
Mick had said.

Hana later discovered it was to allow Danika time to go in
and set up a special holiday table for two with gleaming china
and ready-to-light tapers. "I feel so treasured," she told Mick.

They drifted into a routine after the first of the year that
suited them both. As the weeks passed, they bought a few
items for the makeshift nursery. They slept together in Mick's
room, but since the alcove was off Hana's old room, they
decided to exchange the beds. As time wore on, it became
more difficult to be creative without making love. But Dr.
Walsh still hadn't given Hana the okay.

Jack continued to thrive, and one day in mid-February Dr.

Mancuso told them he could go home with them the next day. "Two o'clock," she said. "Mick, will you stick around while Hana sees Dr. Walsh? I have some weight and height charts I'd like you to take with you to fill out, and we also need to go over the timetable for starting solid foods and so forth."

Mick had been accompanying Hana to her checkups. He slowly released her hand. "You okay to go by yourself?"

"Sure, Mick. And if there's anything we need for the baby that we haven't bought, why don't you go to the store afterward. It's a gorgeous day. I'll walk home after my appointment."

"Okay." Mick thought they had any- and everything a baby could need. But, he discovered, they didn't have a scale. "We need this particular brand?" he asked Dr. Mancuso. "Who stocks them?"

She named a store, and handed Mick the phone book to look up the address. "But it's two suburbs away and I'll get caught in rush-hour traffic. Maybe I'll wait and go in the morning."

"You'll have to listen to Hana fret all night. Mark my words."

Mick reluctantly gathered the instructions and took off for the store. He was right; he got tied up in stop-and-go traffic. He phoned home. "Sorry, babe, the San Diego Freeway is backed up to hell and gone. If you're hungry, eat without me. How did the appointment go?"

"Oh, fine. How long will you be?"

He glanced at his watch and saw it was later than he'd thought. He sighed. "If I get home by seven o'clock it'll be a bonus."

"That's okay. Take your time."

"Hana, are you sure you're okay? I should've waited to pick up this baby scale another day."

"I'm fine. I only meant I don't want you getting in a wreck."

He got home at ten after seven. The scale was big. He bumped and battered the door going in. "Honey? Where are you?"

"In our room."

The house was dark except for a sliver of light coming from under their bedroom door. He banged his way in, expecting Hana to be sitting in the rocker reading. She stood looking in the round mirror on the antique dresser. Only, she was watching Mick. And she had on a slinky, backless nightgown in come-hither red.

He dropped the box with the scale, and swore when it hit his toe.

Hana smiled. "Good thing Grandmother Rose isn't around."

"What gives?" Only the base of the lamp was lit. Candles in dishes flickered throughout the room. The bed was turned down. White sheets gleamed. Satin. And were those rose petals spilling off the bed onto the floor?

"What gives is that Dr. Walsh gave me clearance today."

"Clearance?" Mick edged slowly across the room.

"Yes, Mick. I'm healed…everywhere. Tonight you can truly make me your wife."

Her words were music to Mick's ears—and other parts of his body as well. He couldn't shed his shirt and jeans fast enough.

Hana's laughter tinkled delightedly as he tumbled her into the bed of rose petals. The floral aroma permeated the room as Mick rolled her atop him, and his back crushed cool, delicate petals.

Though his blood pounded in his ears and raged through his veins, Mick didn't rush. He took his time, kissing the tiny straps down her arms, until she was as naked as he was and they were both dying for completion. "The last thing I ever want to do is hurt you, Hana. If I get too rough because it's been so long—and I've imagined this moment for longer than you know—say halt and I will."

She didn't.

They made love not once, but twice that night.

"I feel as if tonight is our honeymoon," she breathed into his ear later.

"A short honeymoon," Mick lamented. "Tomorrow we hit the ground running as new parents."

But they were prepared. They'd been planning and waiting to bring Jack home for eight weeks.

FOR ANOTHER month and a half they reveled in the job of parenting, but also in the sheer joy of being husband and wife.

"I'm anxious to get back to Montana," Hana said one day in early April as they were in the middle of packing their few belongings. "I'm scared, too. What if, after all this, your friends and family don't like me?"

"They'll love you. Honey, you're not having second thoughts? Montana's in my blood. Flying for Cloud Chasers is in my soul."

"If I said I wanted to stay here in California, would you go anyway?"

"Are you kidding? I don't know what I'd do to pay our bills, but I'd stay, yes. You and Jack are my life."

"It was mean of me to tease, Mick. Part of me is still that abandoned little girl. I have to pinch myself every day when I look up and you're still here."

Mick passed her the white leather album he'd bought her for Christmas. She traced a finger around the words *Our Family*.

"Look inside."

She turned back the cover and page after page, and discovered Mick had taken photos of her, of her and Jack, of the three of them. She hadn't realized, hadn't seen him snapping pictures. But there it was in color, their life together.

"When this album's full, we'll fill another, and another until we're old and gray. Then we'll take pictures of Jack's kids."

Closing the book, Hana hugged it tight. She set it carefully in the last of the boxes. "I understand, Mick. You really mean this is forever. I'm ready. Take me home."

STELLA HAD Welcome Home signs along the runway. She'd baked an apple pie and left a casserole warming in the oven. Homecoming was like the culmination of a lifelong dream for Hana.

Mick led her by the hand through the house. Jack gurgled in a cloth carrier strapped to his father's chest. "If you don't like the nursery, we can do something else, Hana. I had Stella get Kent to help her bring down half the nursery set from the attic. This is what the folks used for Marlee and me."

"No wonder you fell in love with the cradle you bought Jack. It looks as if it matches this set. This has such history." She trailed a finger over the dresser. "I need history. I can't fathom changing a thing. Well, maybe a few ruffles here and there in the kitchen. The house is just as you described it, Mick. A man's domain."

"Yeah. Marlee wasn't here long enough to add a feminine stamp. You have free rein to do any and all of that you want."

She barely had time to get a feel for her new home before it was time to fly up to the Ames place for Easter weekend.

The whole Ames clan—Wylie, Marlee, Dean, Jo Beth and pudgy little Bridget Eve—awaited them on the path when Mick landed the Arrow.

Mick, Hana and Jack looked tanned and healthy next to the winter pallor of Marlee and the kids. Wylie, thanks to his Native American roots, had skin that looked tanned year-round.

Under the trees there were still patches of snow. Hana shivered, and Marlee herded them all back to the house.

The kitchen smelled of cinnamon and baked ham. Wingman and Piston bounded up, barked a greeting at Mick and sniffed Hana and Jack's kicking feet.

"Uncle Mick, now that you have a son are you going to want to take Wingman home again? My dad thought you might."

"Dean, I said the animal shelters are filled with good dogs. Wingman's yours. Hana and I will get another dog once Jack's walking and is steady on his feet."

The boy flung his arms around his uncle. Then Dean and Jo Beth tore off somewhere to play with their pets.

Wylie hauled out a new fishing rod to show Mick. "I've been checking the calendar. I figure a couple of years down the road, you and I can teach Bridget and Jack all they need to know about the good fishing holes between here and Whitepine."

Mick nodded and then cast a warm smile in the direction of the women. "Hana's given me leave to teach Jack to fly. I've been thinking twelve's a good age. We'll have to see if Dean's interested in the Callen family trade."

His sister threw a cushion and her aim was true. "You'd leave out Jo Beth and Bridget? Why, Mick? Because they're girls? What macho lies have you told your wife?" Marlee turned to Hana. "I outflew him until we went to the Naval Academy. I wouldn't want to accuse them of being sexist, but Mick got the better appointments and ended up a fighter pilot, which was the job I coveted. Let me remind you that Angel

Fleet didn't turn either of us down as volunteers. They were certainly happy with how I flew."

Wylie popped the tops off two beers and handed one to Mick. "I could tell you about the landing your sister made on her first trip here. But I won't. She has assets you don't, buddy."

Marlee threw a couch pillow at Wylie, too. He ducked and they all laughed.

Hana hardest of all. She finally had a real family. Listening to the men blithely talking about teaching the kids to fish and fly, her heart sensed that Mick's love for her and Jack was lasting. More content than she'd ever been, Hana settled back with a cup of coffee her once pretend-sister, now sister by marriage, handed her. She smiled and warmed her hands on the cup.

And Hana Lee Callen considered herself the luckiest woman in all of Montana.

* * * * *

Ambience is everything. Imagine eating a foie gras at a luncheonette counter or a side of coleslaw at Le Cirque. It's not a matter of food but one of atmosphere. Remember that when planning your dining room design.
—Tips from *Teddi.com*

"Now that's the kind of man you should be looking for," my mother, the self-appointed keeper of my shelf-life stamp, says. She points with her fork at a man in the corner of the Steak-Out Restaurant, a dive I've just been hired to redecorate. Making this restaurant look four-star will be hard, but not half as hard as getting through lunch without strangling the woman across the table from me. "*He* would make a good husband."

"Oh, you can tell that from across the room?" I ask, wondering how it is she can forget that when we had trouble getting rid of my last husband, she shot him. "Besides being ten minutes away from death if he actually eats all that steak, he's twenty years too old for me and—shallow woman that I am—twenty pounds too heavy. Besides, I am *so* not looking for another husband here. I'm looking to design a new image for this place, looking for some sense of ambience, some feeling, something I can build a proposal on for them."

My mother studies the man in the corner, tilting her head, the better to gauge his age, I suppose. I think she's grimacing, but with all the Botox and Restylane injected into that face, it's hard to tell. She takes another bite of her steak, chews slowly so that I don't miss the fact that the steak is a poor cut and tougher than it should be. "You're concentrating on the wrong kind of proposal," she says finally. "Just look at this place, Teddi. It's a dive. There are hardly any other diners. What does *that* tell you about the food?"

"That they cater to a dinner crowd and it's lunchtime," I tell her.

I don't know what I was thinking bringing her here with me. I suppose I thought it would be better than eating alone. There really are days when my common sense goes on vacation. Clearly, this is one of them. I mean, really, did I not resolve less than three weeks ago that I would not let my mother get to me anymore?

What good are New Year's resolutions, anyway?

Mario approaches the man's table and my mother studies him while they converse. Eventually Mario leaves the table with a huff, after which the diner glances up and meets my mother's gaze. I think she's smiling at him. That or she's got indigestion. They size each other up.

I concentrate on making sketches in my notebook and try to ignore the fact that my mother is flirting. At nearly seventy, she's developed an unhealthy interest in members of the opposite sex to whom she isn't married.

According to my father, who has broken the TMI rule and given me Too Much Information, she has no interest in sex with him. Better, I suppose, to be clued in on what they aren't doing in the bedroom than have to hear what they might be doing.

"He's not so old," my mother says, noticing that I have barely touched the Chinese chicken salad she warned me not to get. "He's got about as many years on you as you have on your little cop friend."

She does this to make me crazy. I know it, but it works all the same. "Drew Scoones is not my little 'friend.' He's a detective with whom I—"

"Screwed around," my mother says. I must look shocked, because my mother laughs at me and asks if I think she doesn't know the "lingo."

What I thought she didn't know was that Drew and I actually tangled in the sheets. And, since it's possible she's just fishing, I sidestep the issue and tell her that Drew is just a couple of years younger than me and that I don't need reminding. I dig into my salad with renewed vigor, determined to show my mother that Chinese chicken salad in a steak place was not the stupid choice it's proving to be.

After a few more minutes of my picking at the wilted leaves on my plate, the man my mother has me nearly engaged to pays his bill and heads past us toward the back of the restaurant. I watch my mother take in his shoes, his suit and the diamond pinkie ring that seems to be cutting off the circulation in his little finger.

"Such nice hands," she says after the man is out of sight. "Manicured." She and I both stare at my hands. I have two popped acrylics that are being held on at weird angles by bandages. My cuticles are ragged and there's marker decorating my right hand from measuring carelessly when I did a drawing for a customer.

Twenty minutes later she's disappointed that he managed to leave the restaurant without our noticing. He will join the list of the ones I let get away. I will hear about him twenty years from now when—according to my mother—my children will be grown and I will still be single, living pathetically alone with several dogs and cats.

After my ex, that sounds good to me.

The waitress tells us that our meal has been taken care of by the management and, after thanking Mario, the owner, complimenting him on the wonderful meal and assuring him that once I have redecorated his place people will be flocking here in droves (I actually use those words and ignore my mother when she rolls her eyes), my mother and I head for the restroom.

My father—unfortunately not with us today—has the patience of a saint. He got it over the years of living with my mother. She, perhaps as a result, figures he has the patience for both of them, and feels justified having none. For her, no rules apply, and a little thing like a picture of a man on the door to a public restroom is certainly no barrier to using the john. In all fairness, it does seem silly to stand and wait for the ladies' room if no one is using the men's room.

Still, it's the idea that rules don't apply to her, signs don't apply to her, conventions don't apply to her. She knocks on the door to the men's room. When no one answers she gestures to me to go in ahead. I tell her that I can certainly wait for the ladies' room to be free and she shrugs and goes in herself.

Not a minute later there is a bloodcurdling scream from behind the men's room door.

"Mom!" I yell. "Are you all right?"

Mario comes running over, the waitress on his heels. Two customers head our way while my mother continues to scream.

I try the door, but it is locked. I yell for her to open it and she fumbles with the knob. When she finally manages to unlock and open it, she is white behind her two streaks of blush, but she is on her feet and appears shaken but not stirred.

"What happened?" I ask her. So do Mario and the waitress and the few customers who have migrated to the back of the place.

She points toward the bathroom and I go in, thinking it serves her right for using the men's room. But I see nothing amiss.

She gestures toward the stall, and, like any self-respecting and suspicious woman, I poke the door open with one finger, expecting the worst.

What I find is worse than the worst.

The husband my mother picked out for me is sitting on the toilet. His pants are puddled around his ankles, his hands are hanging at his sides. Pinned to his chest is some sort of Health Department certificate.

Oh, and there is a large, round, bloodless bullet hole between his eyes.

Four Nassau County police officers are securing the area, waiting for the detectives and crime scene personnel to show up. They are trying, though not very hard, to comfort my mother, who in another era would be considered to be suffering from the vapors. Less tactful in the twenty-first century, I'd say she was losing it. That is, if I didn't know her better, know she was milking it for everything it was worth.

My mother loves attention. As it begins to flag, she swoons and claims to feel faint. Despite four No Smoking signs, my mother insists it's all right for her to light up because, after all, she's in shock. Not to mention that signs, as we know, don't apply to her.

When asked not to smoke, she collapses mournfully in a chair and lets her head loll to the side, all without mussing her hair.

Eventually, the detectives show up to find the four patrolmen all circled around her, debating whether to administer CPR, smelling salts or simply call the paramedics. I, however, know just what will snap her to attention.

"Detective Scoones," I say loudly. My mother parts the sea of cops.

"We have to stop meeting like this," he says lightly to me, but I can feel him checking me over with his eyes, making sure I'm all right while pretending not to care.

"What have you got in those pants?" my mother asks him, coming to her feet and staring at his crotch accusingly. "*Baydar?* Everywhere we Bayers are, you turn up. You don't expect me to buy that this is a coincidence, I hope."

Drew tells my mother that it's nice to see her, too, and asks if it's his fault that her daughter seems to attract disasters.

Charming to be made to feel like the bearer of a plague.

He asks how I am.

"Just peachy," I tell him. "I seem to be making a habit of finding dead bodies, my mother is driving me crazy and the catering hall I booked two freakin' years ago for Dana's bat mitzvah has just been shut down by the Board of Health!"

"Glad to see your luck's finally changing," he says, giving me a quick squeeze around the shoulders before turning his attention to the patrolmen, asking what they've got, whether they've taken any statements, moved anything, all the sort of stuff you see on TV, without any of the drama. That is, if you don't count my mother's threats to faint every few minutes when she senses no one's paying attention to her.

Mario tells his waitstaff to bring everyone espresso, which I decline because I'm wired enough. Drew pulls him aside and a minute later I'm handed a cup of coffee that smells divinely of Kahlúa.

The man knows me well. Too well.

His partner, whom I've met once or twice, says he'll interview the kitchen staff. Drew asks Mario if he minds if he takes statements from the patrons first and gets to him and the wait staff afterward.

"No, no," Mario tells him. "Do the patrons first." Drew raises his eyebrow at me like he wants to know if I get the double entendre. I try to look bored.

"What is it with you and murder victims?" he asks me when we sit down at a table in the corner.

I search them out so that I can see you again, I almost say, but I'm afraid it will sound desperate instead of sarcastic.

My mother, lighting up and daring him with a look to tell her not to, reminds him that *she* was the one to find the body.

Drew asks what happened *this time*. My mother tells him how the man in the john was "taken" with me, couldn't take his eyes off me and blatantly flirted with both of us. To his credit, Drew doesn't laugh, but his smirk is undeniable to the trained eye. And I've had my eye trained on him for nearly a year now.

"While he was noticing you," he asks me, "did *you* notice anything about him? Was he waiting for anyone? Watching for anything?"

I tell him that he didn't appear to be waiting or watching. That he made no phone calls, was fairly intent on eating and did, indeed, flirt with my mother. This last bit Drew takes with a grain of salt, which was the way it was intended.

"And he had a short conversation with Mario," I tell him. "I think he might have been unhappy with the food, though he didn't send it back."

Drew asks what makes me think he was dissatisfied, and I tell him that the discussion seemed acrimonious and that Mario looked distressed when he left the table. Drew makes a note and says he'll look into it and asks about anyone else in the restaurant. Did I see anyone who didn't seem to belong, anyone who was watching the victim, anyone looking suspicious?

"Besides my mother?" I ask him, and Mom huffs and blows her cigarette smoke in my direction.

I tell him that there were several deliveries, the kitchen staff going in and out the back door to grab a smoke. He stops me and asks what I was doing checking out the back door of the restaurant.

Proudly—because, while he was off forgetting me, dropping by only once in a while to say hi to Jesse, my son, or drop something by for one of my daughters that he thought they might like, I was getting on with my life—I tell him that I'm decorating the place.

He looks genuinely impressed. "Commercial customers? That's great," he says. Okay, that's what he *ought* to say. What he actually says is "Whatever pays the bills."

"Howard Rosen, the famous restaurant critic, got her the job," my mother says. "You met him—the good-looking, distinguished gentleman with the *real* job, something to be proud of. I guess you've never read his reviews in *Newsday*."

Drew, without missing a beat, tells her that Howard's reviews are on the top of his list, as soon as he learns how to read.

"I only meant—" my mother starts, but both of us assure her that we know just what she meant.

"So," Drew says. "Deliveries?"

I tell him that Mario would know better than I, but that I saw vegetables come in, maybe fish and linens.

"This is the second restaurant job Howard's got her," my mother tells Drew.

"At least she's getting *something* out of the relationship," he says.

"If he were here," my mother says, ignoring the insinuation, "he'd be comforting her instead of interrogating her. He'd be making sure we're both all right after such an ordeal."

"I'm sure he would," Drew agrees, then looks me in the eyes as if he's measuring my tolerance for shock. Quietly he adds, "But then maybe he doesn't know just what strong stuff your daughter's made of."

It's the closest thing to a tender moment I can expect from Drew Scoones. My mother breaks the spell. "She gets that from me," she says.

Both Drew and I take a minute, probably to pray that's all I inherited from her.

"I'm just trying to save you some time and effort," my mother tells him. "My money's on Howard."

Drew withers her with a look and mutters something that sounds suspiciously like "fool's gold." Then he excuses himself to go back to work.

I catch his sleeve and ask if it's all right for us to leave. He says sure, he knows where we live. I say goodbye to Mario. I assure him that I will have some sketches for him in a few days, all the while hoping that this murder doesn't cancel his redecorating plans. I need the money desperately, the alternative being borrowing from my parents and being strangled by the strings.

My mother is strangely quiet all the way to her house. She doesn't tell me what a loser Drew Scoones is—despite his good looks—and how I was obviously drooling over him. She doesn't ask me where Howard is taking me tonight or warn me not to tell my father about what happened because he will worry about us both and no doubt insist we see our respective psychiatrists.

She fidgets nervously, opening and closing her purse over and over again.

"You okay?" I ask her. After all, she's just found a dead man on the toilet, and tough as she is that's got to be upsetting.

When she doesn't answer me I pull over to the side of the road.

"Mom?" She refuses to meet my eyes. "You want me to take you to see Dr. Cohen?"

She looks out the window as if she's just realized we're on Broadway in Woodmere. "Aren't we near Marvin's Jewelers?" she asks, pulling something out of her purse.

"What have you got, Mother?" I ask, prying open her fingers to find the murdered man's ring.

"It was on the sink," she says in answer to my dropped jaw. "I was going to get his name and address and have you return it to him so that he could ask you out. I thought it was a sign that the two of you were meant to be together."

"He's dead, Mom. You understand that, right?" I ask. You never can tell when my mother is fine and when she's in la-la land.

"Well, I didn't know that," she shouts at me. "Not at the time."

I ask why she didn't give it to Drew, realize that she wouldn't give Drew the time in a clock shop and add, "...or one of the other policemen?"

"For heaven's sake," she tells me. "The man is dead, Teddi, and I took his ring. How would that look?"

Before I can tell her it looks just the way it is, she pulls out a cigarette and threatens to light it.

"I mean, really," she says, shaking her head like it's my brains that are loose. "What does he need with it now?"

nocturne™

**WAS HE HER SAVIOR
OR HER NIGHTMARE?**

HAUNTED
LISA CHILDS

Years ago, Ariel and her sisters were separated for
their own protection. Now the man who vowed
revenge on her family has resumed the hunt, and
Ariel must warn her sisters before it's too late.
The closer she comes to finding them, the more
secretive her fiancé becomes. Can she trust the man
she plans to spend eternity with? Or has he been
waiting for the perfect moment to destroy her?

On sale December 2006.

Silhouette Desire

Don't miss

DAKOTA FORTUNES,

**a six-book continuing series following
the Fortune family of South Dakota—
oil is in their blood and privilege
is their birthright.**

This series kicks off with
USA TODAY bestselling author

PEGGY MORELAND'S
Merger of Fortunes

(SD #1771)

this January.

Other books in the series:

BACK IN FORTUNE'S BED by Bronwyn James (Feb)
FORTUNE'S VENGEFUL GROOM by Charlene Sands (March)
MISTRESS OF FORTUNE by Kathie DeNosky (April)
EXPECTING A FORTUNE by Jan Colley (May)
FORTUNE'S FORBIDDEN WOMAN by Heidi Betts (June)

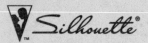